Early praise for Countdown to Jihad

An exciting story...that will satisfy readers seeking thoughtful political thrillers—Kirkus Reviews

In this suspenseful debut...Westmont tells a story full of action and intrigue that readers will recognize is all too plausible in a post-9/11 world. What makes the novel compelling, though, is the care taken to examine the local customs, motivations and histories of nearly all the characters—Western and Middle Eastern. These are characters with doubts and desires, haunted by their personal histories and by their actions in the present. Westmont's investigation of his characters' anger and fear is believable and subtle and adds emotional complexity to his novel.

The novel...is smart and fast paced with well-rounded characters and convincing detail.

Four out of five stars—Clarion ForeWord Reviews

Westmont's novel makes for a good summer read....his plot is clever... and there is a great deal of believable if fast paced action in the book. In many ways, Countdown to Jihad stands a notch above the typical modern Middle Eastern political terror thriller. It is an action novel, but one that attempts to open up the minds of its readers in order to help them consider some of the motivations behind acts of terrorism. Westmont avoids the pitfalls of many writers of the genre who stereotype Arabs, Palestinians and Iranians as inherently evil and instead works to round them out from two to three dimensions. The author tries to explain why terrorists fight the way they do and does so without entirely excusing, condemning or sympathizing with them.

Countdown to Jihad

Jeff Westmont

ISBN: 0-6155-6888-2
ISBN-13: 9780615568881
LCCN: 2011961216
Westwoods Publishing, San Francisco, CA

Dedication

To my incredible wife Sarah, whose patience and encouragement was invaluable. To my Dad, who was a wonderful man and taught me so much.

ACKNOWLEDGMENTS

I want to thank Steve Murphy and Tom Beatty, my writing group, for their invaluable input and encouragement. In addition, I want to thank my mom, Lois Westmont, for being a wonderful mother and passing her love of books on to me at an early age. To Karen Westmont for her excellent editing work.

I

Northern Afghanistan

The Blackhawk helicopter swept low over the valley floor, twisting and turning as it followed the course of a dry riverbed. The rugged terrain was barren and deserted, a jumble of rocky outcroppings, sand and scrub brush. Occasionally a small village flashed past, the forlorn cluster of ramshackle buildings dwarfed by the surrounding mountains. The early morning sky was clear and brightening, the moon a fading crescent on the horizon.

David Harrim looked around at the twenty heavily armed U.S. Special Forces soldiers crowded into the Blackhawk. Most stared back warily, grudgingly accepting his presence yet suspicious of his role. He knew CIA operatives in Afghanistan such as himself were distrusted and disliked—perceived as inexperienced bureaucrats who planned risky missions that were then carried out by soldiers in the field. However, David took pride in leading his missions, drawing on the expertise acquired during a stint in the Special Forces eight years ago.

Tonight was the first time he had worked with this particular unit, so David knew he'd need to prove himself once again. He had already made a favorable impression by volunteering to lead the mission and the practiced ease with which he checked his weapons and donned his gear.

"Five minutes to target!" a voice called out.

Sergeant Billings leaned forward and spat on the floor, narrowly missing David's foot. He was a burly, ten year veteran with a crooked nose, blunt manner and an American Eagle tattoo that wrapped around his neck. "Betcha a 100 bucks this goddamn mission is a waste of time," he growled.

David knew Billings was both resentful and apprehensive about being placed under his command. In addition, David's Middle Eastern appearance, foreign accent and fluency in Arabic and Pashtu had only heightened the Sergeant's uneasiness. Ever since their initial mission briefing an hour ago, Billings had tested David, reluctant to trust a CIA spook that looked like any other 'Camel Jockey', as most U.S. soldiers disparagingly called the locals. After four months in Afghanistan, David had grudgingly accepted such behavior as part of the job.

Without glancing up from loading his M-16, David said, "You got something you want to say to me, Sergeant?"

"What if I did?"

David looked up, his gaze coolly challenging. "I've led a dozen successful missions in the past few months. Each time we found our man. We will again tonight. I'm not here for the damn intellectual stimulation."

Sgt. Billings chuckled, his weathered face split into a rare grin. "Yeah, I don't play chess so good. You sure this Arab we're after is at this village tonight?"

"I'm certain," David replied, even though he knew Afghan informants often sold false information. "The tip came from one of my most reliable sources."

Billings snorted derisively. "That's crap, there's no such thing as a reliable Afghan." He tugged on his bulletproof vest and spat again. "Yeah, if it wasn't for these towel-headed assholes, I could get outta this hellhole, go home and get laid."

"Hey Sarge, I heard you ain't been laid since 'Nam!" a female soldier teased.

The few hoarse chuckles were cut short as the Blackhawk suddenly lurched and slowed.

A loudspeaker crackled to life. "Target in sight."

"Hey Spook," a voice called out. "This guy we're after tonight. He an important guy?"

"Yeah," David replied, although truthfully he wasn't sure. His informant had contacted David that morning about a mysterious senior Al Quada operative who had come down from a sanctuary in the mountains to spend the night in a village about 50 miles north of Basra. Although suspicious his informant was lying for the reward money, David had arranged with the local American military commander for a night raid. A Special Forces helicopter and ground scouts had reconnoitered the village earlier that evening. They had reported nothing unusual, describing it as a typical, desolate Afghani settlement situated in a narrow valley bordered by inhospitable mountains.

The game plan tonight was simple: surround the few buildings, flush out the inhabitants and capture and interrogate any Al Quada or Taliban members.

The problem was, in Afghanistan, nothing ever went according to plan.

"Touchdown in ten seconds!"

The Blackhawk landed with a jarring thud and David checked his M-16 one last time and flipped down his night vision goggles. Billings jumped out first, followed immediately by a dozen soldiers with David the last to emerge. He landed awkwardly, twisting his left ankle and reaching out with his free hand to maintain his balance. The wind from the whirling blades buffeted his back as the helicopter took off again to circle around to the far side of the village to drop the rest of Billings' squad.

Glancing around, David determined they were perhaps 200 yards from the village in a rocky field that offered minimal protection apart from a few scattered trees and large boulders. The settlement was suspiciously dark and quiet. The thirty or so single story buildings were huddled close together, the rocky walls topped either by thatched roofs or corrugated metal. A crumbling, low stone wall encircled the village and a horse corral was on his left. According to the scouting report, the village held mostly women and children, the missing men either serving in the local warlord's forces or killed during the interminable Afghan wars.

Billings silently motioned the unit forward. The soldiers spread out and advanced quickly, darting ahead in alternating waves and using what little cover was available. David moved forward uneasily, feeling exposed even though he knew they were nearly invisible in the early morning gloom. The dark and silent buildings increased his anxiousness—surely the villagers had heard the chopper. David wiped his sweaty hands on his armored vest, tension coursing through his body.

They quickly drew to within 50 yards of the outlying buildings. David stayed close to Billings, who continued on point. A thick band of clouds obscured the moon and the steadily blowing wind brought the faint but pungent smell of a typical Afghan village. Several dogs started barking and a light flickered on in one of the windows.

Billings abruptly gave a hand signal to halt.

"What's wrong?" David hissed.

"Something ain't right."

Suddenly, the night came alive with gunfire. David dropped to the ground and crawled behind a tree. Scanning the landscape, he spotted muzzle flashes near an outlying building. Several bullets whistled past harmlessly overhead and David heard a muffled cry from a wounded soldier on his right. The soldiers returned fire, laying down an intense yet controlled barrage. One of the ambushing gunmen screamed in pain, a high-pitched, inhuman noise that cut through the night. David could see the dark shapes of several soldiers moving rapidly forward to converge on the enemy's position.

Pushing himself to his feet, David ran about 15 yards before diving behind a low stonewall. Peering cautiously over the top, he scrutinized the nearest building—a windowless, single-story structure. He could just make out a gun barrel extending around the corner of the building and a figure writhing around on the ground in pain, crying out in Arabic.

The side of the building hiding the Afghan gunman suddenly erupted in flame, the loud crack of an exploding grenade followed immediately by the detonation of a second one. The gunfire abruptly ceased. The night fell eerily silent, the only sounds the flickering flames and barking dogs. David waited while several soldiers moved forward to check on the two prostrate assailants. One soldier gave the all clear signal and the night was suddenly alive with the remainder of Billings' squad sprinting toward the village.

Cradling his M-16, David headed for the nearest cluster of houses. Several soldiers were preparing to enter one of the buildings, an Afghan translator calling out instructions to the inhabitants. Without stopping, David entered a narrow, pungent dirt alley that ran between several houses. He proceeded slowly, pausing every few steps to listen.

Reaching the end of the alley, David stopped to survey the street, which was lined with ramshackle houses and led to what looked like a community building at the far end. Two soldiers suddenly appeared, one wiping a streak of blood from a gouge on his cheek.

"House to house?" the wounded soldier asked.

"Yeah," David replied. "Where's Billings?"

"Here." Sergeant Billings materialized out of the darkness. "I stopped to make sure those guys shooting at us were dead. We got both of 'em."

"They were the bodyguards," David said, relieved his informant had been correct. "Now we know there's someone important here."

Billings snorted. "Maybe they're just two more Afghan assholes who hate Americans."

"No, the wounded guy spoke Arabic. They're foreigners. That means Al Quada."

Another soldier appeared and shook his head at Billings' questioning glance. "Sorry sir. It's Brown, he took a round in his neck. Doesn't look good."

"Damn!" Billings swore, glancing pointedly at David. "Take care of him. We got a job to finish." He turned to the remaining soldiers. "Standard sweep pattern. Team up and move out. Mr. CIA, you're with Martinez, Tucker and me. We'll take the houses on the left."

They entered the first house cautiously, ignoring the protests of an elderly man who answered the door. Billings and Tucker began searching the premises while David and Martinez remained near the entrance with their guns leveled at the entire family—the older man, sullen younger woman and three frightened children. The large main room consisted of a dirt floor, rough rock walls and an open fire pit.

Billings and Tucker disappeared down the narrow hallway that led to the bedrooms at the rear of the house. Suddenly, a woman screamed followed by a sharp crash. David started moving toward the hallway, but stopped when he heard Billings cursing loudly in exasperation. The Sergeant soon reappeared, ruefully shaking his head and explaining that an old woman had objected to his search of her bedroom and thrown a bowl at him.

There were no fugitives in the house.

Once outside, David noticed the streets remained quiet, indicating that so far the other search teams were equally unsuccessful. Concerned that perhaps their quarry had slipped away, David radioed the helicopter pilot and ordered him to begin a standard search pattern of the countryside. Although he knew a fugitive could easily hide at the sound of an approaching chopper, there was always the chance they might get lucky.

"Heard anything from the others?" David asked Billings.

The Sergeant shook his head angrily, his disappointment clear. David knew Billings was thinking of the wounded soldier and beginning to believe he'd needlessly put his men at risk.

"Our target's here," David stated confidently. "He didn't have time to slip out of the village before we surrounded it."

"You better be right," Billings growled. "Let's finish our sweep and get the hell outta here."

The next house was large and relatively prosperous looking with an enclosed stable attached to the rear. Billings pounded on the door, which opened immediately. A frightened woman backed away, gesturing excitedly and shaking her head. She was dressed in a traditional Muslim black robe, or *abaya*, with her head completely covered by a *hijab*.

"Praise be to *Allah*. We mean you no harm," David said reassuringly in Pashtu. "We're looking for the foreigners we know are here tonight."

The woman shook her head vehemently. "No, no foreigners here."

"We must search your house."

"It's not permitted!"

They argued, David forceful yet respectful, mindful of local customs. Finally, David turned toward Billings, who was staring at him with a mixture of wonder and unease.

"Damn!" he exclaimed. "You sound just like 'em. You Arab?"

David nodded. "That and Jewish."

"No shit! What'd she say?"

"She said there are three strange men in the village. They arrived tonight."

"Where are they?" Billings asked.

"She doesn't know." David smiled wanly. "She said her husband is head of the village and we can't come inside. She has two daughters and we'd violate their honor by seeing them in the privacy of their home. I told her she didn't have a choice."

"Damn right!" Billings moved forward, but the woman blocked his path, her voice rising insistently. David interceded, talking rapidly and soothingly, until she stepped back and allowed them inside.

The large main room was sparsely furnished with several chairs, some floor cushions, rickety coffee table and a worn Tribal rug that failed to hide the dirt floor. A cooking fireplace filled one corner, two black pots hanging over the smoldering coals. The room reeked of unwashed bodies, smoke and spicy food. In the middle of the far wall, a tattered piece of cloth hung over the entrance to the remaining rooms. Billings started toward the doorway, intending to search the rest of the house.

Out of the corner of his eye, David saw the woman suddenly duck behind the front door, just as he heard movement from the hallway.

"Get down!" he shouted.

David dropped to the floor and fired a burst through the hanging curtain into the unseen hallway. A man screamed. Then there was silence, broken only by their ragged breathing. Billings crawled quickly over to the side of the doorway and peered cautiously down the hall.

"I can see one down."

"Think that's it?" David asked.

"How the hell would I know?" Billings cursed.

The Afghan woman pushed her way back inside the house, sobbing and pleading hysterically with David. He could barely understand her, but finally comprehended she claimed to have hidden the dead gunman only to protect her two daughters, who were still in one of the rear bedrooms.

"Billings, she says there was only one man," David called out. "Only one way to find out. Cover me."

David crawled cautiously to the side of the doorway opposite of Billings and peered down the corridor. A body was lying in that peculiar crumpled shape of the dead, a crimson pool of blood spreading across the floor. Rising slowly and staying low to the ground, David rushed down the hallway past the body to the first closed door. Billings joined him. The Sergeant gave a hand count to three and they kicked it open.

The windowless room was empty and undisturbed, the only furnishings a small dresser and a pile of bedding on the floor. They moved quickly to the closed door across the hall. Again Billings kicked it open. Another windowless bedroom, also empty. Billings tapped David's shoulder and motioned to the final door at the end of the hall. They stood on either side and David tried the handle. It was locked. They looked at each other and exchanged nods. Then, in one motion, they kicked the door open.

Two figures dressed in traditional black *abayas* sat huddled on a bed, clutching each other and sobbing. One young woman turned to face them, her tear-streaked face barely visible beneath her *hijab* as the other woman pressed her head even harder against her sister's shoulder. The cramped bedroom was otherwise empty and there weren't any windows or doors.

"I guess that's it," Billings said, lowering his M-16. "I owe you Spook."

David smiled tenuously, beginning to tremble slightly from the adrenaline and close call. "I'll hold you to that."

Billings swatted him on the shoulder and left the room.

David said a few consoling words to the two sisters, who merely nodded in response. The larger, silent one never raised her head. As he turned away, David noticed the quiet sister's exposed hand—it was large, calloused and definitely not feminine. He froze and then tried to unobtrusively swing his gun around to bear on the imposter.

The click of a gun being cocked told him he was too late.

"Close the door," a male voice said in Arabic. The hand holding the pistol remained steady as the man stood and threw off the *hijab*. He had a slight, wiry build, his face drawn and haggard probably from the strain of living for months in the mountains to evade capture.

David shut the door as the sobbing young woman crept over to the corner of the room.

"The village is surrounded," David said. "You can't escape. Give up before it's too late."

"No, it's too late for you."

"Killing me will only bring your own death," David replied, pleased that his voice remained steady.

"As *Allah* wills."

The man moved closer and David could smell stale sweat and smoke, see the jagged scar that ran the entire length of his cheek. His quarry had a thin nose, weak chin and receding hairline while his eyes darted about incessantly, refusing to meet David's gaze. David knew he was Middle Eastern, probably Saudi Arabian.

The man waved the gun. "You're an Arab, a traitor to your own people, to *Allah*."

"*Allah* doesn't condone killing, even infidels. So who's the traitor to Islam?"

The man scowled and placed the gun against David's temple. "On your knees."

"Screw you." David mastered his fear, knowing that only his ability to keep the man talking kept him alive.

"On your knees or I kill her."

David sank to his knees, his gaze darting around ceaselessly looking for an opening.

"You're too late," the man sneered. "The one you seek is already gone."

"It doesn't matter. We'll find him. Al Quada is finished."

The man smiled wickedly. "We're not Al Quada."

Certain the escaped man had an important mission, David decided to bluff. "We know who he is."

"Perhaps, but Al Kabbar will finish his task first."

Now David had a name. "No. Al Kabbar will be killed or captured, just like you will tonight."

The Arab smiled confidently. "But you'll die first, knowing that you failed to stop the coming *Jihad*. Soon Islam will once again rule the world and the *infidels* will be swept from the Holy Land. That day is not far off. And the one who escaped tonight, the one *you* let get away, will make it happen."

The gun pressed harder against David's temple. For the first time, he was truly afraid, all his training forgotten for the moment. He could only recall the image of his favorite beach near Tel Aviv that he used to visit with his mother and father. Those were the good times, the days before the conflicting demands of two religions and two cultures tore his family apart. He closed his eyes, realizing there was nothing else he could do.

Suddenly the door burst open. Startled, David's assailant twisted around and raised his gun to face the new threat, giving David the opportunity to dive forward. The harsh sound of M-16 gunfire filled the room and a body fell across the back of David's legs. He looked up in relief as Sergeant Billings entered the room.

With a slight smile, Billings walked over and extended a hand to help him up. "You okay?"

David got shakily to his feet. "I'll let you know in a moment."

"Figured you could use some help."

"I had it under control. I just wanted to ask him a few questions."

Billings chuckled. "You're a cool son of a bitch."

"Just don't ask if I wet my pants."

"You wouldn't be the first." Sergeant Billings prodded the crumpled body with his boot. "Nothing like a successful mission."

"It wasn't," David replied, recalling what the dead man had said about the escaped terrorist named Al Kabbar and an impending *Jihad*. For some reason, the Saudi's parting words left him with a sense of foreboding and dread. David didn't believe the warning was just the empty boast of a condemned man.

David sighed heavily, knowing he would spend sleepless nights considering the possibilities. "No, this time, we failed."

2

Abrahim Al Kabbar walked down the deserted alley, glancing over his shoulder to make sure no one was following him. Satisfied, he ducked into the rear entrance of a restaurant and passed through the bustling kitchen, ignoring the staff's questioning glances. He left via the front door, hailed a cab and directed the driver on a deliberately winding course through the crowded streets. Twice Al Kabbar had the cab pull over to the side of the road while he looked out the rear window for any pursuers.

He knew perhaps he was overly cautious, but even after eight years as a terrorist, his face and real name were unknown to the authorities, although his bloodiest triumphs had garnered attention worldwide. Al Kabbar was the shadowy figure behind shadowy figures, a facilitator and planner, careful to distance himself from actual terrorist attacks. To maintain his effectiveness, Al Kabbar avoided any notoriety or accolades, preferring to toil unobtrusively for the glory of *Allah* and Islam. The network which he had founded and painstakingly built provided better-known organizations such as Al Quada with information, funding and weapons.

Al Kabbar had dedicated his life to eradicating the American cancer that permeated his former home and Islamic holy land, Saudi Arabia. The American military presence in Saudi Arabia and influence over the government was an affront to *Allah*, defiling the holy cities of Mecca and Medina. Al Kabbar's unyielding hatred in all things Western and American was driven by religion, Arabic pride and, above all else, personal tragedy.

Eight years ago, he was one of the many bitter, unemployed Saudi college graduates, resentful of his status but at least happy with his pregnant wife. Then one night a drunken American driving recklessly through the streets of Riyadh hit and killed her. Distraught, Al Kabbar turned for solace to the Wahhabism, the ultra-conservative Saudi Arabian form of Islam. Although the Saudi government promoted Wahhabism, Al Kabbar followed those *imams*, or prayer leaders, who portrayed the royal family that ruled Saudi Arabia as corrupt and illegitimate. He soon believed there were two enemies of Islam—the *infidels* and the royal House of Saud.

Since then, Al Kabbar had plotted against both the U.S. and Saudi governments. His successes had been noteworthy—a boat filled with explosives ramming a U.S. Navy carrier in a Qatar harbor, several car bombs outside U.S embassies and the assassination of two members of the House of Saud while they slept with their lovers. Al Kabbar didn't consider himself a terrorist. As a Muslim, he felt his people were already under attack in Palestine, Afghanistan, Chechnya, Kashmir and Iraq and that the West supported illegitimate secular Arab governments. Thus, he viewed his actions as defensive. Even after eight years, Al Kabbar's rage still burned and he dreamed of the day the *infidels* would be driven from Saudi Arabia and he could return home.

The taxi dropped him in the *Harrim Abdullah* district, an area of budget hotels and small shops near the old Roman amphitheatre in the city center. Al Kabbar walked aimlessly around for a few blocks, past the busy shops filled with decadent merchandise. He was impatient to have his meeting and leave Amman. He hated the Western influences that had corrupted Jordan, even leading the government to embrace its pariah neighbor, Israel. Amman now catered to infidel tourists and greedy businessmen, the streets filled with bars, American fast food chains and improperly attired women. The only redeeming feature about Jordan was that its attempts to mimic the West had led to unusually open borders for an Arab country, which enabled Al Kabbar with his fake Jordanian passport to move about freely.

Glancing around one last time, Al Kabbar entered a small, decrepit hotel. He walked through the lobby, past the desk clerk and up the stairs to the third floor. The hallway was dark and musty, filled with murmuring voices from behind the closed doors and the smell of spicy food cooking on hot plates. He stopped before a door at the end of the hall and knocked three times, then twice more, saying in English, "I understand you come from America."

"No, from Pakistan," answered a voice.

"Then perhaps you know my cousin, Masharrif?" Al Kabbar replied, completing the coded response.

"Enter."

Al Kabbar stepped inside the dark room and closed the door. A bright light was shone directly into his face and he was forced to avert his gaze.

"You're late," said a male voice angrily, as the light was switched off.

"My apologies," said Al Kabbar. "I wanted to be sure I wasn't followed."

"*Salam 'alaykum.*"

"*Wa alaykum as-salam. Al-hamdu lillah 'al as-salama.*"

The man stayed in the shadows, his head covered by a traditional white Arab *keffiyeh* secured by a black cord, a beard masking his features. In their previous meetings, the man had never revealed his face, nationality or anything about himself, only saying that he should be called Abdullah, a common Arabic name. Al Kabbar guessed he was a well-educated, wealthy Saudi, probably a senior government official or perhaps even a religious leader. For the past four years, Abdullah had unquestioningly funded Al Kabbar's activities. Al Kabbar had no way of contacting Abdullah and their rare meetings usually preceded one of Al Kabbar's major attacks. Upon receiving Abdullah's most recent meeting request, Al Kabbar had left Afghanistan immediately, sticking to back roads to avoid the American military patrols and checkpoints. He had spent the last two days traveling across Iran before flying from Tehran to Jordan.

Al Kabbar walked across the sparsely furnished room and sat in a chair near the bed.

"You heard your bodyguards were killed by U.S. soldiers the night you left Afghanistan?" Abdullah asked.

Al Kabbar nodded. "Yes. It means my contact in Kabul sold me out."

"Then I'll have him killed," Abdullah said matter of factly. "Do the Americans know who you are or where you went?"

Al Kabbar realized he wouldn't leave the room alive if his answer was unsatisfactory. He understood and approved because he would have reacted in the same way if their positions were reversed. "No. Even my guards knew nothing important, only that I'd return soon. They were killed before they talked to the Americans."

"How fortunate," Abdullah replied, intentionally ironic. "What news from Afghanistan?"

Al Kabbar was sure Abdullah had arranged their meeting to discuss something more important, but restrained his impatience. "We've aligned ourselves with the local warlords, enabling us to move about freely in most areas. Soon, Afghanistan will be like it was before the Americans arrived—the government ineffective and the country split into areas of influence. Then we can come down from the mountains and return from Pakistan to re-establish our training camps."

"And the Americans?"

Al Kabbar chuckled grimly. "They still think they can use money and their military to build a Western society in Afghanistan. The fools! But the Afghans have grown tired of the Americans and are once more backing the Taliban. The Americans have grown weary of the struggle and will soon leave. They're weak and don't have the stomach for a long fight."

Abdullah shook his head. "You're wrong. Like many before, you've underestimated them. Americans aren't weak, but strong; not soft, but violent. Have you forgotten they've fought more wars in the past 100 years than any other country? That they didn't hesitate to invade Iraq and Afghanistan? That their society is one of the most violent in the world? They're killers, murderers. Once roused, they won't hesitate to kill to get what they want and keep what they have."

"But they stand for nothing, believe in nothing," Al Kabbar protested.

"They believe whole-heartedly in their way of life and are prepared to die to defend it. Just as we are willing to die to defend Islam."

"You can't compare defending the true faith and word of *Allah* to *infidels* spreading perversity!"

Abdullah sighed. "I was merely pointing out that *infidels* can be as committed to their ideals as any Muslim. I'd never suggest they're comparable."

Abdullah walked across the room and picked up a teapot, frowning as if realizing he had revealed too much. He poured two cups and handed one to Al Kabbar. "Do you have any new attacks planned?" he asked.

Al Kabbar shook his head. "No. Security everywhere is tighter, making it more difficult. Although September 11th was a magnificent blow, Osama increased the risk for us all, making our eventual victory that much more difficult. I still mourn his death."

"He and the rest of Al Quada are fools!"

Al Kabbar was startled at the vehemence in Abdullah's voice. "But Osama fought for Islam and the Saudi people."

"And for himself," Abdullah replied. "The *Quran* says, 'Lift not thyself above *Allah*'. What purpose was served by Osama making these videos featuring himself? We should keep the focus on our struggle."

Al Kabbar shook his head in disagreement. "Osama's actions and visibility brought millions to our cause. Most Muslims are with us now."

"And yet, all that's been achieved is insignificant. Al Quada's merely a thorn in the Americans' side, nothing more."

Angered, Al Kabbar stood abruptly. "Are you saying their efforts, the last eight years of my life, have been a waste of time?"

"To drive the infidels from Saudi Arabia and spread *Allah's* word, we must be bolder."

"Bolder than September 11th?" Al Kabbar asked. "That was a master-stroke of planning and execution and struck a huge blow for our cause."

"And what did it accomplish, apart from killing a few Americans and striking fear in their hearts? Nothing. We generated sympathy for the Americans, gave them additional allies. We hardened their resolve and created a more dangerous enemy. They invaded Afghanistan, they invaded Iraq."

Al Kabbar flushed angrily. "What else can we do? We have the support of most Muslims, but without the backing of the Arab countries, we're limited. Most Arab governments are concerned only about remaining in power and will never confront the West."

Abdullah placed his teacup on the table. "The *Quran* says it's our duty to launch a *jihad*, one that's embraced by all Muslims and forces Arab governments to take action against the *infidels*."

"How?"

Abdullah nodded. "There are several things we can use to our advantage. First, most Muslims remain deeply suspicious of the West and their imperialistic ambitions. Many believe the Crusades continue, that Christianity is still committed to destroying Islam. The wars against Iraq and Afghanistan reinforced this notion. This distrust runs deep—which explains why most Muslims believe 9/11 was a plot by the Americans and Israel to discredit Islam."

Al Kabbar smiled grimly. "Even I was surprised at how most Muslims rejected the obvious."

"Then, there's Israel. By continuing to oppress the Palestinians, Israel stirs religious passions and tramples on Arab pride. In her arrogance and ruthlessness, Israel is the perfect enemy, the perfect foil for our task."

"They're too strong to defeat," Al Kabbar protested.

Abdullah leaned forward intently. "I'm not proposing we attack Israel. No, the destruction of Israel will be the *result* of our efforts, not the target. We must use Muslims' hatred of Israel and distrust of the West to launch an unstoppable *jihad*."

"How?" Al Kabbar asked.

"We need a trigger, something so terrible, so enormous that it'll galvanize every Muslim, destroy governments and change the balance of power throughout the world."

"That's too much to ask from a single event."

Abdullah vehemently shook his head. "No, it's not."

For the next half hour, Al Kabbar listened with growing consternation as Abdullah outlined his plan, briefly describing the key aspects and assumptions. Abdullah's calm, rational voice belied the terrible consequences of his proposal, the unimaginable suffering and devastation. Al Kabbar noticed Abdullah's expression was similarly emotionless, as if he were discussing the weather, not outlining a plan that would change the world.

As Abdullah spoke, Al Kabbar rose to his feet to pace back and forth, unconsciously rubbing his hands together and shaking his head. When Abdullah finished, silence fell, broken only by the faint traffic noise from the street below.

"No, no," Al Kabbar finally said, trying to comprehend the sheer scale and ruthlessness of Abdullah's plan. "We cannot! *Allah* would never forgive us. It's not possible, not allowed!"

"It's what must be done."

"We cannot!"

Al Kabbar was in a quandary, his thoughts jumbled and confused. For eight years, he had embraced violence, grown accustomed to callously planning the potential deaths of hundreds and celebrating the casualties of a successful mission. Until that afternoon, death had lost its meaning, for he firmly believed martyrs were rewarded with heaven and the *Quran* blessed the killing of *infidels*. Al Kabbar suddenly realized that for him, death had become merely a statistic, much like a businessman's sales quota. In planning his strikes against the *infidels*, he had focused only on how many might be killed and how many actually were. Far removed from the actual blood and terror, Al Kabbar had become a dispassionate arbiter of life, inadvertently claiming one of *Allah*'s roles.

For the first time, he questioned his chosen course.

Torn by indecision, Al Kabbar finally spoke. "How can this be permissible? How could *Allah* forgive us?"

Abdullah smiled, a mere stretching of his lips. "The *Quran* says, '*If you are killed in the cause of Allah or you die, the forgiveness and mercy of Allah are better than all you amass. And if you die or are killed, even so it is to Allah that you will return.'* To die for one's faith is the highest form of witness to *Allah.*"

"But what you propose is blasphemy, the worst possible offense against Islam and *Allah!*"

"No. The *Quran* tells us that every martyr will ascend to heaven to sit by his side."

Al Kabbar sought desperately to reconcile Abdullah's plan with his twisted sense of Islamic morality. To him, as with most Muslims, the concept of *jihad* was two-fold—the first was the personal struggle against personal ego, selfishness and evil; and the second, the struggle to defend Islam and establish a just Islamic society worldwide. Al Kabbar suddenly recalled the teachings of Dr. Khaled Azzam, his religious studies professor at King Abdulaziz University in Jeddah, who had preached confrontation and conflict: *'Jihad and the rifle alone, no negotiations, no conferences and no dialogue'.* During the past eight years, Al Kabbar had accepted Azzam's viewpoint, much as once had a youthful Saudi named Osama bin Laden.

As he sat there in contemplation, Al Kabbar slowly realized he had long ago made his decision—his actions over the years had cost the lives of men and women, Christians, Jews and Muslims. To turn back now would only render his past efforts meaningless. Abdullah was offering the opportunity to unleash a worldwide *Jihad* that would not only destroy Israel, but drive the infidels from the Middle East as well. If successful, Abdullah's plan would change the course of history and reshape the entire world.

In the end, that was all that mattered.

Al Kabbar expelled his breath slowly. "You're right. I was surprised by the sheer magnitude of your idea. You're certain *Allah* will bless our efforts?"

"Yes. I've consulted with several important *muftis.* They've assured me *Allah* will give his blessing."

"*Insha'Allah.*" If *Allah* willed it. Al Kabbar knew his simple words committed him irrevocably to Abdullah's plan. He found himself staring at Abdullah with newfound respect and fear. Abdullah had always projected a certain quiet menace, as if capable of extreme violence, but in a casually efficient way. Abdullah had obviously spent years painstakingly developing his plan and making the preliminary preparations. For the first time, Al Kabbar feared another man—he knew if he failed or showed weakness, Abdullah wouldn't hesitate to kill him.

"Let's discuss your first task, the trip to Pakistan," Abdullah said.

"I'd like to take one more *hajj* to Mecca before we strike," Al Kabbar replied, longing to seek *Allah*'s forgiveness before the final part of Abdullah's plan.

Abdullah nodded understanding. "You'll be there at the end, at the hour of our victory. Let me tell you in more detail what must be done."

✳ ✳ ✳

The night had long since fallen by the time they finished their discussions and Al Kabbar finally left. As the door closed behind Al Kabbar, Abdullah smiled contentedly. The meeting had gone as anticipated, and the years of planning and maneuvering were about to come to fruition. The goal he had strived for so long was within reach; a goal, however, that was vastly different from the one he had expressed to Al Kabbar. He knew Al Kabbar hadn't detected his deception and believed their objective was the same—triggering a modern day *Jihad*. Although true, it was for vastly different reasons.

Satisfied, Abdullah pulled off his false beard and wig and removed his cloak. Suddenly, the door opened and the front desk clerk entered the room.

"My apologies, sir. I saw the other gentleman leave and thought the room was empty." The clerk's eyes widened as he recognized his famous guest and his curious gaze darted around the room, taking in the fake beard and wig lying on the bed.

"I understand," Abdullah replied. "There's a problem with the bathroom. May I show you?"

"Certainly."

The clerk walked toward the bathroom and Abdullah stepped aside to let him pass. Reaching under his robe, Abdullah pulled out a pistol with a silencer and fired twice into the clerk's back. The man slumped to the ground and Abdullah walked over to the hallway door and closed it. The clerk had obviously been curious about them and observing their movements. More importantly, he'd seen Abdullah's face. Abdullah was too well known throughout the Middle East to risk having anyone discover he'd attended a secret meeting in a dingy hotel room.

He replaced his disguise and wrapped himself once again in his robe. Then, without glancing again at the motionless body, Abdullah turned and walked out the door.

3

David Harrim awoke to the *azan*, the haunting Islamic call to worship that preceded each dawn. He lay there for several minutes, listening to the droning prayers broadcast from the minaret of every mosque and unconsciously repeating the ancient phrases he'd memorized in his youth. Now, the words held very little meaning, for David had long ago forsaken the religion and values of his Palestinian father, much as he had rejected his mother's Jewish heritage. He'd turned away from both as the discord between his parents deepened into a bitter enmity. Instead, he had eventually embraced the secular promises of America, his adopted homeland.

A conflicted child of the Middle East, David was the product of a Romeo and Juliet love of a liberal Jewish American and a younger Palestinian intellectual. The early years growing up in Jerusalem were pleasant memories; although David knew now that the different backgrounds, cultures and personalities had gradually created a chasm, which widened irreparably when the first Palestinian *intifada* claimed his younger sister. A stray bullet killed her, fired by which side no one ever knew. Afterward, David could only recall the tears, recriminations and anger.

Finally, his father took a five-year-old David and fled to Saudi Arabia, where he was granted sole custody. David had then grown up under the strict Islamic teachings and stifling rules of the Saudi Kingdom. Four years later, his mother arranged David's kidnapping during a visit to his father's relatives in Jordan. She had then disappeared with David into the vast Southern California suburbs and he never saw nor heard from his father again.

Reluctantly throwing aside the bedcovers, David rose and made his way to the kitchen to brew some sweet Turkish tea. His apartment was simply furnished with Indonesian teak furniture and oriental rugs and filled with artifacts from his extensive travels. Glancing around the comfortable surroundings, he felt content to be back home in Istanbul. Last night had been his first there in months and he'd slept soundly for 14 hours. But he had a suspicion that the reprieve would be short. Yesterday, two days after Sergeant Billings had saved his life, David had received cryptic orders to return immediately to Istanbul to meet with his CIA field controller. An Apache helicopter had airlifted him to Kabul, where a waiting CIA passenger jet then flew him to Istanbul.

For the last four months, David had been on loan to the U.S. Special Forces to assist in the ongoing search for Al Quada and Taliban members and serve as a liaison to the Afghan army. With his Palestinian-Jewish heritage, dark skin, prior Special Forces training and fluency in Arabic, Farsi and Pashtu, David was the ideal operative. Although reluctant to risk such a valuable agent, the CIA had bowed to intense inter-agency pressure and released David for a six-month engagement.

After a two-week refresher training course, David had bounced around Afghanistan, moving from unit to unit. He didn't begrudge his stint in Afghanistan, only the time away from developing his budding Turkish intelligence network. Now, although grateful to be back, he was curious and slightly concerned about the sudden change in plans.

David dressed quickly and left his apartment on the hill above Istanbul's *Beyoglu* district, which overlooked the Bosphorus strait, the sparkling expanse of water separating the Middle East from Europe. The morning sun shone brightly, illuminating the numerous mosques that dominated the surrounding hills. Hailing a cab, David gave an address near the *Kapali Carsi*, or Grand Bazaar. As the cab crossed the Ataturk Bridge, he admired the exquisite Blue Mosque and massive Aya Sofya that dominated the ancient *Sultanahamet* district skyline. For the last six years, David had made Istanbul his home, comfortable with the confluence of European and Middle Eastern cultures that suited his diverse background.

The cab dropped him at an entrance to the Grand Bazaar, a maze of covered streets filled with shops that mostly carried tourist goods such as carpets, ceramics, jewelry and clothing. Passing through the crowds of shoppers, David checked periodically to see if he had attracted anyone's interest. After nearly two years with the CIA, he was becoming increasingly comfortable with the need to look constantly over his shoulder. Yet he still considered his position a temporary one; he was the owner of a small, struggling carpet export company, not a lifelong CIA field agent. Someday, when David felt his services were no longer needed, he intended to once again become just another faceless merchant trying to make a few bucks.

David turned down a narrow alley and ducked into a store named "Holy Land Carpet Merchants". The store was a typical Turkish bazaar carpet shop with several comfortable chairs, a hookah for smoking flavored tobacco, hot plate for making tea and rolled carpets piled into every nook and cranny. The heavyset Turk sitting behind the counter looked up and greeted David with a broad smile.

"David, my friend!" he called out jovially. "I heard you were back! I've been worried about you!"

David repressed a broad smile. "Hello Mehmet. Afraid you wouldn't collect the thousand bucks I owe you?"

"My only concern was your safety," the Turk replied with mock indignation. Perhaps in his early forties, Mehmet looked like a Western businessman with his gray slacks and blue button down shirt. His round face was filled with laughter lines and his eyes twinkled mischievously.

"Then you'll forget about the money?" David asked teasingly.

"Ah, if only I could. I've four children to feed." Mehmet lowered his voice conspiratorially. "I'm glad you're back. My wife has a woman friend you must meet."

David chuckled, knowing Mehmet's wife was determined to find him a bride. "I do fine on my own. Besides, what kind of woman would go out with a friend of yours?"

The shopkeeper gave David an exaggerated look of wounded pride. "Always making fun of me. I swear, this one is beautiful and the perfect Muslim."

"I'm part Jewish, remember?"

Mehmet wagged his finger at David. "I think not. You speak perfect Arabic, Turkish and *Allah* alone knows what other languages. Besides, you've no head for business."

"Which is why you do business with me—to rob me blind."

"And I look forward to once again working with you." Mehmet heaved his bulk out of his chair and walked over to give David a bone crushing hug. Still grasping David's shoulders, Mehmet stepped back to examine him. "You look good. Too thin perhaps, but a few of my wife's home cooked meals and you'll be fine." His expression became serious. "I've been worried about you. I can't tell you how glad I am to see you safe and sound."

"Thanks," David replied awkwardly, touched by the Turk's transparent concern. David was also surprised to find that for the first time, he felt Istanbul was truly his home. "Is Reynolds here yet?"

"He'll arrive shortly."

"Good. I'll wait for him in back."

"What about my wife's friend, the beautiful girl?"

David made a gesture of capitulation as he turned away. "Okay. But don't tell her stories about me. The last one expected a rich, handsome actor from Hollywood."

"If I told the truth," Mehmet called after him. "She'd never go out with you!"

Still chuckling, David walked down a long hallway and unlocked the door to a large, windowless room furnished with a mahogany conference table and several leather chairs. The hand-woven tapestries that hung on the walls concealed sound proofing tiles and the entrance to another room filled with sophisticated electronic gear. Mehmet's shop was a CIA front and field office where David usually met Jack Reynolds, his field controller. David's own carpet export firm provided a convenient explanation for the lengthy meetings. In fact, Mehmet and David often worked together on legitimate business deals. For all his good-natured clowning and idle banter, Mehmet was a shrewd business-man. Equally important, the Turk had opened his house to David, so that he had become friendly with Mehmet's wife and four children and felt there was at least one place he could call home.

While waiting for Reynolds, David recalled their first meeting two years ago. Jack Reynolds had appeared unannounced at the offices of David's floundering and nearly bankrupt company, offering a solution to his financial problems and the opportunity to help his adopted country. David agreed, not because of the money, but because September 11th and threat of more terrorist strikes provided a compelling reason. Although David had lived in the U.S. for only 12 years before 9/11, he'd felt the loss as keenly as any American.

The CIA initially had asked David to develop a network of informants in Istanbul and infiltrate Istanbul's Islamic community, particularly the ultra-conservative Wahhabi mosques. To do so, he had distanced himself from his few American friends in Istanbul and began to bitterly denounce the injustices in Israel, Iraq and Afghanistan. So far, David had been very successful. Before leaving for Afghanistan, he had prevented two terrorist attacks on American targets in Turkey.

The door opened and a tall, middle-aged man dressed in distinctly European clothes and carrying a French tourist guidebook appeared. His thin face was filled with sharp angles and his lips drawn tight with intensity. David knew Jack Reynold's shuffling gait and slightly stooped frame were deceptive; his piercing green eyes were watchful and alert and more than one person had ruefully underestimated his intelligence.

"Welcome home David," Reynolds said, striding across the room with his hand extended. "It's great to see you."

"Thanks," David replied, knowing Reynolds's comment was perfunctory. "It's good to be back."

They shook hands, Reynolds' grip firm and challenging. Serious and intense, the career CIA officer rarely smiled or became animated. With his unkempt hair, wire rimmed glasses and pronounced slouch, Reynolds more closely resembled a professor than the CIA's station chief in Turkey. Even though Reynolds was extremely shrewd, David had always felt he was best suited to sitting behind a desk at Langley.

"First, congratulations are in order," Reynolds said. "The reports on your stint in Afghanistan were very complimentary."

"I worked with some good people, both in the Special Forces and the SOG," David replied modestly. The Special Operations Group was the CIA's paramilitary arm. "But I've wasted valuable time by not being in Istanbul. I've lost contact with my informants and it'll take time to rebuild my network."

Reynolds frowned. "I know. I fought against your deployment to Afghanistan. But Langley and the Pentagon were insistent. They think highly of you. You impressed a lot of people last year back at Peary."

"Peary was a summer camp compared to Special Forces training," David said.

Reynolds gave a ghost of a smile as he sat down in one of the armchairs. "I wouldn't tell Langley that."

After agreeing to join the CIA, David had trained for six months at the 'farm', the Agency's 9,000 acre Camp Peary training center near Williamsburg, Virginia. There, along with other new CIA case officers, he had learned skills of the trade such as infiltrating hostile countries, communicating in codes, retrieving messages from dead drops and recruiting foreign agents. He had also studied other Middle Eastern languages to complement the several in which he was already fluent. David had been an exceptional student and his Special Forces training gave him a ruthless competence unmatched by most new agents.

Reynolds leaned back in his chair. "You've exceeded my highest expectations. I must admit, I had some doubts when I first recruited you."

"At the time, you were persistent."

Reynolds shrugged. "Recruiting a good agent is a crapshoot. You had the right background and tools, but I wasn't sure you'd stick with it."

David knew Reynolds was referring to the restlessness that had characterized the last 12 years of his life. Anxious to leave his teenage years in Southern California behind, David had attended NYU on a languages scholarship. But he found New York stifling and college uninspiring. After two years of struggling to fit in, he had dropped out and joined the Special Forces. There, he sought the discipline and sense of belonging he'd lacked for so long. His decision was influenced by his Jewish grandfather, who had often talked fondly about his army days and the confidence it once instilled in a directionless young man. In the end, David grew to hate the rigid regime, incessant training and demands for blind obedience. When his tour of duty ended, he declined to re-enlist. After that, he went through a series of dead-end financial jobs in New York before moving to Istanbul.

Now, at the age of thirty, David had finally found a place where he was comfortable with the culture and people and, more importantly, himself.

David shrugged. "I admit it's been hard at times. I didn't realize the extent of the isolation or that I'd always be looking over my shoulder. But I don't have any regrets."

"I'm glad to hear it," Reynolds said. "You're one of our most valuable assets. We've maybe a dozen agents in the Middle East who are American, speak Arabic fluently and look the part."

"That's your second compliment this morning," David said with a wry smile. "Not to mention the sudden flight home. Something important must have come up."

Reynolds shifted uncomfortably, looking slightly embarrassed. "You're right. But first I've a question about Afghanistan." He reached into his briefcase and pulled out a manila file folder. "I read your report about the raid two days ago where the four terrorists were killed. Any leads on Al Kabbar, the man that got away?"

David shook his head. "No. My Kabul informant knew nothing and the only information we got out of the villagers was that Al Kabbar was the leader and a Saudi. The five men had arrived that afternoon to pick up supplies. Several hours before our raid, Al Kabbar headed for the Iranian border, leaving his guards behind. We tried to pick up his trail, but never found any trace of him."

"Do you think Al Kabbar is important and a threat?"

David grimaced, frustrated he was unable to answer the question. "I don't know. The guy who nearly killed me claimed Al Kabbar was leading a critical mission; but he may've been lying. Then again, Al Kabbar *did* have four bodyguards."

Reynolds sighed and ran his hand through his hair. "I'm concerned about Al Kabbar. One more threat to worry about and no leads."

"Actually, I have a lead," David ventured. "We searched the man Sgt. Billings killed and found a *Quran* that was a gift from the *ulama* of the largest mosque in Riyadh."

"So?"

David leaned forward intently, wanting to convince Reynolds of the importance. "Inside the front cover, the *ulama* inscribed a quote from the *Quran* that read, *'When the sacred months have passed, slay the idolaters wherever you find them, and take them, and confine them, and lie in wait for them at every place of ambush'*. The *ulama* signed and dated the inscription. It was only a month ago."

"You think the dead man recently met with this *ulama*?"

"Exactly. If so, the *ulama* may know something about Al Kabbar. Perhaps the *ulama's* even involved in planning whatever operation is underway. As head of the largest mosque in Saudi Arabia, he's got tremendous influence."

Reynolds returned the manila file to his briefcase while he considered his response. Finally, he looked up and nodded. "I agree, it's worth pursuing. You'll need to go to Saudi Arabia to find out more. Fortunately, that fits with your next assignment. We brought you back from Afghanistan for something important."

David leaned back warily in his chair, mentally preparing for another long mission outside Turkey. He found the prospect troubling, as he wanted to focus on rebuilding his Turkish network. Not to mention that he was weary after his Afghanistan deployment and needed to relax for a few weeks. Then again, Reynolds' worried, intense expression indicated he was deeply concerned about something.

Reynolds stood and began pacing, his gaze focused on David. "These are troubling times. We're losing the war on terrorism. Sure, we've killed or captured a number of Al Quada operatives and disrupted their funding. But the fact is every day more recruits join the cause against America. For every terrorist we kill or capture, five more are created. Goddamn bastards are worse than cockroaches."

"Yeah, I know," David said, resisting the urge to point out America's inconsistent and naïve policies in the region, in particular the ill-fated decision to invade Iraq, were much to blame.

"Both Washington and Langley are worried the entire Middle East is set to explode."

"Do you mean the Iranians and their nuclear ambitions?" David asked.

"No, something more. As you know, recently there've been violent public demonstrations in Egypt, Jordan, Syria, Pakistan and Saudi Arabia calling for a fundamentalist government and a *jihad* against the *infidels*. The casualties from these riots have been staggering—nearly a thousand people died in last week's Cairo riot."

David whistled softly. "I didn't know casualties were so high."

"The state-controlled Egyptian media underreported the deaths to avoid more riots. In any event, we think the governments of several moderate Arab countries are close to collapse."

"That's been true for some time. What's changed?"

"We believe these aren't spontaneous demonstrations, but orchestrated by Islamic fundamentalists to take down secular Arab governments and install an Islamic one."

"They'd still need the military's support and most military officers in the region distrust the fundamentalists," David pointed out.

"True, but it'll take only a few co-opted senior officers to lead the military in supporting a rebellion. We suspect that whomever is behind these recent uprisings has been recruiting key military officers for several years. These are patient, dedicated adversaries."

"Al Quada?" David asked, although Reynolds's description didn't quite fit. Al Quada typically used terror and force to achieve their goals; subtlety and working through the political system weren't their trademarks.

"We don't think so. It could be one of a dozen different groups or even a new group that we know nothing about." Reynolds sighed and sat down again. "What's also disturbing is that in the past few weeks, the "chatter" has grown dramatically. Our communications listening posts have intercepted several messages indicating something significant is underway."

"Much like the increase in communications you saw before 9/11?"

"Exactly. Needless to say, both Langley and Washington are very concerned."

"Are there any hard leads?" David asked, beginning to share Reynolds' apprehension.

"Not from our end," Reynolds replied, frustration evident in his tone and expression. "But the Saudis contacted us three days ago to say they have important information to share with us. What, I'm not sure."

David nodded. "And that's where I come in."

Reynolds took a sip of tea and replaced his cup on the table. "Yes, that's why I recalled you from Afghanistan. They want to work with someone they can trust, one of them. You're a perfect go-between—you lived there as a child, understand Islam and speak Arabic fluently."

"I'm also Jewish," protested David. Even though he once lived in Saudi Arabia, he didn't have many fond memories—not because David was Jewish, but because as a Muslim, he'd experienced the heavy-handed influence the religious extremists had over Saudi citizens.

"Something we'll conveniently forget to mention."

David felt a surge of annoyance. "Jack, if I do this, I'll compromise my cover here in Istanbul. I can't recruit and build an intelligence network if I keep running all over the world."

"Langley believes this is more important," Reynolds replied. "The Saudis are insistent and we have to take their warnings seriously."

"Are you sure I'm the right guy?" David asked, still unconvinced. "A more experienced agent with Saudi contacts would be a better fit."

Reynolds chuckled. "That doesn't sound like the cocky SOB who once told me I didn't know squat about the Middle East and to stop treating him like a rookie."

David smiled ruefully. "After a year of working for you, I realize now what I don't know."

Reynolds nodded, looking pleased. "Which means you're on your way to becoming a pro."

"Who do I meet with in Saudi Arabia?" David asked resignedly, knowing further protestations were futile.

"Khaled ibn Saud, the head of the GDI special investigative police. What do you know about the GDI?"

"Enough to meet with Khaled." David knew the General Directorate of Investigation, more commonly called the *mabahith*, or secret police, was responsible for Saudi Arabian domestic security and counterintelligence functions. "Their reputation is decidedly mixed."

Reynolds shrugged. "They've done a great job maintaining domestic order and protecting the monarchy, but their tactics can be brutal. Mass arrests, torture and, if rumors are true, even murder."

"Sounds like our kind of partner," David replied sarcastically. "When do I leave?"

"Tonight. I've a plane waiting at the airport," Reynolds said.

David winced, wishing he could relax for a few days more in Istanbul. "You coming?"

Reynolds smiled. "Of course not. I'm a desk jockey, remember? At least that's what some hot headed agent called me a few months ago."

David laughed. "That was a term of endearment. Don't forget, you invoked the worst curse possible on a desert Arab."

"May the fleas of a thousand camels infest your armpits," Reynolds said, chuckling. "I've used that curse successfully several times since."

David turned serious. "In Saudi Arabia, I want to follow up on the autographed *Quran* I found in Afghanistan."

"Of course. One more thing." Reynolds hesitated, clearly anticipating David's response. "I want you to work with the local CIA office."

"You know I like to work alone," David replied with a scowl. So far, he'd found most of the local CIA offices were staffed by incompetent agents, further evidence the Agency was overly dependent on technological surveillance and sadly lacking in strong human intelligence networks. He always had the sneaking suspicion that some of the CIA's Middle East agents served more than one master.

"Not this time. It's far too important for heroics."

"It's a mistake," David replied testily. "But if that's an order, then I'll do it."

But he was unable to shake the feeling that relying on his own abilities was the only way he would make it home in one piece.

4

Raising his binoculars, Al Kabbar scanned the road in both directions for approaching vehicles. But the roughly paved, two lane highway remained stubbornly empty, the only sign of movement several deer grazing in the distance. Scowling, Al Kabbar lowered his binoculars and stood to stretch his limbs, stiff from lying there and observing the road for nearly five hours.

A tough-looking, heavyset Pakistani wearing military issue camouflage pants and shirt and carrying an AK-47 suddenly appeared. His full beard partially obscured a heavily pockmarked face, but failed to hide his cold and calculating eyes. Bahadur Noor was an intense, ruthless former mercenary with a gruff, violent demeanor.

"Still nothing?" Noor asked.

Al Kabbar shook his head. "No. Are your men in position?"

Bahadur Noor spat noisily, obviously irritated at the question. "Yes. As we discussed many times before—six men on this side of the road, six on the other."

Al Kabbar glanced involuntary at the wooded hill across the road, but was unable to spot any of Noor's men. Raising his binoculars, he stared once more at the highway. Connecting two remote mountainous regions of Pakistan, the road was lightly traveled, typically by buses or an occasional freight truck. From the valley below, it wound steadily upward through a thick pine forest before reaching the mountain pass where they now waited. There, the road ran through a narrow, heavily wooded ravine that was ideal for an ambush. Al Kabbar was positioned perhaps fifteen feet above the road, behind a cluster of trees and several boulders.

Al Kabbar turned back to Noor. "It won't be long now. Our target is already half an hour late. Keep your men alert."

"I know my job," Noor replied testily. "You just make sure I get paid afterwards."

Shouldering his weapon, Noor disappeared back into surrounding forest.

Al Kabbar settled down to wait. He detested Noor, but needed him for the ambush. According to Azam Tariq, an *imam* from a *madras* in Peshwar, a military convoy transporting important cargo from one base to another was scheduled to pass through this remote mountain pass around dusk. Their quarry would consist of four vehicles: two jeeps, a troop transport truck and a small Mercedes van.

The only cargo: a single suitcase nuclear bomb.

Al Kabbar had been surprised to learn from Abdullah that the Pakistani military had managed to secretly construct a portable nuclear bomb. It was widely known that Pakistan maintained a nuclear arsenal at the Sargodha military base 40 miles away as a deterrent to their arch enemy, India. According to Abdullah, the Pakistanis had also manufactured several suitcase nuclear bombs to provide a second deterrent—the ability to send undercover officers into India's largest cities carrying a single bomb. Not surprisingly, the portable nuclear bombs were a closely guarded secret, known by only a few Pakistani military leaders. Fortunately, as a former senior military officer, Azam Tariq had known about the weapon and, through his contacts, the time and location of the transfer that afternoon.

Al Kabbar's mission was simple: ambush the convoy to steal the bomb and then use it to carry out Abdullah's plan.

A month ago, Abdullah had hired Bahadur Noor to lead the operation and recruit a team of ex-Pakistani military mercenaries. Two days ago, Al Kabbar had met Noor for the first time to review his plan and observe his team stage several dry runs. Although impressed with Noor's ambush plan and painstaking attention to detail, Al Kabbar found the former Pakistani special forces commander irritating, arrogant and, above all else, extremely violent. Yesterday he'd watched as Noor shot one of his men in the leg for disobeying an order. Still, Noor's leadership and experience were beyond reproach.

So far, everything had gone according to plan. Now all they had to do was wait for the convoy to arrive.

His radio crackled to life and Al Kabbar answered. "Yeah?"

"Four vehicles approaching," said his scout, who was stationed a mile away. "It's our target."

As Al Kabbar signed off, he heard the rumble of approaching vehicles. Raising his binoculars once again, he studied the road, feeling relieved as a military jeep containing four soldiers appeared. A troop transport truck and white Mercedes van soon followed with a second jeep bringing up the rear.

Al Kabbar picked up the remote control that would detonate the explosives Noor's men had planted earlier under the road. He waited patiently as the vehicles approached, until the lead Jeep drew parallel to his hiding place.

Then he pushed the button.

The ground beneath the first Jeep erupted, creating a huge crater and turning the vehicle into a fireball. In a desperate attempt to avoid the burning vehicle, the troop transport truck swerved off the road and smashed into a tree. The remaining two undamaged vehicles came to a jarring stop. A second explosion lit up the night, destroying the road behind the convoy and effectively sealing off any chance of escape.

For a moment, there was stunned silence, broken only by the sound and light cast by the flickering flames. Then the early evening became alive with the screams and shouts of the ambushed Pakistani soldiers and sporadic automatic rifle fire. Several figures emerged from the pine trees on either side of the road and began to converge slowly toward the vehicles.

Grabbing his AK-47, Al Kabbar rose and half ran and half slid down the rocky slope to the road below. Glancing at the burning lead jeep, he noticed two dead soldiers lying nearby, their uniforms smoldering. There were additional shouts and screams, all cut short by gunfire. The crackling flames cast an eerie glow, backlighting the shadowy figures flitting across the scene.

Al Kabbar moved quickly toward the green troop transport truck, noticing that while the bumper and hood had crumpled upon impact, the rest of the Toyota was unscathed. The rear of the truck was covered with a canvas top, the rear flap slit down the middle.

Suddenly, the canvas flap was pulled back and a Pakistani soldier staggered into view, his mouth working soundlessly, a rifle loosely held in his hand. Raising his AK-47, Al Kabbar fired. The soldier threw up his hands and crashed to one side. Al Kabbar then directed a stream of bullets into the canvas top, squeezing the trigger until his clip was empty. He reloaded quickly, intently looking for further movement.

There was none.

Al Kabbar approached the rear of the truck cautiously, listening and watching for any threat. Pulling back the canvas flap, he surveyed the carnage inside. Broken bodies lay strewn about the compartment, which was smeared with streaks of blood. One soldier moaned softly, his hand groping toward his rifle.

Without hesitation, Al Kabbar fired several bullets into the soldier's head.

Turning away, Al Kabbar jogged toward the Mercedes van that he knew held the nuclear device. Glancing around, Al Kabbar noticed with satisfaction Noor's men checking the bodies of the Pakistani soldiers scattered amongst the vehicles and along the road. The sound of gunfire had ceased and Al Kabbar could hear only scattered voices of his men and the sound of crackling flames.

All the Pakistani soldiers were dead.

Reaching the Mercedes van, Al Kabbar was met by two of Noor's men dressed in black fatigues and wearing ski masks.

"Any problems?" Al Kabbar asked, referring to the van. He had issued strict instructions to Noor's men to not fire any shots in the vicinity of the van and leave it untouched.

"No," replied the taller one. "We killed the driver as he tried to escape. But we haven't searched the vehicle."

"Good." Al Kabbar walked around to the rear of the van and opened the door.

The van was empty.

For a moment, Al Kabbar was stunned. Whirling around, he accosted Noor's two men. "Where the hell is the case?"

Both men stared back blankly. "What case?"

Al Kabbar stared up at the embankment to his left. There, he saw a soldier, clutching a small case, disappear into the surrounding forest.

Al Kabbar fired several shots at the escaping figure, but knew he missed with the darkness and distance.

"Follow me!" he ordered.

Sprinting across the road, Al Kabbar began to scramble up the rocky slope that led to the forest. His feet kept sliding backward in the loose shale, but he moved doggedly forward, fearful the Pakistani would escape. Reaching the crest of the hill, he paused momentarily to look for his quarry. To his left, near where he'd last seen the soldier, he noticed a few swaying branches. He sprinted forward, his rifle held ready. Behind him, he could hear the ragged breathing of his two men.

"Spread out!" he called.

Al Kabbar moved swiftly through the pine trees, following the faint noises ahead. Tree limbs swept across his face and he stumbled occasionally on exposed roots and pine needle covered depressions. Fortunately the setting sun was still high enough in the sky to light his way. Once he caught a glimpse of his quarry, who was making laborious progress, clearly weighed down by the nuclear bomb case.

Al Kabbar climbed a slight hill and then plunged down the other side. As he reached a small grove of trees, he heard movement to his left. He began to spin around, but it was too late.

"Drop your gun!" came a harsh voice.

Turning slowly, Al Kabbar saw the Pakistani soldier standing next to a tree holding a pistol. There was a large black case at his feet.

"Just give me the case and you can go," Al Kabbar said quietly. "My men will be here any minute."

The soldier licked his lips and nervously glanced around. "No. I swore to protect it with my life."

Al Kabbar chuckled. "In exchange for what? A hundred rupees a month? I'll pay a hundred times that if you give me the case."

The Pakistani looked intrigued. "But what..."

To their left came the sound of breaking branches. The Pakistani soldier whirled around, but a short burst of automatic rifle fire slammed into his chest. He staggered backwards and tripped over a log before falling to the ground.

Al Kabbar looked over to see one of his men holding an AK-47. Nodding his thanks, Al Kabbar walked over to the black case next to the dead Pakistani soldier. It appeared unscathed, the black metal unmarked and the latches still locked. He picked the case up gingerly, surprised at the relatively light weight, before replacing it on the ground. Kneeling down, Al Kabbar searched the dead soldier until he found a key inside a jacket pocket. Turning back to the nuclear bomb case, he inserted the key into the lock.

It fit perfectly.

He smiled victoriously. Now nothing could prevent Abdullah's plan from succeeding.

5

David arrived early the next morning in Riyadh after sleeping for most of the four-hour flight. Dressed in a traditional desert robe, David strolled through the crowd, trying to determine if he'd attracted anyone's interest and looking for his local CIA contact. The Riyadh airport, one of the largest in the world, reflected the dichotomies and tensions of modern Saudi Arabia—the vast modern, glass and steel structure was filled with Western businessmen dressed in suits and ties; women wearing the *hijab*, or traditional long black cloak, veil and gloves; Islamic pilgrims dressed in an *ihram*, two white seamless pieces of cloth; and Saudi men wearing traditional *thawbs*, the ankle-length shirt woven from wool, their heads covered by a *ghutra*, a large square of cotton held in place by a cord. David passed several carpeted areas where the religious were praying on their hands and knees, silently repeating the *shahada*, 'There is no God, but *Allah* and Muhammad is his prophet'.

He continued through the wide corridors until he reached the baggage claim area. As he waited for his luggage, a short man wearing a robe approached.

"Are you David Harrim, the jeweler from Istanbul?" he asked David in Arabic. The stranger's thin face, acne scars and uncertain smile gave him the appearance of a callow youth.

"Yes, but I'm a carpet merchant," David replied.

The stranger made an apologetic gesture. "My mistake. My boss asked me to pick you up as he unexpectedly had to fly to Dubai."

"Then you must be Zacarias," David said.

"No. I'm Sayyid. I've a car waiting outside."

"Thanks, we should go," David replied, acknowledging the correct coded response. He was still disconcerted Reynolds had insisted he contact the Saudi GDI through Sayyid, who headed the CIA's Riyadh office. In his short career, David had already learned about the CIA's propensity for leaks and the value of working alone.

He followed Sayyid outside to a white BMW parked near the terminal entrance. Sayyid introduced the driver, a heavyset Saudi in an ill-fitting suit, as

Hamid. After throwing his luggage in the trunk, David climbed into the back seat with Sayyid.

"I thought we'd first go to your hotel to check in and then to your meeting with Khaled ibn Saud," Sayyid said.

David nodded and leaned wearily back into his seat.

The freeway to downtown Riyadh was relatively empty, the surrounding desert filled with sprawling housing developments, office buildings and scattered palm trees. Riyadh was a marvel of engineering and impersonal modernism, the unnatural product of vast oil wealth. It had changed dramatically from the dusty, backwards city David had known in his youth. Yet, there were constant reminders of the uneasy coexistence with Islamic traditions—the numerous mosques, vigilant religious police patrols and the rare sight of a woman allowed in public and clothed from head to toe in a *hijab*. The wind blew steadily, filling the sky with a light brown haze of desert sand that obscured the hot morning sun.

"Are you a Palestinian?" Sayyid asked, evidently trying to make light conversation.

"Yes," David replied simply, knowing he could never reveal his Jewish ancestry to any Saudi Arabian. Taller and with broader shoulders than most Middle Eastern men, David's face also contained evidence of his mixed heritage—a broad nose with a square jaw and full lips. So, Sayyid's uncertainty didn't surprise him. Still, wearing a robe and a *keffiyeh* over his head, David's dark skin and hair enabled him to easily pass as an Arab.

David switched subjects. "Tell me more about Khaled, I understand he's seventh in succession behind the King." King Abdullah bin Abdul-Aziz Al Saud, grandson of Abdul al-Aziz ibn Saud who had founded Saudi Arabia, was the hereditary monarch and head of the House of Saud.

"That's pure speculation since the King picks his successor," Sayyid replied. "Still, Khaled is considered one of the leaders of the Royal Family, which today consists of nearly 800 grandsons and great grandsons with claim to the throne."

"How long has Khaled headed up the GDI?"

"Six years. The Saudi Royal Family is obsessed with domestic security and always has family members in key positions in the military and intelligence services."

"Where do his sympathies lie?" David asked.

Sayyid smiled. "Like all House of Saud members, with self preservation. Khaled's known to have liberal tendencies, but he's tolerated religious extremists and terrorists like Osama bin Laden for years, afraid to precipitate a confrontation. Still, I think he's favorably inclined toward the U.S. Equally important, he doesn't appear to have designs on the throne, which means we can trust him—at least more so than some of his relatives."

"How do the *ulama* view him?" David asked, referring to the powerful Muslim religious leaders.

"With suspicion," Sayyid replied. "Khaled was schooled in the U.S for ten years. He returned to marry a local girl selected by his family and have four sons. He still maintains residences in Europe and America."

"Is he religious?"

"He does and says all the right things, but I don't think so. I think his conservative image is for show."

"Any idea why Khaled insisted on this meeting?" David asked.

"He wouldn't say," Sayyid replied, clearly irritated. "He contacted us last week and asked to meet a CIA agent from outside Saudi Arabia, someone who understood the country and culture and spoke Arabic."

"What do...", David broke off and glanced again at the rearview mirror. "Don't turn around, but we're being followed."

"You sure?"

David nodded. "Dark blue Mercedes, two cars back. He's good, but he's been on our tail since the airport. Let's find out his intentions."

David leaned forward to tap the driver's shoulder. "Hamid, turn off at the next exit."

"I'm afraid we can't do that."

David turned to find Sayyid pointing a pistol at him.

"Don't try to reach for your gun and place your hands where I can see them," Sayyid said.

David swore loudly and placed both his hands on his knees.

"Do you even work for the CIA?" he asked bitterly.

Sayyid nodded. "For five years. But someone else pays a lot better."

"What now?" David's throat was dry and his voice slightly shaky.

"I'm afraid you must disappear," Sayyid replied, almost apologetically.

"Why is it so important that I not meet with Khaled?"

"All I know is that you're deemed expendable."

David desperately tried to think of a way out of his predicament, but for the moment his thoughts were jumbled and diffuse.

With a shiver down his spine, he also realized he was afraid.

The BMW took an exit toward the old section of Riyadh, leaving behind the gleaming high-rises and broad, palm tree lined avenues of downtown Riyadh. They passed through a decaying, older part of town inhabited by the numerous foreign workers who filled the menial and labor intensive jobs most Saudis deemed beneath them. The store signs were in a multitude of languages, the shoppers a mix of Middle Easterners, Asians and even a few Africans. The sidewalks were crowded with pedestrians and men hawking wares displayed on blankets spread on the ground.

"How will you explain my disappearance?" David asked, realizing he needed to keep Sayyid talking.

Sayyid shrugged. "Simple. I never saw you at the airport. Since I run the office, no one will question my story."

"Who hired you?" David glanced over his shoulder and saw the Mercedes was still following.

Sayyid chuckled. "I like your optimism, believing you'll escape and can use the information. Even I don't know his name. But he's got his tentacles everywhere."

"Is his name Al Kabbar?" David asked, mentioning the name of the man who had escaped in Afghanistan.

Sayyid only shook his head and remained silent.

The BMW turned down a filthy, deserted alley and parked near a single story, decrepit warehouse with crumbling concrete walls. The Mercedes pulled up beside them and a heavyset Saudi wearing a grey robe and *keffiyeh* emerged.

"Now open the door slowly and get out," Sayyid ordered, waving his gun. "Hamid, wait for me."

David climbed out of the backseat. He was acutely aware of the feel of the concrete beneath his feet and smell of the pungent, hot morning air, as if his senses had become more acute with his desperation. He glanced around, looking for an opening. The alley ran between several industrial-looking buildings and warehouses and was empty apart from some large garbage bins.

"Get inside," Sayyid said, motioning toward the warehouse door with his gun.

David walked slowly forward as Sayyid followed. He noticed Hamid remained with the BMW and the driver of the Mercedes had stopped to get something from the trunk. Upon reaching the padlocked warehouse door, David stood to one side. As Sayyid passed by, David lunged for him. They fell to the ground in a heap, David desperately trying to grab Sayyid's gun. He managed to wrench it away and rolled to one side, his gaze searching for the other two men. He spotted the Mercedes driver rushing forward with a pistol in his hand.

David snapped off two quick shots and, without even bothering to see if they struck home, turned to look for Hamid. He was getting out of the BMW and David fired again. Hamid threw up his hands and fell backwards against the open door.

Suddenly, David's head exploded with pain as Sayyid's blow connected. David lost his grip on the pistol, which spun away. He tried to fend off the Saudi's punches with his arms, but Sayyid landed two more blows. David grabbed the Saudi and they fell to the ground, rolling around and each trying to land a decisive blow. David's superior strength and weight enabled him to pull his right arm free. He punched Sayyid in the face several times, causing the smaller man to cry out in pain.

David rolled away once again, his hand scrabbling in the dirt for the gun. His hand struck steel and he grasped the pistol just as Sayyid charged again. Raising the gun, David fired. The bullet caught Sayyid in the chest, stopping the Saudi in his tracks.

He collapsed, twitched and then lay still.

Lowering the gun, David rose shakily to his feet. He glanced over at the Mercedes driver, who was lying groaning in the dusty alley, blood staining his robe. Hamid was lying huddled and unmoving against the BMW, a pistol lying harmlessly a few feet away.

Clearly both men were no longer a threat.

He walked over to Sayyid and knelt down. "Who sent you?" he demanded.

Sayyid only coughed once, red spittle flecking his lips.

"Who sent you?" David demanded again, deliberately touching his assailant's wound.

"No, no," Sayyid whimpered in pain. "They'll kill me."

"I'll kill you first!"

The wounded man suddenly broke into convulsions before lapsing into incoherent babbling. David could only make out one word, 'Abdullah'.

"Is that who sent you? The King?"

"No," Sayyid managed to gasp.

"Then who is Abdullah?" David demanded, knowing Abdullah was a very common Arabic name.

But Sayyid could only give a half nod before passing out.

David stood slowly and walked over to the BMW and got in, grateful to find the keys were still in the ignition. For a few moments, he just sat there, letting the adrenaline and fear seep slowly away. Fortunately, aside from a few bruises, he was unhurt. Feeling nauseous, he stared at his hands which gripped the leather steering wheel, his knuckles white with the effort. There was a roaring sound in his ears and he swallowed hard, trying to erase the images of the dead bodies from his mind.

He suddenly leaned over and retched onto the passenger seat. His head was pounding, both from Sayyid's blows and the knowledge that he'd just killed several men. Unlike Afghanistan, this time he'd been face to face with his victim, felt the closeness of death. So different than the rather impersonal nature of a gun.

After a few minutes, David finally composed himself, knowing he needed to drive to his hotel to contact Reynolds about Sayyid's attempt on his life. Perhaps Reynolds could dispatch a team to interrogate the still breathing Sayyid and find out the identity of the mysterious Abdullah and why he wanted David dead. But David doubted they would find out anything more. He felt that Sayyid was far too low on the totem pole to have any important information.

David started the car. Wearily, he tried to focus on his task—he still had a job to do. After speaking with Reynolds, he would shower, change and meet with Khaled ibn Saud.

He could only hope his meeting would be both productive and enlightening. After all, Sayyid had been willing to kill him to prevent it.

He knew one thing for sure: he wasn't going near the CIA's Riyadh office.

❋ ❋ ❋

David's meeting with Khaled ibn Saud was in a small, unobtrusive building near the Masmak Fortress, the renovated mud citadel in the heart of old

Riyadh. Two unsmiling, heavyset guards in the lobby searched David before allowing him to take the elevator to the top floor. Once there, another guard escorted him down a long hallway into a large room luxuriously furnished with antique Persian rugs, gold-framed 19th century impressionist paintings and two Rodin statues. A wet bar lined one wall and several leather chairs were arranged around a coffee table in the middle of the room.

David was standing and admiring a Monet painting when the door on the far side of the room opened and a slight man wearing a white robe trimmed with gold lace entered. Khaled ibn Saud was younger than David expected, perhaps in his late thirties, his face unblemished except for a thin mustache. The Saudi had the unconscious grace of someone powerful and his casual movements and self-assured bearing spoke of wealth, power and privilege. His face wore a slightly bemused expression, as if finding David an interesting diversion, instead of the response to Khaled's urgent request for a meeting with the CIA.

"David, I'm pleased to meet you," Khaled said in English, his cultured voice and faint New England accent confirming the years spent at American boarding schools and Harvard.

"The pleasure's mine. Thanks for pushing back the meeting time," David replied as they shook hands. He had called Khaled earlier to delay the meeting, but hadn't mentioned why.

"Certainly. Please sit down." Khaled said, nodding toward the chairs arranged around the coffee table. "Can I offer you anything to drink? Perhaps some whiskey or wine?"

David smiled, knowing many Saudis, particularly those who had lived abroad, drank alcohol despite the legal and religious prohibitions. "No thanks. Perhaps some tea."

"Of course." Khaled walked over to the wet bar and picked up a tea pot. "I appreciate your willingness to come all this way from Istanbul."

"I understand you've something urgent to discuss."

"Yes." Khaled poured the tea, but remained silent as if waiting for David's questions.

David decided to be blunt, even though he knew custom dictated they talk politely and learn about each other before easing into the reason of his visit. In this respect, he sensed Khaled was more Western than Middle Eastern. "Why'd you ask to meet with someone other than your local CIA contact?"

Khaled handed David a tea cup. "Actually, it wasn't my idea, but the King's and his advisors."

"And you disagreed?" David asked, sensing Khaled's resentment.

"I'd prefer to work through the CIA in Riyadh. But my hand was forced. Some of my people are concerned the CIA office here is compromised. What I'm about to discuss must remain in the strictest confidence. So we asked for a contact that has influence with the key people in Langley and understands Islam and my country."

David nodded. "I presume you know my background."

"At least what I was told," Khaled replied pointedly.

David wondered if Khaled was implying he knew David was part-Jewish. "I'm here to help in any way I can."

"I wouldn't expect anything less from our American friends. Together, perhaps we can defeat these terrorists and restore some sanity in the world."

"Saudi Arabia could do a lot more to stop terrorism," David replied, deliberately provocative. He felt most American officials treated Saudi Arabia far too deferentially, fearful of alienating the world's largest oil producer. David also believed a confrontational approach might increase Khaled's respect for him while keeping the Saudi off balance.

Khaled sat down in a chair opposite David. "My country treads a difficult road."

"Only because you've chosen it."

Khaled shrugged theatrically, his gaze focused on David. "We've little choice. The Islamic fundamentalists block any progressive programs my government tries to implement. On the other hand, as guardian of the holy places of Islam, we need to legitimize ourselves as an Islamic government."

David nodded, aware the 1.5 billion Muslims worldwide considered Saudi Arabia, site of the holy cities of Medina and Mecca, the Holy Land. Mecca was the city where the Prophet Muhammad, the founder of Islam, was born. Each year millions of Islamic pilgrims embarked on a *hajj*, or pilgrimage, to Mecca.

"Yet the House of Saud continues to fund the Wahhabi movement, the most conservative interpretation of Islam," David pointed out. "It's one thing to support Islam; another to promote its most radical version."

Khaled shook his head. "Obviously you know Saudi history. Saudi Arabia and Wahhibism will always be inextricably linked."

David knew Abdullah ibn Saud, founder of modern Saudi Arabia, had allied himself with the Wahhabi movement in the late 1930s to gain legitimacy and adherents to his cause. Prior to the consolidation of power under Abdullah, Saudi Arabia had been a loose collection of warring tribes allied by blood lines and geography. Indebted to the conservative *mullahs* and to minimize social unrest, the Saudi government continued to lavishly fund Wahhabi organizations.

"I understand the tightrope you must walk," David replied. "But at the same time, your government has paid bribes to terrorists such as Osama bin Laden to stay out of Saudi Arabia and unleash their violence elsewhere."

Khaled motioned vaguely with his hand. "We no longer pay anyone. That was an unfortunate policy, something we deeply regret."

Satisfied he had put Khaled on the defensive, David shifted gears. "How can I help?"

Khaled took a deep breath and came directly to the point. "We've uncovered a plot to overthrow the Saudi government."

"That would be devastating," David said, extremely concerned.

Khaled nodded grimly. "It'd be a catastrophe felt around the world. Today we supply nearly 20% of the world's oil production. Even the perception of a heightened coup threat would roil world oil markets and have significant economic, political and military repercussions. If the House of Saud were actually overthrown, that, combined with the ongoing unrest in the Middle East, would cause chaos."

"Is it a secular or fundamentalist plot?"

"Fundamentalist."

"What are the particulars?"

Khaled stood and walked over to a side table. "During a routine traffic stop, the police searched a car belonging to a young religious student. They found this in his briefcase."

He picked up a piece of paper and handed it to David. "This is a *fatwa*, or formal legal opinion, of a *mufti*. As you probably know, a *mufti* is a religious scholar or legal expert who specializes in Islamic law. Only a *mufti* can issue a *fatwa*, which is an authoritative legal interpretation that provides the basis for a Saudi court decision or government action."

David nodded. "I know a legitimate *fatwa* has enormous influence on most Muslims."

"Particularly Saudis. For instance, my government once obtained a *fatwa* from a council of *muftis* to legitimize the presence of non-Muslim American troops in the country."

"What does this *fatwa* say?"

Khaled grimaced. "The *fatwa* declares that the House of Saud has failed in its duties to promote Islam and protect the religious holy places of Mecca and Medina. It goes on to state the present government is illegal and must be replaced by an Islamic one."

"Was this *fatwa* actually issued by a *mufti?*"

"No. It's a draft and there's no signature."

"Then it's worthless," David said.

"Right now, yes," Khaled replied. "The point is that someone clearly is preparing to have such a *fatwa* issued."

"If I'm not mistaken, *fatwas* are issued all the time and many are ignored or other *muftis* issue contradicting ones. Even if this particular *fatwa* were issued, would it have any affect?"

"It depends on who signs it," Khaled replied. "If, for example, someone persuaded the Saudi Council of Senior *Ulama* to issue this *fatwa*, then it'd be taken seriously and my government threatened."

"Is that likely?" David asked. "I know the Council advises the King on religious matters. But I thought the King appointed the members of the Council and that most are beholden to him."

"Yes, and normally I'd agree it's unlikely the Council would issue a *fatwa* threatening the King. But what I didn't mention is that the young man who had this document is the son of the head of the Council."

David understood Khaled's concern. "Did you interrogate his father?"

Khaled smiled grimly. "One does not 'interrogate' the leader of the Council of Senior *Ulama*. We respectfully requested his 'opinion'. He said nothing, other than he'd never seen the *fatwa* before."

"Do you believe him?"

Khaled shrugged. "Maybe, maybe not. He was persuasive; then again, so is the evidence against him. The *ulama* and his son were close, so I suspect the worse."

"Are you watching the *ulama?*"

"We've tapped his phones, house, cars and even his mosque. So far, nothing."

David mulled it over. "I take it you want me to put our sources to work to find out who might be behind this *fatwa*."

Khaled nodded, clearly relieved David quickly grasped the seriousness and potential threat of the situation. "Yes. I'm concerned there'll be an attempt to overthrow the government during the *hajj*. At that time, Saudi Arabia will host nearly 3 million Muslim pilgrims, including many from countries hostile to our government. If this *fatwa* were delivered during the *hajj* by an important *mufti*, it could spark a full fledged revolt. We can't allow a repeat of the violence of 1979, or even the riots of the 1980s."

David understood his concern, aware that in 1979, Muslim extremists, protesting the Saudi Royal Family's ostentatiousness and the growing influence of Western culture, had seized the Grand Mosque at Mecca. Saudi security forces had removed them only after much bloodshed. In the 1980s, followers of Ayatollah Khomeini sparked several riots during the *hajj* in which hundreds died. These incidents had only heightened the concern of many Islamic fundamentalists that the Saudi Arabia government, one that was already considered too sympathetic to the Christian West, was failing in its stewardship of Islam's holiest shrines.

"Do you think many Saudi citizens would join in a revolt if this *fatwa* was issued?"

"In some respects, Saudi Arabia is ripe for revolution," Khaled admitted, surprisingly candid. "In recent years, our growing population has forced us to largely dismantle our welfare state despite the influx of petrodollars. As a result, many unemployed Saudis have embraced Wahhabism or radical Muslims such as Osama Bin Laden. Equally important, many Saudis are distrustful of Western morals and consumer culture and long to return to a simpler time governed by Islamic law and ancient Saudi traditions."

"In other words, between the pilgrims, guest workers and disgruntled citizens, Saudi Arabia is a powder keg waiting to explode."

"Precisely." Khaled took a sip of tea. "There's another reason why this *fatwa* should concern you. It also calls for a *jihad* against the West and the expulsion of all foreigners from Saudi Arabia and their troops from the Middle East."

"I'm not surprised. If the existing Saudi government were declared illegitimate, then obviously so would any strategic alliances they had with the U.S."

"The end result would be chaos," Khaled said. "At best, the expulsion of foreign oil workers would significantly curtail Saudi oil production. At worst, such actions could spread across the Middle East, topple governments and bring the entire Middle East oil industry to a grinding halt."

"I agree." David thought it over. "When does the *hajj* start this year?"

"As always, during the twelfth month of the lunar calendar. This year, it occurs in February, a week from now."

"Can I speak to the young scholar you arrested who had this *fatwa?*" David asked.

Khaled shook his head. "No, regrettably he's dead. He committed suicide."

"How unfortunate," David replied dryly, assuming that the suspect had died during a brutal interrogation. It was widely known that the Saudis sometimes tortured suspects, particularly those perceived as threats to the House of Saud.

"He died as I explained," Khaled insisted, obviously aware of David's suspicions. "We didn't want to see the son of a senior *ulama* die in our hands. He clearly had something to hide."

David once again examined the *fatwa* document, carefully reading the Arabic text. Curiously, the *fatwa* accused the Saudi government of betraying Islam, yet remained silent on the complicity of the Royal Family, which effectively *was* the government. David wondered if that were deliberate. If so, did it mean that someone from the Royal Family—one of Khaled's relatives—had helped draft the *fatwa*, intending to illegitimize the government, but not members of the House of Saud? If true, then one of Khaled's relatives was planning to take control once the existing government was deposed.

"I'll see what we can find out," David said. "Unfortunately, you may be right that our network here has been compromised."

Khaled smiled ruefully. "There are other organizations operating here beside the CIA. Perhaps the British or Israelis could be helpful."

"We'll consult our allies." David stood and handed back the *fatwa* to Khaled. "Before I go, one good turn deserves another. I need a favor."

"Of course."

David put his briefcase on the coffee table and pulled out the *Quran* he had taken from the dead man in Afghanistan and handed it to Khaled. "I took this from a suspected terrorist in Afghanistan. The *Quran* is new and in the front is a handwritten quote from the *Quran*. It's signed by Turki al Faisal, a Saudi Arabian *ulama*. I'd like to find out if Al Faisal knew the man I killed and what he can tell me about him."

Khaled looked up at David with a dazed expression. "Merciful *Allah*. Such an unbelievable coincidence."

"What coincidence?" David asked, uneasy at Khaled's reaction.

"And the inscription he wrote, '*When the sacred months have passed...*,'" Khaled mumbled, as if talking to himself. "I've heard him use the same verse during prayers."

"Care to fill me in?" David asked impatiently.

Khaled handed the *Quran* back to David. "I know the man you seek very well, the *ulama* who wrote this inscription. Al Faisal's an important man, perhaps the most revered religious leader in Saudi Arabia."

"Then you're surprised he has ties with a potential terrorist?"

Khaled shook his head. "Actually, no. Because of one other fact."

"What?"

Khaled looked grim. "He's the father of the young religious scholar we arrested. The young man who possessed the *fatwa* and then committed suicide. Turki al Faisal heads the Saudi Council of Senior *Ulama*."

David whistled softly. "Is it possible he'd be involved in this coup attempt?"

"If true, it'd be a significant blow. Al Faisal is a powerful man. Seeing this, I'm absolutely convinced that the threat to my government is very real."

"Can you can set up a meeting with Al Faisal for me? Perhaps tell him I'm a Turkish rug merchant looking to donate money to his mosque."

Khaled nodded. "I'll call in a few favors to get you a meeting with Al Faisal tomorrow. Then perhaps you can coax the snake from his hole."

6

The ancient mosque was bathed in moonlight, illuminating the golden dome and blue tiled walls. The slender minarets stood like wary sentinels guarding the deserted plaza that stretched before the imposing entrance, the emptiness somehow unnerving in the early morning hour. A warm wind blew steadily, carrying the sand and grit of the surrounding desert. The silence was broken only by the occasional barking dog and distant rumble of a passing car.

Keeping in the shadows, David moved stealthily along the far edge of the plaza. Drawing parallel to the mosque, he then darted across the plaza and climbed the steps to the main entrance. David tugged on the enormous door, but wasn't surprised to find it locked. He hurried around the side of the mosque to look for another entrance. In the rear, David found a smaller door, which he assumed was a private entrance for Muslim clerics. Removing a set of skeleton keys from a pocket of his robe, he tried several before finally hearing a satisfying click.

The inside of the mosque was pitch dark and David pulled out a flashlight and switched it on. The light illuminated a barren hallway that led to another door at the far end. David moved down the corridor, listening carefully for any movement. After opening the door, he entered another hallway, this one much larger and lined with hand woven tapestries. David paused briefly to get his bearings, realizing he had reached the main passage that led from the clerics' offices to the _haram_, or prayer hall, of the mosque. He moved down the hall away from the _haram_ toward Turki al Faisal's office.

At the end of the hall, David opened another door and entered a conference room with a large table, leather chairs and paintings depicting scenes from the _Quran_. For the second time that day, David paused to admire the painting of Abraham slaying disbelievers with thunderbolts delivered by his fingertip. He had seen the painting earlier that afternoon during a meeting with the _ulama_, Turki al Faisal. The meeting had been arranged by one of Khaled ibn Saud's contacts, who told Al Faisal that David was a rich Turkish rug merchant and devout Muslim who wanted to make a substantial donation to further the cause of Islam.

They had met earlier that afternoon in the same conference room, the elderly *ulama* Al Faisal accompanied by an intense young *imam*. After conveying his condolences over the recent death of the *ulama's* son, David had turned the conversation to the possibility of an Islamic *jihad*. They had discussed the ongoing struggle against the West, David expressing his approval of strikes against American targets. At the appropriate moment, he brought out the *Quran* he'd taken from Said Bahajji, the man who had nearly killed David in Afghanistan.

"Bahajji left this *Quran* with me for safekeeping," David had said. "But I haven't heard from him since. I noticed you'd written a prayer for him on the inside cover and thought I'd ask if you'd heard from him recently."

"Said Bahajji is a very religious man," Al Faisal replied, nodding fervently. "I pray every night for his safe return."

"Is Said in danger?" David asked.

Al Faisal was about to respond when the younger *imam* reached out and grasped the *ulama's* shoulder. The younger man spoke instead. "We don't know. To us, he's just a devout man who worships in our mosque."

David nodded knowingly. "I'd like to follow in his footsteps. I know he's fighting for the *jihad*."

The younger *imam* smiled. "One day, perhaps soon, we'll be victorious."

"I'd like to do more than just give my fortune," David said. "I'm willing to die for *Allah*."

The two Saudi men had exchanged glances before Al Faisal spoke. "We don't countenance violence, even to defend Islam."

"So you've said publicly. But Said Bahajji said you are involved with the *jihad*." David's implied meaning was clear.

"He's mistaken," the young *imam* replied, scowling, his eyes narrowing with suspicion. He glanced at Al Faisal and made a nearly imperceptible gesture. Both men rose to their feet, indicating the interview was over. David cursed silently, knowing he'd pushed too hard and aroused their suspicions.

"Please excuse us," Al Faisal said. "We must get ready for prayer."

Although frustrated he hadn't learned anything, David's only choice had been to leave. On the way out, David had noticed the armed man guarding the entrance to the clerics' offices. Desperate for any additional information, David had decided to search the mosque later that evening. About an hour ago, he'd donned dark clothes and driven there, parking in a nearby alley. He had then cautiously made his way through the empty streets to the mosque without seeing anyone other than a few stray dogs.

David left the conference room and walked down the corridor toward the clerics' offices. Suddenly, he heard the sound of someone approaching. Glancing around, he spotted a nearby door. He opened it and darted inside, shutting the door just as the approaching footsteps drew near. David listened with trepidation as the intruder stopped, as if having seen the door shut. Glancing around the room for an exit, David realized there was none. He slid his hand inside his robe and withdrew a pistol, moving to the side of the door.

Suddenly, the door was kicked open and a shadowy figure appeared.

"Don't move," David commanded, his gun pointed at the intruder. "Drop your gun."

A weapon clattered to the floor.

"Hands high above your head!"

The man slowly raised his arms.

"Come inside, close the door and turn around."

The man did as he was told, careful not to make any sudden movements. David didn't recognize him and assumed he was a patrolling guard.

"Sit down in the chair closest to you. Keep your hands on your head."

The guard sat down. David moved up behind the man and struck him viciously on the head with the butt of the gun. The guard slumped forward, his head slamming into the table. Checking the prostrate figure, David was satisfied he was breathing, but out cold. Although he wanted to interrogate the man, David feared there were other patrolling guards.

He needed to search the *ulama's* office quickly and get out.

Returning to the hallway, David walked swiftly on, stopping occasionally to listen for any movement. Upon reaching Turki al Faisal's office, David opened the door and shined the flashlight around the room. Although fairly large, the office held only a desk, leather reading chair and several file cabinets against the far wall. David walked over to the desk and began to search, looking for something that might connect the *ulama* to Said Bahajji or even Al Kabbar or the mysterious Abdullah. He leafed through a large stack of papers, principally drafts of fiery speeches. A trickle of sweat soon appeared down his back, born of fear and carried by exertion.

Finding nothing interesting, David moved over to the file cabinets. He ignored the unlocked drawers and instead focused on a short file cabinet with two locked drawers. Again, he pulled out his skeleton keys and picked the lock.

The first drawer held mostly magazine and newspaper clippings. The second drawer was much more illuminating. An entire section of hanging files labeled 'Pakistan' was filled with memos, bank statements, purchase orders and lists of names. David quickly scanned the memos. Most were from Azam Tariq, the head of a *madras*, or religious school, in Peshawar, Pakistan called the 'Fist of *Allah*'. According to the memos, the school also operated a military training camp somewhere in the mountains for both its own students and young men sent from Saudi Arabia. The list of names apparently was that of those who had attended the camp. David wondered if the Saudis trained by the *madras* were either members of Al Faisal's mosque, part of the *mutaween* or both.

The second file held five years of bank statements that showed large transfers of money from a Dubai bank to another bank in Pakistan. The purchase orders were for North Korean weapons, mostly rifles and a few surface-to-air missiles, and, most disturbingly, raw materials that could be used to construct chemical weapons.

David put down the papers and pondered the information. The Pakistani *madras* 'Fist of *Allah*' presumably served several purposes—similar to most *madrasas*, it probably taught poor Pakistanis radical Islamic theology and converted them to *Wahhibism*. The *madras* was located in Peshawar, Pakistan; a city that harbored numerous Islamic fundamentalists and Al Quada members. He wondered if Said Bahajji had trained at the *madras* military training camp and if Al Kabbar had returned either there or to the Peshawar *madras*.

David realized he needed to go to Pakistan to investigate both the 'Fist of *Allah*' *madras* and its training camp. If he were lucky, he'd find Al Kabbar.

He continued going through the papers, scanning each quickly before a letter from Azam Tariq caught his attention. The Pakistani *imam* had written that he had put a man named Abdullah in touch with a former Pakistani army General.

All in an effort to "obtain the weapon that will ensure our ultimate victory."

David shivered slightly as it was well known the Pakistani military possessed nuclear weapons. Was that the weapon Tariq was referring to? David was also fairly certain that Abdullah must be the same mysterious man who had ordered Sayyid to kill David in Riyadh. Abdullah was clearly a much more dangerous, important person than he had initially thought.

David now knew it was imperative he quickly learn more about Abdullah.

"Stop what you're doing and turn around *very* slowly," a voice said.

David froze, silently cursing himself for not maintaining his vigilance. David raised his hands and turned to find himself looking down the barrel of gun held by the young *imam* he'd met that afternoon.

"I thought it might be you," the *imam* said. "Step away from the desk and come slowly out of the office."

David complied, desperately searching for either a good excuse or an opening to escape. He found neither, only the knowledge he'd left himself far too vulnerable.

"I can explain," David said desperately.

"Later," the *imam* replied, backing slowly out of the office, his gaze never leaving David. "No talking. Start moving."

The *imam* directed David along a long corridor, then down a steep flight of stairs into a damp and musty basement. The concrete walls were pitted and crumbling and the low roof pressed close overhead. A dim bulb dangled from a cord at the end of the hallway. David attempted to turn and speak, but the *imam* gave him a sharp jab with the gun.

"In there," the *imam* said, pointing to an open door.

David stepped inside a small room with a rickety table, two chairs and several metal book shelves against the far wall. A heavyset man turned in surprise as they entered.

"Kamel, I found him looking around Al Faisal's office," the *imam* explained. "He's the stranger I mentioned to you this afternoon. Search him."

Kamel roughly searched David, removing his skeleton keys, pistol and small knife. David remained alert for any opening, but there wasn't one. Kamel pushed David into a chair and tied his wrists and feet together with a piece of rope, before wrapping it tightly around the chair's metal frame. David considered struggling, but the *imam* kept the gun trained on him.

"Kamel, leave us," the *imam* said. "I want to talk to him alone."

After Kamel departed, the *imam* turned to David and smiled. "Now, we'll talk. Who are you and why were you searching our offices?"

"I'm worried about Said Bahajji," David lied, gazing unflinchingly at the young *imam*, trying to convey the impression he had nothing to hide. "I knew you didn't tell me the truth about him today and I thought if I searched your offices, I might find out what happened to him."

The *imam* pushed back the hood of his robe, revealing a thin face, slitted eyes and mocking grin. "A nice story, but a lie. You see, through some friends, I checked up on you. I'm told you have a legitimate Turkish rug business, but also work for the American CIA."

"You're mistaken. I'm just a carpet merchant from Istanbul."

"And I'm a Jew from America." The *imam* smiled again. "I need answers, but can see I'm wasting my time."

David remained silent, desperately fighting to subdue his fear.

"Talk," the *imam* said, striding forward and striking David across the check with the gun. Then twice more. David tasted blood in his mouth and spit out a tooth.

"I'll kill you," the *imam* said, his expression cold.

David merely ducked his head, desperately wondering how to escape. He cursed himself for his predicament—his earlier smug confidence was replaced by the sickening knowledge he was alone and no one knew David had gone to the mosque that evening.

The cavalry would not arrive; David's fate was in his own hands.

"As you will." The *imam* walked over to a box on a shelf, opened it and pulled out a syringe and small bottle filled with a clear liquid. He inserted the needle into the bottle and filled the syringe.

"Now," the *imam* said, holding up the syringe into the light. "Perhaps we'll get a few answers from you. This is sodium pentothal, better known as truth serum. Crude perhaps, but effective. Although some prefer pain to get people to talk, I find this is much more effective."

"I thought you're a religious man," David said.

The *imam* scowled. "I do this to defend Islam against our enemies. You're the worst of all. You've clearly been exposed to Islam, yet have rejected it. There's no mercy for someone like you."

The *imam* jabbed the needle into David's arm and injected the contents. Satisfied, he replaced the syringe in the box. His expression was both gleeful and victorious, as if he was about to finally vanquish an ancient enemy.

"I'll be back shortly. Then we'll talk."

The *imam* left, closing the door behind. David looked desperately around the room for a way out of his predicament. He found nothing. He tried pulling on the rope binding him to the chair, but succeeded only in cutting his wrists and ankles. After a few minutes, the drug began to take effect and he slumped over in the chair. He began to drift off, his thoughts growing hazy and his eyelids heavy.

He saw his father, a broad shouldered and imposing man for a Palestinian, his face stern as he lectured about the perfidy and betrayal of the Israelis. Although David had loved his father, he had also been old enough to blame him for his parent's separation. Once settled in America, David wrote his father many letters, but his mother refused to mail them. A year after his arrival in America, his mother revealed that his father had died. David never quite forgave her, for he knew she didn't mourn his death. He still had a picture on his bedroom dresser of his father standing before the Dome of the Rock in Jerusalem and proudly holding a two-year old David.

Another face swam into view, that of the tight-lipped, intense woman who had directed David's training back in Langley. She was talking about the importance of conducting searches in pairs so that one person could always keep watch. David knew he had violated a basic tenet of intelligence gathering, but, with Sayyid's betrayal, he'd been left without backup, certain that the entire Saudi CIA office was compromised. Tonight, his lack of experience had shown. He recalled his instructor talking about the necessity of killing, of always being prepared. At the time, sitting in the air-conditioned classroom surrounded by well-dressed young men and women, David had believed such moments were extremely rare for undercover agents.

Now, David knew what he was doing was more than a game; it was possible, even likely, he would die in that musty, dark basement.

The door opened and David struggled to turn his head. A figure in a flowing black garment approached and knelt by his side. He felt something sharp against his wrists and ankles and he realized the rope tying him had been cut. A strong, steady hand pulled him to his feet.

"Can you walk?" a soft voice asked.

"Yes." David wasn't sure why, but it seemed urgent he keep moving.

"Lean on me," the voice said.

David was conscious only of a steadying arm and movement. His vision was blurred and everything seemed dreamlike and slow. He felt stairs beneath his feet and soon was vaguely aware they were on the main floor of the mosque. He heard voices and his mysterious companion opened a door and pushed him inside another room. Leaning gratefully against the wall, David struggled to make sense of the situation.

His companion opened the door again and hustled David down several corridors until they were outside in the cool desert night. David gulped down the clear air, trying to drive away the effects of the drug. He heard shouts coming from the mosque and smiled, aware for a lucid moment that his escape had been discovered.

David wanted to sink to the ground and rest, but the unknown figure pushed him forward. After what seemed hours, but was surely only a couple minutes, they arrived at a car parked in a nearby alley. The driver got out and David heard a hurried exchange of greetings.

"Get in," his unknown benefactor said, opening the rear door.

David chuckled, for some reason finding the situation funny.

"Quiet," someone hissed. "Hurry up and get inside."

David grew conscious of shouting voices and the flat crack of a pistol. David's companion forced him inside the car and climbed in behind. The car lurched forward, the wheels squealing in protest. David leaned back against the soft leather, drowsily reflecting on his good fortune. He wondered vaguely if he had gone from the frying pan to the fire and turned to speak to his unknown benefactor. Even in his drugged condition, he recognized the *hijab* of a woman.

She turned to speak to him and that was the last thing he remembered.

7

Vasily Ivanhov flashed his employee identification to the bored security guard, who gave it a cursory glance before turning back to reading his newspaper. Ivanhov walked quickly through the entrance gate, relieved the guard had failed to notice that his pass expired several weeks ago, about the same time Ivanhov had been fired for theft. The dismissal still rankled Ivanhov. He had only taken a few boxes of office supplies, but the new plant supervisor had vowed to end such entrenched employee habits and made an example of Vasily. At first, he had been devastated to lose his comfortable, well-paid position, knowing few employers could use his specialized skills. Now, Vasily believed that losing his job had been the biggest break of his life. Tonight, he would become wealthy beyond his wildest dreams.

The enormous dome covering the nuclear reactor loomed ahead, the aging structure covered with industrial grime from the numerous nearby factories. The entire plant complex consisted of seven buildings, including offices, warehouses and a cavernous spent nuclear rod holding facility. The nuclear reactor was an old Soviet water-cooled design, extremely inefficient and nearing the end of its life cycle. In the past five years, there had been two accidents; both had nearly caused a nuclear core melt-down potentially far more lethal than Chernobyl. Ivanhov knew that Ukrainian officials were trying to essentially extort money from concerned European governments to shut down the facility and fund a new gas fired power plant. Soon, the entire complex would be dark and silent, a radioactive mausoleum testifying to the failed promise and unforeseen cost of nuclear power.

Ivanhov walked briskly forward with his head down, hoping the gathering darkness would hide his identity from his former co-workers. Fortunately, the biting cold and late hour kept most of the few remaining workers inside. He couldn't help but notice further evidence of the nuclear complex's continued decay—the rubbish piles, discarded broken machinery and sagging building walls. Just before he reached the reactor dome, Ivanhov turned and climbed a flight of stairs that led to the entrance of a large concrete-walled warehouse.

Glancing around nervously to make sure he was unobserved, Ivanhov opened the door and went inside.

The warehouse contained a large open floor filled with hundreds of steel and concrete containers, each the size of a small chest and prominently marked with the international symbol for radiation. Ivanhov was relieved to see a man standing near a delivery van on the far side of the building. He walked across the floor, glancing around the dimly lit building to ensure they were alone.

"Everything ready, Mikhail?" Ivanhov asked as he drew near.

"You got the money?" Mikhail asked nervously, his pale face shiny with sweat. He was a short, rather stout man with bad teeth and an unruly hairpiece that looked like the end of a mop. Mikhail delivered supplies every few days to the nuclear facility and was well known to the plant workers for his willingness to smuggle stolen equipment in his van. Ivanhov had bribed him to load one of the containers into his van and take it out through the main entrance.

Ivanhov scowled. "I told you before, you get paid after we're done. Even I don't get paid until later tonight."

Mikhail nodded reluctant acknowledgement and gestured to the surrounding containers. "Which one you want?"

"Doesn't matter—they're all full. The closest one will do."

Mikhail opened the rear doors of his battered delivery van. Together, Ivanhov and Mikhail picked up the nearest container, which proved to be surprisingly light. They lifted it into the rear of the van and Ivanhov threw a tarp over the container before slamming the door shut.

"You could lift it by yourself," Mikhail said. "Probably only weighs 50 kilos."

Ivanhov merely grunted acknowledgement.

"What if they find out the container is missing?" Mikhail asked nervously.

Ivanhov waved his arm dismissively toward the sea of deadly containers. "Nobody'll ever miss one; they don't even know for sure how many there are. In fact, if they knew one was missing, they'd probably be happy. This reactor waste is good for nothing and just gets buried somewhere in Siberia."

"Is it dangerous?"

"Only when out of the container."

The driver gave a perceptible sigh of relief. "Where's it going?"

"You're being paid not to ask those questions."

Ivanhov got into the passenger side of the van. He pulled his hat low over his forehead and slumped against the door, as if he were sleeping. Mikhail climbed into the driver's seat and started the engine. The van lurched forward and out the warehouse loading dock doors. Mikhail drove slowly, waving several times to acquaintances who were trudging toward the exit, their shoulders hunched and jackets pulled tight against the cold. The van passed unchallenged through the exit gate, the lackadaisical guard waving to the familiar driver. Once on the access road, Mikhail accelerated, clearly anxious to put some distance between them and the facility. As the lights of the nuclear power facility faded, Ivanhov and Mikhail exchanged relieved smiles.

"Easiest money I ever made," the driver said.

"And the most," Ivanhov replied, slapping Mikhail on the back.

Mikhail grinned broadly. "Yeah, this should pay for a long vacation on the Crimean coast with a very pretty girl—not my wife, that old hag."

Ivanhov laughed heartily, relishing the thought that after tonight he could afford a permanent vacation from this godforsaken place.

They drove for nearly twenty minutes, occasionally passing a lone sedan or freight truck. Finally, they reached a roadside bar with a large flashing sign overhead and a dozen parked cars outside. Mikhail pulled into the far end of the parking lot and turned to Ivanhov.

"The van is all yours," the delivery driver said. "My cousin will pick me up here."

"Remember. I'm paying for your silence too."

Mikhail nodded. "When I get the money, you have it."

Ivanhov slid across the seat and took the wheel. As he pulled away, he noticed Mikhail head straight for the bar, probably to celebrate his good fortune.

Ivanhov drove for another half hour, passing several silent and dark factories that spoke accusingly of the former Russian empire's disastrous transformation to a market economy. Most of his friends now survived either through odd jobs or by bartering their services for food. His parents, struggling to survive on a pitiful pension, were forced to spend the day by the side of the road selling old magazines, clothes and anything else they could scavenge from the city dump or neighbors' trash. Ivanhov had long ago vowed never to stoop to such desperate measures. Once settled overseas, he could send for his parents and provide them with the retirement they deserved.

Several nights after losing his job, Ivanhov had been downing cheap vodka in a bar and grimly imagining a similar fate for himself when a stranger offered to buy him a drink. They had chatted over a bottle of the best Russian vodka provided by the dark, slight foreigner. By the end of the evening, Ivanhov had agreed to steal a container of nuclear waste. The bribe offered was more than he could have made during twenty lifetimes at his old job. Ivanhov did not ask, nor did he want to know, why the stranger wanted the container. He thought only of how the money would let him escape to Western Europe and a life of luxury.

Vasily was certain the stranger who had hired him was from the Middle East—his dark skin, eyes and hair were that of an Arab. Ivanhov didn't much care for Arabs; after all, they supported the Chechen Muslim rebels who waged a brutal civil war against Russia. But Ivanhov knew that if he refused, dozens of his former co-workers would have gladly taken the money. In the end, he negotiated a slightly higher price, as if to compensate for his guilt. In the ensuing weeks, he hadn't experienced any second thoughts.

In the new Ukraine, it was every man for himself.

Twenty minutes later, Ivanhov reached the outskirts of a forest and turned down a partially overgrown road toward an abandoned factory that had once made kitchen appliances. The rough and rocky road had fallen into disrepair, forcing him to drive slowly. After reaching the main building, Ivanhov parked the van and turned off the engine. The dark, silent night and remote location suddenly seemed ominous. Ivanhov hesitated and then reached down for the pistol Mikhail usually kept taped to the underside of the seat. Fortunately, it was still there. Ivanhov removed the gun, stuffed it into his waistband and pulled his coat over the bulge. It always paid to take precautions. Feeling more secure, he got out and stood waiting next to the van.

A light suddenly shone in his eyes.

"You have it?" the stranger asked, materializing from the shadows. The Arab was dressed as a construction worker, a hat pulled low over his face. Ivanhov almost failed to recognize him until he saw the bright flash of the stranger's gold front tooth.

"Of course."

The stranger stepped past Ivanhov and looked inside the front of the van, making sure the Ukrainian was alone.

"Everything went smoothly? You told no one?" The stranger's harsh voice chilled Ivanhov. With a terrible premonition, Ivanhov realized his promised wealth might come at an astronomical price. His hand inched toward the gun in his belt.

"Everything went fine, but several people know that I'm here," Ivanhov lied. "My friend, the one who got me inside the plant, should be here shortly to get his share of the money."

The stranger glanced at the entrance road, but saw there were no telltale headlights. He turned back to face Ivanhov, a knowing look crossing his face. Ivanhov shivered again with fear, certain now he had made a mistake in agreeing to meet in this god forsaken location.

"Show me the container!"

Ivanhov walked around to the rear of the van, vainly trying to see the stranger's expression. But the flashlight stayed pointed at his face and Ivanhov could only blink furiously, his eyes tearing in protest at the bright light or perhaps at what was to come. He thought longingly of his favorite smoke-filled bar, the long, satisfying nights spent drinking with his friends and discussing the latest soccer match. Terrified now of the stranger and their isolated surroundings, Ivanhov figured that if the Arab planned to kill him, he'd at least wait until after examining the radioactive container. Ivanhov decided to pull out his gun while the stranger was looking at it, demand his money and then drive away, leaving the man and his container behind.

Unfortunately for Ivanhov, the stranger had a different plan.

As the Ukrainian turned to open the rear door of the van, the Arab pulled out a gun. He fired three times. Mercifully, Ivanhov never heard the pistol shot nor felt the slugs tear through his back and enter his heart.

Vasily Ivanhov was dead before his body hit the ground.

Ivanhov's murderer calmly put his gun away and dragged the body about 30 feet to a previously dug grave beneath several pine trees. He tumbled the body into the shallow hole and filled it with dirt, breathing heavily at the rare physical exercise. Satisfied at last, he took a branch and smoothed away the footprints and loose dirt, before throwing some more branches across the grave. Then he climbed into Ivanhov's van. A check of his watch told him he had four hours to reach the airport and the waiting plane, which left plenty of time for an early breakfast.

As he started the engine, for the first time that night Hazan Qwasama smiled.

8

David walked slowly along the deserted street, enjoying the surprisingly cool night and breathing deeply of the desert air. Although tired, he was unable to sleep, his thoughts turning to his miraculous rescue the previous evening. His face was bruised and swollen where the *imam* had struck him with the gun and he was still feeling the effects of being drugged.

He had awoken alone earlier that morning in an unfamiliar cheap hotel near the Riyadh airport, nursing a splitting headache and unharmed other than his pride. He was unable to recall anything after escaping from the mosque, other than his mysterious benefactor had been a woman. The hotel front desk clerk could only tell him that David had been brought in during the night by another man, who paid cash for the room and asked that his drunken friend be allowed to sleep uninterrupted.

Grateful but bewildered, David had returned to his original hotel. There, he found his room had been searched—the threads he'd carefully placed in strategic locations around the room were disturbed. He had immediately gone to the U.S embassy to call Jack Reynolds in Istanbul. David's information, particularly his meeting with Khaled ibn Saud, had greatly concerned Reynolds.

"If true," Reynolds had said, "The entire Middle East will be thrown into chaos and oil prices would soar."

"You need to put Turki al Faisal and the young *imam* who drugged me under surveillance," David had said.

"Agreed. Any thoughts on the identity of your mysterious rescuer?"

"I think she's a member of a Western intelligence agency. Islamic groups rarely use women agents."

"Too bad she didn't stick around," Reynolds had groused. "Perhaps she could've told us more about Al Faisal."

"I'm more concerned about the "weapon" Azam Tariq referenced in his letter. It could be a Pakistani nuclear bomb."

"It *is* alarming," Reynolds had admitted. "You need to go to Pakistan to follow up on it."

David had agreed. "I thought I'd go to Peshawar to investigate Azam Tariq and the *madras* mentioned in the papers I found in Al Faisal's office. I'll also try to find out more about the training camp and hopefully find some trace of Al Kabbar."

"What about this Abdullah who ordered Sayyid to kill you?"

"I don't know anything about him. He may be behind everything, but I don't have any leads about who he is and where I might find him."

Reynolds had agreed with David's proposed plan and arranged for a CIA jet to fly David that evening to Pakistan.

For the past hour, David had killed time by wandering through the streets surrounding his hotel. His return to Saudi Arabia had stirred up too many, mostly unhappy, memories. After fleeing Israel, David and his father had lived only a few miles from where he now wandered. Alone in a foreign land, David had deeply missed his mother, friends, Israel and even the comforting rituals of Judaism. Even as a young boy, he found Saudi Arabia far too restrictive and somber, even slightly frightening. His father had enrolled him in an Islamic school where David became fluent in Arabic, knowledgeable about Islam and the target of frequent teacher whippings. Once his classmates became aware of his mixed heritage, David had been subjected to constant taunts and petty humiliations. Not surprisingly, the isolation and lack of close friends had become a recurrent theme of his life.

After his mother had spirited him away to America, David never saw his father again. Although he missed his father, David had been initially delighted with his newfound freedom. At times, he became bewildered at the discrepancy between the lessons of his early Islamic schooling and those of a Southern California teenager. He had coped, but not always prospered. Part of him missed the traditions, historic setting and restrictions of his former life—teenagers in the Middle East weren't confronted by such a diverse range of lifestyles and personal choices. David spent most of his teenage years lost in the asphalt jungle of L.A., rudderless and adrift. Although his mother never remarried, she rarely spoke about his father. She only told him that his father had returned to the West Bank and died a year later from cancer. She herself had passed away shortly after he went off to college.

So he was truly alone in the world.

David was suddenly aware of a Chevy Suburban driving toward him, the dark silhouette somehow menacing. He hesitated for a moment before instinct sent him sprinting for the walled compound of a large mansion to his right. Upon reaching the security wall, he was relieved to find the top of it wasn't covered with broken glass like so many. Glancing over his shoulder, he realized the Suburban had stopped and disgorged two men dressed in black robes.

Each was carrying a pistol.

David leaped up and grasped the top of the wall. As he pulled himself up and over, he heard the crunch of several bullets striking the rough concrete.

He fell awkwardly, landing on one foot and tumbling forward to break his fall. Pushing himself to his feet, David pulled out a gun from his shoulder holster. He was standing in a large garden with numerous trees, dense bushes and several flower beds. He ran down a crushed rock path that led toward the mansion, overhanging palm fronds and tree branches clutching at his body. The path fed into a large lawn containing several marble statues. As David ran across the grass, he glanced over his shoulder.

So far, there was no sign of his pursuers.

David looked hurriedly around, searching for the best avenue of escape. The dark and seemingly empty white French chateau-looking building lay straight ahead, the exterior faintly lit by second story flood lights. A large brick terrace adjoined the rear of the chateau with a water fountain in the center. The compound wall extended unbroken on either side, without any sign of an exit gate.

Unfortunately, the moon was bright and shining, leaving him far too exposed.

David ran toward the building, intending to circle around to the front to find an exit. Suddenly, he noticed movement near a small outbuilding to his right. Diving to the ground, he steadied his elbows on the grass and looked for a target. A black robed figure emerged from down another path, his right arm longer than his left.

David fired twice, the flat crack of his pistol overloud in the warm night air. His assailant dove into some nearby bushes, a controlled movement that suggested David had missed. Crawling rapidly forward, David took shelter behind a statue of a horsemen. Peering around the base of the statue, he scanned the bushes where his assailant had disappeared. Spotting movement, he snapped off several more shots. There was a guttural cry from the bushes and then silence.

David didn't take any chances. Keeping the statue between him and his assailant, he sprinted across the lawn, breathing easier only once he'd reached the shelter of the mansion's walls. He moved swiftly along the side of the building, listening intently for any further movement. Turning the corner, he saw a long, curving brick driveway that led to a large iron gate.

There was a solitary figure standing on the other side.

David darted to his left toward the encircling security wall, moving swiftly but silently. Once there, he holstered his pistol and then leaped up to grab the top of the wall. Struggling intently, he managed to pull himself up. At the top, he paused to survey the other side. The street that ran alongside the wall was empty except for several parked cars and faintly illuminated by the light cast from the nearby houses. Glancing back into the mansion grounds, he saw nothing threatening.

David lowered himself to the other side, but stumbled on the uneven ground as he landed. As he reached out with his hands to break his fall, his pistol fell out of the shoulder holster and spun into the street. As David moved forward to reclaim it, a figure in black robes stepped out from behind a parked van.

His gun was pointed at David's chest.

"You led me on a hell of chase," the stranger said in Arabic. "But it ends here."

David closed his eyes, steeling himself for a bullet smashing into his body.

There were several soft popping sounds and David opened his eyes to see his potential killer falling backwards, his gun still clutched in his hand.

David looked up to see two more men in dark Western suits walking toward him.

"Come with us," the first said.

"Who the hell are you?"

The other man smiled as he holstered his gun. "As we just proved, friends. Someone wants to speak with you."

A limousine appeared at the far end of the street and drove up to them.

"Please," the second man said respectfully, opening the rear door. "We're not your enemies."

David hesitated, realizing the invitation meant his cover was blown and might be a trap. Then again, if these men had wished him harm, they could have already done so. He shrugged acceptance, his curiosity proving stronger than his caution.

David walked over to the limousine and climbed inside. The luxurious interior smelled of cigarettes and whiskey, which he took as a good sign. The door slammed shut and David found himself looking at one of Saudi Arabia's best known businessman.

"I apologize for the dramatics," the man said, gesturing vaguely as the limousine accelerated.

"Good evening Mr. Yousef," David said.

"Splendid. You know who I am. And please, call me Ramzi." Ramzi Yousef was practically a legend in the Middle East, a former goat herder who had built one of the largest companies in the region from his humble beginnings. His business interests ranged from construction to textiles and many Middle Eastern political and business leaders sought his counsel. Yousef's picture appeared frequently in the Arab weekly magazines, along with his Egyptian wife who was the most glamorous singer in the Middle East. Reportedly he now spent most of his time in Europe at his oceanfront estates in Greece, Italy and Malta.

David recalled what little he knew about Yousef's personality. The Saudi businessman had a ferocious, cutthroat reputation, a win at any price mentality. Yousef was known to consider business to be a chess game, viewing the companies, competitors and employees involved as so many board pieces that should be manipulated or taken. Legend had it that in the early years of his career, his competitors' businesses sometimes suffered mysterious accidents or delays. Yet he had a generous and compassionate side, consistently rewarding loyal employees with generous bonuses and funding housing projects for the poor. He was also one of the few in the Middle East, in particular Saudi Arabia, who refused to publicly embrace and subject himself to Islam.

"Your reputation precedes you," David said.

"As does yours."

David shrugged. "I'm just another Turkish rug merchant trying to get by."

Yousef shook his head. "Please. Let's be frank. I'm aware of the *Ephesus* episode. "

Six months ago, David had learned that a terrorist bomb had been placed on the *Ephesus*, a U.S. passenger ship based in Istanbul filled with hundreds of

Americans about to embark on a Mediterranean cruise. David had managed to slip onboard the ship and capture the two terrorists as they prepared to detonate the bomb. Although the incident had become public knowledge, David's name and role had never been mentioned.

"Rumors, not very good ones at that," David replied.

Yousef smiled, a mere stretching of his lips, his gaze unblinking and direct. His tailored suit emphasized his stocky, powerful frame, the white hair the only sign of his advancing age. Set beneath a furrowed brow, his eyes burned with an uncomfortable intensity, as if his youthful impulses were only temporarily restrained. Although softened by the passage of time, his face was still remarkably chiseled, the jutting jaw and tight mouth suggesting a stubborn, determined man.

"As you wish," Yousef replied. "Can I offer you something to drink?"

"Got a beer?"

Opening a small refrigerator, Yousef handed David a Heineken.

David took a sip, grateful his hands remained steady. "So who were the men chasing me?"

"The same people who tried to kill you yesterday."

"And they are?"

"I'll tell you in a moment."

"Why were you here?"

"I wanted to talk to you. To warn you. And ask for your help."

"About what?"

Yousef sighed and reached for a tumbler filled with a dark liquid. David couldn't help notice Yousef's gnarled yet powerful hands. "These are dangerous times for my country. Lately there've been numerous demonstrations against the House of Saud, both by Islamic fundamentalists and Saudi liberals."

"Maybe Saudi Arabia should try democracy," David replied pointedly. "It might eliminate the violent protests and reduce the fundamentalists' appeal."

Yousef waved his arm dismissively. "There's a good reason why there aren't any Arab democracies. Most Muslims are uncomfortable with democracy because it establishes people as ultimate decision makers instead of the will of *Allah* as found in Islamic law. There are no true democracies in the Middle East—not because Arabs are incapable of it, but because our religion doesn't encourage democracy."

"Then I'm afraid it'll end badly for Saudi Arabia and the Royal Family—your government can't continue to placate both sides forever."

"Of course not," Yousef replied. "But the liberal reformists aren't a real threat. They recognize the alternative to the current government—a theocracy—is far worse. In the end, it's the fundamentalists who'll bring down the House of Saud."

"Perhaps." David wondered where the conversation was headed.

"It could happen very soon. Did you know there was an attempt on the King's life last month?"

Surprised, David leaned forward. "That's the first I've heard about it."

"Very few know. Three men dressed as chefs entered the palace and made their way into the King's personal quarters. Fortunately, one of his guards saw them and raised the alarm. Five people were killed and the King very nearly was as well."

"Why haven't we heard about this?"

Yousef gave a mirthless chuckle. "Because your intelligence network is extremely ineffective. That's always been the case for the U.S in the Middle East. You Americans don't understand the region, culture or religion."

David knew Yousef spoke the truth. Then again, he also now knew the CIA in Saudi Arabia had been compromised, which confirmed Yousef's charge the U.S intelligence network was ineffective. "I'm surprised I didn't learn about the assassination attempt this afternoon."

"During your meeting with Khaled ibn Saud?"

David looked at his host calmly; inside, he was seething at the evidence of more CIA leaks. "How'd you know about our meeting?"

Yousef took a sip of wine. "I keep close tabs on Khaled. He's a very dangerous man."

"Why?"

Yousef shifted uncomfortably in his seat. "He's an Islamic fanatic. Everything he does is for the good of Islam and the Prophet."

David frowned. "That's impossible. I've never heard that, nor did I see any indication of it during our meeting."

Yousef leaned forward and tapped David's knee. "There's more. His goal is to overthrow the Saudi government and install a fundamentalist Islamic regime that he'd lead. Then Khaled would expel all Westerners from Saudi

Arabia and perhaps one day from the entire Middle East. His ultimate goal is a Pan-Arab Islamic state, with Mecca the capital."

David studied Yousef, noticing the industrialist's confident expression. "Are you sure? I saw nothing in his file indicating that Khaled's a fundamentalist or interested in overthrowing the government. Our intelligence may be poor, but we couldn't have missed something of that magnitude."

Yousef's eyes flashed and his voice became forceful. "He's a very clever man. Publicly, he curries favor with both sides. Privately, Khaled continues to build up his resources in preparation for seizing control."

"Do you have any proof?" David asked skeptically. If Yousef's charges were true, then why did Khaled ask for his help that afternoon in preventing a potential Islamic plot against the Saudi government? Why would he reveal the *fatwa*'s existence to David? Then again, if Khaled *were* planning an Islamic revolution, he could be using David and the CIA to foil a competing Islamic faction. Or Khaled might be pretending to thwart a potential coup to remain above suspicion while receiving valuable intelligence from the CIA. If true, Khaled could be using the CIA against the very American interests the intelligence agency was supposed to protect.

"I don't have tangible proof—yet." Yousef's voice left little doubt he'd have it soon. "But I can point out one of the instruments he plans to use to sweep into power. What do you know of the *mutaween?*"

David placed his beer bottle in a cup holder. "They're the ultraconservative Saudi religious police who ensure people comply with the rules of *sharia*, the Islamic law. The *mutaween* enforce the prohibitions on smoking and drinking alcohol, ensure women are properly dressed and that men participate in the five daily prayer services. They publicly flog or beat violators. They're also extremely conservative: a few years ago, they prevented a group of girls from fleeing a burning school because they weren't accompanied by a male guardian or wearing robes or headscarves—about 20 died."

"Not a proud day in Saudi Arabian history," Yousef acknowledged grimly. "Did you know the *mutaween* now report to the head of the GDI; in other words, to Khaled?"

"No." David was shocked, as one of the functions of the GDI was to monitor the activities of the *mutaween*.

"A few months ago, Khaled gained control of the *mutaween*. There are now nearly 60,000 *mutaween*, twice as many as several years ago. In Saudi Arabia, that's a significant force, perhaps a third of the size of the military. Recently, some *mutaween* went to camps in the Pakistani mountains for basic military training. I think they're being trained in preparation for an Islamic revolt."

Although concerned, David remained unconvinced. "Even if true, the *mutaween* wouldn't be strong enough to take over Saudi Arabia. The army and the King's personal guards are still a formidable force."

Yousef leaned forward, the headlights from passing cars flickering across his face. "As long as the leaders of those institutions continue to support the House of Saud. If they don't or if a few key leaders defect..."

David remained silent, mulling over what both Yousef and Khaled had told him. The *mutaween* not only represented a substantial numerical force, but their fanaticism would make them formidable indeed. If a *fatwa* were issued by the Council of Senior *Ulama* and embraced by the *mutaween*, the military and King's personal guards conceivably could lose control. The Saudi government would fall and the unrest could spread across the Middle East, bringing down other governments and stifling oil production. It was a significant potential threat. David resolved to have the CIA's network examine everything about Khaled and begin tracking his movements.

"If you want more proof, then think about the men who tried to kill you yesterday and tonight."

"The *mutaween*?"

"Yes and aided tonight by the Saudi internal security forces. All, I might add, under the control of Khaled ibn Saud."

"Proof?"

"You'll have to take my word."

"Why do you care?" David asked. "Your business interests are spread across the world and you live outside of Saudi Arabia."

"I still have many investments in Saudi Arabia. Furthermore, I'm still a Saudi citizen and," Yousef waved carelessly at the luxurious surroundings, "I'm not exactly enamored with the fundamentalists. Islam has been hijacked by fundamentalists who twist the Prophet Mohammad's own words to support their goals."

"In calling for a *jihad*?"

Yousef sighed. "*Jihad* is central to Islam. Unfortunately, the West views *jihad* as meaning a holy war against the *infidels*. In truth, *jihad* defines the personal struggle of Muslims to follow the *Quran* and become the best person possible."

"And yet many Muslims *do* advocate a holy war, or *jihad*, against the unbelievers."

Yousef nodded. "For two reasons. One, they believe permissive Western values are corrupting their societies. Second, the West props up secular Middle Eastern governments that ruthlessly suppress Muslims and Islam."

"But the *Quran* advocates violence against non-Muslims," David pressed.

"As someone who has studied Islam, you should know better," Yousef scolded, clearly irritated. "There are Old Testament passages that are just as violent as any from the *Quran*. Those Muslims advocating violence and a *jihad* take quotes from the *Quran* out of context."

David knew Yousef was right. Islam, like most religions such as Judaism and Christianity, could be twisted to fit the goals of extremists. In fact, most non-Muslims didn't realize that the three religions shared many features, including the same patriarch—Abraham, the Old Testament and God.

"I appreciate the warning about Khaled," David said. "I'll see what I can find out."

"That's all I can ask for from someone who claims to be just a rug merchant," Yousef replied, smiling. He rapped on the partition separating them from the driver and the limousine stopped.

"You'll contact me if you find out anything else?" David asked.

"Of course. How can I reach you?"

David pulled out his wallet and removed a business card. "This number goes to a switchboard that can reach me anywhere in the world. My cell phone scrambles the signal, so the line is secure on my end."

Before Yousef could answer, his cell phone rang. The industrialist answered, listened intently and then swore as he hung up.

"What is it?" David asked.

"The Pakistani government has been overthrown. Muslim extremists have seized control and declared an Islamic Republic."

"It's started then," David said, realizing an Islamic revolution in Pakistan could easily spread to other countries.

"I'm afraid it has," Yousef said, shaking his head. "This'll only increase the pressure on Saudi Arabia. There's just one thing missing."

"What's that?"

"A trigger. An event so momentous and terrible as to inflame the entire Middle East and turn Saudi Arabia upside down."

Unfortunately, David could think of far too many possibilities. He resolved to press Reynolds to find the answers to the questions raised by both Ramzi Yousef and Khaled ibn Saud. But they needed to move quickly.

With a sinking feeling, he sensed time was running out.

9

The man some knew as Abdullah stood beside the unused airstrip deep in the Egyptian desert, periodically glancing at his watch. The plane and its lethal cargo were late. He wasn't particularly worried about the delay, or even the possibility of failure, for he was a patient, calculating man. He prepared his plans after methodically evaluating every possible obstacle and potential outcome, satisfied he had done everything possible to ensure success. This meticulous approach, together with his formidable personal and professional powers, ensured he was rarely unsuccessful. Failure simply meant the intervention of factors beyond his control. In those rare instances when he was not initially successful, he dispassionately tried again, supremely confident next time he would triumph.

Throughout his life, Abdullah always had.

A small passenger jet suddenly appeared on the horizon, a growing white speck against the vast blue desert sky. Abdullah glanced again at the runway, evaluating the plane's ability to land safely on the uneven surface of rock and sand. The illegal airstrip, once used to smuggle cigarettes and alcohol into Egypt, hadn't been used in years and had fallen into disrepair. But he judged it safe enough.

The Lear Jet circled several times before landing, bouncing erratically along the rocky runway before rolling to a stop. The passenger door swung open and a slight Palestinian appeared, looking disheveled and tired. He leaped to the ground and waited for the pilot, a pale blond haired man with a crooked nose, to emerge. Together, they walked over to Abdullah.

"*Salam 'alaykum,*" the Palestinian said to Abdullah.

"*Wa alaykum as-salam. Al-hamdu lillah 'al as-salama.*"

"Boris, I'm grateful for your assistance," Abdullah said, extending his hand to the pilot.

Boris grinned. "It was easy."

"Any problems?"

The Russian pilot shook his head. "No. Everything went as planned. We first flew down the Adriatic Coast to the Beirut airport, where we refueled. Then we skirted Israeli airspace to cross the Mediterranean to the Egyptian coast before turning inland."

"Will this landing show up on Egyptian radar?" Abdullah asked, concerned the Egyptian air traffic control might notify the local police. He didn't completely trust Boris, who was a mercenary hired through the shadowy Ukrainian criminal underground.

Boris shrugged. "Yes. I radioed the Cairo airport to tell them I was having engine problems and needed to set down. Once airborne, I'll call back to tell them I fixed the problem."

Abdullah nodded and turned to the Palestinian. "Hazan, any problems with our cargo?"

Hazan Qwasama shook his head. "No. The Ukrainian delivered it as arranged."

"You left him in good spirits?" Abdullah asked, with a veiled look suggesting otherwise.

"I paid him as we discussed," Hazan said with a wolfish grin. "He won't contact us again."

"Good. Let's unload the cargo."

They walked over to the plane and opened the rear cargo hatch. The pilot and Hazan lifted out the metal container that had cost Vasily Ivanhov his life, the yellow radiation symbol now covered by a coat of black paint. Hazan carried the container to the waiting Range Rover and loaded it in the rear cargo bed. He threw a tarp over the dangerous cargo and tied it down before turning to face Abdullah.

"That's it. We're ready to go."

Abdullah reached into the rear seat of the Range Rover, pulled out two suitcases and handed them to the pilot. "Here's your money and a bonus. Good work."

The pilot opened the first suitcase and nodded approvingly at the bundles of American $100 bills. "My pleasure. Call me next time you need a pilot who can keep his mouth shut."

"Just remember you never met either of us."

"Of course." Boris snapped the suitcase shut and gave a mock salute.

Hazan and Abdullah silently watched the pilot walk away and climb back in his plane. They returned his wave as he revved up the engine and turned the plane around to prepare for takeoff.

"Now?" Hazan asked.

"After he's airborne." Abdullah pulled a small remote control device from his pocket. The plane taxied down the runway and lifted off, banking sharply to the right in the direction of Cairo. They could see the pilot adjusting his headphones and consulting his instruments.

"I think it's time." Abdullah pressed a button on the remote control. The plane exploded, disappearing in a bright red and orange flame fed by the fuel remaining in its tanks. The wreckage turned over and plummeted to the ground, leaving a trail of black smoke behind. The mass of twisted metal struck the ground perhaps a half-mile away and exploded again upon impact.

"Looks like he had engine trouble," Abdullah wryly observed.

"I never did like flying," Hazan replied, chuckling.

They climbed into the waiting Range Rover and drove off, passing the burning wreckage without so much as a glance. They had a long drive ahead and their attention was focused on their destination.

An Egyptian warehouse 20 miles from the Israeli border.

✳ ✳ ✳

Islamabad, Pakistan

Abrahim Al Kabbar looked down at the Pakistani nuclear device and shivered, awed that the small metal case was capable of such terrible devastation. Since he had long ago ceased to fear death, Al Kabbar was surprised to find the deadly power intimidated him. He picked up the steel case, his heart pounding violently when the handle slipped in his sweaty grasp and he nearly dropped it.

He carried the case over to the Toyota truck and carefully placed it in the rear cargo area. Then he arranged pillows and blankets around the case, ensuring it was well protected and cushioned against the rough Pakistani roads.

Satisfied at last, he began walking back to the front of the Toyota when his cell phone rang.

"It's me," came Abdullah's voice. "Everything went well with the operation?"

"Perfect, as well as I could've hoped. I've got our product and paid our employees."

"Good. You'll follow the same plan: driving across Pakistan and Iran until you reach the Red Sea. My boat will meet you there. That will enable you to avoid customs."

"I understand."

"Before you leave Pakistan, I want you to tie up one last loose end."

"Of course."

Abdullah's voice was cold. "Azam Tariq has become a liability. The Americans know of him."

"Then he must resign, permanently."

"I'm glad you understand."

"Consider it done."

There was merely a click as Abdullah hung up. Al Kabbar lowered his satellite phone, wondering if one day Abdullah would also consider him a liability. Although certain that day was inevitable, Al Kabbar unhesitantly accepted his fate.

Just as long as he was able to first successfully carry out Abdullah's plan.

Satisfied and humming a popular Arabic *nashid*, or song about *jihad*, Al Kabbar climbed into the Toyota, engaged the clutch and drove off into the night headed for Azam Tariq's *madras* to eliminate one more loose end.

10

"Do you have a good feel for the layout and number of guards?" David asked, as they drove past the _madras_ for the third time.

Nawaz Sharif, the auto-rickshaw driver and head of the CIA's local office, nodded. "Yeah. Pretty straightforward. The only guards are at the front entrance. Best way in is through the vehicle entrance in the rear."

From the back seat, David scanned the crowded street and _madras_ for anything unusual. Trucks, buses, cars, auto-rickshaws, motorcycles, donkey carts and bicycles fought in the road for supremacy, the incessant honking and roar of passing traffic deafening. Occasionally a pedestrian would dart recklessly across the street, each brief dance with death unnoticed. A curtain of dust from the unpaved street hung overhead, darkening the late afternoon sun and bringing an early dusk. Low slung, crumbling concrete buildings lined the street, most unpainted and caked with dirt. Pedestrians crowded along the edge of the road, weaving through the street vendors selling everything from shoes to a few ears of corn to bags of betel nuts. Most men carried rifles slung over their shoulders or pistols tucked into the waistband of their tribal trousers. The relatively few women were dressed head to toe in black _chadors_ and accompanied by solemn looking men who glared at any who glanced at their female companions. To David, Peshawar was an eclectic mix of the Middle East and old American Wild West.

He had arrived only four hours ago, intending to learn more about Azam Tariq, the senior _imam_ of the Fist of _Allah_. After landing in Peshwar, David had been met by Nawaz Sharif, who headed the local CIA office. David was favorably impressed with the Pakistani—he was bright, capable and steadfast, all critical qualities a CIA agent needed to survive in Peshawar. Located near the Afghanistan border, Peshawar was an extremely dangerous place for foreign intelligence agents. The city and surrounding area contained numerous violent anti-American groups and Al Quada members, most of whom had been driven out of Afghanistan. According to Jack Reynolds, Nawaz Sharif had developed a strong intelligence network that spread through the refugee camps clustered along the Afghan-Pakistani border.

"Let's get back to our room."

Nawaz parked the auto-rickshaw and they made their way upstairs to the hotel room Nawaz had rented just across the street from the *madras*. David walked over to the window to study the *madras*. The religious school was housed in a prosperous looking two-story concrete and brick structure set back from the street and surrounded by extensive grounds. A chain link fence encircled the compound and the front gate was guarded by several men wearing cleric robes and carrying AK-47s. So far, David had only seen students and several elderly men, presumably teachers, enter and leave. Still, he was certain the *imam*, Azam Tariq, could answer some of the questions that continued to haunt him.

"Nawaz, come here and take a look."

Nawaz walked over the window. "What is it?"

David pointed to a large Toyota truck that had just pulled up to the building. The driver was standing nearby lighting a cigarette. He was dressed in a Middle Eastern robe, not the typical tribal shirt and trousers favored by most Pakistani men.

"Looks like a Saudi," Nawaz observed.

"That's what I thought. But I can't make out his face from here."

The driver climbed back into the truck, which lurched forward and turned down the alley that led to the parking area at the rear of the *madras* compound.

David instinctively felt the unknown driver was someone important. "Nawaz, do you think he's a go-between between Al Kabbar or Abdullah and Azam Tariq?"

"Could be. We can find out tonight. I'd also like to know what's in the truck."

David wandered over to the hot plate Nawaz had brought earlier and made another cup of tea. He found the room depressing, with its single sagging bed, peeling wall paint and smell of mildew. He also felt weary, a deeper fatigue that went far beyond the effects of the long plane flight.

David looked back out the window, noticing some of the lights in the *madras* compound had been turned off. "What'd you learn about the *madras*?"

Nawaz stretched out on the bed and clasped his hands over his head. "Not much. It's a typical Pakistani Wahhabi school funded by the Saudis. I'm scheduled to meet with Tariq in a couple hours."

Nawaz, posing as a rich Pakistani businessman seeking to donate funds to the Fist of *Allah*, had set up an evening meeting with Azam Tariq. Nawaz had persuaded David to not try his Turkish rug merchant routine, fearful Tariq was aware of the events in Riyadh and would be suspicious.

Nawaz cleared his throat. "I think we should cancel the meeting and instead just search the building after everyone's gone."

David shook his head. "No. I need to question Tariq about the training camp and his memo about the 'weapon'. Equally important, I need to learn more about Abdullah. He could be the key to all this. Plus, if we're lucky, we might discover something about the man who just went inside."

Nawaz looked doubtful. "It's risky. Our meeting with Tariq is too early; I doubt the building will be empty."

"We'll risk it."

"And if we run into someone while prowling the halls unescorted?"

David smiled. "I'm confident you'll think of something."

David settled back into his seat by the window, thankful Nawaz was willing to take risks. He knew the safest course of action was to wait until the early morning hours after everyone had left and then search the *madras*. But David had been fortunate in Riyadh—this time, he couldn't count on the search of an empty office uncovering incriminating evidence. He instinctively felt Azam Tariq could answer his growing list of questions. Who were the Saudis training in the camp in the Pakistan mountains run by the 'Fist of *Allah*'—*mutaween* or members of Al Faisal's *Wahhabi* mosque in Riyadh? What was the connection between the *madras* and Turki al Faisal's mosque? What did Tariq's letter to Al Faisal mean about 'obtaining the weapon that will ensure our ultimate victory'? Was he referring to nuclear weapons or was it something else, perhaps chemical weapons? Who was Abdullah? And what was his connection to Al Kabbar?

David could only hope Azam Tariq could answer some or all of these questions.

He hardened himself for the task ahead, knowing they might need to torture Tariq to get answers. When the time arrived, David hoped he could do what was necessary. Despite his misgivings, he was growing increasingly sure of his ability to do just that. Although his reticence made his job more difficult, he preferred it that way, having seen too many in his Special Forces unit become inured to human emotions. When he joined the CIA, David had been willing to give his time, commitment and loyalty, but vowed to keep his humanity.

As he settled back to wait, for the first time David wondered if that were still true.

✳ ✳ ✳

Two hours later, David and Nawaz stepped outside into a bitterly cold night under a sky shrouded with a threatening layer of clouds. The street was relatively empty, the occasional passing car or truck stirring up a choking cloud of dust from the unpaved surface. As they walked past the *madras'* front entrance, David noticed there was now only a single guard. They turned down the alley that circled behind the *madras* compound. The chain link fence enclosing the grounds of the religious school marked one edge of the road while a dark warehouse formed the other. David peered through the fence at the *madras* grounds, but saw neither a patrolling guard nor watchdogs.

After perhaps a hundred yards, they reached a gated vehicle entrance that was locked but unattended. David scaled the chain link fence, grateful there wasn't any barbed wire along the top. He landed easily on the other side, rolling forward to absorb the impact. Glancing around, David saw no one, only several small structures that looked like storage sheds. Nawaz landed nearby, his cry of pain overloud in the night.

"You okay?" David whispered.

Grimacing and rubbing his ankle, Nawaz nodded affirmatively.

David led the way up a short driveway into a dirt parking area at the rear of the *madras.* The building was dark and quiet, the only light spilling from several second story windows. He was pleased to see the Toyota truck that had arrived earlier that afternoon was parked there. Glancing inside the locked cab, David could see only crumpled food wrappers and empty water bottles. He tried the rear gate of the truck, but was disappointed to find it was also locked. He debated about breaking in to see what was inside, but decided to wait until they'd interrogated Azam Tariq. He then joined Nawaz, who was trying to pick the lock of the building's rear entrance. After a minute, Nawaz managed to open the door.

Once inside, Nawaz led the way down a dark corridor past a series of classrooms. At the end of the hallway, they reached a staircase that led to the second floor.

"I was told Tariq's office is upstairs at the end of the hall," Nawaz whispered.

They moved stealthily up the stairs, the only sound that of a distant radio playing a popular Islamic song. Sweat dampened David's shirt and he felt naked without a gun in hand. The second floor corridor was lined with framed paintings of scenes from the *Quran*, most depicting a triumphant Muhammad slaying the *infidels*, an approving *Allah* by his side. Nawaz led the way down the hallway, pausing every few steps to listen. At the last door, Nawaz motioned to David to stay out of sight and knocked.

"Yes," a quavering voice asked.

"It's Asam Muggol. I'm here for our appointment."

"Oh." David could hear someone move around. "Just a moment. The guard didn't call to let me know you were here."

David nodded to Nawaz, who yanked the door open and they rushed inside. An elderly man turned to face them, simultaneously dropping several pieces of paper on the floor. He stood next to a wall safe, which had been hidden behind a painting that had swung away from the wall.

"What's the meaning of this?" the *imam* cried out, outraged. "Leave at once!"

A gun appeared in Nawaz's hand. "Move away from the safe and sit down."

Although clearly confused, Azam Tariq did as Nawaz instructed. He dropped the remaining papers on the desk, straightened his black robe and white turban and sat down.

"Who are you?" the old man asked testily.

"It doesn't matter," Nawaz said, as David pulled a strand of rope from his pocket and began tying the *imam*'s arms to the back of the chair. "Not another word from you for the next few minutes while we look around. If you call out, I'll kill you."

"Take a look at the pages he dropped on the floor," David said. "I'll check the safe."

Nawaz picked up the scattered pages and began reading. David walked over to the wall safe and pulled out a leather ledger and black leather case. He put them on the desk and opened the case, whistling softly in amazement when he saw the precious gems and diamonds.

"Quite a haul," David observed, putting the case aside and opening the ledger. He scanned the pages quickly and saw they recorded payments to various bank accounts around the world. He felt a surge of excitement, realizing the payments could be disbursements to members of Islamic terrorist groups. By tracing each account, the U.S. might be able to locate the individuals and, at the very least, place them under observation. David glanced over at the *imam*, who appeared panic-stricken at the sight of the open ledger.

"Tell me about these bank accounts." David demanded.

The *imam* merely bit his lip and looked away.

Nawaz walked over and handed David a piece of paper. "It's a list of the weapons purchased by the military training camp he runs in the Pakistani mountains."

David glanced quickly through the list, his concern growing as he realized the weapons were sufficient to arm at least 15,000 men with substantial firepower.

Nawaz looked at David. "I think it's time we ask some difficult questions."

"You're right." David turned to the *imam*. "To start with, perhaps you can tell us about the letter you wrote a couple weeks ago to Turki Al Faisal."

The *imam* shrugged, a curious gesture with his arms tied securely to the chair. "Please, I don't know what you're talking about. I just run a school that teaches students about Islam."

David chuckled grimly. "I suppose the diamonds are tuition from your students."

"Family heirlooms."

David leaned close. "Answer our questions or we'll make it *very* painful."

Nawaz reached inside his coat and pulled out a small electrical cattle prod. The *imam's* eyes widened and he looked ill, his mouth moving soundlessly in terror.

"You recognize this, don't you," Nawaz said. "Shall I plug this in and get started? Or will you tell us about Turki al Faisal and the letter that said you were obtaining a weapon."

"Please! I don't know anything!"

"What weapon? A nuclear bomb?"

But Tariq only shook his head.

"Who is Abdullah? Do you know Al Kabbar?"

Looking frightened, Tariq began repeating the *shadada*, "*La illaha illallah, Muhammador rasulallah.*" There is no God except *Allah* and Muhammad is his messenger.

David sighed and turned to Nawaz. "We don't have a choice."

"We never did. Shall I get started?"

"Yes." David quickly subdued his distaste for their next task. To hide the sounds of their interrogation, David switched on a radio on the desk and turned up the volume. Nawaz plugged in the cord for the cattle prod. The *imam* began struggling violently against his bounds and then started shouting. His quavering voice quickly dissipated when Nawaz struck his face, causing the old man to lower his head and begin weeping. David felt some remorse, which disappeared when he thought of the dozens of terrorists Azam Tariq had probably trained and funded.

"Let's get this over with," he said grimly.

Suddenly, the door opened and a man stepped inside.

His mind still focused on the interrogation, David reacted slowly to the threat. His hesitation proved costly. The intruder reached beneath his robe and pulled out a gun.

"Don't move!" the man ordered.

David froze, but Nawaz lunged for his pistol lying on the nearby table. There was a spitting sound and a red patch blossomed on Nawaz's shirt. He looked astonished before he reeled backwards, arms flailing. He crashed against the wall, fell to the floor, twitched once and lay still.

"Shit!" David cried out. "Nawaz!"

The man pointed the silencer equipped gun at David. "I told him not to move."

"Let me tend to him," David pleaded, consumed with guilt and anger.

After closing the door, the Arab walked over and prodded Nawaz with his foot. "Too late. He's dead."

"You bastard!" David swore in English.

"Interesting," the gunman said, turning his attention back to David. "Although you appear to be Middle Eastern, Palestinian even, you swear in English. I'd guess you're something much, much more. American perhaps?"

David clenched his teeth and struggled to remain calm, realizing he'd need all his cunning, skill and a great deal of luck to escape his predicament. He stared at the intruder, noticing the ill-fitting coat and trousers, as if they were borrowed from someone else. The gunman's thin Middle Eastern face was undistinguished. His eyes were sunken beneath half closed eyelids, as if observing a contemptible world was wearying and hardly worth the effort. Yet he was light on his feet and moved quickly, as the unfortunate Nawaz had already learned.

"Merciful *Allah*," Azam Tariq cried. "They wanted to know about the training camp and the weapon. But Al Kabbar, I never…"

"No names!" Al Kabbar hissed. "This one isn't dead yet. Now you," he said, waving the gun at David. "Untie the *imam*."

"So, you're the man we nearly caught in Afghanistan," David said to Al Kabbar, desperately gauging the distance between them to see if he could successfully attack. But the gun remained pointed directly at his chest and David knew any attempt would be suicidal. He stared at the Arab's face, knowing he'd never forget the features—the flattened nose, thin lips and high forehead. But it was the man's eyes that stood out—cold, brown and flecked with yellow, similar to a cat's.

"You were there?" Al Kabbar said, looking interested. "You've come a long way. I don't know how you found me, but it'll be the last thing you accomplish. Azam, tie up this American. Make sure the rope is tight enough to cut his circulation."

The *imam* complied, using the same rope that David had used earlier. David surreptitiously tugged on his bonds, but the rope held fast.

"What now?" the *imam* asked nervously when he finished. "Why are you here? Shouldn't we interrogate this man?"

"I don't have the time and there isn't anyone here I trust to do it," Al Kabbar replied, his expression hardening. "Besides, I have my orders about you."

Al Kabbar raised his gun and fired, the bullet striking the *imam* in the chest. The old man crashed backwards into the desk and fell to the floor. Al Kabbar turned to David.

"I wish I had time to interrogate you, but I don't. I've more important things to do."

David ventured a guess. "Does it involve a nuclear weapon? One that Abdullah managed to obtain through Tariq?"

Although Al Kabbar didn't answer, David could tell by the furrowing of the Arab's brow that his question had struck a nerve.

Turning around, Al Kabbar left the room and returned several minutes later carrying a gasoline can. He doused the room with gasoline, including the inside of the safe and the two bodies. He then threw the can to the floor and looked at David.

"This way, the evidence is destroyed."

Al Kabbar picked up a book of matches, smiled wickedly at David and struck a match. He lit a piece of paper on fire, then threw it into a corner. The flame ignited the gasoline and began spreading rapidly.

"Goodbye my friend. I'd kill you, but," Al Kabbar shrugged, his hands spread outward, "I'd rather have you watch the flames approach and know the meaning of terror. It won't be long before you see *Allah* and get an opportunity to explain your failings."

With that, he left.

David watched in fascinated horror as the flames streaked across the floor, crawling up the wall into the open safe and onto the desk top. He smelled burning flesh and knew the flames were beginning to consume the bodies of the *imam* and Nawaz. He struggled against his bonds, trying to free either his arms or legs. For the first time in years, David began praying, neither to the *Allah* nor Jehovah of his parents' religions, but to a nameless God he'd long forsaken. His mouth grew dry and throat constricted, both from fear and the choking smoke. He wondered vaguely why with death so close, his life wasn't flashing before his eyes; he could only see the flickering flames, hear only the pounding of his heart.

In desperation, David managed to lift the chair off the ground and propel himself backwards to crash against the wall. The chair shuddered and there was the sound of cracking wood. The rope binding his wrists to the chair loosened slightly. Again and again, David slammed the chair against the wall. Finally, he could move his wrists. He managed to pull his left arm free and reached across to fumble with the rope binding his other arm. The flames were licking greedily at the walls and floor and smoke filled the room, making it difficult to breath.

David knew time was short.

The next time he slammed the chair against the wall, his right arm suddenly came free. Reaching down, David untied the rope around his legs. The rope fell away. The flames were close now, the smoke and smell of burning flesh nearly causing him to pass out. He leaped up and stumbled through the door into the corridor. The empty hallway was filled with smoke and he pulled his shirt over his mouth to ease his breathing. Squeezing his eyes nearly shut against the burning smoke, David made his way along the hallway and down the stairs. The first floor was relatively smoke free and David managed to take a few deep breaths.

Suddenly, a figure carrying a rifle appeared. David kicked out with his right leg, striking the man's chest and knocking him to the ground. Without stopping, he rushed past the prostrate figure and down the corridor toward the door he and Nawaz had originally entered.

Fortunately, no one else appeared.

Reaching the exit, David stumbled outside into the cold, clear air. He managed to make it into some bushes a short distance away before his legs gave out and he sank gratefully to the ground. Glancing around, he realized with bitter desperation that the truck he'd examined earlier was gone.

Al Kabbar had escaped.

David sat there for a few moments, tears streaming down his cheeks and racked by deep coughs. Something moved in the shadows and he looked up. A figure in a dark robe and *hijab* suddenly materialized out of the darkness. The light cast by the burning building reflected off the delicate cheekbones of a woman.

She looked down at him and pulled out a gun, whether to protect or guard him, David didn't know.

II

Dava avid stared transfixed at the pistol pointed at his head, the cold steel reflecting the flickering light cast by the burning building. He looked up at the hooded and cloaked woman, unsure of her intentions and loyalties. She remained silent, her gaze boring into his. Moving very deliberately, he got to his feet.

"I need to get out of here," David said in Arabic

"Who are you?" she asked, glancing around to ensure they were still alone.

David sensed she wasn't associated with the _madras_ and instinct told him to answer truthfully. "An American agent."

She smiled grimly. "You're right, it's time to go."

They ran down the driveway that led to the gated vehicle entrance. David occasionally stumbled, his legs still stiff from being lashed to the chair. When they reached the perimeter fence, David scaled it first while his companion waited impatiently behind, brandishing a pistol and looking back at the burning building. Fortunately, there still wasn't any sign of pursuit. Dropping down to the other side, David waited as she adroitly climbed the fence, her skirt pulled tight by an elastic cord she'd removed from her pocket. She landed lightly, her athleticism apparent. Before David could speak, a Mercedes sedan pulled up.

"Get in," she ordered.

David hesitated, aware the street was now alive with people rushing toward the fire. For a moment, uncertain about his mysterious companion, he considered disappearing into the crowd. But he decided to trust her. His mind was brimming with too many unanswered questions and he knew he'd regret not learning something about her. Besides, he sensed she might be the woman who had rescued him from the Saudi Arabian mosque.

If so, he had even more questions.

After David climbed into the back seat, the Mercedes raced ahead, wheels squealing in protest. Looking out the rear window, David saw the fire had spread and now engulfed most of the second floor of the *madras*, flames shooting through the roof. The night was filled with the sound of crackling flames, the cries of the watching crowd and, growing nearer, sirens.

Turning back to face his companion, he wasted no time. "Who are you?"

She removed her veil and turned to face him, her face still partially masked by the shadows. Her features were Middle Eastern, perhaps Persian, with dark eyes, a perfect nose and prominent cheekbones. Her smile, even in the dark, was warm and genuine. "For now, a friend."

"And later?" David asked, certain she was an agent with one of the many Western intelligence agencies in Pakistan.

"Perhaps an enemy."

"Then I'll worry about that later." David was intrigued by her comment. Evidently, she worked for a Middle Eastern country. For now, he'd trust her— finding Al Kabbar and learning the truth was worth the gamble. David leaned over and began coughing, the convulsions wracking his body. His lungs still hurt from breathing in the smoke from the fire.

"We must find the truck and the Arab who was driving it," he insisted.

"Why? Who is this Arab?"

"A man named Al Kabbar. He killed my partner and set the fire."

"What kind of truck was he driving?"

David closed his eyes and recalled the truck that had been parked in back of the *madras*. "A mid-size, black Toyota diesel with a canvas top over the rear bed. Unfortunately, there weren't any distinguishing markings."

His companion frowned. "We can try, but I doubt we'll find it."

She leaned over the front seat and spoke quietly to the driver. David overheard enough to realize she spoke Farsi. The driver picked up a radio and spoke urgently into it.

"You're Iranian?" he asked, when she turned back to face him.

"Yes."

David wanted to ask more, but decided to focus on the task at hand. "What do you suggest we do?"

"We can drive to the main road leading out of town and see if he's taken that route. After that, there's not much we can do. I have several people in the city that can search for the truck. But it's a common vehicle and I doubt we'll find it. Most likely, your Arab will dispose of it and get another truck."

David knew she was right. Given the murders and fire, Al Kabbar would probably take extra precautions, including ditching the truck. Al Kabbar had struck him as careful and calculating; but he'd made a serious mistake not killing David immediately. The Arab's judgment had been impaired by his desire to not just kill, but torture his enemy. At this point, David realized his best alternative was to contact Nawaz's subordinate to get the CIA's Pakistan network to search for the truck and Al Kabbar.

"If we fail to find the truck, I have a proposition for you," she said. "I need to return to Tehran. You should come with me."

"Why?"

"We can talk about Khaled ibn Saud, the *mutaween* and the situation in Saudi Arabia."

David looked appraisingly at his temporary colleague, certain now she was the woman who had rescued him in Saudi Arabia. "You're full of surprises."

Her smile chased away the worry lines etched around her eyes and mouth. "I've a plane waiting at the airport and we can be in Tehran in two hours. There, you can rest before we talk."

Frowning, David placed his hand on the door handle. "I'm free to go whenever I want?"

"And contact anyone you desire—and I mean anyone."

David nodded acceptance, relieved that for the moment he had found an ally. Removing his hand from the handle, he smiled wryly. "In all the excitement, you never introduced yourself."

She extended her hand. "Parissa."

"David."

She smiled again, although her gaze remained watchful and guarded. "CIA?"

"Or something similar," he reluctantly allowed.

"And your dead companion?"

David's eyes clouded over and he felt another stab of anger and guilt. "Nawaz Sharif. He was a good man."

Parissa shook her head. "I knew of him. He had a good reputation."

David turned toward the window, not trusting himself to say anything more at that moment. There was still much left to discuss with this mysterious Iranian agent and her silent companion. But David felt himself begin to shake slightly, a delayed reaction to the events of the past half hour. First, the guilt assailed him, the weighty responsibility for another's death. Although his actions were reasonable and defensible, David knew his impatience and aggressiveness had put them in a risky situation, one a more experienced agent might have avoided. He also knew the CIA would applaud his initiative while simultaneously chiding him for the death of another agent. Once David acknowledged the lesson learned, they would merely send him out there once more to seek, gather and report. CIA agents were like a string of Christmas lights that continued to shine brightly even as the burned out individual bulbs were replaced.

David knew he'd survived only because Al Kabbar had sadistically wanted David to burn alive. That knowledge, the nearness of death, shook him. In Afghanistan, he had always confronted danger with a gun in his hand and he'd rarely seen the face of his enemy. There, death and danger had seemed impersonal and distant. Now, it had a name and face that could, and would, inflict pain or death. He found the rawness of life as an undercover agent still somewhat overwhelming. He had expected phone calls and meetings; not stealthy searches, guns and death. In short, he felt ill-equipped mentally for the task at hand. He was learning, but not fast enough and at a very high price.

David realized that unless he quickly became much tougher and smarter, he would never make it.

12

Abrahim Al Kabbar wearily climbed out of the Brahma diesel truck. He was exhausted, having driven non-stop for ten hours since leaving Peshawar. He cursed again the necessity of transporting the nuclear bomb overland by truck instead of flying, but knew the tight airport custom controls might result in the discovery of the Pakistani weapon. His overland route was lengthy but straightforward, perhaps a thousand miles across both Pakistan and Iran to the Red Sea coast. There, he would catch a boat to his final destination.

He glanced around the small village, detesting the hopeless scene—the dusty, rutted road, stray chickens and mangy dogs wandering through the windowless concrete buildings and pervasive odor of human waste and general decay. It was a familiar sight for Al Kabbar, who all too easily could remember his own indigent upbringing. His wealthy Saudi father had accused his mother of infidelity before divorcing her and disowning her newborn son. In Saudi Arabia, a woman was shunned after such a charge. There, a man's slightest word always carried more weight than even the most vociferous protestations of any female.

Al Kabbar had grown up knowing only hunger and hardship, his mother unable to hold a job for very long before whispers about her past unerringly followed. Without much in her life, his mother had turned to Islam. Encouraged by his mother, Al Kabbar had also become deeply religious, Islam providing both structure and escape for a young man desperate for both. He grew to hate the smug, wealthy Saudis who drove around in their European sports cars and American SUVs, their disdain for the less fortunate, their immoral indulgences.

At Saudi International University, he had met similar young men who were angry with their lives and jealous of the wealthy and successful. Congregating in tea houses, they whiled away the hours engaged in endless political and religious discourse. Upon graduation, Al Kabbar was unable to find any meaningful employment, his religious studies degree considered a potential liability. He had entered into an arranged marriage with a poor, uneducated girl who played the subservient, obedient role the *Quran* demanded. Still, he'd never quite known what to do with his anger until that fateful night a drunk American driver had killed his wife. Subsequently, through the mosques, Al Kabbar had sought out those fighting the West. There were many. Three years ago, he'd been introduced to Abdullah by a contact at Turki Al Faisal's mosque.

Since then, he had followed only Abdullah.

For the first time in years, he was apprehensive about his mission due to the debacle in Peshawar. Again, Al Kabbar cursed his misfortune in stumbling into the two intruders at the *madras* and the need to kill them. Al Kabbar wondered again about their identity. The first man he had shot was clearly Pakistani, while the other appeared to be either Jordanian or Palestinian. He was certain both men worked for the Americans and he thanked *Allah* for his escape.

He would have enjoyed torturing and questioning the second man, watching him cry out for mercy. It would've been payback for all the indignities Muslims had suffered over the years. Al Kabbar sensed the man was a dangerous adversary—he had reacted professionally to both his companion's death and the prospect of burning alive. In hindsight, Al Kabbar wished he'd killed the man instead of leaving him to die in the fire. Still, the *madras* was burning fiercely when he left. Surely the American agent was dead.

But he couldn't shake his uneasiness and the ridiculous feeling they might meet again.

Al Kabbar was brought back to the present by the ringing of his satellite phone.

"What's your status?" It was Abdullah.

"I'm on schedule to deliver the package, but something went wrong."

"What happened?" Abdullah's voice threatened consequences.

"At the *madras*, before I could deal with Azam Tariq, I was interrupted by two strangers. I think they were working for the Americans. They've since resigned—permanently. One was Pakistani. The other looked like he was from either Palestine or Jordan, but I think he was an American."

There was a dangerous, poignant pause before Abdullah's harsh response. "This American, was he broad shouldered, about six feet tall? Handsome but light skinned for an Arab?"

"That sounds like him."

"I know this man." Abdullah remained silent for some time. "He's no longer working for them? You're sure?"

"Yes." Al Kabbar could picture the American spy struggling with his bindings while the room around him burned brightly.

"Too bad," Abdullah replied. "He could've been used to our advantage. Have you left Pakistan?"

"Not yet. I'll cross the border in an hour."

"Contact me again when you board the boat."

Al Kabbar replaced the phone in the truck, relieved the phone call with Abdullah had gone as well as he'd hoped. Pulling a wad of U.S. hundred dollar bills from his pocket, he peeled off several thousand. He had already made several trips across the Iranian-Pakistani border and by now the guards knew him well. Each time he'd paid substantial sums to avoid a search of the truck, implying that Al Kabbar was illegally importing televisions to avoid the Iranian duty.

Anxious to reach his destination, he climbed back into the truck and drove off toward the Iranian border.

13

The Ayatollah Khomeini mausoleum was imposing, the enormous gilded dome at least twenty stories high and surrounded by four towering minarets. A sea of humanity filled the immense plaza, listening intently to the impassioned clerics, whose amplified voices reached even the far edges of the crowd. Roars of approval greeted the speeches as the crowd was whipped into a frenzy both by the speakers and the occasion—the annual day of mourning for their fallen leader. An enormous pile of flowers lay near the stairs that led to the mausoleum entrance, tokens of the respect the Ayatollah still commanded.

David stood near the edge of the plaza, listening and observing the crowd. A short, stout Iranian man approached and nodded a greeting.

"Is Parissa ready to see me?" David asked.

"Yes. I'm to take you to a restaurant on the other side of Tehran."

The drive back into Tehran took nearly an hour. The heavy traffic moved slowly even though it was early evening. David looked out the window, distressed to see the once charming city had morphed into a sprawling mass of roads, cars and block after endless block of concrete apartment buildings. Men in western style pants and shirts crowded the streets while most women wore a bulky cloak and headscarf. Although people were still occasionally publicly flogged for having premarital sex, David knew most Iranians longed for reform and return to a more normal society. Unfortunately, the American invasion of Iraq and continued threats about Iran's nuclear program had alienated many moderate Iranian voters and strengthened the religious right. Even the contested election several years ago and massive street protests by the moderates had failed to weaken the control of the conservative _mullahs_ and the bizarre conservative President, Mahmoud Ahmadinejad.

Leaning back against the seat, David reviewed the whirlwind of events since Nawaz's death and his narrow escape from the burning Pakistani _madras_. Before leaving Peshawar, he had directed the local CIA office to initiate a search for the Arab, Al Kabbar. The subsequent plane flight to Tehran was uneventful and he had slept for most of the flight. He had talked briefly with Parissa, his newfound companion, who revealed only that she'd been an Iranian agent for seven years. Otherwise, she remained cagey with her answers, although her probing questions conveyed her strong interest in David and his presence in Peshawar.

After landing in Tehran, David had been taken to a hotel near the former U.S. embassy, now a teaching facility for the Revolutionary Student Association. The walls surrounding the compound were covered with slogans and paintings depicting the struggle of the Iranian people against American hegemony. The hotel itself was a pleasant, older building and David was amused to find there was at least one listening device hidden in his room.

Earlier that morning, Parissa had called to make dinner plans and tell David a guide and car and driver were at his disposal for the day. David had accepted reluctantly, knowing the men were Iranian agents sent to monitor his movements. He went first to the Swiss Embassy, which oversaw American interests in Iran since the two countries still didn't maintain diplomatic relations.

David had used the embassy's coded communications facilities to contact Jack Reynolds. His control agent informed David that unfortunately Al Kabbar and his truck had vanished. Reynolds had encouraged him to learn what he could from the Iranians without revealing too much. Above all, David wasn't to mention his search for the mysterious weapon Azam Tariq might have obtained for Abdullah.

David's chauffeured car finally arrived at a mansion with graceful columns and blue tiled façade. The beautifully maintained garden contained rolling lawns, extensive flower beds and a winding creek lined with willow trees. Parissa was standing next to a pond and greeted David with a warm smile.

"You look well rested."

"Thanks. I needed the sleep." David looked around the deserted garden, surprised they were alone. "Where are my guards? Did I bore them today?"

Parissa chuckled. "They were offended you didn't use the car phone and instead went to the Swiss embassy."

"It was my uncle's birthday and I wanted to call him."

She laughed. "How is Uncle Sam?"

"Grouchy," David replied lightly. "He's afraid I might get delayed here."

She shook her head. "As I said in Pakistan, you're free to leave whenever you want."

"It's his concern, not mine." He looked approvingly around the garden. "Then again, you keep bringing me to places this nice, I may never go home."

"Where do you live now?"

"You know better than that," David chided gently. Even though his face was now known to the Iranians, he would try to shield his identity as long as possible. He and Reynolds had earlier agreed that finding Al Kabbar—and potentially a nuclear device—was worth the risk of compromising his cover in Istanbul to the Iranian Secret Service.

"I didn't mean to pry," she said. "You won't believe it, but I asked from personal interest, not professional."

"I'm sorry. I don't mean to be rude. But under the circumstances..."

She waved her arm dismissively. "Please, don't apologize. I shouldn't have asked. Shall we go inside?" she asked, taking David's arm. Her touch sent tingles up his spine.

"You look beautiful tonight," David said, surprised at her appearance. In public, Iranian women were required to wear black robes and a veil or, at least, a bulky overcoat and head scarf. Parissa was wearing a green dress that although modest, still showed off her shapely body and legs. Her long dark hair was tied back in a single pony tail, which wiped away most of the years that gathered in small lines at the corner of her eyes. So far, her actions had suggested a sophistication and experience surpassing his own. David guessed she was five years older than he, perhaps in her mid-thirties.

"Thanks," she replied, blushing faintly. "You should be careful—in parts of Iran, your compliment might offend a woman's male relatives."

"And the woman?"

"She'd like to hear more."

David smiled. "With you, that'd be easy."

There was an awkward but warm silence. Her grip tightened slightly on his arm.

"The garden is gorgeous, very peaceful," David finally said, not wishing to break the companionable silence. "How often do you come here?"

"As much as I can," she replied. "The owner is an old friend of the family. Here, there isn't a female dress code. Maybe someday that will become a part of the past in Iran."

"Strange words coming from a representative of an Islamic government."

She shrugged. "The conservative clerics governing Iran will one day be replaced by more moderate politicians. Unfortunately, the invasion of Iraq set back the Iranian reform movement, which was viewed as too close to the Americans and their ideals and policies. The recent election turmoil was also blamed on the Americans, which weakened the reformers. I'm sure that at some point the government will reflect the people's wishes."

"And you'll no longer be a part of former President Bush's Axis of Evil?"

Parissa scowled, but then laughed when she saw David was kidding. "I know most Americans still think we're terrorists because of our takeover of the U.S. embassy 30 years ago and our nuclear program. And I must admit, our government still supports many fundamentalist Islamic organizations, some that the U.S considers terrorist."

"Perhaps now isn't the right time to discuss politics," he said with a smile, knowing it could only create friction.

"Agreed, although my personal politics are probably closer to yours than you think."

As they entered the restaurant, the elderly proprietor greeted Parissa like a beloved daughter, complementing her appearance and asking about her family. They were seated in a private area away from prying eyes, although David assumed their conversation was being recorded. He was pleasantly surprised when the waitress brought a bottle of wine. They were soon exchanging stories about their childhoods and college years. Parissa dropped her guard somewhat, revealing glimpses of a vibrant, humorous woman who adored her family and tolerated the demands of Islam. The drinks, conversation and beautiful setting created an unexpected intimacy David hadn't felt in some time.

Once they ordered dinner, David turned to Parissa. "I hate to talk business, but I've a lot of questions."

She met his gaze unflinchingly. "I'll answer those I can."

"Have your people found out anything more about Al Kabbar?"

She shook her head. "No, he disappeared without a trace. We think he left Peshawar and probably switched vehicles somewhere outside the city."

"Do you think he's still in Pakistan?"

"It's possible. If so, he may've gone to the mountains. The Fist of *Allah madras* runs a training camp near the Afghanistan border."

"Then it's possible he's there." David had already come to the same conclusion. "Let's come back to Al Kabbar later. I've never thanked you properly for saving my life that night in Turki al Faisal's mosque in Riyadh."

Parissa looked blank, her hand distractedly pulling on her hair. "Mosque, what mosque?"

David looked at her suspiciously, wondering why she was pretending amnesia. He tried again. "Several days ago, you pulled me out of the interrogation room in the basement of the Wahhabi mosque outside of Riyadh."

"I haven't been to Saudi Arabia for a month," Parissa replied, her expression innocent.

Stunned, David leaned back and considered her response. As far as he knew, there wasn't any reason for Parissa to lie and she appeared genuinely surprised. If true, then another woman had rescued him that night. But who? And what was her role? He mastered his surprise and curiosity and instead focused on Parissa.

"Why were you in Pakistan?" he asked.

Parissa sighed. "Because we don't trust Islamic fundamentalists."

"Why not? Iran's a fundamentalist Islamic republic."

"But we're Shiites, not Sunni Muslims." Parissa reached for the bottle of wine and poured another glass. "As you know, most Iranians are Shiite Muslims. We've been persecuted for a thousand years by the Sunnis, even massacred on occasion. More importantly, Mecca and Medina are under the control of the Saudis, who are ardent Sunnis. We fear that not only is the persecution and violence against Shiites increasing, but that we may soon be prohibited from taking the *hajj* to Mecca."

David knew Islam was split into two primary branches—Sunni and Shiite—the religious schism dating to the first few years after the death of the Prophet Mohammad. Most Muslims were Sunnis, as were most Arabs. The two sects had feuded for centuries and still occasionally clashed violently over Islamic ideology and the Sunnis treatment of Shiites. Iran and Iraq and several smaller countries were largely Shiite while most of the Middle Eastern Islamic countries were Sunni. Occasionally, the Sunni fundamentalists controlling Mecca would limit the number of Shiites during the *hajj*. In fact, just 20 years ago, after several clashes with Iranian pilgrims, the Saudis had significantly restricted visas for Iranians embarking on the *hajj*.

"For the last few years," Parissa continued, "we've become increasingly concerned about the growing fanaticism of many Sunni Islamic organizations. Some of these organizations view Shiite Muslims as much the enemy as Christians or Jews. So we monitor the most dangerous organizations closely."

"Such as the Fist of *Allah madras* in Peshawar?"

She nodded. "Yes. They're teaching the strict, Wahhabi interpretation of Islam to their students. In effect, the Fist of *Allah* advocates *jihad* against anyone who doesn't adhere to their beliefs—including Shiite Muslims."

David recalled Khaled's warning. "Is the *madras* involved in a movement to overthrow the Saudi government?"

"We've heard rumors *someone* is plotting to do so, but I don't know if they're true or not. It's very possible the *madras* is involved." Suddenly Parissa abruptly switched subjects. "Did you know that Azam Tariq was a former senior Pakistani military officer who was closely involved with Pakistan's nuclear weapons program?"

"Yes," David answered tersely, noticing Parissa was carefully observing his reaction. He maintained a neutral expression, wondering if perhaps the Iranians knew something more; obviously, he couldn't ask without disclosing the contents of Tariq's letter. And Jack Reynolds had been very clear—under no circumstances was David to reveal they were concerned about a nuclear weapon. Among other reasons, Reynolds was concerned the Iranians might pursue such a weapon for their own arsenal.

Parissa leaned forward. "It's my turn to ask you a question. Why were you at the *madras* that night? Were you chasing Al Kabbar?"

David quickly told her about the information he'd found at Al Faisal's mosque in Saudi Arabia that implicated the *madras* in the training of potential terrorists and, more importantly, the overthrow of the Saudi government. He also mentioned briefly his meetings with Khaled ibn Saud and Ramzi Yousef, the Saudi industrialist.

"Khaled ibn Saud heads the GDI and, according to Yousef, is preparing to use the *mutaween* to overthrow the Saudi government," David concluded.

Parissa looked grave. "That's a serious charge. Khaled's very bright, very capable. If anyone could successfully overthrow the Saudi government, Khaled would be my choice."

"What can you tell me about both men?"

She shrugged. "Nothing more than the usual background. We don't have either man under observation. If Khaled really controls the *mutaween* and can create a crisis of confidence in the Saudi government by getting a *fatwa* issued then..."

"...staging a coup would be easy," David said, finishing her thought.

Parissa leaned back in her chair. "Especially if it happens during the *hajj* when there are over three million foreign pilgrims in Saudi Arabia."

They remained quiet while the waiter cleared the table, each lost in thought. David tried to figure out how he could find Al Kabbar, knowing the man was the key to finding out about Tariq's 'weapon'. Al Kabbar might also be able to shed some light on Abdullah's identity and role, the *mutaween* and the activities of the Fist of *Allah madras*.

When the waiter finally left, David leaned forward. "Parissa, if Al Kabbar is still in Pakistan, it's possible he went to the Fist of *Allah* training camp."

She mulled it over before replying. "It's a long shot."

"It's the only chance we have of finding him."

"Even if true, you don't know the location of the training camp."

"I'm betting you do."

Parissa's slight smile confirmed David's hunch. "I'll have to check with my superiors before I give you the location. What would you plan to do?"

"Do you have a man inside?" he asked.

She hesitated before nodding. "Yes. But we only communicate by pre-arranged meetings every two weeks. Our agent doesn't want to get caught with sophisticated communication equipment."

"I need to visit the camp. If Al Kabbar is there, then perhaps your agent can tell me something more about him. I could even try to grab and interrogate Al Kabbar."

"Not much of a plan," Parissa said pointedly.

"Got a better idea? Azam Tariq is dead and his papers destroyed by the fire. Al Kabbar is my only lead."

"You're a typically persistent American, I'll give you that," she said, her smile softening her words. "I'll see what I can do."

David pushed away his wine glass. "Why were you at the *madras* that evening?"

"We were observing the building when we saw you climb the fence. I decided to follow to find out what you were up to. As for my showing up in time, that was pure luck. I suppose you could say that *Allah* was watching your back."

"I wish I'd been watching Nawaz's," David replied quietly, his guilt surging once more. Ever since arriving in Tehran, he'd fought to forget his role in Nawaz's death.

Parissa reached over to touch David's hand. "He was a professional, he knew the risks. You can't blame yourself."

David knew it wasn't that simple. "Perhaps, perhaps not."

She squeezed his hand and continued to hold it. David looked down at her hand and then back up at Parissa. She smiled and pulled him to his feet.

"Are we going somewhere?" David asked, as they moved away from the table.

"Outside for a walk."

"Tired of having your every word recorded? Where was the microphone? Under the table?"

She laughed. "In the flowers."

"Not very original."

"The CIA would've insisted on the same thing."

"Not true. They would've recorded *and* videotaped us."

She smiled. "You Americans and your technology."

They walked outside. The night had grown crisp and cold, a curtain of stars having swept across the sky. In companionable silence, they walked along the meandering brick path alongside the gurgling creek. Parissa tucked her arm under his and drew closer. He could smell her perfume and her hair, feel the softness of her breasts as she leaned against him.

He found Parissa's curious mixture of East and West, Islamic and secular, both appealing and sexy. Her story, at least as much as she had chosen to reveal, was simple. As friends of the deposed Shah, her family had once known wealth and privilege. After the revolution, the new government had stripped her family of their assets and monitored them closely for years. Parissa had known only stories of a luxurious past and the realities of a harsh religious school. While she had superficially embraced her religion, Parissa was more interested in the cultural aspects of Islam than the teachings of the *Quran*.

Her gift for languages, intelligence and desire to see beyond an Iranian woman's limited horizon had led her to the intelligence world. David sensed her successful career and years abroad gave her an independence that intimidated most Iranian men, who were used to more pliable companions. Clearly there had been liaisons, but few, if any, lasting relationships. Despite her independence, David sensed that at some level Parissa still sought a traditional role. The conflict was evident in her occasional deferential remarks and the way she sometimes eagerly sought David's opinion. But most of the time, she came across as an independent Western woman, toughened by her experiences and the constant danger of her profession. She had chosen her path, as opposed to David, who had his thrust upon him.

Her gentle tug on his arm brought him back to the present. "Why don't you have a girlfriend?" she asked, her soft tone indicating her caution in asking such a personal question.

David tensed but then forced himself to relax. "I did, until about two years ago."

"About the time you became a part of all this?"

David nodded. "I thought I could balance both, but I was wrong. When I returned from training in the U.S, she decided to move on. Since then, I guess I've been too busy. There've been dates but..."

"It's a lonely life."

"So I've discovered." David felt the urge to reveal himself to Parissa. She was the first woman he'd spoken with who understood his situation. He knew he was becoming increasingly isolated and more like the veteran field agents he'd met in Langley—the kind whose eyes remained wary and calculating above perfunctory smiles. They were cold and distant, as if interacting with others was both a chore and a potential threat. David had felt their air of superiority hid insecurities and a gnawing fear—the kind that David sometimes now felt when he went to bed at night, locking the doors and windows and wedging a chair under the bedroom doorknob.

But not tonight. Tonight, he recalled the gentler, quieter moments of his youth.

He realized he had stopped walking and that Parissa was staring up at him.

"Sorry," he said. "I was thinking. I haven't been this relaxed in a long time."

"One of the agents who trained me said something I never forgot."

"Don't take life too seriously?" David joked.

Parissa smiled wistfully. "Something almost as simple. He said if you constantly look into the shadows, you never see the sun."

"Like tonight?"

"Yes." Parissa turned and kissed him. Her lips were soft and inviting, her body filling the hollows in his.

David drew back and looked down at her. "Thanks for a wonderful evening."

"You make it sound as if it's over."

"I was hoping that it had just started."

"It has."

Which she proved over and over again for the remainder of the night.

14

Ramallah, Occupied West Bank

The young woman trudged down the dusty road, a basket filled with apples and oranges tucked under her arm. Her tattered *abaya* hung loosely on her thin frame, as if her struggles to survive under the Israeli occupation had taken both her health and prosperity. Although she was not beautiful, her face was memorable—a strong jaw line, aquiline nose and piercing grey eyes. She moved slowly, avoiding the scattered piles of trash and debris that were further evidence of the economic and social malaise that now permeated the Palestinian territories and the infrequent nature of even the most basic municipal services.

"See them?" inquired the voice in her ear.

Rachael Barak dropped her chin to whisper into the hidden microphone in her *abaya*. "Yes. There are two guards in front of the house and I saw a third head for the rear."

"Good. All units, get ready to move in. Rachael, thanks. Time to turn around."

Rachael felt a surge of anger. "Not a chance Ehud. This one's mine."

"Dammit Rachael, get your ass back here!"

Rachael ignored the command and continued to move forward. The unpaved street was lined with flimsy houses poorly constructed from whitewashed concrete walls and rusting tin roofs, interspersed with trash-strewn empty lots and an occasional struggling olive tree. Two dogs wrestled playfully in the street before an audience of several children, their grubby faces delighted at the spectacle. A battered blue BMW sedan was parked in front of the house Rachael was approaching. Two Palestinian men sat on a porch bench, carefully observing the passing traffic and pedestrians. Despite the warm weather, they wore bulky jackets, which Rachael assumed was to hide their weapons.

Her ear microphone crackled to life once more. "Rachael, I know you want Shadi Muhana's head, but this is too dangerous. You're not equipped properly for the assault."

"It's my decision," she replied calmly. "I haven't forgotten Meacham."

Several hours earlier, a Palestinian informant had warned the Mossad that Shadi Muhana, a wanted Hamas militant, had taken refuge in the house, guarded by four loyal men. Muhana was suspected of masterminding dozens of Palestinian rocket attacks and bombings over the years, including a car bomb that several years ago had killed Rachael's lover, Meacham. Vowing to find the man responsible, she had dedicated all her waking hours to tracking down Muhana.

"The rest of you follow my lead, I'm moving in," Rachael whispered into her microphone.

As Rachael drew near to the guards, she pretended to stumble and dropped her basket. As it hit the ground and tipped over, the apples and oranges spilled into the dusty road and rolled in different directions. The younger of the two guards jumped to his feet, set down the rifle that suddenly appeared from under his coat and walked toward Rachael.

"Here, let me help you," he called out, as he drew near. "You're far too pretty to be groping around in the dust."

"Oh thank you," Rachael gushed.

The young Palestinian smiled and kneeled down to pick up the wayward fruit. He was barely a teenager, the soft dew of an attempted mustache straggling along his lip. The other guard watched silently, reaching into his shirt pocket to pull out a pack of cigarettes. When the young man extended his hand filled with apples, Rachael leaned forward as if to take the fruit from him. She suddenly reached out and grasped his arm.

"What are you doing?" he asked with a frown.

She stubbornly retained hold, preventing him from standing.

Eight soldiers dressed in full combat gear and carrying assault rifles suddenly materialized from behind a neighboring house. There were scattered shouts and screams as the soldiers sprinted forward. As the young Palestinian guard kicked frantically at Rachael, she suddenly let go of his arm. He stumbled backward and nearly lost his balance.

"You bitch, you're one of them," he snarled.

He pulled out a pistol tucked in his waistband, but Rachael had already brought out an Uzi from under her loose robes.

"Drop it," she yelled in Arabic.

With a look of hatred, the Palestinian dropped his gun and raised his arms. The remaining guard on the porch pointed his Ak-47 at Rachael, but was cut down by the approaching soldiers before he could pull the trigger.

"Cover me," Rachael yelled to soldiers as she sprinted up the dirt walkway to the house.

She darted onto the porch and flattened herself against the wall of the house. Two soldiers joined her on the other side of the front door, while four more sprinted down the walkway that led to the rear of the building.

The first soldier held up his hand and motioned her down to the ground. He then gave a silent hand count to three before kicking in the door. The flimsy wood around the lock gave way and the door sprang open. Before the soldier could move back to the safety of the wall, a burst of automatic rifle fire struck his shoulder and spun him around to the ground.

The remaining soldier pulled a stun grenade from his vest and threw it inside. The deafening explosion sent a plume of smoke and debris pouring out the doorway. Rachel and the soldier fired blindly inside. There was a scream and then silence. From her prone position on the concrete floor, Rachel waited patiently for any further movement. She could hear gunfire and yells from the rear of the house. She glanced down at the wounded soldier, who lay groaning incoherently in a spreading pool of blood.

Rachael knew they needed to end the raid quickly to get him medical attention.

"Ready?" she called out softly to the remaining soldier.

He nodded. They rose to their feet and rushed through the doorway, plunging into a swirling cloud of smoke. Rachael tripped and nearly fell over a man's body, an AK-47 lying near his outstretched hand.

"Down!" her companion cried.

Rachel hit the floor, feeling bullets tear through the air where she'd been just a moment before. She returned fire, calmly squeezing the trigger and laying down a precise pattern. There were shouts and curses in Arabic and she crawled forward, her companion moving alongside. Reaching the bottom of a staircase, they fired another burst up into swirling smoke. Stifling an urge to cough, Rachael waited patiently for any return fire or movement. They heard and saw nothing threatening. The gunfire from the rear of the house ceased.

"All clear!" shouted a voice from outside.

Rachael and the soldier exchanged glances and then rushed up the stairs, their Uzis leveled. Another bloody body lay unmoving at the top, an AK-47 lying nearby. Glancing around, Rachael realized the hallway contained two closed doors. They moved cautiously toward the closest one. Rachael stopped on the near side of the doorway and nodded to her companion. He kicked the door open and they peered inside.

The small bedroom was empty, the only furniture a bed and dresser.

They moved down the hall to the next closed door. Again, the soldier kicked it open and they looked inside, Uzis held at the ready. There was a sudden movement and Rachael's finger tightened on the trigger.

The Palestinian stood still with his arms raised high above his head. His face was still covered in shaving cream and he was naked, a bath towel flung over his shoulder.

Rachael lowered her Uzi. "Muhana, it must be very, very cold. Your manhood is so small that if I were your wife, I'd demand a divorce."

The naked man shot a look of hatred at her, but remained silent.

Although disappointed she didn't have a chance to kill him, Rachael consoled herself with the thought of Shadi Muhana's interrogation. It would be brutal, bloody and hopefully last a long, long time.

❄ ❄ ❄

The windowless two story building was rather non-descript and shabby, the numerous armed guards in front the only indication that it was a critical component of Israel's national security. The building held the Mossad's interrogation center, which had been deliberately located in an industrial district far from the prying eyes of the international community and the scorned Jewish 'peaceniks'. Every Palestinian dreaded the place, for many had disappeared inside—a few never to be heard from again and the remainder often returning home broken in both spirit and body. Those released to return home were never completely trusted again, because it was said a Palestinian never exited the building other than in a pine box or as an Israeli spy.

Rachael Barak moved quickly down the dank basement corridor, anxious to get started on her interrogation. Shadi Muhana was being held in the bowels of the building, in an underground room known simply as the "hole". There, no one heard the screams and cries of suspected Palestinian terrorists, who were subjected to a wide variety of interrogation techniques. There was never any hesitation to use force or borderline methods such as water boarding or electrical shock—too many Israelis had died in Palestinian terrorist attacks. The Mossad simply fought the war on conditions and terms their enemy would understand.

Rachael was one of the Mossad's most experienced and effective agents. A *sabra*, or native born Israeli, she had grown up an orphan on a kibbutz in the West Bank near the Lebanese border. Her parents had originally come from Yemen, members of the 'lost tribes' of Israel. When Rachael was eight, a Hezbollah-backed guerilla group sneaked across the border and raided the kibbutz, taking seven hostages, including Rachael and her parents. She had watched as the guerillas executed the adult hostages one by one, her parents the final two murders. Although she was rescued, Rachael never forgot the sight of her parents' bloody bodies lying on the ground, their eyes staring blankly back at her. It was that image that had driven her to join the Mossad as soon as she was old enough. Her Middle Eastern looks and fluent Arabic enabled her to spend significant time abroad, gathering intelligence on Israel's enemies and, on occasion, even 'terminating' potential threats.

Although Rachael occasionally returned to visit the kibbutz, she now considered Mossad headquarters as her home and fellow agents her surrogate family. She admitted this freely and without regret, satisfied with the knowledge that she was preventing other young Israelis from a similar childhood fate such as hers. Yet the years of brutal interrogations and dangerous undercover assignments had taken an inevitable toll—she had become callous, brusque and somewhat removed, as if she were viewing everything from a slight distance. Although aware of the change, she chose not to fight it, thankful that her remoteness made each day easier to bear. Her days as a Mossad agent were drawing to a close, a point hammered home after her most recent department psychological assessment. In her heart, Rachael agreed, knowing she could only retain her compassion and humanity if she soon stepped aside from field work.

Still, she was desperate to complete one more task—the capture of Shadi Muhana, who had murdered her former lover, Meacham. Only in his late-twenties, Meacham had been filled with passion and hope. Rachael had drunk greedily from his reservoir of youthful enthusiasm, delighting in his affection and sexual desire. During their months together, she had begun to glimpse a life beyond the one she had only known since her parent's death. Those were heady days, when almost anything seemed possible, perhaps even a family of her own.

Then, tragedy struck, as it so often does to those who have known nothing else. Several years ago, Meacham was killed by a suicide bomber in a Jerusalem café—a bomber sent by Shadi Muhana. Since then, Rachael had dedicated her life to capturing the Palestinian. But until that morning, he'd always managed to slip away.

Outside the interrogation room, Rachael paused to gather herself before opening the door. She had asked to speak briefly with Muhana before the professional interrogators began. Rachael hardened her resolve, reminding herself the man inside was a murderous coward, responsible not only for the death of someone she loved, but for the deaths of numerous innocent civilians. There could be no mercy, no second chances.

She opened the door. The brightly lit interrogation room contained two chairs, a wooden table and two-way mirror along the far wall. A naked Shadi Muhana was tied to a steel chair anchored in the cement floor, his face a welt of bruises and cuts. A slight man with indistinct features, Muhana had bandages on both arms. He raised his head and stared at her defiantly.

"Don't bother to get up Muhana," she said. "I can see you're tied up at the moment."

He spat on the floor. "What do you want, you Jewish bitch?"

"To talk," she replied, her meaning clear. "By the marks on your face, I see you've had a chance to meet some of my friends."

"They're cowards. Very soon, all of you will die."

She walked over to him and pulled up a chair. "When you were naked, I couldn't believe you were that small. I actually felt sorry for you."

He scowled. "If you and I had a moment together, I'd make you a real woman."

"If you don't behave, I'll make it very unpleasant for you."

"I'm not afraid to die."

"I think you're a coward. If you weren't afraid to die, we never would've captured you."

"You surprised me," he said. "I was in the shower."

Rachael chuckled humorlessly. "What, you didn't hear the gunfire? You had plenty of time to grab a gun."

"Screw you!"

"I have a few questions to ask you."

Rachael leaned back in the chair and for the next few minutes questioned him about his cohorts and plans. Not surprisingly, Muhana refused to answer any question or even meet her gaze. He merely stared straight ahead, not even shaking his head in response.

Certain that further questioning would be useless, Rachael stood and signaled to the unseen Mossad agents watching from behind the mirror.

"Muhana, I have a surprise for you," she said.

The door opened and a man walked in, pushing a cart loaded with what looked like an electrical generator. Rachael looked deliberately at the cart then back at Muhana. He was frightened, obviously recognizing the contents of the cart. For the first time, a few beads of sweat appeared on his forehead and his eyes blinked rapidly.

"That's right Muhana," she said. "We're going to hook you up to this machine and give you the thrill of your life. I'm told it's very, very painful and the best part is that it doesn't leave a single scar. But it works wonders with your memory, sort of 'sparks' people to remember things. Afterwards, assuming you're still functioning, we'll pump you so full of drugs that you'll tell us everything you didn't before." She gave him a practiced smile, thankful she never had to witness these brutal sessions. "This is your final chance."

He looked around the room and then nodded. "Okay."

Surprised, Rachael remained suspicious. Muhana's assent was too fast and easy—something wasn't right.

"I'll tell you something," Muhana said, with a wicked, gap-toothed smile. "Something that'll keep you up at night. Something that will haunt your every waking moment until the day it happens, knowing you're powerless to stop it."

"And what is that?" Rachael asked calmly, although his assured voice worried her. By now, he should have been intimidated—not staring back at her as an equal. A surge of foreboding shook her.

Shadi Muhana leaned forward and gave a small laugh. "I can see it now, thousands and thousands of dead Jews. Burned and charred from a bomb. *My* bomb. A nuclear bomb. Remember me when you die."

He clenched his jaw shut and then slowly slumped over, held upright only by the wire binding him to the chair. Rachael rushed forward and lifted his head off his chest. His eyes were closed and muscles slack—he was clearly already dead. But how? She recognized the faint aroma of bitter almonds. Cyanide! She realized there must've been a capsule hidden in a false tooth and he had bitten down hard to crack it.

Rachael let Muhana's head fall back on his chest and stood there, her mind racing over his final words. Were they the meaningless taunts of a doomed man or the knowledgeable warning of a deadly terrorist? Damn him to hell! She wanted to dismiss his warning outright, but knew Muhana's bloody track record required her to consider every possibility. She kicked the dead man and cursed him for stealing her moment of triumph. Rachael knew she'd spend the next few weeks tracing Muhana's final movements and contacts, trying to discover if his threat had any merit.

At the very least he had been right on one count—his words would keep her up at night and haunt every waking hour until she discovered their meaning.

15

The Blackhawk helicopter settled down gently in the dry river bed, the rapidly whirling blades kicking up a plume of dust and sand. Through the gathering darkness, David could see a waiting silhouette standing near five horses. The figure raised his arm and a flashlight flickered on and off three times in recognition. David gave a thumbs up signal to the pilot, who cut the power, the helicopter shuddering as the blades whirled to a stop. After a two hour flight, they had finally arrived at the staging area for David's journey through northern Pakistan to the Fist of *Allah* training camp.

David began collecting his gear. He was dressed in a *shalwar kameez* outfit, the traditional knee-length shirts and pants combination worn by many Pakistani tribesmen. He was also wearing a false beard. He knew a closer examination would reveal his deception, but from a distance or in dim light he could pass as a Pakistani. His equipment was minimal—a thick coat, change of clothes and several Russian AK-47s—standard issue for northern Pakistan tribesmen. His equipment included a satellite communications system, cunningly hidden inside a water container. David was also wearing a cheap looking watch with a tracking device, a belt that concealed a thin stiletto and small gun strapped to his ankle.

"You got everything?" asked the Air Force corporal.

"Yeah," David replied. "Thanks for the ride, Max."

Max smiled. "This was a milk run. Don't feel right without someone shooting at my ass."

David turned to Parissa, who was still pulling together her gear. "Need a hand?"

She scowled. "I'm perfectly capable of handling myself."

David smiled, realizing Parissa was masking her uneasiness over the flight. She had spent the entire flight gripping the side of the fuselage, leaving David to conclude she'd never flown in a helicopter before. Then again, even he found that the incessant din and vibration made the flight seem endless.

The past 24 hours since their dinner together in Tehran had passed quickly. Once Parissa received permission to guide David to the Fist of *Allah* camp, they had left Tehran immediately. Fortunately, there was a regularly scheduled meeting the next day with the Iranian agent inside the camp. According to Parissa, their agent, who had been in place nearly six months, passed along a variety of information, including the names of those, mostly Saudis, who trained there. The Iranian agent had also identified perhaps 20 Iranian Sunni Muslims who attended the camp—men who were quietly arrested upon their return to Iran.

David had been forced to allow Parissa to accompany him. She had visited the camp once before and, in fact, had recruited the Iranian agent inside. Once their temporary alliance was forged, David and Parissa flew from Tehran to Kabul. From there, they took a helicopter to a U.S. Special Forces base near the Pakistan border. Unfortunately, the U.S. military was prohibited from flying inside Pakistan and the training camp was nearly 40 miles from the border. They would need to travel the remaining distance by horseback. Parissa had arranged for one of her colleagues—the man who regularly met with the agent inside the camp—to meet them with horses and supplies for the journey.

David dropped from the helicopter to the rocky ground before reaching back to grab the tattered cloth sack offered by Max.

"Remember, this is as far as we can go into Pakistani air space," Max said. "If you get in trouble, you're on your own."

"Understood." The Pakistani North-West territory was a remote, harsh region, ruled by tribal alliances, rivalries and ancient laws. The Pakistani government largely left the entire region alone, effectively allowing the tribes to govern themselves. U.S. CIA drones constantly monitored the area and the few Pakistani soldiers in the region rarely ventured from their bases.

"Good luck," Max said. "See you in two days, unless you contact us sooner."

David jogged across the uneven ground toward the waiting figure with Parissa close behind. As the helicopter took off, David could feel the wind from the accelerating blades whip against his back.

"Greetings, my friend," the stranger said in Pashtu, straightening up slowly and tossing away a cigarette butt. "I'm Afrasiab Khattak. Welcome to Pakistan."

"I'm David. Any problems?"

The Pakistani shook his head. He was a sinewy, rough-looking man, his coarse skin deeply lined from the sun and wind. A full beard covered most of his face and wisps of graying black hair escaped from beneath a travel-stained turban. The black stumps and missing teeth in his mouth spoke of a hard existence, as did the vivid scar that streaked along his jaw.

"No trouble," Khattak replied. "I passed one tribesman several kilometers back. He eyed my horses, so I just made sure he saw this." He patted the AK-47 slung over his shoulder. "That made him think twice."

Parissa and Khattak exchanged formal greetings. David was surprised to see Khattak treat Parissa almost as an equal, which was unusual for women in Pakistan, particularly in the North-West Frontier Province. In general, women rarely left their homes and weren't allowed contact with unrelated men. For this trip, Parissa would pose as David's wife and Khattak's daughter. She was forced to travel under the constraints of *purdah,* which was Persian for curtain, and wear a *chador,* a loosely draped cotton cloth used as a head covering and body veil. During the helicopter flight, David had teasingly reminded Parissa to walk several steps behind him and never look another male in the eyes. She hadn't been amused.

David looked over the five horses, noticing two were carrying baggage—heavy cloth sacks filled with clothes and a few household items.

"Why the baggage?" David asked.

Khattak laughed. "Our cover story. Merchants traveling through the area. I even make some extra money this way."

"How long until we reach our destination?" Parissa asked.

Khattak shrugged, his gaze focused on David as he sized him up. "The trails are poor, so perhaps 16 hours. We'll ride for six hours tonight, then make camp. The meeting with my contact is scheduled for tomorrow evening."

David strapped his cloth sack on one of the horses and slung a rifle over his shoulder. He mounted easily, thankful he'd grown up riding horses at a friend's ranch in Southern California. His horse was thin but tough, his flanks covered with the scars of whips and years of carrying poorly-fitting baggage. A full moon was just rising over the horizon, providing sufficient light to follow the trail. Khattak led the way, the two pack horses immediately behind, then Parissa with David bringing up the rear.

"Very romantic, David" Parissa said, looking over her shoulder. "You take me to all the best places."

"No expense spared," he replied. "Wait until you see the hotel room."

They had never spoken of their night together, the tacit understanding that the sex, much as their alliance, was merely fleeting and temporary. Even so, David felt a certain tenderness toward Parissa and, in the rare moments when she let her guard down, he sensed she felt the same way. Still, he vowed not to let his feelings interfere with the task at hand. It wasn't the time or place to become sentimental; besides, Parissa was clearly capable of handling herself.

They rode along the valley floor, following the winding course of a shallow river. The trail was exposed, since many of the trees had been cut down for firewood. The surrounding mountains loomed close, the steep slopes mostly bare and rocky. The terrible beauty of the unforgiving landscape spoke eloquently of the harsh tribal life of the North-West Province. They stayed alert, scanning the countryside for any movement. Occasionally they passed a sign of habitation—a small hut perched on a hillside or the discarded refuse from previous travelers. The horses kicked up clouds of dust, forcing David to place a scarf over his mouth. The handmade saddle was rough and ill-fitting and he knew he'd soon have saddle sores.

They rode in silence for the next few hours, David's thoughts drifting in and out of no particular place. The sun disappeared below the horizon and a bone-chilling cold descended, their breath leaving white misty trails. The early evening was deathly quiet, unnerving in the utter silence and stillness.

Suddenly, Khattak held up his hand for them to stop. David listened carefully, hearing only the wind. A wolf howled on his left, a mournful sound that even to David's untrained ear was too concise and low pitched.

"I fear we're heading into a trap," Khattak said.

"The wolf?" David asked.

Khattak nodded. "Tribesmen often use it as a signal. The man I saw earlier may have gathered others."

"Are they after us because they saw the helicopter?"

Khattak shook his head. "I think the horses. Usually I take no more than two."

Parissa leaned forward. "Is there another trail?"

"No. This is the only one. See that rocky outcropping ahead? Where the trail narrows?"

Perhaps a half mile ahead, the mountains squeezed closer together and the valley became a narrow ravine. In the gathering darkness, David could just make out a cluster of rocks that overlooked the trail as it passed out of the valley. The surrounding slope was intermittently covered with brush, trees and large boulders.

"If there's an ambush, it'll be there," Khattak said. "The trail drops down on the other side of the pass and the next valley is wide open."

"What do you suggest?" Parissa asked.

"In about ten minutes, the clouds will hide the moon and it'll grow darker."

David glanced up and noticed a large band of clouds drifting towards the moon.

"I'll go ahead and work myself around behind the rocks. In about a half hour, you head down the trail. Be prepared to jump off the horses when the shooting starts."

"That's your plan?" David asked angrily, shaking his head in disbelief. "Let us be targets and draw their fire so you can see where they're hiding?"

Khattak shrugged. "We've no choice, this is the only trail. I know this valley and have the best chance of reaching them unseen."

"It's the best plan," Parissa interjected, looking at David. "Go ahead."

David bit back his response and nodded tersely. The Pakistani slid off his horse and disappeared into the underbrush, his passing leaving barely a ripple of moving branches. David gathered the reins of the pack animals and Khattak's horse and pulled them closer.

"As we approach, lie flat on your horse and keep the pack animal on the uphill side for protection."

"And you?" Parissa asked.

"I'll be shooting at anything that moves."

Parissa swung her rifle off her shoulder and adroitly loaded it. She looked up at David. "I can handle myself, thank you."

David smiled, feeling a surge of affection and admiration. They sat in companionable silence, David occasionally checking his watch. The night grew darker as the clouds passed over the moon. The only sounds were the night insects and the occasional snort from their horses.

"It's time," Parissa finally said.

David kneed his horse forward and Parissa followed. They rode slowly down the trail, which began to climb toward the end of the valley. The foliage and brush grew sparse, replaced by a stunted forest, the trees slight and sickly looking with the altitude and dryness. David's palms were sweaty and even the horses seemed more alert, as if sensing something was about to happen. David held the reins in one hand and his rifle in the other.

Ahead, the trail switch-backed several times up a steep slope before disappearing past the rocky outcropping that Khattak had pointed out earlier. David maneuvered so that he kept the pack horse between himself and the rock outcropping and Parissa followed his example. They began to climb up the slope, still perhaps fifty yards from the potential ambush.

The moon suddenly broke through the clouds, bathing the valley with light. David saw the glint of steel from the slope above. He stopped his horse and raised his rifle.

The night came alive with gunfire. David aimed at the muzzle flash from the rocks and returned fire. His horse shuddered with the impact of a bullet and another caught David in the chest, knocking him to the ground. He lay there for a moment, listening to the gunfire, the horses whining with fear, their hoofs churning up a cloud of dust.

"David, you okay?" Parissa called.

"Yeah." He rolled over on his stomach and peered back up the mountain, thankful he was wearing a bullet proof vest. Parissa was lying behind a rock, firing intermittently at an unseen target.

David's horse was lying still and the remaining horses had sprinted in terror down the trail. Peering over a boulder, David determined that there were at least two gunmen hidden near the trail and a third was further up the mountain. He couldn't see Khattak, who clearly wasn't close enough to take out the attackers.

"Parissa, cover me," David said.

He sprinted up the trail. A hail of bullets bounced off the surrounding rocks and he dove forward behind the shelter of a cluster of trees. He waited for the gunmen to refocus their attention on Parissa before climbing up the hill directly toward the gunmen, using the trees and rocks for cover. The night suddenly grew dark again as the moon disappeared once more behind the clouds. Steady bursts of gunfire continued to pierce the night, the muzzle flashes betraying the positions of their attackers.

David reached the edge of the tree line. The ambushing gunmen were hidden in the rocks straight ahead. Suddenly, one of the attackers screamed in pain. David waited until the gunfire intensified before sprinting the remaining distance. He saw three prone figures—two huddled and unmoving and the third firing back down the hill at Parissa. The lone remaining gunman turned at the sound of David's pounding feet. David stopped and fired a long burst. Dropping his AK-47, the gunman fell backward and lay still.

David walked closer and looked down at the three men. One was still alive, although badly hurt; the other two were now greeting *Allah*. The wounded man was a sallow youth, with a sparse beard and a thin, malnourished appearance. David kicked the weapons away from the bodies. Glancing around, David noticed three horses tethered to a nearby tree. Looking back at one of the dead men, David noticed something on his arm that caused deep consternation.

Khattak suddenly materialized from the darkness. "Nice shooting," he observed.

David bent down and turned over the wounded attacker. The man's eyes widened at the sight of David and he tried to reach inside his shirt. David kicked the man's hand away and placed the muzzle of his gun against the Pakistani's forehead.

"Khattak, ask him why the ambush?"

"I told you earlier. It was the horses."

"I don't think so. Look over there, at the dead man's arm."

Khattak whistled softly. "He has a tattoo. The insignia of the Fist of *Allah madras*."

"Exactly. Ask him!"

Khattak began questioning their captive, who only stared blankly straight ahead at Khattak's increasingly insistent voice. Infuriated, Khattak finally pulled out his gun and shot the man in the leg.

"Damn it!" David cried out. "Give him a chance to answer."

Ignoring David, Khattak raised his gun again. The wounded man waved his arms desperately and broke into a torrent of words. Khattak nodded understanding and asked several more questions before turning around.

"He said they're a patrol from the training camp. They saw the helicopter land and waited for us here. Fortunately, they weren't in radio contact with the camp."

"What do we do now with him?"

Khattak shrugged. "If he doesn't die from his wound, we kill him."

David wasn't surprised by his answer. After all, they were in the lawless northern mountains of Pakistan, a place where everyone carried a gun and deadly blood feuds began over a mere misunderstood glance. Although uneasy about the necessity of killing their captive, David also knew they had little choice. He fervently hoped they would find Al Kabbar or some other useful information once they reached the training camp. Otherwise, all the deaths were in vain.

He hadn't yet grown calloused enough to ignore death, even that of his enemies.

Parissa arrived and quickly took in the situation. "What do we do with the wounded man?"

"We're not taking him with us and we can't leave him here," David replied quietly, with a nod to Khattak. With a shrug, the Pakistani pulled out a knife.

Ignoring Parissa's shocked expression and violent protestations, David turned and walked away. Despite his best efforts, David realized he had already commenced down the path he'd resisted for so long. While his feet had been traveling steadily down the path, his gaze had been focused on the past, of who he once was and imagined he still remained. With a sense of sorrow and loss, David knew he had taken one more step away from innocence and toward becoming more like a seasoned agent, even capable of acting much like Khattak.

Then again, he just might stay alive longer.

16

D avid focused the binoculars on the newly-arrived Toyota pickup truck and tried to ignore the ants crawling down his shirt. He was lying behind a large boulder on a mountain overlooking the Fist of _Allah_ training camp. Parissa was crouched next to him, also surveying the camp. About twenty yards away, Khattak was standing guard to watch for roving patrols, even though they were well hidden amidst the rocks and brush.

The training camp was located in a small valley set in the rugged foothills of northern Pakistan. They had arrived there about an hour ago, weary from riding hard for most of the day. After the unsuccessful ambush last night, they had only traveled another hour before setting up camp. They had forgone a fire, fearing it might attract another patrol. In the bitter night cold, David and Parissa had slept huddled together for warmth. He had awakened to find her face next to his, her lips inviting. His kiss had roused her and she had given him a warm and winning smile. In the bright morning light and warmth of her presence, David almost believed the deadly ambush and Khattak's execution of the wounded gunman was just a bad dream.

Unfortunately, it was reality.

They had set out early that morning intending to cover the remaining 30 miles to the training camp by nightfall. The trail had been rough, but clearly marked. Gradually, the trees fell away until they were riding through rugged, sparse terrain populated primarily by lizards and hardscrabble brush. The cool mountain air was refreshing and smelled faintly of smoke from distant dung fires. Twice, they had encountered groups of silent, heavily armed men wearing tribal clothing. David knew the tribesmen of the region were fiercely independent and distrusted any outsiders. Each tribe and clan still implemented their own laws and justice, a code that had remained virtually unchanged for centuries. As strangers, David and Parissa could have been stopped and interrogated. But Khattak was well known and they were allowed to pass unchallenged. Nevertheless, David noticed both groups of tribesmen had stared after them until they were out of sight.

After tethering the horses to some trees perhaps three miles away, Khattak had led them along a strenuous trail over a mountain ridge to the rear of the camp. Fortunately, the rugged terrain was covered with enough brush and trees to conceal their approach. Upon their arrival, they had settled down at this observation point that commanded a view of the entire valley.

Lying there, David focused his binoculars once more on the training camp. The narrow valley containing the camp was heavily wooded with pine trees and split by a dirt road. The compound was a clear-cut area consisting of 15 individual huts and one large building, which held the kitchen and meeting hall. Several firing ranges and obstacle courses were scattered throughout the grounds.

Since their arrival, David had seen only a handful of men wandering around. The unfenced compound didn't appear to be guarded nor had they seen any patrols. The arrival of the Toyota truck a few minutes ago had been the first meaningful sign of activity.

David lowered his binoculars. "Parissa, when will your man break away and meet us?"

"After dark," she replied. "Durrani usually goes for a walk at that time each day, so that his absence never appears unusual. He knows to meet us here."

David turned back to observe the Toyota. Several men greeted the driver and then they all walked over to the main building. David trained his binoculars on the group, but was unable to determine if one of them was Al Kabbar. He was desperately hoping to find the man—out here, there were no rules. Once Al Kabbar answered his questions, nothing could stop David from avenging Nawaz's murder. His guilt and hatred had steadily grown during the past few days to create a burning desire to wring the Arab's neck and watch his face twist with pain. David knew he should remain dispassionate, but he was unable to forget he'd insisted on searching the Peshawar *madras* over Nawaz's objections.

Guilt was a heavy burden to carry.

"Khattak, any idea who might be in the Toyota?" David asked.

The Pakistani shrugged. "No, never seen it before. Perhaps our man inside will know."

The men disappeared inside the large building. David lowered the binoculars and settled down to wait. He and Parissa had agreed that before attempting to infiltrate the camp, they'd first speak with Akram Durrani, the

Iranian undercover operative. Although David was tempted to radio the U.S. Special Forces in Afghanistan and arrange for a team to storm the compound, he knew the camp was too far inside Pakistan—any potential target was left to the few American agents operating in the region.

In the meantime, there was nothing to do but wait.

✳ ✳ ✳

David was awakened by the touch of Parissa's hand on his shoulder. Rousing himself, he found Khattak deep in conversation with a haggard looking Pakistani, who was oddly dressed in a U.S Army camouflage shirt and baggy Pakistani pants, or *shalwar*. David glanced down at the camp, which was quiet and dark, except for the light flickering from several huts.

As David approached, the stranger turned to greet him.

"David, this is Akram Durrani."

"May *Allah* keep you and your family in his care," David said, nodding slightly.

"Sleeping soundly like that will get you killed," Durrani said brusquely, looking David up and down as if he'd seen something distasteful. His beard and hair were long and unkempt and his nose was squashed flat, as if it had once suffered a terrible blow. Although Durrani appeared gaunt and careworn, David knew that Pakistani tribesmen were capable of great feats of endurance. They were also fierce warriors, as the mountain tribal culture highly valued fighting skills, bravery and cunning.

"Only a few men could fall asleep out here," David replied, implying he deserved respect for being that fearless.

Durrani turned to Parissa. "Why is he here? Since when do we work with Americans?"

"This time, we do," Parissa answered firmly.

"They'll betray us once we're no longer useful," Durrani complained.

Parissa smiled at David. "And we'll do the same. Now, tell us what you know."

Glaring back at David, Durrani made an impatient gesture that David would've found offensive under different circumstances. "Tonight, there are only 20 men here, perhaps half are teachers. Most recruits left a week ago."

"Did Parissa tell you about the man we're looking for?" David asked.

The Pakistani cleared his throat and spat, wiping his mouth with the back of his sleeve. "No one named Al Kabbar has been here."

"What about anyone fitting the description?"

Durrani shrugged. "She described many visitors. Saudis all look same."

"What about the man who arrived this afternoon?" Parissa pressed.

The Pakistani squatted and rubbed his beard thoughtfully. "I didn't meet him. Perhaps he's the man you seek. I was told he's someone important from Riyadh."

"Do you know who provides money for this camp?" David asked.

"The Saudis."

"A mosque? A religious group? An individual?"

"They say it's one person, a wealthy man. The man who came tonight works for him."

David felt a flicker of hope. "This man, the one who provides the funding, has he ever been here? Is his name Abdullah?"

"Maybe, maybe not."

David scowled, certain Durrani was being deliberately vague. "These men from Saudi Arabia that train here. Are they *mutaween*?"

"Yes, I've heard that name."

David wondered if Khaled ibn Saud was behind the camp. The presence of the *mutaween* and Durrani's description of a single, mysterious Saudi backer was suspicious. Still, there was no proof Khaled was funding the camp and sending the *mutaween* there for training. It was possible the *mutaween* were sent there by someone else.

"Where's the new man sleeping tonight?" David asked.

Durrani stood up, his gaze boring into David's. "I know what you thinking. Trying to capture him is foolish. The risk is too great."

"Let me worry about that. Show me which hut the stranger is in."

Scowling, the Pakistani crept over to the rocky outcropping overlooking the camp and pointed. "That one closest to us. New arrivals usually sleep there. But I doubt he's the man you seek."

"I'll take that chance."

The Pakistani shrugged and turned away. "I must get back."

"Thanks for the information," David said.

The man spat one more time, narrowly missing David's foot. "I don't wish you luck, American. One day, we'll be at war."

"Perhaps. But until then, we work together," David replied.

Durrani scowled again and pointedly turned his back on David. After nodding to Parissa and Khattak, he disappeared into the darkness.

"You're not seriously thinking about sneaking into the camp tonight?" Parissa asked, looking incredulous.

David nodded. "First, Al Kabbar may be here. If not, then I want to grab and interrogate the new arrival. Perhaps he can tell us about the *mutaween* and the Saudi who funds this camp."

"It's too risky. Tomorrow, Durrani may know more about these new arrivals."

"What if Al Kabbar uses a different name? What if the new man leaves tomorrow? What if 50 new recruits arrive tomorrow; then it'll be far too risky to sneak into the camp."

"And what will you do if you manage to sneak in undetected and Al Kabbar is there?"

David's expression was grim. "Kidnap and interrogate him."

Parissa shook her head angrily. "Forget it. It's too risky. I won't let you."

They argued for some time and, in the end, David prevailed. Parissa reluctantly agreed to accompany him into the compound and stand guard outside the hut while Khattak covered them from the woods. She was mystified at David's insistence on searching the camp, asking bluntly at one point if he was concealing something. But David merely insisted his reasons were obvious—Al Kabbar was his only lead and had murdered a fellow CIA agent. What he didn't tell Parissa was that Al Kabbar might have obtained a Pakistani nuclear weapon. Discovering the truth about Al Kabbar made nearly *any* risk worth taking. Still David knew it was unlikely Al Kabbar was in the camp and there was a much greater chance he'd be caught during his search.

Unfortunately, he had no other choice.

At the end, Parissa had grumbled something that David asked her to repeat out loud.

The Iranian scowled in response. "I said, you're a typical American. Self-righteous, a bully and used to getting your way."

"Yeah," David replied, for the first time in hours breaking into a smile. "Ain't life a bitch."

✳ ✳ ✳

In the early morning hours, they crept down the mountainside to the edge of the training camp compound. The narrow footpath wound down the steep slope, occasionally veering perilously close to the edge of a sharp drop off before disappearing into clusters of pine trees. Even though David wore night vision goggles, he had to pick his way down the trail with his rifle slung over his shoulder to keep his hands free in case he stumbled. Parissa and Khattak followed, remaining at least 20 yards behind in the unlikely event David encountered someone. The moon was obscured behind a band of clouds and the steadily blowing wind hid the sound of their passage.

After reaching the valley floor, David moved cautiously through the trees toward the camp, staying parallel with the dirt road. Fortunately, the undergrowth was sparse and he was able to move quickly and quietly. Every so often, he would stop to listen for voices or anyone moving about. The night remained still and oppressive; even the crickets were quiet. Still, David couldn't shake the feeling they were being watched.

His plan was simple: capture and force the new arrival into the woods, where Khattak could employ interrogation tactics that David still couldn't bring himself to use. Even if the man wasn't Al Kabbar, then perhaps their captive could provide information on either the *mutaween* or the mysterious Saudi financing the training camp. David knew his plan was risky, but he was confident in his abilities and training.

Besides this time, as opposed to Peshawar, there wasn't any other choice.

After reaching the outskirts of the camp, David crouched behind a clump of bushes. He rapidly scanned the unfenced dark and quiet compound. Nothing was moving. The earlier open pit fire was merely glowing embers and a dog was sleeping nearby. David could see the hut housing the new arrival straight ahead, across perhaps 30 yards of open ground and separated from the other huts.

After Parissa and Khattak joined him, David waited for ten minutes to ensure there wasn't a guard patrolling the camp. Finally, he dropped his AK-47, pulled out a pistol and looked at Parissa.

"Ready?"

She nodded.

David sprinted across the open ground, staying low to minimize his profile. The uneven ground was difficult to traverse and he slowed to ensure he didn't stumble. He passed by a shooting range, noticing the targets were the caricature of an American Uncle Sam.

After reaching the hut, David paused to catch his breath. The building was crudely constructed from mud bricks, rough hewn logs and a corrugated steel roof. Parissa materialized a few seconds later. She was breathing hard, her face grim with tension. David put his hand out, indicating she was to remain there. Parissa nodded and crouched down, trying to blend in with the wall.

David edged his way around to the front of the hut. Reaching the entrance, he grabbed the door handle, pausing once more to listen. Still nothing. As he began to open the door, it creaked loudly. He froze, listening intently for any movement. There was none. He proceeded to open the door and make his way inside. He paused to let his eyes adjust to the darkness, the only light provided by the moonlight filtering through the windows. The room reeked of stale sweat and was simply furnished with six cots, several chairs and a table.

Two of the cots were occupied.

Surprised there were two sleeping men, David considered aborting the mission. But he had come too far—he needed to find out if one was Al Kabbar. He moved across the room to the first occupied bed, treading carefully to prevent the floorboards from creaking. Glancing down at the sleeping figure, he felt a stab of disappointment at the unfamiliar face. Cursing silently, David crept over to the second cot. Again, he was disappointed—the man wasn't Al Kabbar. But David had seen the man before. He stood there for a few moments, trying to recall where. Then it hit him.

David had met the man in Riyadh at Khaled ibn Saud's offices.

The sleeping man was Khaled's assistant.

One more connection. David was now beginning to believe Ramzi Yousef's warning about Khaled ibn Saud.

Although tempted to wake Khaled's assistant and force him outside, David knew it'd be foolish to try unless he first killed the second sleeping man. But he just couldn't do it—in spite of everything, David hadn't yet reached that point where he could do those things that must be done; he could only do those things that felt 'right'. Killing an unarmed, sleeping man didn't qualify.

Reluctantly, he decided to leave.

As David turned away, he noticed a briefcase at the foot of Khaled's assistant's bed. He picked it up and tucked it under his arm. As he moved toward the door, his foot caught an empty cup near the bed and sent it clattering across the floor. Kneeling quickly, he pointed his gun at the sleeping men. Both squirmed in their sleep, then remained still. Relieved, David rose and quickly crossed the room to the door.

Once outside, David began to breathe easier. He nodded to Parissa, who rose to her feet. They began jogging across the open ground toward the safety of the trees. Suddenly, the door of another hut opened and a man stepped outside. They froze, unsure whether to keep running for the trees or drop to the ground and wait. Their indecision proved costly. Although the moonlight was faint, there was enough to illuminate their silhouettes.

"*Masa al-khayr. Kayf halak,*" the man called out. "What are you doing out here?"

"Taking a walk," David replied, trying to keep his voice low.

"What's that on your face?" the man asked, referring to their night vision goggles. His voice tailed off as he realized that the slender, short figure next to David was a woman and she was also wearing goggles.

"Help! Help! Enemies!"

They sprinted for the trees. David cringed at each step, expecting any moment to feel a bullet slam into his back. But they reached the trees without a shot being fired. By now, several voices were raising the alarm behind them.

Khattak was standing by a tree, his rifle shouldered. "What happened?"

"We ran into someone taking a piss," David replied. "Al Kabbar's not there."

"We must move. Hurry!"

They ran through the trees and up the trail that led back to their observation point. Parissa led the way with Khattak bringing up the rear. David cursed his impetuousness, realizing he'd put everyone in danger for nothing. He could hear shouts and even a few shots in the woods behind them. Glancing over his shoulder, he saw the flicker of flashlights, indicating a search was underway.

For nearly twenty minutes, they climbed up the mountain trail. The crumbling rock path was slippery and tree limbs and brush tore at their clothes and exposed skin. Finally, Parissa paused to let them catch their breath.

She looked over at David. "We'll be fine. I know you did what you felt you had to."

Grateful, he managed a meager nod. "Thanks. Think they'll organize a search party?"

She frowned. "I don't know. Hopefully they think it was a thief."

"The man who saw us could tell we were wearing night goggles."

She shrugged. "Even out here, there are a few pairs floating around."

David looked back down in the valley. The camp was roused and figures were moving around the now lighted compound. In the woods surrounding the camp, he could see the movement of flashlights and hear an occasional shout. Then, David noticed several flashlights begin to move along the trail they had just climbed.

"Trouble coming," he said.

Parissa looked back down the mountain. "We'd better go. If they find us before we reach the horses..."

With that, she turned and plunged into the night.

17

Abdullah let out a sigh of satisfaction and put down his fork. The hovering servant silently cleared the fine English china from the table and presented Abdullah with a Cuban cigar before disappearing. The enormous dining room was expensively decorated with an elegant antique dining table, luxurious Persian carpet, two chandeliers and several valuable 17th century paintings, including a Rembrandt. Abdullah lit the cigar and breathed deeply of the aromatic smoke, feeling sated with excellent food prepared by his chef and a rare bottle of Bordeaux from his extensive cellar. He leaned back in his chair, thinking about his next appointment.

So far, given the complexity of his plan, everything was going as well as could be expected. Al Kabbar had successfully procured the Pakistani nuclear device and was winding his way across Iran toward the Red Sea. Hazan Qwasama had delivered the radioactive waste from the Ukraine and was waiting for further instructions at the warehouse in the Sinai desert near the Gaza Strip. In addition, Abdullah's female "sleeper" operative in Jerusalem was patiently waiting instructions.

The capture and suicide of Shadi Muhana in the West Bank had been a difficult blow, but not fatal. Abdullah had already contacted a replacement, a Palestinian named Ziad Abbas whom he had used before. Like a Grand Chess master, Abdullah had maneuvered his pieces skillfully until they were positioned to strike together. In general, Abdullah was extremely pleased with the progress of his ingenious and multi-staged plan.

Soon, he would change the world.

The only person who knew all the details of his plan was Al Kabbar, although even the Saudi terrorist didn't suspect Abdullah's final objective. Al Kabbar, like everyone else involved, believed Abdullah was driven by religious fanaticism. In fact, Abdullah detested religion, sharing Marx's view it was an opiate for the masses. Abdullah had developed his plan to further his own goals. For years, he had worked alone developing and implementing each carefully orchestrated step. During a rare moment of weakness, Abdullah had revealed the full details of his plan to Al Kabbar, primarily because he'd felt the need to tell one person and bask in the awe and incredulity that followed. It was vain and foolish, but Abdullah had permitted himself just the one indiscretion.

No one else knew or even guessed there were two parts to his plan. That the impact of the second would dwarf the first.

Abdullah rose and rang for his driver, telling him to bring the limousine around to the front of the mansion. He went upstairs and changed, replacing his suit and tie with a simple white robe. Once outside, he found his limousine waiting. As they drove out the entrance gates, he looked back with satisfaction at his mansion—a smaller copy of the Versailles palace outside Paris, constructed by some of the finest European craftsmen. Eight years in the building, the mansion was an elegant and powerful statement of the heights he had achieved.

Abdullah sat silently reflective during the thirty minute drive to the center of Riyadh. He was going to see the *ulama*, Turki al Faisal, who was the one man who knew his true identity. He was supremely confident in his ability to continue to manipulate Al Faisal. Abdullah considered himself a master puppeteer of people, similar to the Prophet Muhammad and other great leaders; for all of his life, Abdullah had been able to control others. Two years ago, he had approached Al Faisal offering to provide funds to further the Islamic cause. Once Abdullah determined he could bend the *ulama's* fanatical beliefs to his benefit, he had recruited Al Faisal to play a critical role in his plan. Although Al Faisal knew Abdullah's real identity, the *ulama* had never guessed the second part of Abdullah's plan.

The limousine entered an older industrial area of Riyadh filled with warehouses and an occasional light manufacturing facility. The streets were deserted, the foreign laborers who thronged the area by day having retired to their squalid apartment buildings. They turned down a dark and narrow street, the only sign of movement a stray dog scrounging in a garbage bin. Finally, the driver pulled over and Abdullah got out.

He walked down a short alley, wrinkling his nose at the fetid smell of sewage and rotting garbage. Reaching a small, deserted looking building, Abdullah knocked on the only door.

"Yes?" came a cautious voice.

"Allah works in mysterious and wonderful ways," Abdullah replied.

The door opened and he was ushered inside by an Arab in black cleric robes. The man nodded a silent greeting before leading Abdullah down a barren corridor and into a small wood paneled room with luxurious oriental carpets. The furnishings were simple—cloth tapestries on the wall, floor cushions piled around the room and a low table for tea. The elderly man sitting on the floor rose and greeted Abdullah.

"It's good to see you again my friend," said the *ulama*, Turki al Faisal.

"It's been far too long since we last met."

The *ulama* touched Abdullah's lowered head. "May *Allah* bless your every day and grant you the privilege of living forever at his side."

"May I be deemed worthy in his eyes."

They embraced and then sat together on the floor.

"I'm sorry about your son," Abdullah said, his expression appropriately sorrowful. He hadn't seen Al Faisal since his son's death and knew he needed to stroke the *ulama's* ego while acknowledging his loss. "He was a fine, upstanding man and a credit to Islam."

Turki al Faisal made a gesture of appreciation, his eyes suddenly watery. "He died trying to bring about the *jihad*. I miss him every day. Still, I'm comforted knowing he's with *Allah*."

"And surely by his side, *In'shallah*." Abdullah took a sip of tea before delicately raising his most pressing concern. "Are you sure he revealed nothing to the Saudi authorities?"

Al Faisal's face clouded with irritation before he nodded with understanding. "No. He killed himself before they could interrogate him. Unfortunately, as you know, he was found with a draft of the *fatwa* that illegitimized the House of Saud."

"Do the GDI or police suspect your involvement?" Abdullah asked, looking for the slightest hint of deception. Even though he needed Al Faisal, Abdullah wouldn't hesitate to kill the *ulama* if his identity was at risk of being revealed.

Al Faisal shrugged. "They suspect. But that's all they can do. My position as the head of the King's Council of Senior *Ulamas* prevents them from probing further."

Abdullah nodded, believing his assurance. "Then everything is finally in place, including the 20,000 men we discussed months ago?"

"Those and ten thousand more, all waiting to revolt against the House of Saud. Once the *fatwa* is issued, they will follow where I lead."

Abdullah restrained a broad smile. Everything was going even better than expected. "Excellent, you've done well."

Al Faisal repressed a smug smile. "All we need is your signal to start the revolt. It's time to reveal it to me."

Abdullah shook his head. "I'm sorry my old friend, but I believe no one should know, in case we're betrayed. When the moment arrives, you'll have no doubt."

"*Insha'Allah*," the old man said, bowing his head but clearly disappointed. "I've no doubt your plan will succeed. *Allah* blesses us and will watch over it."

The plan was simple: During the *hajj*, Abdullah would ensure that a terrible calamity befell Islam and the House of Saud. Once the signal was given, Turki al Faisal, together with several members of the Council of Senior *Ulama*, would issue a *fatwa* declaring the House of Saud could no longer be trusted to safeguard the holy land and must be replaced. At strategic locations throughout Saudi Arabia, members of the *ulama*'s Wahhabi mosque and the *mutaween* would take to the streets and riot against the government. Whipped into a religious frenzy by Abdullah's manufactured crime against Islam, hundreds of thousands would join the revolt. Shaken by the popular uprising, the military would be indecisive and stand by helplessly. Some co-opted officers would command their units to support the revolution. The chaos and violence would cause the Saudi government to fall and the members of the House of Saud to flee. The events in Saudi Arabia would quickly trigger a worldwide *jihad*, as Muslims everywhere would join their brothers and rise up against their secular governments and the *infidels*.

Although Abdullah had painstakingly developed the plan and approached Turki al Faisal with the idea, it was the *ulama* who had used his power and influence to assemble the disparate Saudi components. Abdullah had remained in the background, providing advice, encouragement and, of course, money. After three years of planning, everything was ready and awaiting the triggering event known only to Abdullah.

"When should I go to Israel?" the *ulama* asked.

"In two days. I'll have a private plane take you there. Are you prepared?"

The *ulama* smiled patronizingly, as if at a child. "Of course."

"It's important that you return immediately afterwards. My plane will wait for you at the airport." This aspect of his plan worried Abdullah—if Al Faisal was delayed or even killed in Israel, the second part of his plan might be jeopardized. Still, even if the *ulama* was dead, Abdullah controlled enough members of the Council to ensure that a *fatwa* would be issued against the House of Saud.

"I understand," Al Faisal replied. He got stiffly to his feet and walked over to a table and picked up a large *Quran*. "And now, let us read from the holy book and ask *Allah* for his blessing."

Abdullah bowed his head, not in prayer, but so that the *ulama* could not see his smile of satisfaction and triumph.

Nothing could stop him now.

18

"They're getting closer!" Parissa shouted.

David looked back over his shoulder at the pursuing troop of horsemen. They were perhaps a mile behind.

"Khattak, how much further?" he called out.

"Perhaps ten kilometers," the Pakistani yelled back. "I hope the American helicopter is waiting there."

"They'll be there!" Earlier, David had radioed the U.S. Special Forces base in Afghanistan to request an emergency airlift from the drop off point. "Keep riding hard!"

They had been riding virtually non-stop for six hours. After their failed excursion into the training camp, they had hiked laboriously for two hours on the difficult trail over the mountain to reach their horses. From there, they had ridden back along the trail that wound alongside the shallow river. Khattak had pushed both David and Parissa, neither of whom were strong riders. Fortunately, Khattak's ragged looking horses were deceptively strong. Occasionally David had seen lights on the trail behind, as their pursuers checked for signs of their passage.

After they had been riding for several hours, the dawn broke—clear, bright and far too illuminating. When their pursuers realized David and his two companions were within sight, they had fired a fusillade of shots that had little chance of hitting the mark, but were merely intended to create fear. David had counted five men on horseback, all of whom wore turbans and tribal clothing. They were being chased not by city dwellers, but hardened Pakistani mountain men. With their lead rapidly evaporating, David knew the three of them would be within easy rifle range very soon.

Ahead, the trail wound up the side of a mountain, before veering off to the side and running along the crest of a ridge. David recalled that the trail then plummeted down into the next valley, which was where the helicopter had dropped them two days ago. He could only hope that his confident words to Khattak proved prophetic.

Suddenly, Parissa's horse stumbled and nearly fell down the steep slope to their left. She pulled up on the reins and dismounted.

"I think he's hurt."

Khattak dismounted and looked at the horse's foreleg.

"Broken," he said succinctly. Removing his rifle, he placed the muzzle against the forehead of Parissa's horse. The gunshot echoed loudly and the horse collapsed to the ground.

"Better ride with David," Khattak said. "His horse is stronger. Hurry!"

As if to emphasize his point, there was the crack of a rifle and a bullet whined off the nearby rocks. Parissa swung up in the saddle next to David. David kicked the flanks of his horse, which surged forward. As they rode up the mountain, David realized they needed to reach the ridge crest soon to get out of range of their pursuers. The harsh, largely treeless terrain offered minimal protection, other than scattered boulders and rock formations. Occasionally, a shot would ring out. Down to two horses, David knew it was only a matter of time before their pursuers drew closer and found the range.

Dispassionately analyzing their situation, David grimly realized their prospects were bleak—capture or even death appeared inevitable.

Finally, they reached the ridge crest. Reining in his horse, David looked in dismay down the other side. The trail wound down in a series of switchbacks to the valley floor and the barren mountainside offered minimal cover. If they failed to reach the safety of the forest below before their pursuers reached the top of the ridge, they'd be shot like fish in a barrel. David knew the men hunting them were far too close. His trembling horse was covered with sweat and clearly spent.

"We must make our stand here," David said quietly.

Khattak glanced down at the trail and then back at their pursuers. "I agree. Parissa, you ride ahead and meet the American helicopter. See if you can bring back reinforcements."

Parissa looked like she was going to object, but Khattak's logic was irrefutable. She reluctantly nodded agreement.

David dismounted and Parissa handed him her rifle and ammunition belts. "You'll need these." She tried to smile and then leaned over to kiss his cheek.

"Good luck," she said, trying to make light of the situation. "Remember, I expect you to take me to dinner after all this."

David smiled. "Now that's what I call an incentive."

Parissa wheeled her horse about, plunging down the trail leading to the valley below. David turned to see Khattak grinning at him.

"She's quite a woman."

"Yeah," David replied, knowing words were inadequate. "You could say that."

They tethered the remaining horse and ran back along the trial until they reached an ambush location that overlooked the trail and provided sufficient cover. David found a protected position about 20 yards from Khattak that enabled them to protect each other's flank with a withering cross-fire. The trail section they had chosen to defend was well suited to their purposes—a sheer rock wall formed one side and it dropped off steeply to the valley below on the other. Their pursuers would be forced to remain on the trail or backtrack to try to find another way up the mountain. David knew time was on their side. They only needed to hold out until the Special Forces helicopter arrived and Parissa directed the U.S. soldiers to their position.

Assuming, of course, they were coming and on time.

David readied himself, loading his weapons and placing two extra rifles within easy reach. Breathing deeply and steadily to calm his nerves, David reviewed his preparations to see if he'd missed anything. He was clear-headed and unafraid—his training and Afghanistan experiences had prepared him well. Rather than fearful, he was merely anxious for the waiting to end.

Hearing the sound of approaching horses, he peered over the top of the rock. A single horseman led the way, the remaining four men following about fifty yards behind. Clearly, they were wary of an ambush. David hesitated—if he waited to open fire until the main group drew near, the leader would have passed David's hiding place and be in position to attack from behind. If David opened fire now, then the other four men would have time to take cover.

Suddenly, Khattak opened fire, his first few shots dropping the lead horse and rider. David joined in, but the remaining men were too far away for accuracy and they quickly took cover. David fired several more shots just to let them know they were facing more than one ambusher. He then held his fire, not wanting to disclose his position or waste ammunition.

Several minutes of silence followed while their pursuers assessed the situation. The lead rider and horse lay unmoving on the trail.

Khattak called softly over to David. "Two of them have backtracked and are climbing the mountain to circle around us. I'm moving over to cover them."

"Okay."

The two tribesmen remaining on the trail began firing periodically, clearly intending to distract David and Khattak. David could just make out their gun barrels protruding from behind the rocks, the sun glinting off the metal. He glanced down into the valley and his heart nearly stopped. Perhaps three miles away, a plume of dust rose from the trail. Another group of horsemen was coming, riding hard and fast. Their attackers must have radioed back to the training camp to ask for reinforcements.

The wrong cavalry was about to arrive.

David heard gunfire on his left and realized Khattak had engaged the men trying to outflank them. Suddenly, the two men remaining on the trail darted forward, weaving from side to side. David fired. One of the men immediately dove to take cover behind a boulder. David continued firing. The other Pakistani continued running for a few more steps before throwing up his arms and falling forward.

David felt a grim satisfaction. He figured the remaining Pakistani would stay put for awhile, giving David an opportunity to check on Khattak. He crawled backwards until he was out of sight of the trail, before rising and sprinting along the mountain side. The loose, rocky ground was difficult to traverse and David was forced to slowdown.

Suddenly, there was intense gunfire from Khattak's location and an exultant yell. David ran along the ridge, staying low and his AK-47 ready. He came over a slight rise only to see a man standing over an unmoving Khattak. David fired, but the AK-47 jammed. Without thinking, David charged forward. The Pakistani glanced up and tried desperately to bring his gun around.

David crashed into him, sending Khattak's killer flying. David's momentum carried him forward so that he landed on top. He grabbed the man's turban and slammed his head into the ground. The Pakistani cried out in pain. Shoving his assailant away, David pulled out the knife strapped to his belt. But his adversary was already on his feet and also held a knife. They circled for a few moments, David careful not to stumble on the uneven ground. Suddenly, the Pakistani leaped forward while simultaneously slashing at David with his knife. Leaning backward, David felt the knife tip slice his left forearm. As his opponent stumbled, David pounced, bringing his knife upward in one motion to strike soft flesh just below the rib cage. The man screamed and David twisted the knife free, blood running down the length of the blade.

The Pakistani fell to his knees and dropped his knife. He grabbed his bleeding stomach with both hands before looking up in surprise at David. Then he slowly toppled over and lay still.

Stunned, David stood there for a few moments. He had never fought, let alone killed, in hand to hand combat. He had reacted from adrenaline and his military training. In a daze, David stepped back as if to distance himself from his actions. There was a roaring sound in his ears and his gaze went blank, as if he were the one bleeding to death on the ground.

The harsh voice behind him brought him back to reality.

"Turn slowly around. Hands high."

David turned to find another Pakistani walking toward him with his rifle pointed at his midsection.

"Step away from the body."

David did as asked, realizing the man was the survivor from the trail. The Pakistani must have seen David leave his position and followed.

Now, David would pay with his life.

The man smiled wolfishly and raised his AK-47. There was a gunshot. The tribesman stood still for a moment and then toppled forward.

In disbelief, David turned around. Standing twenty yards away with a raised M-16 was a U.S. Special Forces soldier. Stunned, David just stood there, expecting to look down and see blood seeping out of his chest. Lowering his rifle, the soldier walked toward him.

"Where'd you come from?" David asked, his mind still not functioning properly. "God?"

The soldier grinned. "We were dropped off a couple of hours ago to keep a lookout for you. Your buddy Sergeant Billings thought you might need some help. We ran into your friend Parissa on the trail and she told us where to find you."

"Thanks," David said slowly, still unable to believe his luck. "I owe you both."

"Hell, you're square with me. Billings said you saved his ass a week ago. The son of a bitch owes me a hundred bucks, so you did me a favor. Ready to get out of here?"

"You bet."

As if on cue, David heard the thump of helicopter blades and saw the U.S. Special Forces Blackhawk sweeping toward them.

19

Hazan Qwasama angrily slammed the mug of tea down on the table and began pacing back and forth, considering his alternatives. For the past two days, Hazan had waited with growing impatience for Abdullah to return or at least phone to give an update. Although Abdullah hadn't revealed his plan, Hazan knew combining the radioactive isotopes in the stolen Ukrainian container with a conventional explosive device created a "dirty bomb", capable of killing thousands and contaminating a large area with radiation.

The fact he was ten miles from Gaza Strip left no doubt their target was Israel. But what was the target inside Israel?

Scowling, Hazan leaned back against the seat to wait. His mind wandered, taking him back to his youthful days in the refugee camp, when life was so very hard and he was surrounded by death and despair. His father had worked as a day laborer in New Jerusalem, cleaning the homes of Jewish immigrants. Despite their poverty and bleak prospects, those were happier times; his parents, four brothers and two sisters had been a close knit family. Once his older brothers became swept up in the first *intifada*, it all changed. Hazan could still remember the violent arguments with his father, whom they accused of being a Jewish lap dog. When he was 14, Hazan had left his father's house to go live with his brothers. Now, Hazan missed his brothers, missed the fact he'd never have a family or a son of his own. It was a rare moment of personal reflection, for Hazan had long ago buried his desires and emotions. He couldn't afford any, needing to fuel the flames of hatred and revenge.

Since his youthful years in the Jenin refugee camp, Hazan had been trained to hate the Israelis. In school, the Palestinian textbooks gave credence to outlandish lies about the Jewish people and his teachers had enthralled their students with even more outrageous stories. He had learned the Jews used Arab blood for their religious ceremonies and exploited their vast wealth to control not only the world media, but many governments as well. He was taught the sad history of Palestine, how the Jews manipulated the U.N. into establishing a Jewish State and then started a war to steal Palestinian land. In his youth,

Hazan plastered his bedroom walls with pictures of young Palestinian suicide bombers and terrorists, with an Adolph Hitler poster occupying the place of honor over his bed.

Three years ago, he had left Gaza after finally realizing that to strike a mortal blow against his enemy, he needed a more powerful ally. There had to be a final solution, much like Hitler had envisioned. So he sought out every Islamic radical group in the Middle East, searching for someone who not only shared his dream, but could fulfill it. His wanderings led him through Jordan, Syria and finally to Egypt. There, he joined a radical branch of the Muslim Brotherhood, planting bombs in tourist hotels along the Red Sea and obtaining arms for the Palestinian *intifada*.

Four months ago, Abdullah had recruited him, offering an opportunity to strike a fatal blow against the Israelis. Although Hazan was never able to find anything out about Abdullah, he assumed Abdullah was someone very important in Saudi Arabia. Abdullah hid his identity behind a false beard, sunglasses and overlarge *keffiyeh*. They had only met twice: once when Abdullah had recruited him and again when Hazan had returned from his trip to the Ukraine.

Now, he waited impatiently for Abdullah to return.

Noticing the satellite phone lying on the table, Hazan thought of his half-brother, Shadi Muhana, who also worked for Abdullah. Muhana was an old comrade in arms; they had grown up together throwing stones at Israeli soldiers, graduated to the occasional sniper attack before turning to smuggling explosives for Palestinian suicide bombers into Gaza. Hazan decided to call Muhana to find out if he'd heard from Abdullah recently and get news of home.

He picked up the satellite phone and dialed. The phone on the other end rang twice before someone answered.

"Hello?" an unfamiliar male voice said.

Momentarily confused, Hazan demanded, "Who's this?"

"Ahmad Yassin. Shadi asked me to answer his phone. He's unavailable."

"Who are you?" Hazan asked warily.

"I'm one of his guards. I took Yassir's place."

Hazan knew the Israelis had recently killed Yassir with a helicopter missile that destroyed his car. "Where's Shadi?"

"Why should I tell you? You haven't even told me who you are."

"Hazan Qwasama." He hesitated, still suspicious of the stranger. "Never mind. I'll call back."

"Please, wait," the stranger's voice pleaded. "He'll be angry if I don't take a message."

Hazan smiled. "Just tell him I will soon strike a tremendous blow against the Israelis."

With that, Hazan Qwasama hung up.

* * *

"Did you get it, Benjamin?" Ariel Rosenberg asked, as he put down the satellite phone and looked over at his colleague sitting at a nearby computer terminal.

"Yes, Ariel," Benjamin replied, scrutinizing his computer screen and typing furiously. "The call came from Egypt, near the Gaza Strip. Perhaps ten miles from the border."

"My instinct tells me that the caller is dangerous. We must track him down." Ariel felt a surge of excitement and satisfaction. After arresting Shadi Muhana two days ago, the Mossad had discovered an unregistered satellite phone that tapped into Israel's cellular network. Ariel had been assigned to answer the phone, hoping another terrorist, unaware of Shadi Muhana's capture and subsequent death, would call. This was the second time someone suspicious had called looking for Muhana.

Ariel looked at his companion. "Pull up the satellite map to see if you can find the caller's location."

"It's coming up now."

Ariel walked over to Benjamin and looked over his shoulder at the computer screen. A satellite picture of perhaps thirty square miles of desert suddenly appeared, a solid black line demarking the Egyptian border with the Gaza Strip. A blinking curser marked the spot where the call had originated.

"Can you enlarge the picture?"

"Yeah. Hold on." Benjamin typed a few commands, zooming in on the key area. "There, that'll do it."

"Looks like a warehouse," Ariel said. "What do you think?"

"I think we need to nail the asshole. Call Rachael."

"She'll be pleased," Ariel said, picking up the phone. "Muhana killed himself before she could interrogate the bastard. She's been desperate to find out what he was up to before we caught him."

Benjamin grinned. "Tell her to get her gear ready and Uzi loaded. I'll call for the helicopter."

✳ ✳ ✳

Hazan Qwasama replaced the satellite phone on the table, worried about the conversation. He'd never heard of the man, Ahmad Yassin, who answered the phone. There was something about the man's voice that troubled Hazan; the man sounded educated and his flawless Arabic lacked the slang of a refugee camp Palestinian. Hazan wondered if Muhana had been arrested and if he had just spoken with an Israeli agent. Cursing his impetuousness for ignoring Abdullah's warning, he tried to convince himself that since the conversation had been brief, the call was untraceable.

Still, he knew it was a possibility and there was nothing to do but wait nervously.

Perhaps an hour later Hazan was resting on the cot when he heard a vehicle approach. Leaping to his feet, Hazan grabbed his AK-47 and knelt down behind a row of boxes. Although he assumed it was Abdullah, Hazan wasn't taking any chances. Footsteps approached and someone fumbled with the lock, as if trying different keys.

The door opened slowly and someone peered inside.

"Abdullah!" Hazan cried out in relief. "*Allah* be praised. I was afraid something had happened to you."

Abdullah walked inside, his gaze darting around the dark interior. "I've been busy finalizing our arrangements. I brought another man with me, his name is Farid."

Hazan set his gun down. "I was worried."

"We must move quickly. Open the garage door. Farid will pull the truck inside so that we can load our cargo."

Hazan resisted the impulse to ask Abdullah the questions that came to mind; instead, he opened the garage door and watched as Farid drove an Egyptian Army jeep inside, the doors and canvas top clearly marked with a military insignia. Farid got out and nodded a greeting. Wearing the uniform of an Egyptian Army captain, Farid was a slight Palestinian youth with a horribly disfigured face, as if an explosion had taken the better part of his looks along with his innocence. His expression echoed that of so many disaffected, alienated Palestinian youths—barely contained rage beneath a cold, uncaring exterior. Hazan knew the type well.

Abdullah reached into the front seat and pulled out a bundle of clothes that he tossed to Hazan.

"Put these on."

The bundle contained the uniform of an Egyptian Army corporal.

"Where are we going?" Hazan asked, as he dressed.

"Farid will take you and our cargo to the border. There, a man named Ziad will smuggle you into Gaza. He'll take you to a safe house, where you'll receive further instructions."

Hazan frowned. "How will I enter into Gaza? The Israelis have sealed the border."

"The Egyptian army also patrols the border, so you won't raise suspicion in the jeep and uniforms. Farid will lead you to a tunnel that will take you into Gaza."

Hazan nodded, knowing weapons were constantly smuggled into Gaza through elaborate tunnels that terminated inside buildings built near the border. A small strip of harsh, unforgiving land about ten miles by 50 miles jammed between Israel and the Egyptian Sinai, Gaza was home to a million Palestinians. Gaza was now controlled by Hamas, who had seized power during a bloody dispute with Fatah. Despite Israel's withdrawal from Gaza, the Israeli army still patrolled Gaza's Egyptian border to prevent weapons smuggling and the return of fugitive Palestinians.

"What will you do next?" Hazan asked.

Abdullah smiled coldly. "Many things, but you don't need to know. Now load the cargo."

Picking up the radioactive waste container, Hazan loaded it into the back of the jeep. He pulled a tarp over the container and turned to face Abdullah, who was holding the satellite phone.

"Did you use this?" Abdullah asked.

"Yes," Hazan answered reluctantly. "Just before you arrived."

Abdullah's eyes flashed and he spoke with a silent fury. "You idiot! I told you not to call anyone. We must hurry. It's possible the call was traced. Tell

Farid to drive the jeep outside and close the garage door. I'll be there momentarily."

Hazan was thankful Abdullah still needed him, realizing he might have paid for his indiscretion with his life. He nodded and disappeared outside.

Abdullah walked over to several boxes stacked near the entrance. He reached inside the top carton and removed an explosive device equipped with a motion detector. Setting the timer for two hours, he placed the device on the ground. Abdullah then locked the garage door and walked outside to the Egyptian military jeep to speak with Hazan and Farid.

"Don't return here under any circumstances," he warned. "I've wired the building to explode. Hazan, Farid will drive you to the border. When you get to Gaza, Ziad will tell you what to do."

Content, Hazan didn't ask anything more about his mission. In the cold-blooded planning of murder and mayhem, he had unshakeable confidence in Abdullah, who exuded a calculating ruthlessness few possessed. Abdullah never raised his voice nor expressed emotion; his every word was concise and thoughtful. There was something more dangerous about him than even the most committed Palestinian terrorist—as if Abdullah was coldly dispassionate about everything, even the cause for which they were willing to sacrifice their lives.

"Let's go," Hazan said to Farid, anxious to return to Palestine. "It's time for Palestinians to finally strike a blow."

✳ ✳ ✳

"Can't you go any faster?" Rachael demanded angrily, leaning over the shoulder of the driver of the unmarked Israeli Army Range Rover.

Without taking her gaze off the terrain, the woman shook her head. "The ground is too rough and I can't see much in this light. If I go any faster, I'll either crash or bend the axle."

Rachael scowled. "I'm more worried about an Egyptian patrol or giving our target time to escape."

"We can outrun the Egyptians. As for the target, I'm doing my best to get us there. Now shut up and let me drive."

The Range Rover continued to hurtle through the night, Rachael holding on tightly to prevent her head from slamming into the roof when the vehicle struck a hole. Fighting to restrain her impatience, she concentrated on the mission. Immediately after being contacted by the surveillance team monitoring Shadi Muhana's phone, Rachael had assembled a six-person strike team from the Israeli Defense Force (IDF) to raid the building where the call had originated. The team had flown by helicopter over the Egyptian border where they were met by two undercover Mossad agents who lived in the Egyptian Sinai. Her team had separated into two unmarked Range Rovers the Mossad stored in an Egyptian warehouse.

Although the Egyptians jealously protected their territory, there was an implicit understanding the Israelis could occasionally cross into the Egyptian Sinai in pursuit of Palestinian terrorists. To avoid an embarrassing diplomatic situation, the Israelis were always judicious with their forays. Tonight's mission had been approved only after Rachael had relayed to her superiors the deadly threat contained in Shadi Muhana's final words.

Unfortunately, the drive across the open desert had taken longer than anticipated and they were already twenty minutes behind schedule.

"There's the road we're looking for," the driver called out.

Rachael let out a sigh of relief, knowing they were only a couple miles away. The Range Rover skidded down a sand dune and bounced onto the road, which was nothing more than packed sand and dirt. They drove in silence for another few minutes, passing the occasional ramshackle building or oncoming vehicle. The light had disappeared from the sky, leaving the surrounding desert cloaked in darkness. One of the agents in the back seat remained hunched over the GPS monitor that plotted their position relative to their target.

"We should see the building any minute now," he called out. "It'll be on our left."

"There, I see it," the driver said with relief.

Rachael switched on her radio to call the other vehicle. "Tomer, we'll go in first and swing around to the rear to make sure no one gets out that way. You and your team take the front entrance."

"Sure thing Rachael. Anything the boss wants."

She restrained a smile, knowing Tomer hated taking orders. A fiercely patriotic *sabra*, Tomer Ron was an efficient, enthusiastic and highly regarded soldier. They had flirted for several months, ever since he had become her liaison with the IDF. Tomer had been respectful of her need to let the relationship develop slowly, although Rachael knew it was only a matter of time before they become lovers.

Perhaps tonight after this mission.

A sharp jolt brought her attention back to the present. Her left hand tapped the Uzi in her lap impatiently as the two Range Rovers turned off the main road and sped down the narrow track that led to the warehouse. The building was a simple structure with tilt up concrete walls, metal roof and a garage entrance sufficiently large enough for a truck. As her gaze swept across the empty parking lot and dark building, Rachael felt a sharp pang of disappointment. Their quarry was gone. The surrounding desert remained barren, dark and quiet. Their headlights illuminated the tire tracks of several vehicles and her hopes rose once more as she realized they led to the solitary garage door.

Perhaps their target was still inside.

Her Range Rover turned sharply to drive around to the rear of the building. Rachael glanced back at Tomer's vehicle, watching with satisfaction as it stopped near the garage door to disgorge several armed figures. They spread out quickly and moved toward the entrance.

Rachael held on as the Range Rover roared down a rutted road to the rear of the building. There was another parking area next to a small outlying building perhaps 30 yards away.

"Park there!" she ordered.

The Range Rover stopped and Rachael jumped out, followed by her three team members. Glancing around, she looked in vain for a rear entrance to the warehouse. She motioned for her team to spread out, both to present a more difficult target and search for an emergency exit tunnel. She paused every few steps to listen, intending to circle around to the front to meet up with Tomer and his team.

Suddenly, the building exploded. The ferocious sound and accompanying shock wave knocked Rachael to the ground. The warehouse roof disintegrated into a fireball of smoke and flames and the concrete walls buckled. Ears ringing, Rachael was faintly conscious of chunks of the building falling all around her. She could only lie there, her senses numbed both by the blast and terrible sight. Fortunately, she'd been far enough away from the building to escape any serious injury from the explosion.

Rachael knew Tomer had already led his team inside and was not so lucky.

Tears begin to stream down her face and sobs shook her body. In the depths of her misery, Rachael was unable to find the strength for the anger and recriminations she knew would soon follow.

It appeared their quarry had escaped, but left a calling card behind.

20

David stood at the entrance to the supply hut and gazed around the U.S. military base where he had spent much of the last four months. The helicopter and fighter jet storage hangers, concrete and steel barracks and several administrative buildings signified a permanent presence that invited comparisons with stateside military facilities. Yet the encircling barbed wire fence, numerous manned watchtowers and incessant perimeter patrols spoke of the unsettled situation and constant danger in Afghanistan.

The regrouped and reinvigorated Taliban had adopted many of the tactics used by Iraqi insurgents; as a result, the Taliban had made significant inroads recently, despite the continued presence of foreign troops supporting the democratically elected Afghanistan government. The ongoing cost of maintaining peace in Afghanistan was measured in both dollars and American lives. Nevertheless, despite his misgivings about the U.S. invasion of Iraq, David believed Afghanistan was worth the sacrifices. Here, unlike Iraq, Al Quada had always maintained a significant presence.

He turned as a hand lightly touched his shoulder.

"What's the American saying…penny for your thoughts?" Parissa asked.

David sighed. "Thinking about those guys I knew who didn't make it."

"I'm sorry," she said softly.

David shook his head, his gaze unfocused. "I spent four months here working closely with these soldiers. A better group of dedicated, honest and likeable men and women you'll never meet. It makes me proud to be an American—and sorry that such incredible talent dies in this god forsaken, desolate place."

They stood in companionable silence for several moments more before he glanced back at her. Even dressed in a flowing black robe and *abaya*, Parissa was still remarkably lovely. Her high cheekbones, delicate nose and full lips would have done justice to many models. Her bright eyes sparkled with intelligence, compassion and a hint of lively mischievousness. When she glanced up and smiled, he felt himself grow warm with pleasure.

"Looking forward to going home?" she asked.

"Yes, I need to clear up some things there. Then I'll go wherever they need me. And you?"

Parissa shrugged and crossed her arms across her chest. "I'm off to Tehran to report in. Then to Saudi Arabia to look into the address we found in the briefcase and meet with Khaled ibn Saud."

A few hours ago, shortly after their return from Pakistan, they had opened the briefcase Mark had stolen from Khaled's assistant. Unfortunately, it was virtually empty. The only item of interest was a Riyadh address scribbled on a piece of paper and the words, "Delivery on Tuesday" next to it.

They had agreed that perhaps the address was the delivery point for the illicit weapons purchases that David had found mentioned in both Azam Tariq's and Turki Al Faisal's files. Given David was a marked man in Saudi Arabia and the CIA's Riyadh operations were compromised, they had agreed Parissa and her organization should look into the address. Parissa would also try to meet with Khaled ibn Saud to see if she could learn anything more. She was scheduled to hitch a ride on a supply helicopter to Kabul in about an hour.

"I'll call Ramzi Yousef shortly to get him to set up the meeting with Khaled," David promised, then hesitated before continuing. "I'm worried about you. You could be headed into a hornets' nest."

"I'll be fine," Parissa said, reaching out to touch his shoulder again.

Silence fell between them again, comfortable yet also slightly awkward.

Parissa then gave a low, soft laugh. "You know, I feel clumsy standing here, like a teenager at the end of a first date."

David smiled. "Because you're afraid that your date might try to kiss you?"

"No. Because I'm afraid he won't."

David reached for her hand and pulled her inside the supply tent. Then, she was in his arms, her body pressing hard against his. They kissed passionately, her tongue entwined with his. He breathed deeply of her scent and felt the softness of her breasts against his chest. David knew he'd miss her; she was the first woman in a long time that had reached past the surface and made a part of him feel alive. Their night together, the mission and death of Khattak had brought them even closer together.

David knew the distance he'd maintained with other women was largely of his own doing, not necessarily due to his CIA duties, but because of what *he* was deep inside. With Parissa, his concerns and emotional baggage fell away with her touch, steady voice or her warm gaze across the dinner table. Almost imperceptibly, she had penetrated his defenses with the right gesture or word at every critical junction until she occupied a prominent place in his thoughts. Yet David also knew now was not the right time to take their relationship further.

Perhaps someday, just not today.

David was the first to break their embrace.

"Will we see each other again?" she asked.

He felt his natural defense mechanism rise, but tried to fight it. "As colleagues or personally?"

Parissa looked hurt. "If you need to ask, then I guess not."

David sighed. "I'm sorry. That was uncalled for. I'd like to, but I don't know if we can."

"Because of us or them," she asked, referring to their superiors.

"Them. I'd very much like to see you again. I'll miss you."

She smiled. "That's the answer I was looking for."

As she reached up to kiss him again, a voice from outside the tent called out. "David Harrim, you in there?"

David pulled away, but kept his arms wrapped around Parissa. "Yeah. What is it?"

The tent door opened and someone made their way through the shelves and stacks of equipment. A female corporal appeared. "Oh, sorry to interrupt. Phone call for you. Said it was urgent."

"Who?"

"Some guy named Reynolds."

"I'll be right there."

"By the way, he told me to get a plane ready for you."

"To where?"

"Israel. He's to meet you there."

Suppressing his surprise, David merely nodded.

The corporal disappeared.

"Why Israel?" Parissa asked.

"Not sure. Something must have come up." David smiled wistfully at Parissa. "I'm sorry. I'll be back shortly. Will you wait here for me?"

"Yes, but hurry back. We've only got an hour or so. I'll be waiting by the cot over there," she added provocatively.

David grinned. "In that case, Reynolds will just have to wait. After all, I'm working hard to improve Iran-U.S relations."

"And doing an admirable job," Parissa said, taking his hand and pulling him close once again.

21

Tel Aviv, Israel

Walking slowly down the street, David stared around blindly, lost in his thoughts. Returning to Israel always brought a conflicting surge of emotions. Overriding all others was his anger at the interminable Israeli-Palestinian conflict, mostly at the extremists who had polarized the situation. He was discouraged by the intractability of both sides and the senseless violence that raged unchecked by their so-called leaders.

Although his mixed heritage prevented him from taking sides, David's neutrality also stemmed from his ability to dispassionately analyze the situation. He understood the Palestinians' desire for a homeland and anger about the unceasing seizure of their land. He also realized the Israelis feared for their very existence—a valid concern after being persecuted for thousands of years, four invasions by their Arab neighbors and the growing Iranian nuclear threat. Even 60 years after Israel's founding, many Palestinians still refused to recognize Israel's right to exist and Hamas was committed to the nation's destruction.

To David, the arguments didn't matter—the simple fact was that both the Palestinians and Israelis were destined to share the historically rich land and needed to accommodate and make peace with each other.

Despite his heritage and the fact he'd been born in Jerusalem, David felt virtually nothing for the land of his ancestors. He had fond memories of growing up near the Old City of Jerusalem—the quaint neighborhoods, diverse inhabitants and the grandeur and mystery of the ancient religious sites. Yet, in his return visits to Israel, the sights and sounds left him cold and distant, as if he were trespassing on a private street protected by a locked gate. Somehow, he knew his years growing up in America were to blame—there, he was taught the past held little meaning, for the unlimited opportunities meant one could rise anew, much like a Phoenix from the ashes. David knew most Americans found such sentiments a cliché; but for those such as himself that sometimes found the past served as shackles and chains, the thought was liberating.

It also helped explain why he'd drifted for so long, never quite able to find his place.

David's destination was a non-descript two story office building separated from the road by a row of concrete barriers. After showing his identification to the lobby guards, David was searched before passing through a metal detector.

He took the elevator to the third floor and walked down a narrow hall to the conference room. The cheerless, spartan surroundings and severe expressions of the few people who hurried past matched the deadly purpose of those who worked at Mossad headquarters. Reaching his destination, he stopped to catch his breath before stepping inside.

Opening the door, he found himself in a conference room that was simply furnished with a large table, leather chairs and a chalkboard along one wall. Two people stood near the solitary window—Jack Reynolds and an older man.

"David, welcome back," Reynolds said, striding forward to greet him.

"Thanks Jack," David replied, shaking his hand. "I uncovered some disturbing information. There's a lot to be concerned about."

"I know. I've been on the phone constantly since your report," Reynolds replied. "Let me introduce you to Moshe Rabin."

David shook the outstretched hand, studying the Israeli intelligence officer. Rabin was a stocky but imposing figure, his hair cut short in military fashion and a crooked nose that had obviously been broken on several occasions. His gray green eyes burned with an uncomfortable intensity and his abrupt movements and powerful physique suggested an explosive personality.

David had heard numerous stories about Rabin, who was almost a mythical presence in the intelligence community. A *sabra*, or native born Israeli, Rabin was fanatically devoted to Israel's security. As a youth, Rabin had spent years undercover as a member of various Arab terrorist organizations. Supposedly he had foiled the sale of a nuclear device from a rogue Russian general to Palestinian terrorists about twenty years ago. He was also rumored to have been one of the Mossad's best assassins, slipping into various countries to execute Israel's enemies. At one point, he had even assassinated Saddam Hussein, only to find out later he'd killed one of the former Iraqi dictator's many doubles.

David and Rabin exchanged polite greetings, the older Israeli agent making several comments that indicated he was familiar with David's background.

David wondered if the file the Israelis kept on him contained all the details of his mixed heritage.

"David, take us through the events of the past week," Reynolds said, motioning David toward an empty chair. "I've given a summary of your reports to Moshe, but he should hear it directly from you."

"Before you do, I'd like you to meet someone else," Rabin said. He spoke into an intercom. "Rachael, please come in."

The door opened and an attractive, young woman strode confidently into the room.

David stepped back in surprise. Rachael was the mysterious woman who had rescued him from Turki Al Faisal's mosque in Saudi Arabia.

David extended his hand to her. "Thanks for pulling me out of a tough situation. I wouldn't have made it without you."

"I was just doing my job," she replied, in a low, husky voice that recalled a young Lauren Bacall. Her dark features and brunette hair betrayed her northern African ancestry as did her generous nose and full lips. She was wearing a blue sweater and gray pants, which highlighted her taut and muscular physique. Her features were solemn and unmarred by laughter lines, as if humor were a rare visitor. Returning David's intense gaze, she managed a tight lipped smile. "Fortunately for you, we were watching the mosque that night."

"Why?"

"We've been concerned for some time about Turki al Faisal," Rabin interjected. "We think he and his mosque are funneling money to terrorist organizations around the world."

"After you went inside," Rachael said, "I decided to follow to see what you were up to."

"Why didn't you identify yourself?" David asked.

"There wasn't any reason to do so," she replied evenly.

Reynolds cleared his throat. "Now David, tell us what you learned."

For the next hour, David described everything that had occurred during the past few days, leaving out only his romantic interlude with Parissa. He was peppered with questions, mainly on his conversations with Khaled ibn Saud and Ramzi Yousef. Although Reynolds complemented David for his courage and important information, David could tell from his tone that later, when they were alone, Reynolds would criticize some of his decisions, including his impulsive search of the Pakistani *madras* that cost Nawaz his life.

Finally, Reynolds leaned back in his chair. "David, what are your conclusions?"

"First, I believe the threat to the House of Saud is real. We need to do everything in our power to uncover who is behind the threat."

"I agree," Reynolds said. "Our intelligence network is searching for more information and we've asked our allies for help. We've also put a round-the-clock watch on the Riyadh Wahhabi mosque, Turki al Faisal and the young *imam* who caught David searching their offices. So far, we've uncovered nothing unusual."

"We should also put a tail on Khaled ibn Saud," David said. "Ramzi Yousef was adamant that Khaled's a threat to the monarchy. And I saw Khaled's aide in the Pakistani training camp."

"I think Yousef is mistaken," Reynolds replied. "Khaled has always been a friend of the U.S."

"We can't ignore Yousef's warning and what I saw."

"True, but I need to figure out how to handle it politically. Langley will have my hide if I approve surveillance on Khaled without clear justification. But I'll get it done."

Rabin walked over to the side table and picked up a coffee pot. "Next, the events in Pakistan."

David nodded. "There are numerous questions—What was the "weapon" referred to in Azam Tariq's letter? Nuclear? Chemical? Did they actually manage to obtain it? Does this Al Kabbar have the weapon? And what is his connection to Turki al Faisal, the *mutaween* and Tariq? Finally, who is Abdullah? Is he the mastermind behind all this?"

Reynolds shook his head. "I doubt a Pakistani nuke was stolen. First, the Pakistani military guards their nukes closely. Second, the missiles are very large; our intelligence network would've spotted their transport out of Pakistan."

David tapped his hand on the table. "Actually Jack, there's another scenario to consider. You're assuming all of Pakistan's nuclear missiles are traditional ICBMs. But what if they've developed a suitcase nuclear bomb?"

Reynolds shook his head vehemently. "Not a chance, we would've learned about it. We pay some of their officers a lot of money to keep us informed."

"We've been wrong before," David replied pointedly.

"David's theory about a Pakistani suitcase nuclear bomb is worth considering," Rabin interjected, his voice suitably grave. "It fits with a tip we got recently that Pakistan has developed smaller nukes. There's something else. Two days ago, we arrested a former Hamas member named Shadi Muhana. During the interrogation, just before he committed suicide, he taunted Rachael, saying a nuclear bomb would soon explode in Israel."

The room fell silent, the only sound the distant hum of the street outside. Deeply concerned and with his mind racing, David realized his worst fears might come true. Rabin's news, together with everything he'd uncovered recently, convinced him Al Kabbar had stolen or purchased a Pakistani suitcase nuke.

Reynolds finally broke the silence. "Did Muhana say who was behind the bomb?"

"No. He left Hamas about six months ago to work for someone else. We don't know whom, but we're certain it's not the Palestinians."

Reynolds stood and began pacing. "Then it's possible he was working with the same Saudi organization that's connected with Al Faisal's mosque and the Fist of *Allah*."

Rabin nodded. "Yes. There's more. Rachael, fill them in."

Rachael leaned forward and placed her hands on the table. "Yesterday, we intercepted a phone call to Muhana from his half-brother, Hazan Qwasama. He refused to talk to our agent, but did say that in a few days, he'd kill many Israelis."

"Which would indicate Muhana's threat is real and Hazan knows about the bomb. Where's Hazan?"

Rachel's grim expression betrayed her answer. "We don't know. He left Gaza a year ago. We traced his call to a warehouse on the other side of the Egyptian border with the Gaza strip. Yesterday, we raided the building, but Hazan was already gone. But he'd left behind a sensor bomb that killed three of our men."

"I'm sorry," David said, sensing that Rachael had known the victims well. His suspicion was confirmed as Rabin reached out and gripped her shoulder compassionately.

"I'm okay." She paused, as if struggling to regain her composure. "There's more. Since Hazan was already gone, it seemed strange the building was booby trapped. On a hunch, we brought in a Geiger counter. We found faint traces of radiation in the building wreckage."

"Damn!" David swore, realizing why everyone was so grave. "Was the radiation from a nuclear bomb? Or was it from enriched uranium that could be used to construct a nuclear bomb?"

"It could be either as both would leave traces of radiation," Rachael replied. "So would low-grade radioactive isotopes used for a dirty bomb."

Rabin rubbed his chin wearily. "For now, we're assuming a nuclear bomb was the source of the radiation, not uranium or low grade radioactive material."

David looked around the table. "What do you think happened to whatever was in the warehouse?"

"We believe it was taken into the Gaza Strip," Rabin replied. "The border is 20 kilometers away and there are numerous tunnels to smuggle arms between Gaza and Egypt."

"Have you heard anything from your Mossad sources in Gaza?" David asked.

"No. We're obviously cautious about telling anyone what we're looking for, as we don't want to start a panic."

"Do the Palestinians have someone who can build a nuke or dirty bomb?" Reynolds asked.

Rabin sighed. "Probably. It's not hard to build either once you get the material. You can even download plans from the internet."

"Then it's possible that the weapon referred to in Azam Tariq's memo was whatever was radioactive in that warehouse. Which means that Al Kabbar could be the key to finding it."

"David, who is Al Kabbar? An Al Quada operative?"

"I don't think so," David replied. "He never mentioned Al Quada to me. I think he's part of another unknown organization, a much smaller one. Al Kabbar clearly is connected with the 'Fist of *Allah*' *madras*, which we know is funded by Turki Al Faisal's mosque. We also know the *madras'* training camp is supported both by the mosque and an unidentified Saudi man. That suggests another, smaller terrorist group—Al Faisal's mosque, the *madras*, the unidentified Saudi backer and Al Kabbar, all working together."

"Is Abdullah the mastermind? And who is he?"

"I'd say yes," David replied. "Abdullah may—and I stress may—be Khaled ibn Saud."

There was a disbelieving silence in the room and David noticed Reynolds shaking his head in disagreement.

"David, you're the key to this," Rabin said. "If Al Kabbar has a bomb, he'll certainly come here. And you're the only one who knows what he looks like."

David felt like someone had punched him in the stomach as he realized he might be responsible for the fate of thousands of innocent people. He would've preferred to be back on the mountain ridge in Pakistan facing a dozen hostile gunmen than having such an enormous responsibility. His stomach churning, he stood abruptly, stumbling slightly as if under the weight of their expectations.

"Finding Al Kabbar will take a miracle," David said.

Rachael smiled grimly. "Everything about Israel is a miracle. What's another one?"

"There's one thing more." Rabin began pacing, his hands clasped behind his back. "The *ulama*, Turki al Faisal, is here in Jerusalem. He flew here yesterday from Saudi Arabia."

"Has the *ulama* been to Jerusalem before?" David asked.

"No. That's why we think something is up," Rabin replied.

Rabin and Reynolds exchanged meaningful glances. David looked shrewdly at the older Mossad agent. "Moshe, you didn't ask me here this afternoon just to brief Rachael about Pakistan. What else do you need me for?"

"Very prescient," Rabin said, offering a brief smile for the first time. "Two things. First, you're the only one who knows what Al Kabbar looks like. I want you to sit with a police artist to draw up a mug shot. But there's another way you can help."

David didn't have any idea what Rabin meant, but he braced himself for something unpleasant.

Rabin walked back from the window to stand near David. "Shadi Muhana is the name of the man who told us about a nuclear bomb before committing suicide. Do you recognize the name?"

"No, I can't place it," David replied cautiously.

"Muhana is a close friend of Sufian Ashrawi, a Palestinian who lives in the Jenin refugee camp."

"And?" David asked, not giving any sign he recognized the name as that of his cousin. David felt a surge of anger, both at the Israelis for their presumptiveness and at Reynolds for revealing the details of his background. He just wanted to be left alone, to do his job. He suddenly realized that was one reason he found the CIA appealing—he was pretending to be someone else, which enabled him to avoid or postpone certain questions or choices that everyone was forced to confront at some point. That of who he was and would become.

Rabin leaned forward. "I took the liberty of checking your background, with Reynolds' permission of course. We know Sufian Ashrawi is your cousin."

"I haven't talked to him in over twenty years."

"But he *is* your cousin. Family is very important in Palestine."

"You mean the occupied West Bank don't you?" David asked, deliberately trying to provoke Rabin.

The Israeli intelligence officer's eyes flared but he ignored David's barb. "We'd like you to ask your cousin Sufian if he knows where to find Muhana's half-brother, Hazan Qwasama. Sufian also knows Hazan very well."

David realized the Israelis must be desperate to ask him to pursue such an unlikely source of information. He hadn't spoken with any of his father's relatives since his mother had taken him to America over twenty years ago.

"This is crazy," David said, shaking his head. "Sufian won't talk with me. I'm an American, part Jewish and I work for the CIA."

"Given the circumstances, it's worth a shot. We know where he is."

"You've kept tabs on him?" David asked.

Rachael pulled some pictures from a manila envelope and handed them to David. "You ought to see these pictures before you contact him."

David looked at the first picture, which showed a handsome young man holding a copy of the *Quran* and explosives strapped around his waist.

"That's Sufian's brother and your cousin, Yassar. He took this picture before launching a successful suicide mission on a Jerusalem bus six years ago that killed eight Israelis, including three children."

David felt ill. He recalled playing hide and seek with Sufian and Yassar so many years ago and their childish cries of delight and excitement. Yassar was two years younger, but had insisted on always following Sufian around. He had been a bright, irrepressible boy who loved chocolate and pirate stories. David was unable to picture him as a cold blooded terrorist capable of killing other children.

David looked at the second picture, which showed a man lying comatose in a hospital bed, the rumpled sheets failing to disguise the fact that his legs were missing.

"Your cousin, Sufian," Rachael said softly. "Unfortunately, he associated with the wrong people. He was riding in a car with a Hamas leader in Gaza that was targeted by one of our helicopters. He survived, but lost his legs. He's been involved with Hamas for years."

David felt a surge of anger at the sheer stupidity of the unending killing, the loss of life on both sides. "Goddamn it!" he snarled. "When does it all end? How many more have to die?"

There was an uncomfortable silence and David clenched his fists, straining against a further outburst. He realized that despite his desire to distance himself from the Israeli-Palestinian conflict, there were too many ties for him to become a dispassionate observer.

"David," Rachael said, breaking the uncomfortable silence. "I know how you feel. We've all lost friends and family to this conflict. We're asking you to prevent even more."

"Why the hell do you think Sufian will even see me, let alone tell me what you want to know? My God, how he must hate all Israelis and Americans. He'll see me as one of you, not a Palestinian."

"We're desperate. You've *got* to make him understand that if a nuke is detonated in Israel, no one wins. The Palestinians can forget about *ever* getting a nation of their own."

David knew Rabin was right. Each terrorist attack on Israel only reinforced the notion that the Palestinians were untrustworthy. If a nuclear bomb were ever detonated, Israel would never risk further attacks by permitting the establishment of a Palestinian state. The Palestinian situation would only get worse.

He gave in. "I'll try. Can I tell Sufian about the nuclear threat?"

"Yes," Rabin replied. "I don't like it, but it's probably the only way to get his cooperation. Sufian knows Hazan very well. Whatever it takes, we must find Hazan."

"I'll do it." As David handed Rachael the manila folder, another photograph fell to the ground. Picking it up, David stared curiously at the slightly out of focus picture, which showed an older Palestinian sipping tea at an outdoor café, apparently somewhere in Saudi Arabia. He was wearing a traditional *keffiyeh* and dark sunglasses and the way his head tilted to one side, as if listening to something far away, reminded David of someone.

"Who's this?" David asked, staring at the photograph. Suddenly, his heart started pumping and he knew the answer before Reynolds broke the news gently.

"It's your father."

David thrust the pictures angrily back at Rachael. "I don't know what game you assholes think you're playing, but my father is dead," David said furiously, even as he sensed that what Reynolds said was true. "He died fifteen years ago in Ramallah from a heart attack."

"As hard as it is for you to accept, David, it's not true," Reynolds said, shaking his head. "His death was faked. I didn't know it until yesterday, when Rabin informed me."

"This is bullshit. Why the hell would he fake his death?" David said angrily. "Why wouldn't he contact me for 20 years!"

"I think I can answer both questions," Rachael said quietly, putting her hand on David's shoulder. "Here's the best as we can figure it. Nearly 25 years ago, he lost your sister in an accidental shooting. Nobody ever knew if the bullet was an Israeli or Palestinian one."

"I know. It drove my parents apart."

"When your parents separated, your father took you to Saudi Arabia. Three years later, both of you returned to the West Bank to visit his family. Your mother found out and had the police seize you. Then the two of you emigrated to America and vanished without a trace. At that point, we believe your father committed himself to the Palestinian cause. He changed his identity and became a Saudi citizen, which gave him significantly greater freedom to move about and procure money and weapons for the Palestinians."

"How long have you known?" David asked quietly, accepting the explanation.

"We've had our eye on him for years, but we always thought he was a Saudi citizen," Rabin replied. "A year ago, we learned otherwise and it was only this week that we connected the two of you."

David looked away, afraid that the tears so near at hand might start flowing at any moment. He was rescued by his anger, which surged through him and found numerous targets. First, the people standing there—Reynolds for betraying his past, Rabin for trying to use him and Rachael for casually revealing the truth of his father's deception. Then his parents, for falling in love in the first place and their inability to stay together. Finally, he was coldly furious at his father, both for never attempting to track David down in America and for becoming a terrorist who was responsible for the murder of innocent civilians.

He suddenly grew conscious of everyone waiting for his response. Determined not to succumb to his emotions and their expectations, David fought to get himself under control.

"Why'd you tell me this now?" David asked angrily.

"We thought you should know," Reynolds replied gently. "It's possible your cousin Sufian is aware of this, maybe not. But you may stumble across your father at some point."

"And if I do?" David asked, glancing around at the concerned, yet hardened faces.

There was a prolonged silence before Reynolds answered. "Just remember, he's a terrorist. You'll have to treat him like one. Because he'll see you only for what you've become—an enemy to his cause."

"But I'm his son!"

"Unfortunately David, as much as it hurts, your father decided years ago the Palestinian cause was more important. It's your turn to remember the same."

It was good advice and something David kept repeating to himself during his lonely cab ride back to his hotel. Once there, he ordered a bottle of Scotch and proceeded to drink alone into the early morning hours before mercifully slipping into a drunken, restless sleep.

A deep sleep in which he was unable to avoid the ghosts of his past and present.

22

Ziad Abbas entered the windowless garage and flicked on the light switch. The room was nearly overflowing with tools, spare automobile parts and two worktables. A white ambulance emblazoned with a prominent red Islamic crescent was parked to one side. Piled against the wall were four small green medical cases and four large duffle bags, all marked with a Red Crescent. Next to them was the steel container Hazan had brought from the Ukraine.

Ziad picked up a medical case and put it on the table to examine the explosive device inside. He checked the timer, connecting wires, ignition device and forty pounds of C-4 explosive material. Satisfied the bomb was in working order, he locked the case and put it aside. He then proceeded to check the other three medical cases, all of which contained a similar explosive device. Finally satisfied, he put the cases back on the floor and tucked the key away beneath his shirt.

Next, Ziad examined the radioactive Ukraine container and found the opening sealed shut by a bolted steel plate. Using a wrench, Ziad removed the bolts. The container was filled with radioactive material sintered in metallic pellets. With a plastic trowel, Ziad scooped out a handful of pellets and placed them on the table. Using a mallet, he pulverized the pellets into a fine powder. He repeated the procedure again and again until the mound of crushed radioactive material covered the top of the table. Then he took the four duffle bags and filled them with the powder.

Ziad knew he had just signed his death sentence. But he had researched the effects of radiation and found it would take several days before he grew ill and weeks more before the radiation killed him.

It was enough time to complete his mission.

Ziad didn't fear death itself, only the thought his demise wouldn't advance the Palestinian cause. Although Ziad had never spent any time with Hazan, he knew what drove him. They were both dedicated to the Palestinian cause, came from a similar background and burned with hatred, rage, despair and frustration. In this, they were as close as any brothers or sisters.

Ziad placed his hand on one of the medical cases, feeling a surge of pride in his mission. He couldn't recall the specific event or moment when he became a man of violence. But he had grown up without hope or direction, much like the disaffected youth in America's ghettos portrayed on television. Until recently, he'd never left the dusty, squalid confines of the Gaza Strip; his few youthful excursions were to the trash strewn Gaza City beaches or an occasional drive into the desert.

Since most Palestinians glorified and admired those who fought the Jews, Ziad had never considered another path. His father had died years ago in a workplace accident and his mother quickly lost any influence over the handsome young teenager. After joining Hamas, Ziad had completed his ragged military training in a cellar or during the night deep in the desert to escape Israeli spies. But his commanders quickly realized Ziad was too valuable to waste as a simple foot soldier. His good looks, winning smile and fluent Yiddish made him an ideal operative to slip between Israel and Gaza. For the past year, Ziad had completed numerous missions inside Israel, each time never expecting to return home.

Ziad put all the medical cases and duffle bags in the rear of the ambulance next to the gurney. As he finished, there was a knock on the door. Ziad closed the ambulance doors and walked over to the garage entrance.

"Who is it?" he called out.

"Hazan."

Ziad unlocked the door and Hazan Qwasama slipped inside. He was dressed as a Palestinian farmer in a bedraggled robe with his head covered by a red and white checkered *keffiyeh*.

"Are you finished?" he asked.

"You shouldn't be here. There's still too much radiation in the air."

Hazan smiled, his gold tooth flashing even in the dim light. "It doesn't matter, our mission ends soon. Show me what you've done."

Ziad took him over to the ambulance and opened the rear door. "I've made four traditional bombs and put them in medical cases. Because I used highly concentrated plastic C-4 explosives, the bombs are very powerful. The four duffle bags are filled with radioactive powder from the container you brought. I crushed the radioactive pellets into a fine dust so it would disperse easily. When the bombs explode, radiation will be spread over a large area."

"How many will we kill?" Hazan asked. "Tens of thousands, maybe more?"

Ziad shook his head. "No, the blast won't have much impact, perhaps enough to destroy a small building."

"That's it?" Hazan asked, clearly disappointed.

"The radioactive material doesn't increase the size of the explosion. Instead, the conventional explosion spreads the radioactive powder, polluting the atmosphere and making an area uninhabitable. The impact is not necessarily to kill, but to terrorize. As Abdullah said to me, it is the unseen, the insidious that people fear."

"Then many will die over time from the radiation?"

"Some," Ziad acknowledged. "But that's not Abdullah's intent. It's the act itself that's important, the symbolism of the targets we strike."

"Where will the bombs be placed?" Hazan asked.

"You don't need to know that yet. But it'll be in the two places that'll cause maximum psychological impact. It's the first step of a two-part plan."

"And the second part?" Hazan asked.

"It'll occur several days later. Where or how, even I don't know. Our explosions here in Jerusalem are meant both to destroy and as a signal."

"Are we taking the bombs into Israel in the ambulance?"

Ziad nodded. "The Gaza City hospital isn't very good; the more difficult patients are taken to an Arab hospital in Jerusalem. We'll wait until we have such a victim, preferably a child hurt in an Israeli air strike, then transport him across the border."

Ziad picked up a white shirt and pants from one of the tables. "You'll need to wear this ambulance driver's uniform and Islamic Crescent Society identification badge. Now, I must phone Abdullah to tell him we're ready."

"What do you want me to do now?"

Ziad smiled. "I need to go to Jerusalem to meet with the woman who'll help us. You remain here, quiet and out of sight."

"I'd like to see a friend of mine, Sufian Ashrawi."

Ziad shook his head. "That's a bad idea."

"I'll be quick. He lives in the Jenin refugee camp. The Israelis aren't looking for me."

"No. Stay here and wait for my return."

Hazan shrugged. "As you wish."

Ziad clapped Hazan on the shoulder. "In two days, we will strike a huge blow for our people. The destruction of our targets will devastate both Jews and Christians. It won't be long now before the entire Arab world rallies behind us and Palestine is once again ours."

Hazan grinned. "Then time will pass slowly in anticipation."

23

David woke with the sour taste of whiskey in his mouth and a splitting headache. Rolling over, he peered at the sunlight streaming in through the window, realizing it must be close to noon. Fortunately, he had the entire day to himself. Rising slowly, his head throbbing, David made his way into the bathroom, where he took a cold shower. Afterward, feeling slightly better, he ordered a large American breakfast and a pot of coffee.

He was still extremely bitter over the sudden revelation last night about his father and, to a lesser extent, the insistence of both Rabin and Reynolds that he contact his cousin. While drinking alone in the dark hours of the night, he had directed his anger at everyone and no one, but finally settled on one person—his father. In a sense, he felt as if his father had stolen his childhood or perhaps even part of his sense of self worth. Palestinians considered family ties extremely important, particularly the relationship between father and son. So what did it say that his father had willingly forgone the relationship with his only son? David knew his father initially might have been unable to track him down after his move to America. But later, he could have easily done so, as David had never hidden his identity.

The news his father was alive shook him, but even more so was the knowledge that he was a terrorist. David couldn't reconcile his youthful memories with the blood and terror he now knew his father caused. Even though it wasn't rational, he had a sick feeling in his gut, as if he were partially to blame for his father's actions. The dual shock of the knowledge that his father was alive and his chosen path was something David had yet to fully absorb and would certainly never accept.

The knock on the door startled David out of his reverie. He wasn't expecting anyone and, as far as he was aware, no one knew where he was staying. Pulling out his pistol, David moved across the room to stand to one side of the door. "Yeah?"

"Bellman sir, I've a message for you."

"Door's open."

David tensed as the door opened slowly. A short, dark haired young man wearing a blue doorman's jacket stepped inside, his hand clutching only an envelope. David put away his gun and stepped forward to take it.

"Where'd you get this?" David demanded.

The bellboy shrugged. "It was left at the front desk for you."

David tipped the bellboy and waited until he left before tearing open the envelope. A single white sheet of paper was inside, a one line message written in block letters.

5 PM, Grotto of Gethsemane.

He knew the Grotto well, having visited it during a recent trip to Jerusalem. Located at the base of the Mount of Olives just east of the old city, the Grotto of Gethsemane was supposedly where Jesus had been resting with his disciples when he was betrayed by Judas and arrested by Roman soldiers. With a single narrow entrance, the small cave held three altars and was typically crowded with tourists and pilgrims.

Why meet there?

David pondered the message. Clearly, the note was from someone unassociated with the CIA or Mossad. Then, whom? What person or organization would be following him and know his whereabouts so quickly? Was it a mysterious ally, such as Rachael when she rescued him from the Saudi Arabian mosque, or someone intent on harming him? Was it once again Abdullah?

Questions he was unable to answer. The only sure way was to show up for the meeting, prepared for any potential situation.

One thing David knew for certain—he would be heavily armed.

✳ ✳ ✳

David stared nonplussed at the "Closed Temporarily for Renovation" sign at the entrance to the Garden of Gethsemane. The garden was enclosed by a crumbling stone wall that stretched about 200 feet on each side and contained nearly a dozen ancient olive trees, reputedly direct descendents of those Jesus once enjoyed. The Basilica of the Agony, a modern stone replica of the original 4th Century basilica, was adjacent to the garden. A wizened old man suddenly appeared, shuffling out from a nearby guard shack.

"You David?"

David nodded.

"Friend said you'd be coming. Go on to the Grotto. They paid me for a private showing."

David walked through the garden, alert for any movement. A cool wind blew fitfully, the afternoon sun already low on the horizon, the bright desert light fading fast. The gravel crunching beneath his feet sounded overloud in the still afternoon, broken only by the distant hum of traffic. Reaching the entrance to the Tomb of Mary, another stone façade building, he turned right and down a narrow corridor to the Grotto entrance. Set against a steep, rocky hillside, the entrance was protected by a thick metal fence and wire mesh to keep out the pigeons. The entrance gate was open and he paused before going inside, aware he was about to enter an enclosed area without any other exits.

A surefire place for an ambush.

Taking a deep breath, he plunged inside. The steep stairs led down into a cave, perhaps 60 feet by 20 feet, with an impressive stone vault. The grotto contained three altars with murals over each, including *Jesus Praying among the Apostles* and the *Assumption of the Virgin* and the *Kiss of Judas.* The cool, damp air smelled of smoke and age. The Grotto's center floor was filled with metal chairs used by tourists and the cave walls were worn smooth in many places by the touch of countless hands over the centuries. David walked over to stand next to the main altar, keeping his right hand near to the gun in the shoulder holster beneath his shirt.

A man suddenly materialized from the corner of the cave.

"I wasn't sure you'd show." A short, heavyset man with lank blond hair, he was wearing Khaki pants and a blue shirt. His only distinguishing features were an enormous belly and the gun in his hand.

"I was curious," David replied, his hand edging toward his own gun.

"Don't try," the man said, with a small smile. "You'll be dead before you get it."

David dropped his hands to rest on the wooden table next to the altar. "What do you want?"

The heavyset man chuckled, a mirthless sound that rang overloud in the still air. "To kill you, of course."

"Why?"

"You're getting too close and asking too many questions."

"Khaled ibn Saud?"

His assailant simply shrugged, but gave no sign of recognition.

"Better known as Abdullah?"

This time, a flash of recognition.

David glanced up at the stairs leading out of the Grotto as he heard someone approaching. A second man appeared; a thin, dark youth with a short afro wearing dark trousers and a yellow shirt. He walked over to stand next to the heavyset man.

He held a gun as well.

"Why here?" David asked.

"I thought it'd make you curious, encourage you to come. Plus, no crowds today."

"How do you know I came alone?"

The young man spoke. "I been watching. No one followed."

David slid his hand beneath the table, finding the pistol he'd taped there earlier that afternoon. He then directed his gaze over the shoulders of the two men at the stairs, his eyes widening slightly in surprise. His ruse worked. The two men involuntarily glanced over their shoulders. Grabbing the gun, David brought it to bear on the younger man. He fired twice, red stains appearing in the yellow shirt, his would be assailant's arms flailing as he crashed backward. The heavyset man snapped off a quick shot in response as he dove behind one of the altars carved from the rock wall.

David darted to his left, out of sight behind a thick rock ridge that extended from the wall. A couple bullets whistled harmlessly past, several more striking the protective barrier. Peering around the edge, David could only see empty chairs and the altar his assailant hid behind, which was near the stairs. A fusillade of bullets drove David backwards, a rock chip gouging his cheek as blood immediately spurted forth.

He heard footsteps pounding on wood. Risking another glance, he spotted his assailant sprinting up the steps that led outside. David didn't chance a shot, hoping to catch and interrogate his opponent. Rising, he dashed across the floor of the Grotto to hit the steps at full speed. He hurtled up the 60 or so steps, his thighs burning. As he burst through the metal gate at the top of the stairs, he saw his quarry disappear around the bend of the corridor that led back to the entrance to the Tomb of Mary.

Sprinting forward, David managed to reach the Church in time to see his assailant dart into the Garden of Gethsemane. Rather than follow, David ran along the outside of the rock wall that enclosed the garden, intending to circle around to meet his assailant at the far exit. His breathing was ragged and he unconsciously wiped the blood streaming down his cheek.

He rounded the corner of the wall just as his opponent emerged from the Garden. Launching himself, David struck his assailant in the back and both men crashed to the ground. David wrestled his right arm free and punched the man on the side of the head, followed by several more blows. His assailant tried to strike back, but David managed to deflect the blows with his left arm. Rolling away, David reached down to pull out the small pistol strapped to his ankle.

His assailant was trying to pull out his own gun when David's voice stopped him.

"Freeze! Hands up!"

Breathing heavily and with blood trickling down his face, the heavyset man tentatively raised his hands.

"Who are you?" David asked.

"Just a guy. You can call me Gus." He gave a lopsided grin, as if they'd just met in a bar.

"Who sent you?"

Gus glanced around, as if hoping for a rescue. "I don't know. I'm just hired help."

"Hired for what?"

"To kill you. I get paid when it's done."

"How?"

"Well, it's complicated..." His assailant glanced over David's shoulder. David didn't fall for his own ruse, but still Gus reached down once more for his gun. Just as David fired, aiming for the shoulder, Gus jerked to one side and the bullet smashed instead into his chest. Gus screamed, his hand releasing the gun. He keeled over to one side, blood darkening his white shirt and flecking his lips. Moving forward, David leaned over the wheezing, coughing man. Gus' face was deathly pale, breathing labored and blood poured from his chest wound.

"How do I contact the man who hired you?"

But Gus could only stare up at David, his mouth working soundlessly. Slowly, his gaze grew unfocused and finally his head lolled to one side.

He was dead and David was left to ponder two questions: who wanted to kill him and would they try again?

✳ ✳ ✳

Abdullah was relaxing in his study when his satellite phone rang. Scowling, he answered, sensing the news wasn't good.

"Yes?"

"The two men I hired failed in their task." The caller was one of his contacts in Jerusalem.

"What happened?"

"Not sure. Your target must've got the jump on them somehow. I heard about it through a contact at the police."

Abdullah tried to restrain his temper. "Your incompetence is staggering."

"I've never failed before. Should I do it myself?"

Abdullah hesitated, considering all the alternatives. "No, perhaps it's best this way. I've got another idea. A way we can use this man, instead of killing him." He permitted himself a small smile. "Yes, my idea is perfect. This way, he'll help bring about the very thing he's trying to prevent. So let him live for now. I'll kill him when he's no longer useful."

He hung up, pleased with his plan and once more certain everything was on schedule.

24

David moved cautiously down the narrow alley. The fetid night air assaulted his senses, reeking of sewage, rotting garbage and something else he couldn't place, perhaps the stench of decaying bodies buried beneath the rubble of a house that had been destroyed during a recent Israeli raid. The alley was strewn with piles of rubbish and an open sewer ran along one side. The cinder block houses, originally built as temporary housing for Palestinian refugees 40 years ago, looked weary and forlorn, as if having witnessed far too much despair. The palpable grinding poverty and hopelessness made South Central Los Angeles a relative beacon of prosperity and opportunity.

Jenin was a place where dreams never visited and nightmares never left.

Reaching the end of the alley, David spotted his destination, a three story apartment building poorly constructed from crumbling concrete with a rusting tin roof. The building tilted noticeably to the left and at least half the windows were covered with plywood. David climbed the stairs that wound around the outside of the building until he reached the top floor. He knocked on the only door and stepped back so that he could keep an eye on the street below.

The door opened slowly and he found himself looking at his aunt. She stared at him without recognition for a moment, before a forced smile lightened her weary features.

"Hello Nina."

"Hello Anwar," she said, staying behind the door as if unsure of David's credentials. Anwar had been his father's Palestinian name for David after the divorce. "Sufian said you were coming. It's been some time."

"It's good to see you," he replied, feeling awkward. They had only met several times, the last over twenty years ago. He didn't know her very well, as she was his uncle's second wife. Nina was a dumpy, middle aged woman with the years clearly etched in her deep facial lines and graying hair. When David called Sufian to set up a meeting, she had told him that his uncle, Sufian's father, had died several years ago.

"You look like pictures of your father," Nina said softly.

David merely nodded, unsure what to say.

She held the door open and he walked inside. The apartment was furnished with care, but few possessions—a couch and coffee table surrounded by floor cushions. There were several posters of tranquil meadows taped to the walls and a framed drawing of the Prophet Mohammad holding the *Quran*.

"He's waiting for you," she said, motioning to the other side of the room.

The man sitting in a wheelchair was watching television, a smoldering cigarette lying in a filled ashtray.

"Hello Sufian," David said quietly, appalled at the change in his cousin Sufian had been a bright, handsome boy, clear eyed and energetic with a winning smile and engaging laugh. The man sitting morosely in the wheel chair displayed nothing of the past—his brows were pulled tight in anger, his mouth twisted in a scowl. Where there had once been hope, openness and warmth, David saw only bitterness and despair.

"So, what brings the mighty American Anwar to our hovel?" Sufian asked, without looking up.

"I know you're angry with me, Sufian," David said. "But it was my mother who took me from my father and to America. It wasn't my choice."

"Yet you're older now and never tried to contact us before tonight," Sufian said. "You've made your own choices and decided to ignore your Palestinian family."

David shifted uncomfortably at the truth. He was unsure why he had never contacted his father's relatives; perhaps from anger over David's perception that his father abandoned him or even to put his former life far behind.

Sufian made a dismissive gesture at David's silence. "So, what do you want?"

"I'm not sure where to begin....," David replied, trying not to look at his cousin's legs, which ended shortly above the knee. Sufian's hair was matted and his beard unkempt while his face bore the unmistakable signs of a growing dissipation, courtesy of the empty vodka bottles stacked against the wall.

"Don't...David," his cousin interrupted sharply. "David, that's what you go by now, isn't it?"

"Yes."

"Well, don't try to say how great it is to see me or how good I look," Sufian said. He finally looked up at David. "We both know it's a lie."

"That's not true," David protested half-heartedly. He glanced around the room, looking desperately for a common reference point, a place to begin.

Sufian made a bitter sound that masqueraded as a laugh. "Right. I sit here without my legs, courtesy of a missile from an Israeli helicopter. I drink and smoke too much, causing my beloved stepmother to spend much of her time in the mosque praying for my soul."

David heard a muffled sob from the next room and knew Nina was listening. "Do you want to tell me what happened?"

Sufian shrugged. "It's a familiar story. The Israelis targeted a Hamas leader for execution and fired a missile at his car. Unfortunately, I was also in the car." Sufian looked down and moved the stumps of his legs slightly. "This is what happens when they miss. If they had hit the car, I'd be dead. Now, I'm worth nothing."

"Your life is what you make of it Sufian."

Sufian laughed bitterly. "Spoken like a rich American Jew, one who has never been shot at by Israeli troops. Tell me *David*, have you ever been beaten by the police just because you're a Palestinian? Watched your friends get shot for throwing stones at soldiers? Every week hear of someone you know become homeless because the Israelis have thrown them off their land? Been unable to visit other countries because you don't have a passport and may not be allowed back home?"

David shook his head. "You know the answer to that."

"Exactly. So don't sit there and tell me what to do with my life. You know nothing of it, nothing about me."

"I know enough to know that you're better than what you've become."

"A drunk? A terrorist?" Sufian snarled. "If I could, I'd kill them all with my bare hands."

"Including me?"

"What are you now? You're clearly not a Palestinian. Are you Jewish? Are you an American? Are you both?"

"I'm all of them."

"How can you be one of *them*," Sufian said, literally spitting out the last word.

"I'm neither Jewish nor a Palestinian. If anything, I'm an American," David replied, surprised at his answer. For the first time, he felt it was true.

"That's almost worse," his cousin snarled.

David felt a surge of anger. "Labels, Sufian, you're concerned with labels, not people. It's so easy for you to sit there and criticize, but when have you tried to do something positive? The Palestinian leadership only cares about retaining power and lining their own pockets, not creating a free Palestinian state. You teach your children hatred and send them to die in suicide bombings. You refuse to negotiate, violate every ceasefire and encourage your extremists to kill innocent civilians. Hell, Hamas doesn't even recognize Israel's right to exist; they want to wipe Israel from the face of the earth. Hating and killing won't alleviate your suffering. There's only one solution and that's to learn to live together."

"Live together?" Sufian bit back a bitter laugh. "Every year, the Israelis take more of our land to build settlements. Every year, they annex more of Jerusalem. Every year, they shoot and imprison our young men. They're the problem, not us. They call us animals, say we don't have any respect for life. But they use tanks and helicopters against schoolboys armed with rocks. They're the murderers, not us."

"And how many innocent Israelis have the Palestinians killed? How many times have the Palestinians ended every negotiation with more violence? Suicide bombs or raining rockets down on Israel will never get you your state. It'll only harden their resolve and strengthen the hands of those Israelis who claim the Palestinians can't be trusted."

"You're *wrong!* The Israelis have held our land for 40 years. It's only now that we strike back, that they grow fearful and respect us. We drove them out of Gaza and one day we'll drive them out of the Middle East."

"You're no closer to getting a nation than 10, 20 years ago." David insisted. "Violence is not the right path."

Sufian shook his head. "It's pointless to discuss this with you. What do you want? You said it was important. It's only because our fathers were brothers that I agreed to see you."

David leaned forward. "I need your help. I need to find someone."

Sufian's expression grew angry and he spat on the floor. "Bah! Just as I feared. You've become one of them. My sources were right."

"What sources?" David asked.

But Sufian would only shake his head. "Who are you looking for? And why?"

"I'm looking for Shadi Muhana's half-brother, Hazan Qwasama. I know both men are your friends."

"Why not ask Shadi? The Jews have taken him already."

"He's dead."

"The bastards," Sufian hissed. "They killed him."

"No," David replied. "He took his own life with a cyanide capsule hidden in his tooth." David leaned forward and tapped Sufian on the shoulder. "He was hiding something Sufian. Something so important that he killed himself before they had a chance to interrogate him."

"They killed him," Sufian insisted. "The rest are lies."

"No," David replied evenly. "I spoke to the woman who interrogated him. He died as I said."

"What's it to you?"

David hesitated, unsure if he should reveal he was working for the CIA. Then again, if he didn't, Sufian would never believe there was a nuclear bomb. David decided disclosing most of the truth was the correct approach.

"I work now for the Americans trying to find Al Quada operatives," David said, twisting the truth slightly. "The Israelis asked our help in finding Muhana's half-brother, Hazan."

"Why?"

David again sensed the truth would be far more effective with Sufian. "It's possible that Hazan has a nuclear bomb. The Israelis were trying to track him down, but he escaped. In the building, they found traces of radiation."

Sufian's expression conveyed a look of victorious satisfaction.

David walked over to the couch and sat down. "Sufian, if he does use a nuclear bomb against Israel, there will *never* be a Palestinian state. Not in ten years, not in ten thousand. The Israelis would never allow an independent Palestine because they'd be afraid it would happen again. It would destroy your cause."

Sufian scowled. "The cause will never be achieved until all the Jews are dead."

David slammed his fist against the coffee table. "Damn it Sufian, don't feed me the damn party line. You're smarter than that. I suggest you think about it. It's in every Palestinian's interest that Hazan is found."

Sufian remained silent, although his expression grew thoughtful.

David stood and walked over to his cousin and placed his hand on his shoulder. "Please Sufian," he pleaded. "You know I'm right."

Sufian refused to look at him.

"If you change your mind, here's a number you can reach me at." David took a card from his wallet, but Sufian didn't take it. David put the card on the table and walked to the door. With his hand on the door knob, David turned to face Sufian one last time. For some reason, he sensed it might be their final farewell. He would be unable to tread this path again. Sufian was right—David had entered another world and the only thing that remained between them was the same bloodlines. It was not enough to make up for the years apart and yawning chasm in-between their lives, values and future.

"What have you heard about my father?" David asked suddenly, deliberately trying to catch his cousin unaware.

Sufian looked defiant. "Your father's dead. You know that. Heart attack 15 years ago."

"That's not what I was told."

Sufian gave a twisted smile. "Just like the Israelis—lies, lies and more lies. He's dead. Don't trouble yourself anymore."

With that, he turned back to the television.

"Goodbye cousin," David said softly to the back of the broken body of the boy he had once loved. "May *Allah* watch over you and grant you peace."

David turned and hurried out the door. As he rushed down the stairs, filled with sadness and regret, he heard the door open again and footsteps follow behind.

"Anwar," called a woman's voice. "Wait."

David stopped and turned. Sufian's stepmother stood on the stairs, glancing nervously back at the closed apartment door.

"I must tell you, your father, he's still alive," she said, stumbling slightly over her words in her rush. "You're his son, you should know."

"How do you know?" David asked.

"I overheard Sufian. Just last week."

"Do you know where I can find him?" David asked.

The woman shook her head. "No."

"Will you let me know if you find out?"

"Not if you work for the Israelis."

"Right now, I only want to ask him the same thing I did Sufian."

She nodded understanding. "Is it true? What you said about the bomb?"

"Yes."

She stared searchingly at him, looking for the falsehoods. "I'll talk to Sufian. Perhaps he'll listen to me."

"You'd better pray to *Allah* he does," David said. "Otherwise, no one wins."

With that, he turned and plunged into the night.

25

Parissa settled back against the front seat of her Chevy delivery van, prepared to wait as long as necessary. She was parked outside the warehouse that had been listed in papers she and David had found in the briefcase of Khaled ibn Saud's assistant in Pakistan. Located in a grimy industrial neighborhood of Riyadh, the warehouse was a dreary, rundown building in a quiet, deserted area without any street lights. A chain link fence topped by barbed wire encircled the building while the adjacent parking lot held numerous unmarked delivery trucks and vans.

Her colleague, Zakoria, was there as well, parked down the street in another vehicle. Just a few minutes ago, he had finished dismantling the extensive network of security cameras and alarms that protected the property. Once the two patrolling guards returned to rest in the trailer by the vehicle entrance, she and Zakoria could begin to search the warehouse.

While waiting, Parissa thought about David. She found herself reliving the memory of his touch and features, even suppressing a smile as she recalled one of his corny jokes. She found her feelings slightly unnerving, certainly unusual. During the past few years, she'd had no time or inclination for personal relationships. Parissa knew her natural tendency toward isolation was largely to blame. As an only child, she had rarely sought the company of her peers, inevitably feeling more comfortable with her parents' friends. Then again, the last few years had hardly been conducive to forming any lasting bonds.

Originally a translator for the Iranian Secret Service, Parissa had landed a one-time field assignment that soon led to additional overseas missions. Now, after traveling the world for several years and experiencing both the excitement and dangers of her job, Parissa couldn't imagine anything else. Although she still wasn't sure what her dreams and aspirations were, she knew what she _didn't_ want—that of a traditional Iranian marriage and motherhood—and her chosen profession offered a convenient escape. Although there was still a part of her that craved a traditional role, her feeling came more from habit than conviction.

So far, Parissa hadn't been asked to do much more than observe, listen and, on occasion, even flirt with potential male sources of information. The Pakistan trip had at times both thrilled and frightened her, but she had ultimately felt energized by the danger and uncertainty. Parissa wasn't sure she could kill, even though she had trained extensively for such a possibility. Still the idea both enthralled and repulsed her and she was aware that perhaps a small part of her attraction to David had to do with his ability to do so. Parissa wasn't proud of what it revealed about her, but at least she was aware of her feelings.

Parissa also sensed she and David shared some similar qualities—independence, stubbornness and aloofness. David also failed to completely hide an underlying vulnerability, something Parissa knew dwelled inside her as well. In many ways, David was a conflicted individual—his ability to kill when necessary contrasted with a surprising depth and sensitivity that he seemed constantly struggling to subjugate. Parissa wasn't under any illusions about both the difficulties and probable eventual failure of their relationship.

Still, for now, it felt right and that was all that mattered.

The appearance of both patrolling guards brought her thoughts back to the present. As they disappeared inside the trailer parked at the entrance, Parissa spoke into her handheld radio.

"It's sunset!"

Grabbing her pistol, she emerged from the car and met Zakoria about fifty meters from the gated entrance to the parking lot. Zakoria was already using a pair of bolt cutters to slice through the chain link fence. Like her, he was dressed in tight fitting black pants and shirt with rubber soled black shoes.

Parissa glanced around nervously, but the street remained deserted, the only illumination coming from the floodlights mounted on the warehouse.

"We're in," Zakoria said, peeling back a cut section of the fence.

Parissa crawled through the opening, careful to not snag her clothing. Once inside, she kept watch while Zakoria followed. So far, she was disappointed in the decrepit appearance of the warehouse and relatively lax security, causing her to wonder if there was anything important inside. Then again, perhaps the understated facility was intended to avoid drawing attention.

They made their way across the crowded parking lot, weaving in and out of the dozens of delivery trucks and vans.

"Parissa, have you noticed that all the vehicles are unmarked and practically brand new?" Zakoria said.

Parissa stopped in surprise. "You're right. There must 60 or 70 new vehicles parked here. Most look like they've never been driven and they don't even have license plates."

"Then someone must be planning a large delivery soon."

"Yeah, but of what?"

As they approached the warehouse, Parissa noticed to her left loading docks and large sliding doors wide enough for a delivery truck while the office entrance was on the other side of the building.

"Let's try the door," she said.

The side entrance was a heavy steel door with three dead bolt locks. Zakoria pulled out some skeleton keys and began to try to pick the locks. After a few minutes, he shook his head in exasperation and turned to Parissa.

"I need to drill them open."

"Do it" Parissa ordered, although she hated to leave visible evidence of their break in.

Pulling out an electric drill, Zakoria proceeded to drill into each lock to pulverize the internal mechanism. Once finished, he managed to pry open the door. Parissa went first, stopping just inside to assess the narrow cement and steel framed hallway intermittently lit by bare light bulbs. The two doors at either end were unmarked.

"We've got 20 minutes before the guard does another round and sees the door we drilled open," Parissa said. "Let's split up."

Zakoria nodded and disappeared to the left while Parissa moved quickly down the hall in the opposite direction. Even with her soft soled shoes, her footsteps echoed off the cement floor and steel walls. Reaching the end of the hallway, she opened another door and stepped out into a cavernous open area, perhaps a hundred meters by a hundred meters. Stacks of large wooden crates, some twenty feet high, filled the area. Walking over to the nearest stack, Parissa found the crates were marked in numerous languages, including Korean, Russian, French and Chinese. But the boxes labeled in English were straightforward.

The corporate names were familiar: General Dynamics, Colt and Raytheon, amongst others. The contents were familiar as well: M-16s, ammunition and grenade launchers.

Looking around, Parissa found a crowbar nearby. She pried open the top of one of the wooden boxes with Chinese labels. The box was filled with hand held anti-tank rockets, capable of stopping even the most powerful tanks in the world.

Someone was preparing to arm a very large army with the latest, most sophisticated weapons available.

Glancing over her shoulder, she noticed another door that led to what appeared to be an office. Hurrying over to it, she was disappointed to find the door was locked. Picking up a loose board, she smashed the door's window and reached inside the broken glass to unlock the door. Stepping inside, she glanced quickly around. Unlike the rest of the warehouse, the office was luxurious, furnished with oriental rugs, paintings and sleek modern furniture.

Walking over to several large file cabinets against the far wall, Parissa opened one and began to hurriedly search the contents. There was nothing interesting, mostly copies of bills and shipping manifests for the crates. Most had come from Europe, although clearly many shipments had originated in the U.S. She wondered if the purchased weapons were obtained from the black market, unscrupulous corporations or diverted from legitimate Saudi arms purchases. The vast amount and wide variety of weapons led her to believe it was a combination of all three.

Hoping to find something more illuminating, Parissa turned her attention to the second file cabinet.

"Well pretty lady, what are you doing here?"

As Parissa began to turn, she heard a spitting sound and felt a bullet pass by her head.

"Slowly my pretty lady."

Cursing silently, Parissa turned slowly to find a rotund, slack-jawed man dressed in a suit standing there. His steady hand held a large pistol.

'My, you're better looking than I thought."

"I can explain," she said desperately. "I'm a temporary secretary and…"

"Save it," he snapped. "Good thing I came back to get some papers. Stupid guards aren't worth a damn."

Suddenly, there was a clattering noise behind him and the man partially turned. In desperation, Parissa launched herself across the five meters separating them. Before she could reach her assailant, he staggered to one side before crashing to the floor. He lay there unmoving.

"You okay?"

Parissa looked up at Zakoria's concerned face, a silenced pistol in his hand. "Yeah, thanks."

"Saw him coming down the hallway and thought you could use a hand." He glanced nervously around. "We should get out of here before the guards show up."

"Give me a minute." Parissa knelt down next to the dying man. His dark face had grown slightly pale and a trickle of blood ran from his mouth. "Who are the weapons for?"

"No, no...," he replied, trying to wave his hands dismissively.

Parissa nodded to Zakoria, who walked over and placed his foot on the wounded man's chest.

The Saudi screamed and then managed to spit out almost unintelligibly. "For the *mutaween*, the *mutaween*."

"Who's leading them? Is it Khaled ibn Saud?"

But the wounded man lapsed into incoherent babbling. Zakoria slapped him hard several times across the cheek.

"Do you know Turk al Faisal? And his weapon?"

More unintelligible words.

"Do you know Al Kabbar?"

His eyes seemed to flash recognition. As the man rolled onto his stomach, Parissa was able to catch one word—"Medina Moonrise".

"What's that?"

The Saudi suddenly reached into his suit jacket pocket, clearly for a weapon. Zakoria fired several times, the bullets smashing into the Saudi's chest. The man's hand slid slowly down his shirt and his head lolled to one side, his eyes open and vacant.

He was dead.

With a sigh, Parissa stood and looked at Zakoria. "Any idea?"

The Iranian shook his head.

"Fantastic," Parissa said sourly. "We found enough weapons for a revolution and *Allah* alone knows how many more stockpiles are scattered around Saudi Arabia. The *mutaween* are preparing to do something—what and when we've no idea. And to make things worse, now I've got to figure out the meaning of some half-crazed comment about the moon rising."

For some reason, she sensed the latter was much more important than the weapons. Unfortunately, she just didn't have a clue where to start.

26

Shira raised herself on her elbow and looked down with a smile at her exhausted lover. Her long black hair fell across her breasts, caressing the erect nipples and light sheen of sweat that glistened on her smooth skin. Her face was a perfect oval, her flawless features flowing softly together into loveliness. Her Israeli lover reached out and touched her lips, then moved his finger down along her body, relishing the voluptuous curves.

"Yitzhak, you're such a wonderful lover," she lied, brushing his lips with hers.

"You're incredible," he replied with a sigh. "I've never felt this way before."

"Nor me." She giggled. "You've taken me to places I've never been."

He awkwardly smoothed her hair, his touch betraying his inexperience. "I'm sorry I can't stay this morning. I'm meeting some of the guys to watch the soccer game."

"It'll be good to see your friends." She smiled reassuringly. "I'll be here when you get back."

He leaned over and kissed her again, before disappearing into the bathroom. Shira waited until she heard the shower running, before hurrying over to his black leather jacket that hung over the back of a chair. Picking it up, she searched the pockets and removed Yitzhak's police identification, placing it in a dresser drawer. Although Yitzhak would eventually discover his I.D. was missing, Shira only needed the ruse to work for several hours, after which she would have returned it.

She dressed and made her way out to the living room. The inexpensive furnishings were typical for a young professional woman and recent college graduate—a couch covered in flowery fabric, matching chairs, teak coffee table and vases filled with dried flowers. Several framed prints of Monet's Water Lilies hung on one wall and an entertainment center with a TV filled another. Yet there weren't any personal items such as photographs; because Shira, the Jewish tour guide, didn't really exist.

Her real name was Salwa Mustafa and she was a Palestinian widow.

She picked up the phone and dialed a local number.

"Yes," answered a male voice.

"I'm sorry, I was trying to reach the Horowitz Delicatessen."

"You have the wrong number."

She hung up, knowing she had an hour to reach the scheduled drop point. Yitzhak appeared, half dressed in his police uniform pants and drying his hair with a towel. Salwa repressed a slight shudder at his pudgy body, flabby love handles and bulbous nose set beneath the beady eyes. So different from her beloved Imad, who had been tall, lean and elegant. Salwa closed her eyes, driving the image of her dead husband from her mind, determined to focus only on completing the task that would avenge his murder and her son's.

"Don't forget, we've dinner plans tonight," Yitzhak said, pulling on his leather jacket.

Salwa held her breath, suddenly afraid he would check his pocket and realize his ID was missing. Instead, he leaned forward and clumsily embraced her.

"I'll see you tonight," she promised, breaking away and walking him to the door.

After his departure, Salwa waited several minutes before leaving. Her house was located near the Bukharin Quarter, perhaps three kilometers from the Old City. The area was a disparate collection of modern apartment blocks, older pre-war homes and small local shops. The afternoon was bright and sunny, a recent storm having cleared away the desert grit that occasionally shrouded Jerusalem.

Salwa walked rapidly, ignoring the open looks of male admiration just as she did the entreaties of the street vendors. Salwa was extremely striking, although her beauty no longer gave her any pleasure, but was merely a tool she'd used to ensnare Yitzhak. She had picked him out of a dozen Israeli policemen milling about a bar because his plain appearance and awkwardness indicated someone desperate for romance. It had been easy to ensnare Yitzhak; the only difficult part was the physical act of making love. When it became too difficult, she would close her eyes and recall her husband and son at their funeral as they lay in their plain pine coffins, their pale faces devoid of any expression.

That day several years ago was still etched in her mind—it had been a perfect fall afternoon, a false prognosticator of the bloodshed that would follow. Her husband and four year old son had been walking ahead of her exploring the open air market. Suddenly, there were shouts and screams and the sound of gunfire. She learned later that several Israeli soldiers had fired at a suspicious man who had evaded a checkpoint. The wayward bullets had killed her husband and son instantly. She could still see their limp bodies, the pools of blood painting the broken pavement a vivid crimson. Although it was just one more mistake in an endless cycle of tragic mistakes, Salwa blamed the Israelis. Like most Palestinians, she never considered the impact of her fellow Palestinians' violent actions.

Since then, the thought of revenge had become her constant companion and principal subsistence.

Nearly six months ago, a man named Shadi Muhana had contacted her to ask if she wanted revenge. She had agreed eagerly. He had arranged her cover story, fake identification, new job and house. The man she was on her way to meet, Ziad, had become their go-between a month ago.

Ziad had insisted Salwa take a job guiding tourists around the Church of the Holy Sepulcher, the most important church in Jerusalem and reputedly built over the spot where Jesus Christ had been crucified, buried and resurrected. When Salwa asked why, Ziad had only replied that she must learn everything about the Church, including the security procedures in a medical emergency. Although unsure as to what a sacred Christian monument had to do with achieving her revenge, Salwa had reluctantly agreed, reassured by his promise that soon her vengeance would rock the world.

That was enough to satisfy her.

She hurried through the Old City's New Gate and down the narrow, cobbled streets toward the Wailing Wall plaza. Since she was early, Salwa turned impulsively down the narrow alley that led to the Church of the Holy Sepulcher and went inside.

Although Jesus was also considered a Muslim prophet, Salwa detested the church, finding the gloomy, musty interior morose and cheerless. The main floor and two subterranean rooms were a jumble of architectural styles, the original Byzantine church modified and reconstructed numerous times over the years. The rough hewn walls bore the cruel reminders of the Christian Crusades—paintings glorifying victorious battles and portraits of important Christian kings—even the swords and armor of the Crusaders held a place of honor. The Crusades had been violent, ruthless pogroms launched by Christians to reclaim the Holy Land nearly a thousand years ago. Her tour groups always were unaware the Crusaders had persecuted and attacked Muslims as well as the ruling Turks—murdering and pillaging all in the name of God and their savior, Jesus Christ. As a result, most Muslims had never forgotten the centuries of conflict and persecution and continued to view the West and Christians with suspicion.

Salwa moved across the large main floor of the Church, past the numerous alcoves, golden shrines and candelabras before exiting through the main double doors. At the far end of the entrance plaza, she stopped to gaze once more at the Church. The imposing stone spires reached vainly skyward, the confusing array of angular roof lines reflecting the numerous alterations to the basic structure over the centuries. To Salwa, the thick stone walls represented the imposing battlements of a Christian castle that must be stormed and the inhabitants defeated. She couldn't forget that the Christians continued to give legitimacy to Israel, offering support and financial aid while ignoring the plight of the Palestinians.

Turning away, Salwa walked through the Christian Quarter of Old Jerusalem, soon reaching *Bab as-Silsila* Street, a prominent thoroughfare that ran nearly the length of the Old City before terminating at the Temple Mount.

Stopping for a moment, Salwa mused about the bitter irony that such a small area was considered holy by both Jews and Muslims. The Temple Mount, or *Haram ash-Sharif*, was the biblical Mt. Moriah on which Abraham was instructed by God to sacrifice his own son as a test of his faith. Solomon, David's son and successor, had built the great First Jewish Temple, which was destroyed in 586 BC. The Second Temple was built in the same place, only to be subsequently destroyed by the Romans in 70 AD. For thousands of years, the Jewish people had considered Temple Mount the physical and spiritual center of the prospective Jewish return to Palestine. To Muslims, the *Haram ash-Sharif* was also where the Prophet Mohammed had left his earthly existence to take his place alongside *Allah*. The Dome of the Rock was unfortunately constructed on the same site as the Jewish Second Temple and held the sacred rock on which Abraham prepared to sacrifice his son and from which the Prophet ascended to heaven.

It was both ironic and tragic that two religions and two implacable enemies shared the same holy site.

Although not religious, Salwa viewed the *Haram ash-Sharif* as the unequivocal center of Palestine. Without it, there was no Palestinian State. The Israelis knew it, which was why their sham proposals for a Palestinian state always excluded the *Haram ash-Sharif*. Meanwhile, the Israelis kept expanding their West Bank settlements while claiming they were willing to negotiate. At this point, Jerusalem was almost completely surrounded by Jewish settlements, physically cutting off the Palestinian heart of Jerusalem from the rest of the West Bank.

Glancing at her watch, Salwa realized she must hurry to arrive on time for her meeting with Ziad. After reaching the intersection with the *Al-Wad Road* which crossed beneath *Bab as-Silsila*, Salwa followed the circular stairs that took her down to the lower street. There, she passed through an Israeli checkpoint with a metal detector and x-ray machine. Once through, she entered a long, dark tunnel that led to the Western Wall plaza, more commonly referred to as the Wailing Wall.

Reaching the plaza, Salwa stopped and pretended to be just another tourist taking in the sights. The large stone plaza was crowded, the Jewish Sabbath drawing numerous orthodox worshippers. To her left stretched the Wailing Wall, the last remnant of the great Jewish Second Temple. Directly behind the Wailing Wall was the Al-Aqsa mosque and, further back on the left, was the Dome of the Rock. Straight ahead was the access road to the plaza and the remnants of the fortified wall that once encircled the Old City. Perhaps a dozen vehicles were parked there, mostly police cars and ambulances. To her right rose the rebuilt Jewish Quarter which had been mostly destroyed during the fighting of 1948. The area was filled with small yet expensive yellow sandstone condominiums and Orthodox synagogues.

The Wailing Wall was actually a retaining wall to the Second Temple's esplanade and still formed part of one side of the Temple Mount plaza, providing critical support to the foundation of the Al-Aqsa mosque that had been constructed in the 8th Century. The Wailing Wall was about seventy feet high and stretched for perhaps a hundred yards, bulging in spots from the pressure of holding up the Temple Mount plaza. At the base of the wall, pious Jews were praying, some rocking back and forth and crying out to *Jehovah*. Many were Hasidic Jews, with long braided hair and beards and wearing black hats and pants with a white shirt.

"They look ridiculous don't they?" said a familiar male voice.

"I can't understand why they believe they're *Allah*'s chosen ones," Salwa replied quietly, turning to face Ziad. He was wearing the clothes of a Hasidic Jew, complete with a wig and false beard. Two Torah scrolls were tucked beneath his arm. After weeks of anxious waiting, she was relieved to see him.

"We must speak quickly," Ziad said, guiding Salwa to a deserted spot on the plaza. "I was nearly prevented from crossing over from Gaza today. The Israelis have tightened security."

"Why?"

Ziad frowned. "I'm not sure. But they seem to be looking for something or someone. It's possible our mission has been compromised."

Salwa suddenly found it difficult to swallow. "By Shadi Muhana? You said he was dead and couldn't betray us!"

"I thought he didn't say anything before he died, but now I'm not so sure. So be careful." Ziad rubbed his hands together in anticipation. "Did you bring the identification?"

She brought out Yitzhak's police identification, which enabled the holder access to every important and closely guarded religious and government site in Jerusalem. Ziad had asked her to obtain such identification several months ago and she had spent the intervening time picking her target and getting to know Yitzhak. Two days ago, Ziad had called to say it was time to steal Yitzhak's ID.

"Good," Ziad muttered, turning it over in his hands. "My forger can duplicate this in a few hours. How long before your man misses it?"

"Perhaps two hours."

"That's all I need."

"Then everything is ready?" Salwa asked, fearful their mission was delayed.

Ziad smiled, his eyes alight with anticipation. "Yes. Hazan has arrived from Egypt and brought what was needed."

"When do we strike?"

"Tomorrow."

Salwa felt a surge of excitement and something she recognized as regret, tinged with sorrow. She had never caused another person harm, yet soon she would be responsible for the deaths of many. For the first time, she fully began to appreciate the potential cost of her actions, which would surely violate the word of *Allah*. Yet, Salwa was able to put her concerns aside; she wasn't a particularly religious person, only an angry, vengeful one. Like many, she chose to follow religion when it fit her needs or desires. Even so, she prayed for the strength to continue, knowing she'd reached the point of no return.

"What do you need me to do?" she asked.

"Several things. First, this afternoon you go to the Jerusalem Hilton. There, you'll call on a guest, Turki al Faisal, who's expecting you. He's an important *ulama* from Saudi Arabia. You'll arrange to take him on a tour of the Old City tomorrow afternoon. Next, call your Jewish boyfriend..."

"That pig is not my boyfriend," Salwa interjected vehemently.

"My apologies." He smiled, his expression softening. "After tomorrow, you'll no longer have to see him. Is he working tomorrow?"

"Yes."

"Good. Have him come to your house during his lunch hour. That way, he'll have his police car and be wearing his uniform. You must keep him there until I arrive. We'll be dressed as Palestinian ambulance drivers."

"You'll kill him?" Salwa asked.

"Of course. But make sure he's there."

"Don't worry. He does what I tell him."

Ziad grabbed Salwa's arm and pulled her away from two American tourists who had wandered too near. "After we arrive at your home, you'll pick up the *ulama*, Turki al Faisal, at his hotel. Then, take him through the Old City to the Church of the Holy Sepulcher."

Salwa frowned. "Why there? No self respecting *ulama* would set foot in a Christian church, particularly one the Christians revere so much."

"Jesus is also an Islamic prophet. If asked, that's your rational. You can say the *ulama* views all of *Allah*'s prophets without prejudice."

"And then?"

Ziad smiled. "Once inside, the *ulama* will suffer a fake heart attack. Naturally, such an important Islamic leader must only be attended by a Muslim medic. You'll pretend to call a Palestinian ambulance, except you call me. After my arrival, I'll take care of the rest."

Salwa glanced around nervously, making sure no one was listening. "And the uniform and the police car you take from Yitzhak? How does that figure into everything?"

"Hazan will wear the uniform and drive the car to here. Needless to say, this," Ziad paused dramatically to let his sweeping arm gather in the entire Western Wall Plaza, "will look dramatically different tomorrow."

"You said there is a second part to the plan. That our actions are merely the first step."

"There is. But even I don't know what it is. We must focus on the task at hand."

Salwa nodded, feeling the weight of Ziad's gaze before turning away. "My life ended long ago. Tomorrow I'll finally avenge my husband and son."

"Remember. Your Israeli man *must* be at your place by mid-morning."

Salwa tossed her head irritably. "I heard you. I'll do my part."

Ziad grinned. "Then tomorrow will be the day."

27

For the second time in two days, David moved cautiously down the filthy alley that led to his cousin Sufian's apartment. This time, David carried a pistol in his hand. His cousin had called earlier that morning to tell David he had obtained some information and wanted to meet that evening. Although David had been warned to come alone, Rachael was stationed at the head of the alley and several Mossad agents were scattered throughout the nearby streets. David was also wired for sound, with a small receiver in his ear and a microphone strapped to his chest.

So far, he had seen only a young man who walked past without even meeting David's gaze. The cold night was brightened only by a sliver of a moon. The surrounding buildings were mostly dark and quiet, although a burst of laughter or glimpse of light occasionally escaped. The cold steel of the pistol felt reassuring in David's hand.

Reaching the end of the alley, David moved toward the crumbling three story building that housed Sufian's apartment. Suddenly, from the corner of his eye, David caught a movement in the shadows to his left. Dropping to the ground, he brought the gun to bear on the target. David saw nothing but darkness. He was looking at a small empty lot squeezed between two apartment buildings, the area filled with scattered mounds of trash. He held his position for ten counts. Still nothing.

Suddenly, there was the clatter of metal on metal and movement in the nearest rubbish pile. David's finger tightened on the trigger as he sought a target. To his surprise, a cat suddenly bounded out into the alley. David breathed a sigh of relief and stood. He brushed at the sludge that now coated his clothes and wrinkled his nose at the stench, a combination of human excrement and rotting garbage.

A voice crackled in his ear. "You there yet?"

David tucked his head against his chest before replying. "Almost. I'm at the foot of the stairs."

The apartment building leaned drunkenly to one side, the exposed concrete walls and cinder blocks pitted and crumbling. Steps to the upper floor apartments wrapped around the outside of the building, although the railing had long ago fallen into disrepair.

The rickety wooden stairs creaked with every step, so David would take one step and then stop to listen before taking another. The solitary window on the first floor was dark as was the one on the second. An Arabic pop song wafted through the night air from the building across the street.

Reaching the third floor, David paused outside the apartment door. He heard nothing, not even the sound of a television. He shivered slightly, not from the cold, but the tension and uncertainty. He glanced back into the alley to ensure it was deserted before knocking.

At his touch, the door swung open. The apartment was dark, although a faint glimmer of light came from a room in the rear. He stepped cautiously inside.

Something wasn't right about the unlocked door and dark, quiet interior.

Leaving the door open, David crossed the living room to a hallway he guessed led to the bedrooms. He crept down the hallway, listening carefully. He heard the creak of floorboards and a rustling sound from a room at the end of the hallway. A sliver of light spilled out from beneath the closed door. Raising his gun, David proceeded cautiously forward. Reaching the last door, he heard movement inside once again. He hesitated before deciding to seize the initiative.

Stepping back, he lunged forward and kicked in the door. The fragile wood door frame splintered and the door swung open.

"Freeze!" he ordered.

His cousin Sufian lay huddled on the floor in a pool of blood next to his overturned wheelchair. A slight Palestinian with an unshaven face stood bent over a desk rifling through one of the drawers. Overturned chairs and scattered clothing indicated the room had already been searched.

"Keep your hands where I can see them," David ordered. "Move slowly away from the desk to the bed."

The man lifted his arms in the air and moved slowly to the bed.

"Lie face down! Now!"

The man did as David asked. Keeping his gun pointed at the stranger, David knelt to feel Sufian's pulse with his other hand. He was dead, although the warmth of his skin indicated he'd died only a few minutes ago.

"Who are you?" David asked, not expecting an answer.

The man remained silent. David looked around the room for something to bind the man's hands and feet. There was nothing.

"On your feet," he ordered.

The man rose slowly to his feet, his gaze never leaving David's face.

"Jewish pig," he spat.

David glanced at Sufian, feeling a surge of guilt his questions had gotten his cousin killed.

"David," said a voice in his ear. "Are you alright?"

"Fine," he replied. "Sufian's dead, but I've got his killer."

"We're on our way," Rachael promised.

Suddenly, there was a commotion at the front door and a female voice called out. "Sufian? Sufian?"

Footsteps approached down the hallway. David moved so that his gun covered both the door and Sufian's murderer.

"Sufian?" a female voice asked again.

Sufian's stepmother appeared in the doorway.

"Sufian!" she screamed, rushing into the room.

David moved forward to block her. Too late, he realized he was too close to the stranger. Sufian's murderer lunged at David, knocking his gun to floor. They went down in a heap, David frantically trying to twist his body free. Although he had the wind knocked out of him, David held on desperately, trying to prevent the man from getting up and retrieving the gun.

"Rachael, hurry!" David shouted.

They rolled around on the floor, the screams of Sufian's mother adding to the chaos. David managed to free his arm and swung wildly, grazing the side of the man's head. David's foot struck the gun, sending it spinning across the floor and under the bed. He struggled to get on top, but the man wrenched his arm free and punched David in the face. David rolled away, only to strike his head against the overturned wheelchair. Feeling dazed with blood beginning to gush from a deep cut on his head, David felt his assailant pull free and stand. The man rushed out the door as David rolled to his knees and struggled to rise.

"Rachael, he's getting away!"

"I'm in the alley."

David got to his feet. Sufian's mother was huddled sobbing over the body of her stepson. Pushing past her, David staggered down the hall, only to hear the front door slam shut. Thrusting it open, he peered outside. The man had disappeared. David rushed to the edge of the staircase, but saw only Rachael and two men racing down the alley.

David realized the fugitive must have climbed up on the roof. Grasping the side of the building, he stepped up on the railing and pulled himself onto the roof. As he rose to his feet, David saw a figure jump onto the roof of the adjacent building.

"Rachael, he's on the roof of the next building."

"I'm on it."

David ran to the far side of the roof. There, he could see the man leap to a third building. David gauged the distance to the next building and backed up a few feet to get a running start. Sprinting forward, he leaped the yawning chasm, refusing to look down. He landed awkwardly, twisting his ankle slightly before righting himself. He raced across the tar paper tiles, dodging the ventilation shafts. At the far edge, he leaped the three feet separating the two buildings, this time landing perfectly in stride. Sufian's murderer had already disappeared through the roof access door.

David quickly reached the roof staircase but stayed hidden to one side. Reaching around, he grasped the door handle and flung it open. Peering cautiously around the doorframe, he could only see the darkness of the stairwell.

"Rachael, he's gone inside the second building over."

He moved down the stairs, the only light seeping up from the lobby three flights below. Pausing, David listened intently for his assailant, but heard nothing. He continued down the stairs until he reached the upper floor. There were two doors and he pounded on the first.

"Who is it?"

"Police!"

"Piss off!"

Below, David could hear the sound of Rachael and her team bursting into the lobby and begin to race up the stairs.

"Seal off the building!" David shouted. "He's here somewhere. I'm going to start searching the apartments on the top floor."

"Wait there for backup," Rachael called back.

David heard the Mossad agents climbing up the stairs from the lobby. While he waited, David glanced around the dank hallway, noticing the graffiti that praised Hamas and Fatah and promised death to the Jewish people.

When the two men reached the third floor, David directed the first agent to guard one apartment door and the second to cover him. David slammed his foot against the door of the second apartment, only to find that the wood merely buckled and splintered.

"Open up!" he cried again.

Bullets suddenly ripped through the door and part of the adjacent wall, striking the Mossad agent next to David and sending him reeling backward. David dropped to the floor as did the unharmed Mossad agent. A second burst was fired through the door, sending wood and plaster splinters flying and cutting David's face.

He crawled out of the doorway and behind the safety of the hallway wall. David stuck the muzzle of his gun against the door and returned fire, snapping off five quick shots. The other agent crawled to the other side of the door to return fire. The staccato sound of his Uzi filled the hallway.

David made a cutting motion and they waited for any return fire. A male voice started shouting at them in Arabic. "Okay, okay. I come out now."

David and the Mossad agent remained in a prone position with their guns trained on the door, which looked like a piece of Swiss cheese. The door opened slowly, the butt of an automatic weapon appearing first. The rifle fell to the ground as its owner shouted, "Here I come."

A disheveled youth appeared, his arms raised high. David motioned him into the hallway.

"Down on the floor," he shouted.

The youth lay down, his hands clasped behind his head. Rachael and another agent appeared, their guns drawn.

"Anyone else in there?" David demanded.

The youth shook his head.

The Mossad agent reached into his jacket and pulled out a stun grenade. David nodded and the agent threw it into the apartment. There was a tremendous explosion and smoke billowed from the apartment.

David sprang to his feet and rushed at a low crouch through the door, his gun leveled. The smoke obscured the room, although David could see the outline of furniture. Staying low, he made his way through the smoke and down a hallway, the second agent following behind. David kicked in the first door, but found only an empty bedroom. He moved on to the second door and kicked it in. Another empty bedroom. The third and final room was also empty.

David lowered his gun and returned to the hallway, his eyes burning from the smoke. Rachael and another agent had the Palestinian gunman pinned up against the wall and were slapping him around. Hearing David approach, she turned.

"He's not the one."

"Bullshit!" David replied, although the youth appeared smaller and lighter than the man he'd grappled with at Sufian's apartment.

She shook her head. "I'm sure of it. He thought we were IDF troops coming to arrest him. He's a terrorist alright, but not the guy who killed Sufian."

David closed his eyes to try to picture the face of his assailant. The man had been swarthy and unshaven. The man standing there was much younger and his face was smooth.

"What do you think happened to the guy I was chasing?" David asked.

Rachael shook her head grimly. "When we heard shots, we thought you'd found him. So we stopped our search on the lower floors and ran up here to join you."

David's shoulders slumped. "So the fugitive must've slipped out while we were taking down this kid."

Rachael shook her head wearily. "My apologies. We broke procedure. Unfortunately, your cousin's killer is gone."

✳ ✳ ✳

The face of Sufian's stepmother was swollen from crying and wore faint traces of nails dragged in agony over one cheek. Nina stood as David approached and flew at him, beating his chest with her balled fists.

"Why? Why did you ask that of him?" she cried, tears once again pouring down her face.

Brushing aside his guilt, David gently pinned her arms to her side. "I'm sorry about Sufian."

She spit in his face. "He died helping the Israelis, the same animals that put him in the wheelchair. I curse his decision."

"Please, you must tell me what happened."

"May *Allah* never forgive you for Sufian's death."

David had no choice. He tightened his grip and shook her hard. "Listen to me. Sufian decided to help. If you honor him, you must honor his decision. He was trying to avert the death of thousands."

His aunt pulled away angrily and walked back to stand over Sufian's body, her head bowed. She stood there for some time, sobs wracking her body and refusing to look at David. When she spoke, her voice was muffled as if coming from a long distance. "He made some phone calls after you left. He found out something, what I don't know. He asked me to go to the store when you came. I was worried, so I came back early."

"The man who was here. Who was it?"

Wiping her tears, she sighed, a defeated, resigned sound that succinctly conveyed the years of difficulties. "I think it was Hazan Qwasama, the man you're looking for. He called Sufian this afternoon and wanted to meet. But I'm not absolutely sure."

"Do you know who Sufian called to get the information I wanted?"

She shook her head. "Too many to say for sure."

Distressed, David glanced over at Rachael who had the same thought.

Time was running out and their only real lead was lying dead on the floor.

28

The sullen night sky was heavy with rain, the grey clouds hovering threateningly overhead. Lightening occasionally split the sky, as if the God of Abraham were angry with all his children—Jews, Gentiles and Muslims. The wind, blowing hard from the west, tasted both of the desert and the distant Mediterranean, gritty with salt and sand.

Despondent over the day's events, David wandered aimlessly through the streets just outside the Old City. They had reached a dead end. Sufian was dead, Hazan Qwasama had disappeared and Al Kabbar hadn't surfaced. The *ulama*, Turki al Faisal, still remained sequestered in his hotel. He had met for five minutes with a female tour operator named Shira to arrange a private tour. The Mossad had run a quick background check on Shira, but had turned up nothing suspicious. David hadn't heard from either Jack Reynolds in Istanbul or Parissa in Saudi Arabia. Rachael had disappeared, saying only that she'd pick him up at his hotel early in the morning.

At this point, there was nothing to do but wait.

David was tormenting himself, shouldering the blame for the deaths of two people—Nawaz in Pakistan and Sufian in the West Bank. He knew dispassionately that both men had known and accepted the risks, that he wasn't responsible for their deaths. Still, David was too new at the game to blithely accept the deaths of others. He felt he was responsible for Nawaz's death and believed if he'd been more careful, Sufian would still be alive.

But what disturbed him almost as much was that he had been initially unfazed by the sight of Sufian's body; instead, he'd been thinking only about his next steps and the interrogation of Sufian's murderer. He had felt nothing—no initial shock or dismay. He realized he was beginning to accept such events as almost normal; that sudden, violent death wasn't an outlandish, frightening event. David felt as if in the last few weeks he'd lost something precious, perhaps innocence or even had his moral compass recalibrated. In a word, he was becoming hardened, something always stressed in his Special Forces training.

Oddly enough, it was as a civilian and six years removed from the military that the training finally began to have an impact.

When David drew near to his hotel, a man approached from the opposite direction, striding purposefully as if he were seeking someone. As he drew near, David saw the flare of recognition in the stranger's eyes. Reaching inside his shirt, David grasped the pistol in his shoulder holster and prepared to defend himself.

"You're the American, yes? David Harrim?" the man asked, slowing.

David drew his gun. The man's eyes grew wide, but he managed to smile. "There's no need for alarm."

"What do you want?" David asked, not taking any chances and leaving the gun pointed at the stranger. Another pedestrian noticed the weapon and broke into a run.

The man gave a slight cough. "An old friend wants to see you."

"Who?" David asked again, annoyed that they were playing the guessing game.

The man reached for his jacket pocket and David raised his arm and pointed the gun at the man's head.

"Nice and slow," David said.

The man merely smiled and pulled out a folded piece of paper. David reached for it, keeping his gun trained on the man. Opening it, he was surprised to find a photograph of a very young David with his mother and father.

"This man knows you well. He also knows about the death tonight of Sufian. He can shed some light on the situation."

David looked up from the photograph. "When and where do I meet him?"

"Now. I'll call for a car to pick you up and take you there. Your gun and phone will remain behind. You can't call anyone before we leave."

David knew he had no choice but to agree to the conditions. Although it might be a trap, David figured that if the man had wanted to harm him, he would've already done so. David knew he was grasping for straws, but the proffered meeting was his only lead.

David looked down again at the picture. "Where'd you get this? I've never seen it."

"You can ask that question of the man who arranged this meeting."

David nodded. "Make your call. Let's go."

✳ ✳ ✳

David stood shivering in the cold outside the Jaffa Gate, the imposing, reconstructed gate that had originally been built by the Romans. From there, the rebuilt stone wall of the Old City stretched in both directions, providing an imposing glimpse of ancient Jerusalem. He looked out over the lights of Jerusalem, for the first time feeling as if he had returned home. The death of Sufian had deeply affected him—after all, Sufian was his cousin and David had few remaining relatives. He had no living relatives on his mother's side and he hadn't spoken with his fathers' relatives for nearly twenty years. With a pang of loneliness, David realized he had few ties, even fewer close friends. For the first time, he understood he'd joined the CIA in an effort to become a part of something.

The rumbling sound of a passing truck brought David back to the present. His unnamed escort stood silently beside him, scrutinizing the passing pedestrians and traffic. David assumed the secrecy and elaborate precautions meant that whomever he was going to meet was wanted by the Israelis. Without backup or even a gun, David was at the complete mercy of the mysterious person he was meeting.

A black BMW sedan pulled over and the rear door opened. There were two men in the front and a third in the rear. David got into the rear seat.

"Remove your clothes," ordered the man in the rear seat as the BMW roared away.

David complied, struggling to get his pants off in the tight confines. He could only see the back of the two men in front and the man next to him was wearing a nylon stocking to distort his features. The pungent interior smelled of stale body order, garlic and mildew. Once undressed, David handed over his clothes, which were thrown out the window. Then the man next to him checked David's naked body for any tracking or listening devices. Satisfied, he handed David some clothes and shoes and told him to get dressed again. Finally, David was blindfolded and told to lean his head back and stare only at the ceiling.

They drove for perhaps fifteen minutes. Several times, the BMW took a sharp u-turn and once, judging by the horns and squealing tires, apparently ran a red light. The roads were generally smooth and well paved, indicating they remained in Israeli-controlled Jerusalem. Then the roads became rougher and the driver liberally used his horn. Finally, they turned sharply onto a bumpy road. A minute later, the BMW came to a screeching halt.

"American, get out, " said the man next to David.

The rear car door was opened and David was helped outside. He felt the crunch of gravel beneath his feet and smelled the stench of refuse and sewage, a sure sign he was somewhere in the Palestinian-controlled areas of the West Bank. A pair of hands grabbed his shoulders and steered him roughly into a building and down some stairs. David heard the sound of a radio and a dog barking somewhere nearby.

He was thrust into a chair and his hands untied. Then, the blindfold was removed. David sat there blinking furiously in the harsh light thrown from the single bulb hanging from a frayed wire in the ceiling. As the closest figure swam into view, David gave an involuntary gasp and then bit his lip so hard that blood filled his mouth.

His father was standing there.

For a long time, neither spoke. David felt a rush of emotions—love, hate, regret, anger and remorse—clashing together like the waves on a stormy sea. His emotions were woven into a multi-colored fabric, each thread separate but interconnected. He felt physically assaulted, as if each emotion were both a blow and panacea. Any joy he felt was tempered by the knowledge that the man who stood before him was a terrorist and murderer.

"Hello my son," his father said.

Despite himself, David rose to his feet and moved across the room to embrace his father for the first time in twenty years. He knew what the man had become, but he also knew the man he clenched so tightly was his father. Circumstances, not each other, had driven them apart. There had not been any ugly scenes or bitter words between them—their separation was the result of his parents' acrimonious parting, not theirs.

His father stepped back and held David at arm's length, studying the boy who was now a man. David noticed his father was old before his time, his haggard, worn face filled with deep lines that spoke of years of hardship and stress. His father's eyes moved incessantly, as if seeking something. Perhaps it was from spending so many years on the run, avoiding the scrutiny of others while watching for potential danger. Still, David recognized the way his father's mouth twisted slightly in an unintentionally sardonic grin and the tilt of his head.

"You look good my son," his father said. "There's some of your mother in you and much of my people."

David smiled weakly. "Mom always said that I looked a lot like you."

His father returned his smile. "I like that thought."

"You know she's dead."

He nodded. "Yes. I heard. I'm sorry for you." His tone revealed that his father still harbored ill will toward his former wife.

"Did you ever try to reach me?" David asked.

"Many times in the first few years. I tried desperately to find you, but your mother hid her tracks too well."

"I see."

An uncomfortable silence followed. David was at a loss for words—where did he start? With elementary school, high school? Time in the Special Forces? Then again, what was the point of even starting? His father was a murderer of innocent civilians. This was likely their only meeting. For tomorrow, his father would once again be a hunted man and David would be working for the staunchest supporter of his father's enemy, Israel. They may not have chosen different sides, but opposing sides had chosen *them*. For all practical purposes, this man was a stranger. But David knew his father was the source of much of his inner struggles and restlessness. In that, he was his father's son.

"I'm sorry, Anwar. Sorry for the years apart, for not being there."

David knew it was the only apology he'd ever get. In the Middle East, a father was considered infallible and allowed every latitude in raising his children. David felt himself grow distant and hard as he accepted who his father was and the experiences of the past week took hold. There was a far more pressing crisis—that of a nuclear bomb. David was certain his father had arranged the meeting not for personal reasons, but to discuss Sufian's death and search for Hazan Qwasama.

"Why are we meeting now?" David asked.

"Sufian's mother called me."

David nodded. He was right—the meeting was more than just personal. "The secrecy tonight. Do you fear Sufian's murderers or is it the Israelis?"

"I'm a Palestinian freedom fighter," his father replied, proudly. "The Israelis would love to capture me, but I rarely return here. I spend most of my time abroad working for my people. Our people."

David smiled wearily, realizing debating with his father was useless. "I'm neither Jewish nor Palestinian. I made that decision years ago."

"An American then?" his father asked, looking disappointed.

"As much as anything else," David replied, not wanting to be drawn into a philosophical discussion with a man who was essentially a stranger. "I don't want to discuss it with you. Time is too short."

"What are you?" his father asked. "CIA, FBI?"

David shrugged. "A rug merchant who was asked to try to avert a disaster."

His father chuckled. "I know you're lying. But for now, let us both believe in lies. You, that I am a falsely accused high school teacher of classical literature; I, that you're a Turkish rug merchant."

"Why'd you bring me here?" David asked.

His father turned serious. "I spoke yesterday to Sufian, who told me what you'd said to him. I heard this evening that he was killed."

"Hamas? Fatah? Some other organization?" David asked.

"None of them."

"Why should I believe you?"

"Because you're right about a nuclear bomb destroying our dream of a Palestinian state," his father replied. "We must keep the pressure on the Israelis; remind them that this is our land too. Killing settlers and launching rockets is justified and necessary. But we must never go too far as to destroy any hopes for an eventual peaceful settlement. Setting off a nuclear bomb in Israel would be disastrous for my people. The world would treat us as pariahs and we would lose any moral superiority. We'd no longer be the victims in this struggle, but the killers."

"Is there a bomb?" David asked, although he knew his father's presence there tonight confirmed his suspicions.

His father sighed. "I'm not sure. If there is, then it's controlled by a very secretive group. None of the Palestinian groups, even the violent radicals such as Hamas or Islamic *Jihad*, would be foolhardy enough to use a nuke. Despite their fierce rhetoric, most are also realists."

"Hamas wants to wipe Israel from the face of the earth. Why wouldn't a nuke fit with their plans?"

"True, that's their stated goal and a few will never stop fighting until it's accomplished. But for many—not all—the extreme position is viewed as a way to drive our enemy to the negotiating table."

"What can you tell me about Hazan Qwasama?" David asked.

"He's back in Palestine, but I don't know where."

"Can you find out?"

"I can try."

David felt a surge of anger. "Then what *can* you tell me?"

His father ran his hand through his close cropped, gray hair. "Hazan's name was recently linked to a man named Ziad. A member of Hamas, Ziad is a violent, dangerous man, even by their standards. He recently disappeared. A week ago, I heard Ziad was looking for a Palestinian ambulance."

"Why?"

"That's all I know."

David examined his father's face and saw it was true. There was nothing else he could pass on that would be helpful. But David saw the linkage immediately—a Palestinian ambulance would enable Hazan and Ziad to easily drive around Gaza and West Bank and even into Israel itself.

"Will you get your people to look for Ziad and Hazan?" David asked.

"This is one of the few times we'll work with the Israelis. If we uncover anything, someone will contact you."

"Thanks." David's thoughts turned to more personal matters. "Why'd you risk seeing me?"

"You're my son. When your mother took you away, I had no idea where you'd gone. It could've been Europe, America, almost anywhere in the world. I tried to track you down, but failed. Instead, I turned all my efforts to the Palestinian cause. In a sense, I traded one family for another. I wanted to see you again, just this once."

"It's not too late to stop what you're doing, to become a man of peace."

His father shook his head. "There's no turning back: my hands are too bloody. The Israelis will kill me if they can. More importantly, I believe in what I'm doing. The Israelis will never give us justice, let alone our land unless we fight them for it."

"So killing Israelis is your idea of diplomacy?"

"That's the only language they understand."

David knew arguing with his father would be even more pointless than with Sufian. His father, like many Middle Eastern men, was ruled by emotions and religion, not necessarily logic. An eye for an eye and destroying your enemies were the guiding principles.

"You realize I'll tell them I met with you?" David said.

"Of course, but there's nothing you could say that would lead them to me. By morning, I'll be out of Palestine. Someday, the Israelis will catch up with me. It may be a bomb in my car, an assassin on a crowded street or in the night while I sleep. I don't know. But until then, I'll continue to seek justice for my people."

"Eventually, they'll find you." David was surprised at his matter of fact tone; the flat emotionless voice of a stranger. He realized he was trying to ignore his jumbled emotions, which alternated between happiness at their reunion to anger at being forsaken by his father and, most importantly, the terrorist he'd become. The conflict was so gut-wrenching that he preferred the status quo of 24 hours ago—when David had believed his father died years ago and that he cared for his son above all else. Now, he had to accept the fact that not only had his father chosen the Palestinian cause over his son, but he was also a murderer of innocent civilians.

His father nodded sadly. "Someday, yes, the Israelis will kill me. But I accepted my fate long ago."

The door suddenly opened and the man who had approached David on the street reappeared. "It's time to go," he said.

"Will I see you again?" David asked

His father smiled, a sad, almost desperate expression of a terminal cancer patient forgoing any more treatments.

"If *Allah* wills it. But for now, I'll fade into the background of your life, as before." He reached out and touched David on the head. "I give you my blessing, my son. I can tell that although we may be on different sides, you've become a fine man. For that, I'm grateful."

He walked quickly away, leaving David with a last glimpse of his father's sorrowful face, the tears that were running unchecked down his cheeks.

David turned quickly away to hide his own tears and stumbled outside to the waiting car.

He didn't say another word during the entire ride back to his hotel. Once safely inside his room, he ordered a bottle of Scotch from room service and a single glass.

It was another long, lonely night.

29

Al Kabbar stood on the bow of the luxury yacht, 'Medina Moonrise' and watched the coast of Saudi Arabia draw closer. The flat, featureless landscape concealed very little, although there was nothing of consequence to hide. In each direction, there was only a vast expanse of sand and brilliant blue water under a cloudless azure sky. A few scattered houses stood on the ridge overlooking the Arabian Sea, mostly mansions of rich Saudis who sought this remote location to escape the watchful eye of the *mutaween*. The area had a reputation for wild, extravagant parties with heavy drinking, drug use and prostitutes, most flown in from Europe. Many members of the House of Saud had houses in the region, although most residences were held under false names or by dummy corporations.

Al Kabbar was anxious to land and deliver the Pakistani nuclear weapon to Abdullah. He had grown increasingly nervous something would go wrong just as success was within reach. Fortunately, the boat trip from Iran had been short and uneventful. Al Kabbar had kept to himself most of the journey and avoided the captain, who was the only crew member and merely a mercenary hired for the trip.

The yacht nosed past the outlying jetties and into the harbor, which was filled with hundreds of expensive yachts. The Captain navigated the yacht through the boat traffic and docked at a secluded slip at the far end of the harbor. Al Kabbar went below deck and, after rifling through his duffle bag, pulled out a pistol equipped with a silencer.

"Captain, could you come here to help me?"

The Captain appeared, his heavyset features twisted with annoyance. "What do you want?"

Al Kabbar fired several times, the force of the bullets knocking the Captain against the wall. He slid to the floor, his surprised expression touched with mournful understanding. Satisfied, Al Kabbar dropped the pistol, knowing he'd be far away before the body was discovered. He went into one of the staterooms, lifted the Pakistani nuclear bomb case and lugged it up on deck.

Al Kabbar made his way onto shore, past the harbor master's office and a restaurant, until he reached a parking lot. There, a blue Mercedes limousine with tinted windows stood waiting.

As Al Kabbar approached, the rear trunk popped open. After placing the case inside, he climbed into the rear seat of the limousine. He was greeted by an unsmiling Abdullah who was wearing desert robes, a *keffiyeh*, false beard and dark glasses.

"Your trip was uneventful?" Abdullah asked, as the limousine began moving forward.

"No problems."

As Abdullah rubbed his chin with his hand, a large diamond ring caught Al Kabbar's attention. He had never seen such a large stone, something that could have easily been displayed in a museum as part of the jewel collection of a royal family. Al Kabbar had always known that Abdullah was wealthy, but for the first time he began to appreciate the extent of his fortune. Again, Al Kabbar speculated about Abdullah's true identity; the man must be someone extremely important, perhaps even a senior member of the House of Saud.

A phone suddenly rang and Abdullah pulled a satellite phone out of his suit pocket.

"Yes?" he asked. A man's voice spoke rapidly as Abdullah listened without interruption, his mouth stretching slightly with the hint of a smile.

"Then it'll happen tomorrow afternoon as scheduled?" Abdullah asked. The caller spoke rapidly for a few moments more before Abdullah interrupted.

"I'll wait to hear about your success on CNN. In any event, we won't speak again," Abdullah told his caller and hung up. He rolled down the window and threw the phone away, which bounced several times on the pavement before disintegrating into pieces.

Abdullah leaned back in his seat. "Now, even if the call were traced, they'll be unable to find us."

"Was that our Palestinian friend in Gaza?" Al Kabbar asked. "We're on schedule?"

"Ziad has finished making the dirty bombs. All that remains is to sneak them into Israel and detonate them at our targets."

"The plan is still the same as you outlined to me in Amman?" Al Kabbar asked.

"Yes. One dirty bomb will be placed in the Church of the Holy Sepulcher, where Christ was supposedly crucified and buried. The other will be placed near the Jewish Wailing Wall. Together, the explosions will damage, if not destroy, both monuments and kill many. More importantly, both locations will become dangerously radioactive for years. No one will be able to visit either site without wearing protective clothing for a long, long time."

"Won't one bomb be enough for both sites?"

Abdullah shook his head. "No. The bombs are small and the sites are a half mile apart."

Al Kabbar shook his head in admiration. "The Jews and Christians will explode with anger at the destruction of their holy sites."

"Yes," Abdullah replied smugly. "They'll know the hand of *Allah* has punished them."

"Isn't that enough?" Al Kabbar asked uneasily. "Are you sure we need to carry out the second part of your plan?" Al Kabbar inadvertently glanced over his shoulder at the trunk of the limousine which held the Pakistani nuclear bomb.

Abdullah shook his head, his fierce expression matched by his forceful words. "As I said before, we must trigger a *jihad*, not just strike a crushing blow against our enemies. Destroying the two most important religious shrines of the Jews and Christians will *not* rouse Muslims. The trigger for a *jihad* will be the ruthless response of the Israelis and Christians to the desecration of their holy places. A response that we'll manufacture for them."

Al Kabbar rubbed his eye wearily, still distressed at Abdullah's plan. "Won't Muslims be the logical suspects in the destruction of the Church and Wailing Wall?"

"The Christians and Jews will believe it was an Islamic act of vengeance; but our fellow Muslims won't. The radioactive fallout from the blast by the Wailing Wall will also endanger the Al Aqsa mosque and the Temple Mount, the third holiest site in Islam. No Muslim will believe another Muslim detonated a radioactive bomb near these shrines. Remember most Muslims still believe that either the Americans or Israelis destroyed the World Trade Center to disparage Islam; surely, they'll suspect them of this crime as well. Two days after the explosion in Jerusalem, you'll carry out the second part of our plan."

Al Kabbar remained silent, thinking about Abdullah's plan. The first act, destroying the Jewish and Christian religious shrines, was justified—after all, the Jews and Christians had conspired against Muslims for centuries. In addition, many important *ulamas* had issued *fatwas* justifying the deaths of *infidels* in the name of *jihad*.

Al Kabbar finally spoke. "I fully support destroying the two sacred sites tomorrow. But I'm still concerned about the second part of your plan. Help me to find the words and strength to overcome my doubts. Convince me that the second part of your plan conforms with everything we've been taught and hold sacred."

Abdullah leaned forward, his gaze burning into Al Kabbar's and dominating the younger man with his passionate presence. Once again, Al Kabbar glimpsed Abdullah's inner strength and intensity. He realized Abdullah would have been an exceptional *imam* or *ulama*. Abdullah had that rare gift of both an expressive voice and face, the ability to cajole and reason while dominating with his forceful personality. Coupled with his commanding grasp of Islam and *Sharia* law, he was both impressive and persuasive. Most importantly, he was extremely ruthless and Al Kabbar knew Abdullah wouldn't hesitate to kill anyone who stood in his way.

"The *Quran* says," Abdullah replied, "*If you are killed in the cause or you die, the forgiveness and mercy of Allah are better than all that you amass. And if you die or are killed, even so it is to Allah that you will return*'. Thus, any Muslims that die from our actions will be welcomed by *Allah*. They are the foot soldiers in our struggle to spread the faith and return Islam to its former glory. We will be forgiven, even praised."

Al Kabbar stared out the window. He felt as if his entire life had been merely a prelude for this mission. Abdullah was right—the *Quran* said that if one was killed in the pursuit of *jihad*, then those killed, who were called a *shaheed*, or martyr, went directly to heaven and all previous sins were forgiven. A *shaheed* was so incredibly favored by *Allah* that he didn't require funeral prayers. Those innocent Muslims who might die as a result of Abdullah's plan would give their lives in a worthwhile cause and live forever at *Allah's* side.

At least, those that believed in the one true faith. The others, the *infidels*, deserved to die.

Al Kabbar nodded slowly; Abdullah's words had once again satisfied his desire for forgiveness and the assurance their plan was consistent with *Allah's* will. He also believed the success of their plan so far without any major setback meant *Allah* had indeed blessed them.

"To Mecca?" he asked, looking out at the desert speeding past.

Abdullah nodded. "To Mecca. Let us pray."

While Al Kabbar bowed his head in prayer, Abdullah thought about the last few things he needed to do.

The most important of which would be a series of calls to his contacts around the world to ensure that his real, undisclosed objective would be achieved.

30

The morning sun was already high in the sky before Ziad received a phone call from an orderly at the Gaza City hospital emergency room about an injured child needing urgent medical care. The boy was an innocent bystander who had been accidentally wounded during a raid by the Israelis searching for armed militants in Gaza. The hospital orderly, an old friend of Ziad's, had promised to send an ambulance to the scene, but called Ziad instead.

When the phone rang, both Ziad and Hazan, already dressed in paramedic uniforms, were pacing back and forth impatiently in the garage. They had been up since well before dawn, their nervous anticipation and excitement making sleep impossible. The eight cases and duffle bags containing the conventional bombs and radioactive powder had been loaded into the ambulance and they were ready for immediate departure.

After hanging up, Ziad turned to Hazan and said simply, "It's time."

Ziad drove out of the garage and down the alley that led to the main street, where he turned on the siren. Several pedestrians looked surprised to see an ambulance emerge from the alley. Hazan knew that even if they were suspicious, they would remain silent rather than risk being labeled informers. Palestinians had long ago learned that the reward for cooperating with the Israelis was to be executed by Hamas.

Grateful the moment had finally arrived, Hazan was still shaken over his close call in Jenin the night before. Ignoring Ziad's orders, Hazan had gone there to visit his old friend, Sufian. Hazan had been stunned when Sufian said the Israelis were searching for Hazan and then added he wouldn't permit Hazan to detonate a nuclear bomb. Even after a long, violent argument, Sufian refused to change his mind. Finally, Hazan had been forced to kill his old friend before fleeing. Fortunately, he'd managed to evade the stranger, probably an Israeli police officer, who had surprised him at Sufian's apartment. Hazan knew he'd been foolish and extremely fortunate. Again he silently thanked _Allah_ for his escape and prayed fervently that his luck held throughout his final mission.

For the next few minutes, they raced through the streets of Gaza City, just another ambulance speeding to the site of one more Palestinian casualty. Watching the scenery slide past, Hazan was appalled at the continued deterioration since his last visit a year ago. Even though Gaza was under Palestinian control, the Israelis still guarded the border and Gaza's prosperity was dependent on Palestinian jobs inside Israel. Many pedestrians appeared weary and thin, their shoulders hunched as if carrying a great burden. Israeli raids over the years had damaged numerous buildings, and past battles between the two Palestinian organizations, Hamas and Fatah, had caused significant further damage. Most streets had fallen into disrepair and were filled with potholes, trash and even the occasional burned-out automobile.

"Our people look defeated," Hazan finally observed.

Ziad looked grim. "The Israelis have beaten down resistance. Most don't have jobs and rely on relief agencies for handouts to feed their family. The only ones with jobs are the medical workers, plus a few government employees." Ziad conveniently neglected to blame the infighting between various Palestinian factions, lack of assistance from neighboring Arab nations and the general malaise of the citizens.

Hazan nodded, realizing his people needed a major victory to revive their flagging spirits.

Ziad turned down a narrow street where a crowd milled about at the far end. Hazan rolled down the window to shout at people to move. He could smell cordite in the air, indicating an explosion had occurred recently. The crowd parted and Hazan could see a weary resignation on many faces, as if the scene were all too familiar.

Ziad parked the ambulance and they got out, forcing their way through the sullen crowd. A small boy was laying awkwardly in the street, a weeping woman trying to comfort him. His soccer shirt was torn and bloody, one leg twisted at an unnatural angle. Ziad guessed he was five or six.

'What happened?" Hazan asked no one in particular.

"An Israeli helicopter fired a missile at a car," several voices replied. "The boy was playing nearby and was hit by the debris."

Hazan kneeled down and examined the boy, gently peeling away the remnants of his trousers from the wound. The boy's eyes were wide and unseeing, his breathing labored and shallow. The shrapnel had nearly severed his leg, although someone had applied a rough tourniquet to stem most of the bleeding. Hazan had seen enough injuries to know the boy was dying.

"We must get him out of here quickly."

Hazan gently picked up the boy and carried him to the ambulance to place him on the gurney inside. He climbed into the rear of the ambulance and sat next to the boy, who continued to whimper with pain. Hazan wished he could alleviate the boy's suffering, but he was a man of violence, not medicine. The needles, syringes and bottles in the ambulance were merely props to him. Hazan could only watch as the boy struggled. For the first time in years, Hazan prayed to *Allah*, asking for forgiveness for causing a child pain. Hazan suddenly felt the boy's small hand touch his, which he took as a sign that *Allah* understood and offered forgiveness.

The ambulance raced through the streets of Gaza City, Ziad adroitly weaving in and out of the traffic. Soon, the buildings fell away and the road narrowed to two lanes before entering a barren area that had been cleared of any structures. A security fence topped with barbed wire marked the Israeli border and a deep ditch two meters wide ran along both sides of the fence.

Hazan knew there were two security check points—the first manned by Palestinian security forces and the second by the Israeli Defense Force. The Palestinian check point was merely a small shack by the side of the road manned by twenty armed men wearing ragged, mismatched uniforms and armbands identifying them as members of the Palestinian security force. The Palestinian guards quickly waved them through without checking either their identification or the ambulance.

The road approaching the Israeli checkpoint was filled with both pedestrians and vehicles waiting to cross into Israel. Ziad swung the ambulance onto the edge of the road, siren blaring and honking his horn. The waiting cars and pedestrians moved to the side, allowing Ziad to slip past.

The Israeli checkpoint was a series of concrete barriers set up to allow only one car forward at a time. Four tanks and several machine gun emplacements overlooked the checkpoint and a nearby parking lot held military jeeps, a troop transport truck and two Jewish ambulances. There were at least a hundred soldiers milling about the entrance gate, some checking identification and searching cars and the armed remainder standing guard, poised to repel any potential attack. Palestinian extremists rarely attacked the checkpoint, due both to the heavily armed soldiers and the fact that any assault would seal the border for days and create hardship for those few Palestinians permitted to work in Israel.

"I hope our ID is good enough," Hazan said.

"They are. I bought them from my source at the hospital," Ziad replied.

As they approached the checkpoint, Hazan stuck his pistol under the mattress of the boy's bed. He knew he should have left the gun behind, but he felt naked without it. His greatest fear was to be arrested unharmed by the Israelis; he preferred to go out in a blaze of gunfire.

"Let me do the talking," Ziad said, as he rolled down the window. "I've done this crossing before."

A soldier held up his hand ordering them to stop. Three more soldiers warily approached the ambulance, one pointing an Uzi submachine gun at Ziad.

"*Shalom*," Ziad said in Hebrew. "Please," he continued, switching to English. "We have child hit by helicopter missile. We take him to specialist hospital. To Jerusalem."

"Papers," asked the first soldier, who wore a sergeant's insignia. A curly haired young man with acne, he had an unwavering, steely gaze.

Ziad handed over both IDs. "Please, the boy is very serious. Very hurt."

As the sergeant examined the identification, another soldier walked around to the rear of the ambulance. He peered in through the rear window before banging on the door and asking Hazan to open up.

Fearful the soldier suspected something, Hazan slowly opened the door. As if on cue, the injured boy called for his mother. The Israeli soldier leaned inside the rear compartment and examined the youth's face before pulling back the covers to look at the wounds. Hazan held his breath, fearing the soldier would recognize that the boy's wounds had been cleaned and dressed by an amateur, not a paramedic. Fortunately, the boy's obvious pain and the blood seeping through the bandages convinced the Israeli the wounds were real and needed urgent medical care. The soldier stepped back and nodded to his watching companions.

The Israeli sergeant continued to examine the pictures on the identification cards. "This picture doesn't look like your partner," he said to Ziad.

Hazan's hand inched toward the gun hidden beneath the mattress.

Ziad merely smiled. "He's ugly, never takes a good picture. Even his wife thinks so."

The sergeant chuckled although he still looked dubious. "You look familiar. You came through here yesterday, right?"

"Yes. I'm new driver. I went to Jerusalem to get supplies and learn the route."

The soldier in the rear of the ambulance pointed to the cases and duffle bags holding the bombs and radioactive material. "What's in those?"

"Medical equipment and supplies," Hazan responded.

"Open them," the soldier said, closely watching Hazan.

Hazan knew their deception was about to be discovered, so he decided to appeal to the soldier's guilt.

"We don't have time. The boy is dying!" he cried, gesturing wildly. "You're going to kill him. He needs a doctor!"

"Open it," the soldier ordered as his companions pointed their Uzis at Hazan.

Hazan shrugged, knowing he'd never reach his hidden gun in time. He decided to open the first case, which was actually filled with medical supplies, and hope the soldiers would be satisfied and not search the remaining cases.

Hazan put the unlocked case on the ground. He purposefully struggled with the lock, grateful the wounded boy continued to whimper with pain. The case popped open and the soldier rifled quickly through the contents.

"Now the other cases."

Desperate, Hazan prepared to launch himself at the soldier.

Suddenly, a huge explosion occurred behind them.

Hazan turned to see several cars perhaps fifty yards away consumed in flames and the bodies of two Israeli soldiers lying on the ground. Several nearby cars were trying desperately to drive away while pedestrians fled in all directions. The screams and shouts added to the confusion.

"Get out of here," the Israeli sergeant snapped. "Before I shoot both you damn Arabs."

Hazan threw the medical case back into the ambulance and jumped inside. The soldiers were already running toward the scene of the explosion. Ziad turned the siren back on and drove across the border and into Israel.

"That was fortunate," Hazan said, still trying to control his trembling.

Ziad chuckled. "I don't believe in fortune. Call it good planning and timing."

"You arranged for the explosion?"

"Yes. A car bomb. A friend was waiting in line. When he saw us pass, he got out and moved a safe distance away. I told him to blow up the car after the soldiers had talked to us for several minutes."

"I hope he killed some Jews at the same time," Hazan said.

"Perhaps. But more importantly, we've safely reached Israel."

They drove down the highway that led through Israel to Jerusalem. They had earlier decided to stick to the main road instead of trying to reach Jerusalem through the West Bank. Each route had its risks—a Muslim ambulance on Israeli roads was rare and might be pulled over. But the road through Israel was far more direct, better paved and without roadblocks. The primary West Bank roads were reserved for Israelis and filled with army roadblocks. Although they could take side roads through the West Bank to avoid the roadblocks, the route was much longer and there was always the possibility of temporary checkpoints. Ziad figured the presence of their injured patient and fake identification would satisfy even the most suspicious Israeli soldier or policeman.

Traffic was light and they made good time. Hazan watched the dry, desert landscape roll past, thinking about the thousands of years his forefathers had lived on such historically rich, yet unforgiving land. His grandfather once farmed a small olive tree grove outside Jerusalem, but the land had been seized thirty years ago to house the ever expanding population of Jewish settlers. Prosperous looking small towns dotted the countryside, the detached single family homes similar to those he'd seen in pictures of American suburbs.

Angrily, Hazan contrasted the prosperity of the Jewish state to the harsh conditions experienced by his people. He refused to credit the "Jewish Miracle"—the remarkable accomplishment of the Jewish people in creating a modern, prosperous country from a resource-poor desert while fighting five wars. He never asked why his people continued to farm, trade and live in much the same way as their ancestors did centuries ago. He never admitted that Palestinian women were treated as second class citizens, limiting their contributions, or that Palestinian officials were notoriously corrupt.

Hazan never acknowledged the extraordinary level of Jewish determination, grit and sacrifice, only his envy of their success.

As they drew near to the outskirts of Jerusalem, Hazan stuck his head into the front seat.

"Ziad, the boy is dead."

Ziad sighed. "Then we'll pray for him. He served us well."

"What should we do with the body?"

"We'll keep him in back for now. If we get pulled over, he'll serve a valuable purpose."

Ziad gunned the engine and headed for Salwa's house in the suburbs of New Jerusalem.

In the rear, Hazan vowed vengeance. The Jews would pay for yet another young Palestinian's death.

Yes, this time, they would pay.

31

David stood impatiently on the street corner outside his hotel, raincoat drawn tight against the unseasonable cold. The early afternoon had turned sullen and dark, the sky filled with rare rain clouds that brought temporary life to the exhausted ancient land of Abraham, Moses and Jesus. The roads were slick and filled with puddles, causing traffic to move slowly. Perhaps a dozen people waited to board a nearby bus, a security guard scrutinizing each passenger looking for a possible suicide bomber. Even a toy bear clutched by a little girl was checked for explosives.

For David, the last twelve hours had been a disaster. After returning from the meeting with his father, David had tried to contact either Rachael or Moshe Rabin to relay his father's warning about an Islamic ambulance. Unfortunately, both Mossad agents were unreachable. David had finally tracked down Jack Reynolds in Istanbul, who promised to contact the Mossad. Rachael had finally returned David's call earlier that morning.

After hearing David's warning, she'd expressed her concern that his information might be a red herring. Although she agreed to notify her superiors, she had warned him that the Mossad was leery of information gathered by American intelligence sources. Two hours later, she called back to say the IDF was sealing the Gaza border to automotive traffic. David was infuriated by the delay, fearful that in the interim, the nuclear bomb, if there was one, had already been taken over the border into Israel.

A Mercedes sedan pulled over. The rear door opened and Rachael leaned out. "Get in".

As David settled himself inside, Rachael greeted him with harried smile. Her hair was loose and flowing around her shoulders and David noticed that for the first time she wore a dress, which emphasized her long, shapely legs. If he hadn't been aware of her Mossad background and lethal training, David might have mistaken Rachael for just another young, pretty businesswoman.

"Have you heard anything?" David inquired.

"The Gaza border remains sealed and only pedestrians have been allowed to cross into Israel. If any Islamic ambulance tries to cross the border, the IDF will seize and search them. We've also sent a nuclear bomb detection team to the border that's capable of identifying and disarming a nuclear device."

"Have any ambulances tried to get across?"

"Two so far. Each was searched and nothing was found."

"How many ambulances crossed in the past twenty four hours?"

Rachael shrugged. "We don't know for certain. The checkpoint near Rafeh remembers three coming through—one late last night and two early this morning. Two had patients inside and the third was empty."

"Everyone's papers were in order?"

"Yes. The ambulances were searched. Nothing was found."

"Where was the empty ambulance going?" David asked.

"To a repair shop outside Bethlehem. The Gaza auto shops don't have the necessary parts for ambulances."

David shifted uncomfortably. "That must be the one we're looking for."

Rachael shook her head. "We sent a team to the repair shop. The ambulance was there. No traces of radiation were found."

"Shit," David muttered. "Then it must be one of the other two ambulances."

"Finding them won't be easy. There are numerous Red Crescent ambulances in the West Bank and even some inside Israel. The two ambulances were supposedly taking their patients to see specialists at hospitals in Jerusalem. We're checking the admissions records to see if we can track down the ambulances."

"I wish there was something I could do," David said anxiously. "I feel so helpless."

Rachael cleared her throat. "It's possible, you know, that your father was lying to mislead us and take our attention away from the real threat."

David shook his head. "I considered the possibility. But he recognizes the damage a nuke would do to the Palestinian cause."

Rachael turned so that she could look directly at him. "Don't you find it odd that after all these years, he finally contacts you last night? That he offers up potentially important information to stop a Palestinian terrorist attack?"

David's eyes flashed and he restrained his anger. "Make your point."

"Don't forget he's a sworn enemy of Israel. What better way to mislead us than by passing on false information about an ambulance? Obviously it was emotional for you to see your father again, which meant that you probably didn't ask many questions."

"Are you saying I was compromised? That I didn't do my job properly?" David asked angrily.

Rachael looked at him appraisingly. "Under the circumstances, it's possible."

"Damn it Rachael, he wasn't lying," David said vehemently. "Does the Mossad really believe his warning is just a red herring?"

"They think it's possible. I don't." Rachael frowned, the dark circles under her eyes speaking eloquently of a sleepless night. "I trust your instincts on this one."

"Thanks," David replied gratefully. "But I hope I'm wrong."

Rachael looked out the window. "Look, the border will remain sealed until we can figure out if there really is a nuclear or dirty bomb in Gaza. All our sources are focused on finding a bomb, if it exists. Until then, the border stays closed."

"In the meantime, we should track down those ambulances."

"Don't worry. I said that we don't trust your father, not that we wouldn't check out his information. We'll find those ambulances. We have to. We can't afford to take any chances."

✳ ✳ ✳

Ziad parked the ambulance in front of Salwa's modest house in the outskirts of Jerusalem. He detested the prosperous-looking Jewish neighborhood, the neat row of houses, tidy yards and late model automobiles lining the street. He recalled that years ago the entire hillside had been an open field owned by a Palestinian and filled with flocks of sheep. But after taking the West Bank during the 1967 war, the Israeli government had seized enormous swathes of Palestinian land that were not properly documented. Although Palestinians had farmed or grazed the land for centuries, many did not have the legal paperwork their new Jewish rulers required. As a result, many Palestinians, even entire villages, were thrown off their land. This continuing source of Palestinian anger was a primary reason why many Palestinians would never accept Israel until the land reverted to its original owners.

Ziad was gratified to see the police van of Salwa's Jewish boyfriend parked in front. He had called Salwa about a half-hour ago from the highway, letting her know they'd arrive shortly. After leaving the Gaza Strip, the ride through the West Bank to Jerusalem had been uneventful.

So far, everything was going as planned.

"Stay here until I signal for you," Ziad said to Hazan.

He got out and moved up the walkway to Salwa's house, glancing around to see if any neighbors were watching. He saw only two boys playing nearby, one pretending to be a Jewish soldier and the other a Palestinian terrorist.

Ziad straightened his uniform and knocked. He heard footsteps and the door opened. It was Salwa, her face tense and worried.

"Where is he?" Ziad whispered.

"In the bedroom," she replied.

"His gun?"

"Out in the living room."

"Get it."

Salwa stepped aside to allow Ziad to slip past. She closed the door and followed.

"Darling, who is it?" called a male voice from the rear.

"No one, Yitzhak," she replied. "Just a salesman I got rid of."

"Come on back to bed. I'm getting lonely."

Salwa pointed at the gun and holster lying on the sofa in the living room. Ziad picked up the gun and whispered, "Call him out here."

"Sweetheart, can you come here please?" Salwa called out.

There was the sound of movement in the bedroom before a short, naked man walked into the room. When he saw Ziad, he stopped in surprise, looking slightly ridiculous with his large belly swaying above his shriveled manhood.

"What's this?" Yitzhak asked. "Who the hell are you?"

"On the floor," Ziad replied. "Now!"

"Shira, what's going on? Is this a robbery?"

"Down. Now!"

Yitzhak complied, his eyes never leaving Ziad's face. As he stretched out on the ground, Ziad picked up a pillow and moved across the room. He nodded to Salwa who turned up the stereo. Ziad folded the pillow over the gun and fired, the telltale crack drowned out by the music. Yitzhak lay there unmoving, his skull splattered on the rug from the force of the bullet.

Salwa suddenly grew pale at the sight of the blood and splintered skull. Clutching her hand over her mouth, she dashed for the bathroom. Ziad waited patiently until Salwa returned, still white-faced, but with a determined look as if forcing herself to go forward.

"He was a Jew," Ziad said coldly. "He deserved to die."

"I know. But still..." Salwa replied, her voice tailing away. She was clearly sickened by the death of Yitzhak and the blood.

"I know it's hard," Ziad said. "But we had no choice."

"Won't the neighbors have heard the shot?"

"Not with the music and pillow. Open the front door and give Hazan the all clear signal."

As Salwa walked to the front door, Ziad grabbed a blanket from the couch and threw it over Yitzhak's body. He then went into the bedroom to get the police uniform that hung over a chair. When he returned to the living room, Hazan was waiting.

"Hazan, take this uniform and gun belt and put them on."

As Hazan began undressing, Ziad turned back to Salwa.

"Go to the hotel to pick up the *ulama*. He knows what to do. I'll be waiting for your call in an alley several blocks from the entrance to the Old City. Make sure no one else calls an ambulance when the *ulama* has his fake heart attack."

"I understand." Salwa smiled tremulously; now that the moment had arrived, she appeared somewhat uncertain.

"Go on," Ziad encouraged. "It'll be fine. This is the right thing to do."

Salwa bit her lip, nodded and rushed out the door. Ziad turned to examine Hazan, critically examining the fit of the uniform.

"You almost look like a Jew."

"*Allah* save me," Hazan exclaimed with a smile.

"You understand the plan?"

Hazan nodded. "I wait here. After Salwa calls you about the *ulama's* heart attack, you'll call me. Then I drive the police van down to the Wailing Wall plaza and park in the lot at the plaza entrance. Depending on the situation, I either set the bomb off immediately or set the timer and walk away."

"I don't think you should leave the vehicle," Ziad said. "Should someone get suspicious, you can always set the bomb off immediately."

"I'll manually set the timer," Hazan said calmly. "I know I'll die in the blast, but I'm prepared."

"Come. We still need to move half the cases from the ambulance to the police van."

They walked onto the front porch and stopped to gaze out at the vista spread before them.

"Look!" Hazan cried, pointing toward the Old City.

The clouds overhead had parted, pierced by a ray of light that stabbed down dramatically to strike the Temple Mount. The sunlight sparkled as if alive or trying to say something. For a moment, they stood in silence, certain they were witnessing a message from *Allah*. Although neither man was particularly religious, the panoramic view, light, clouds and moment all came together, lifting them to a higher place than ever before. It was if *Allah* had spoken and blessed their mission. They stood transfixed for a moment before turning to look at each other.

"We must hurry," Ziad said.

They removed four cases and duffle bags from the ambulance—two containing a conventional bomb and the other two containing the Ukrainian radioactive waste—and put them in the rear of the police van before covering them with a tarp.

After he closed the door, Ziad turned to face Hazan. He searched for something dramatic to say befitting the momentous occasion, but the many words became jumbled. Instead, he merely held out his hand.

"Good luck," he said.

"To a free Palestine!"

They embraced briefly before Ziad climbed back into the front seat of the ambulance. Hazan waved farewell and turned back up the path toward Salwa's house to wait for Ziad's phone call.

Neither man noticed that the two boys who earlier had been playing near Salwa's house were now hiding behind a nearby car. Two young boys who were exceedingly curious about the sudden appearance of a Palestinian ambulance and the apparent friendship of an unfamiliar Israeli policeman with the Palestinian driver. Two young, talkative boys who were on their way home for lunch with their father, who was a Mossad agent assigned to watch a visiting Saudi Arabian *ulama* named Turki al Faisal.

32

Salwa took only fifteen minutes to drive from her house to the hotel where the *ulama*, Turki al Faisal, was staying. After leaving her car with the valet, Salwa walked through the hotel lobby until she reached one of the enclosed booths with a house phone. While waiting for the operator to connect her to Al Faisal's room, Salwa looked around the lobby and noticed a man dressed as a tourist surreptitiously watching her. She shivered with nervousness and fear, wondering if the man were following her or if he were just admiring her as a woman.

The *ulama's* aide answered the phone.

"I'm downstairs," Salwa said. "Everything is ready for our tour."

"We'll be downstairs shortly."

Salwa replaced the phone and tried to remain calm. Even if she were being followed, her actions for the next hour wouldn't raise any suspicions. She had decided to follow the typical route of one of her tours—a leisurely walk to the Old City through the Damascus Gate, along the *Souq Khan as-Zeit Street* until they reached the narrow alley that led to the Church of the Holy Sepulcher. Anyone following them would quickly become convinced she was merely taking the *ulama* on a tour of the Old City.

Salwa still was shaken and remorseful about Yitzhak's death A decent man, he had treated her well and even talked about a future together. With a shiver, she recalled the shiny brightness of Yitzhak's blood on the carpet—it looked no different than that of her late husband and child. Salwa closed her eyes, trying to summon up the hatred and despair that had ruled her emotions for the last few years. Repeating the names of her dead loved ones, she felt her resolve return.

The *ulama* swept into the hotel lobby, dressed in the flowing black robes and wearing a haughty expression befitting his position as one of the most important religious figures in Saudi Arabia. His leathery face was heavily lined, but his sprightly step and lively eyes belied his age. Al Faisal was trailed by an unobtrusive aide, a dour looking, young *imam* who glanced around nervously.

Salwa wondered if the *ulama's* aide knew about their plan or if he'd be shocked when his superior suddenly collapsed in the Church of the Holy Sepulcher.

"I see you in *Allah's* good graces," the *ulama* said. "I'm ready to go."

Salwa led the way out of the lobby. As they reached the street, Salwa wasn't surprised to see the man she had noticed in the lobby appear behind them. Ziad had warned her that the *ulama* might be followed. After all, he was considered an ardent enemy of Israel.

They walked along the street, Salwa struggling to focus on giving her typical guided tour speech. She found it comforting to slip back into speaking Arabic after months of speaking only English or Yiddish. Walking along with the *ulama*, Salwa felt at peace, knowing her mission was endorsed by an important religious figure. Although she'd never been religious, there was something comforting about the silent, elderly *ulama* next to her. He didn't speak or even ask questions, his gaze darting around to take in the sights and sounds of Jerusalem.

She was looking forward to the end of her task and seeing her husband and child again.

✳ ✳ ✳

Rachael put down the cell phone and looked at David. "Turki Al Faisal just left his hotel. Shira, the tour guide who met with him yesterday, came by and picked him up. They're walking toward the Old City. The *ulama's* aide is also with them."

"How many agents are trailing them?"

"Just one. They caught us in the middle of a shift change. We also pulled several agents off the *ulama* this morning to hunt for the ambulance."

David nodded and looked down at his coffee cup. He didn't like the fact the *ulama* had left his hotel about the same time that the Palestinian ambulance had disappeared somewhere inside Israel. Then again, if the *ulama* had been ill, perhaps he was just feeling better.

Rachael's phone rang and she snapped it off the table. She listened carefully for a few minutes before hanging up.

"That was one of our men. He said his son was playing down the street and saw a Palestinian ambulance pull up. Supposedly the driver and an Israeli policeman talked and then the ambulance drove off."

David leaped to his feet. "Let's go!"

✳ ✳ ✳

Hazan Qwasama peered out through the flowery window curtain of Salwa's house, more out of habit than curiosity or concern. As a wanted man always on the run, Hazan was used to looking over his shoulder, wondering if the pedestrian following was just a shopper or an Israeli agent. Even in supposedly safe Arab countries such as Saudi Arabia, he always slept with the doors locked and a gun under his pillow. One never knew.

Hazan noticed the man walking past looked familiar. He realized the same man had passed by Salwa's house several minutes before. Hazan watched closely, noticing how the man turned his head slightly toward the house so he could examine everything as he walked past. Hazan stepped away from the window and picked up his gun. He didn't know why the stranger was interested in the house, but he couldn't afford to take any chances. Hazan shoved the pistol into his belt and walked out the front door.

Hazan saw the man had stopped in front of the neighboring house and was talking on his cell phone. Hazan proceeded down the front steps to the police van. There, he opened the door and leaned inside, pretending to look for something. As he had hoped, the stranger walked back towards Hazan to see what he was doing. When the man was perhaps five feet away, Hazan pulled out his gun and turned to face him.

"Keep your hands where I can see them. Drop the cell phone."

Although startled, the man did as instructed. He was a short, dark haired Israeli with a prominent chin and thick lips. Hazan knew by the calm way the man reacted that he was a professional—a policeman perhaps, or, even worse, IDF or Mossad. If so, then his phone call had probably been to his associates.

Hazan might have only a few minutes before the authorities arrived.

"Who were you talking to?" he asked angrily, keeping the gun close to his body so that anyone observing them couldn't see the weapon.

The Israeli just stared back and shrugged.

"Move into the house. Quickly."

Hazan glanced around the street, seeing only a small boy at the end of the block. They began moving toward the house.

"Who are you?"

"Quiet." Hazan snapped.

"I was curious about the police van. Please, I meant no harm."

Hazan was not fooled by the stranger's words or sudden change in the tone of his voice. Hazan was certain the man's sudden cooperation and attempt at conversation were intended to keep him occupied until reinforcements arrived.

Once inside the house, Hazan shut the door. The Israeli walked into the living room, Hazan following close behind. Hazan then fired twice into the stranger's back. The man crashed to the floor, a pool of blood quickly forming. Hazan knew the neighbors had heard the shots and would call the police. But by the time they arrived, he'd be gone. Hazan stepped over the body and grabbed the keys to the police van. He reloaded his pistol and bolted out the front door.

As he ran down the steps, Hazan heard police sirens in the distance.

✳ ✳ ✳

Ziad drove carefully through Jerusalem, realizing a Palestinian ambulance in the Jewish-controlled areas might draw questions. Fortunately, it was the Jewish Sabbath and traffic was light. He passed through the streets of the New City until he reached the *HaTzanhanim Road* that ran alongside the walls of the Old City. There, he turned right until he reached *Jaffa Road*. After driving several more blocks, he turned down the alley he was seeking. He parked in front of a small warehouse with an attached garage. Ziad got out and unlocked the garage door. Then he backed the ambulance inside, leaving the door open so he could leave quickly.

Ziad was following the plan developed months ago by Shadi Muhana and Abdullah. Muhana had rented the garage to hide the ambulance temporarily before it entered the Old City. The garage was located only five blocks from the Jaffa Gate, the primary entrance for the few vehicles permitted inside the Old City walls. Most of the streets in the Old City were limited to pedestrians and any vehicle allowed inside needed a permit. It was one of the reasons Abdullah had selected an ambulance and developed the elaborate plan for the *ulama* to feign a stroke.

Ziad had memorized the short route inside the Old City from the Jaffa Gate to the Church of the Holy Sepulcher. Although difficult to navigate, the narrow streets were wide enough for an ambulance. The guards at the Jaffa Gate wouldn't prevent an ambulance, even a Palestinian one, from entering the Old City to attend to a sick, very important *ulama* from Saudi Arabia. Ziad knew the guards would be fearful of creating an international incident and let him pass without searching the vehicle.

The plan was perfect.

Ziad settled himself against the seat, lit a cigarette and waited for Salwa's phone call.

✳ ✳ ✳

Although Salwa continued to pretend she was just leading the *ulama* on another tour, she was very conscious of the Israeli from the hotel following them. Glancing over her shoulder, she could see the man keeping pace, trying to remain unobtrusive by keeping people between them. They walked along the rebuilt stone walls of the Old City, Salwa pointing out the places along the ramparts where, according to legend, something significant had occurred. When they stopped just outside the Damascus Gate, she leaned close to the *ulama* and spoke softly.

"The man in a dark blue shirt standing by the falafel cart is following us."

The *ulama* almost turned to look, but stopped in time. "Shall we get rid of him?"

Panicked and fearful they might be arrested before reaching their destination, Salwa nodded assent.

The *ulama* had a hurried, whispered conversation with his aide before Al Faisal motioned Salwa forward. They passed through the Damascus Gate, the imposing entrance a witness to so many historical moments. They proceeded down the *Souq Khan as-Zeit Street*, the main thoroughfare that split the Christian and Muslim quarters and led into the heart of the Old City. The cobblestone street was crowded with people, including many Hasidic Jews on their way toward the Wailing Wall to pray on the Sabbath. As they reached a crowd listening to a street musician playing a guitar, the *ulama's* aide moved off to the side. Salwa stopped to wait, but the *ulama* impatiently motioned her forward.

As they continued down the street, Salwa heard a woman scream and then many voices shouting from behind them. She turned to see the *ulama's* aide struggling in the grasp of several Hasidic Jews. At his feet lay the man who had been following them, a knife protruding from his back. Salwa looked up at the *ulama* as he grasped her arm.

Al Faisal nodded grimly. "We're no longer followed. Now, lead me to our destination."

Salwa nodded and turned to plunge into the crowd.

They were free from surveillance and would arrive at the Church of the Holy Sepulcher in ten minutes.

✳ ✳ ✳

Rachael braked and turned simultaneously, sending the Toyota sliding around the corner and nearly sideswiping a parked truck. David held on tightly to his seat, still terrified from their most recent near-accident only two blocks back. Ahead, he could see two police cars parked in the middle of the street, roof lights flashing. Several officers were standing outside a modest house with the front door wide open.

"This must be it," David said, knowing they were too late. Rachael had told the agent who had initially called her about the Palestinian ambulance to phone back after checking out the house. But he'd never called and they feared the worst.

Rachael slammed on the brakes and they jumped out. A police officer ran toward them. Rachael flashed her Mossad identification.

"What've we got?" she demanded.

"We got here five minutes ago. Neighbors reported shots fired. Two dead men inside. One of them a Mossad agent, according to his identification."

"Two!" David exclaimed. "And the other?"

"A policeman. House belongs to a Shira Friedman. We think it was her boyfriend."

"Shit!" David exclaimed, feeling as if he'd been punched in the stomach. "Al Faisal's tour guide!"

"My god, she's part of it," Rachael said.

"Any sign of the gunman?" David asked desperately.

The policeman shook his head. "He's gone. According to two boys play-ing nearby, one man was dressed as a policeman. He invited your agent inside and then re-appeared a minute later and drove off in a police van. Earlier, there was a Palestinian ambulance parked out front."

"Damn!" Rachael exclaimed, looking stricken. "Do you have an alert out for the van?"

The officer nodded. "Citywide."

Rachael grasped his shoulder. "Tell them it's urgent. I want every police officer and soldier in Jerusalem to drop what they're doing and look for both the van and the ambulance!"

The policeman looked uncertain. "I can't authorize something like that."

"Do it!" Rachael shouted, pushing him toward the police car. "We think there's a nuclear bomb in either the van or ambulance!"

The policeman blanched and ran off to his car for the radio. Rachael pulled out her phone and dialed another number. She let it ring five or six times before slamming the phone shut. "I can't reach our agent following the *ulama*."

David was thinking furiously. If his father had been telling the truth, then the ambulance held a nuclear bomb. But why would the driver stop here, kill two people and then take off again in the ambulance? Why take the policeman's van? Unless they moved the bomb into the police van. If so, then why did they take the risk of killing a policeman and taking his van instead of just using another car for the bomb? And why drive off again in the Muslim ambulance?

"Rachael," David said slowly as he was struck by an alarming thought. "Are there areas in Jerusalem that are sealed off to normal traffic, but permit police vehicles and ambulances?"

"Of course. Why?"

"If you were to set off a small nuclear device, what would be your target?"

"A Jewish site of historic or religious significance..."

"...that is only accessible by police vehicle," David finished.

"The Knesset building? Or the *Yad Vashem*?" Rachael said.

"What about the Wailing Wall?" David asked.

"No, no, no," Rachael replied vehemently. "It's too close to the Temple Mount and the Dome of the Rock and the Al-Aqsa Mosque. Those places are sacred to Muslims."

"But for religious significance, there's nothing more important than the Wailing Wall to the Jewish people," David said.

"No, no Muslim would risk it. It's too damn close to sacred Islamic sites."

Rachael picked up her phone and dialed another number. This time, it was answered on the first ring.

"Moshe," Rachael exclaimed to her boss. "We need every agent on the street." Rachael quickly explained the situation, including their suspicions about a potential high profile Jewish target.

David was suddenly struck by a another thought. "Rachael, do you suppose there might be two bombs?"

Rachael stopped dead in the middle of her sentence and looked aghast at David. "It's possible."

"That might explain why they took two cars—the police van and ambulance."

"Tell the police your suspicions," Rachel said, tight lipped. "I'll have Moshe tell the IDF and our agents."

David ran over to the police officer who was on the radio and relayed the warning. He then returned to Rachael just as she was hanging up the phone.

"More bad news," she said, moving toward her car. "They just found the agent following the *ulama*. He's been stabbed and the *ulama* has disappeared somewhere in the Old City."

David nodded understanding. "Then that's where we'll go. I've a hunch that if we can find the *ulama* and his guide Shira, we'll find the bomb."

"*If* there's a bomb," Rachael said, although her tone was pleading, as if accepting David's fears.

"I'm not worried that there's *a* bomb," David said, opening the car door. "I'm worried there are *two!*"

✱ ✱ ✱

Hazan had just turned onto the main boulevard that led out of the New Jerusalem housing development when a police car roared past, siren blaring and headed in the direction of Salwa's house. Hazan knew he'd been fortunate to leave in time. He assumed that either the man he'd just killed had earlier called the police or the neighbors, hearing the gunshots, had phoned. The dead stranger's sudden appearance had nearly been disastrous and Hazan thanked *Allah* for his escape.

The murders meant Hazan needed to deviate from their plan. Realizing the police would quickly make the connection between the dead men and missing police van, Ziad decided to drive directly to his target. Although he was supposed to detonate his bomb after Ziad arrived at the Church of Holy Sepulcher, Hazan knew he couldn't afford to wait. Besides, in the resulting panic and confusion, Ziad might find it easier to drive his ambulance through the Old City to the Church of the Holy Sepulcher.

The accelerated timetable made sense.

Relieved to have made a decision, Hazan headed for the entrance of the Wailing Wall Plaza to detonate his "dirty" bomb.

Hazan turned on the police radio to hear if they were searching for him. So far, nothing. He had already decided to remain with the bomb after he started the timer to ensure nothing went wrong. He envisioned himself standing beside the van watching the Jews praying at the Wailing Wall, moments before the bomb blew the entire plaza into oblivion and changed history.

Hazan left *HaHevi'im Street* and turned left onto *Sultan Suleiman Street*, which divided the northern wall of the Old City from East Jerusalem, still the home of many Palestinians. The reconstructed Old City wall rose imposingly on one side while numerous tourist shops and cafes were on his left. After passing the Damascus Gate, Hazan drove by the smaller Herod's Gate, which was the preferred way for most Muslims to enter the walls of the Old City. He then turned right on *Jericho Road*, the major thoroughfare that paralleled the Western Wall of the Old City and passed through the outer edge of the Valley of Jehoshaphat. From there, Hazan could see the entrance to the Grotto of Gethsemane where Jesus had often met with his disciples and the Mount of Olives, the rocky slopes now covered with ancient Jewish graves. To his right, a medieval Muslim cemetery lay between the Old City walls and the road.

The police radio crackled and a panicked voice announced that a heavily armed Palestinian terrorist was driving a stolen police van that carried a huge bomb. Hazan swore loudly, cursing his luck that the bulletin had been issued when he was perhaps two kilometers from his destination. He accelerated, hoping to reach the entrance to the Old City before being spotted.

Hazan saw the police car coming toward him at about the same time the driver saw him. The police car swerved to block the road, leaving no room to pass between the retaining wall on the right and the guard rail on the other side that prevented a car from plunging to the valley floor. Hazan knew he'd be unable to ram the police car successfully off the road. Besides, he would never be allowed into the Old City if his van were heavily damaged.

So he did the only logical thing—he slammed on his brakes and swerved to a stop, prepared to talk, cajole or shoot his way out of the situation.

✳ ✳ ✳

Salwa hurried along the *Souk Khan as-Zeit* Street, dodging tourists, Jewish worshippers and local shoppers, primarily Palestinians. She restrained her urge to run to their destination, knowing it would only attract unwanted attention. The *ulama* trudged gamely behind, obviously unused to such a rapid pace. His face was a mask of exertion as he strove to match her stride. Salwa slowed down to accommodate him and catch her breath; she was breathing heavily, more from tension than exertion.

Finally, they reached the alley that led up the slight rise to the Church of the Holy Sepulcher.

"Shira!" called a male voice.

Salwa turned and saw an American from her tour group the day before. He was wearing safari shorts, a Red Sox baseball hat and t-shirt labeled 'I love Jerusalem'.

"How are you?" the man asked. "Off on another tour?"

Salwa ignored the man and began walking quickly away.

"Hey, Shira," he called again.

Salwa and the *ulama* disappeared around the corner, leaving behind the jilted tourist, who complained bitterly to his wife about the snub.

Once they were out of sight, the *ulama* stopped to catch his breath. "Are we near?"

"Perhaps another hundred meters."

The *ulama* nodded and again began walking. Enclosed by stone block buildings, the alley's cobblestone surface was worn smooth from the passage of numerous pedestrians. Small shops lined each side, most selling tourist trinkets for all three religions such as clothing, replicas of important buildings and religious artifacts. Salwa couldn't help but notice the paintings of the Church of Holy Sepulcher.

They emerged from the street into the small courtyard that led to the entrance of the Church of the Holy Sepulcher. The *ulama* stopped and mumbled a brief prayer, his eyes taking in the church's stone façade, worn smooth by the passage of the years. Most of the church was hidden behind the surrounding buildings, although the steeple rose high above, beckoning worshippers.

"So, this is where the prophet Jesus was crucified and resurrected," the *ulama* said. "Let's go inside. Slowly, we've got plenty of time."

Salwa nodded a greeting to the two guards as they walked inside the church. The *ulama* spent several minutes wandering around the main floor, taking in the ancient structure and the attached naves. Several times, he offered unintelligible prayers, as if asking forgiveness for the act of destruction that would shortly follow.

Salwa felt an urgency to end it all before she could reconsider. She approached the *ulama* and whispered, "Where will you suffer the stroke?"

"Here, near the entrance," the *ulama* replied, looking around the austere church interior.

Salwa felt her knees grow weak, but she steadied herself.

"Are you ready?" the *ulama* asked.

Salwa merely nodded.

Turki Al Faisal suddenly slumped to the ground, his flailing arm knocking over a large candelabrum. The resounding crash caused everyone in the church to look in their direction.

Salwa knelt down and pretended to feel the *ulama*'s pulse, before placing her head on his chest as if to listen for his heartbeat.

A guard rushed over to them. "Is he all right?"

"It's his heart. He has a weak one. I must call for an ambulance."

"I'll do it."

"No," Salwa said quickly. "He's an important *ulama* from Saudi Arabia. He may only be attended by a Muslim paramedic. I can call a Palestinian hospital."

The guard nodded and Salwa reached into her purse and pulled out her cell phone. She dialed Ziad's number.

"Yes."

"The *ulama* has had a heart attack. We need an ambulance."

"I'm on my way," Ziad said.

Hanging up the phone, Salwa realized she only had a few minutes to live. She glanced around the church, which reminded many Muslims of the Crusades so many years ago. The paintings, statues and weapons hanging on the wall glorified a triumphant age, when the Christian aggressors raped, pillaged and murdered in the name of religion. Even now, most Christians rarely acknowledged their violent past, only the sins of Islam.

Salwa smiled to herself. There, in the house of her enemy, she would have her revenge.

❊ ❊ ❊

Rachael drove like a woman possessed while arguing with David over the potential target for the bomb.

"It's got to be a target in the Old City," David insisted. "According to your agent, the tour guide was taking the *ulama* to the Old City."

"We don't know that the van or ambulance will meet them there. We need to follow the vehicles—they've got the bomb. I think it's more likely they strike a target in the New City, which is filled with Jewish people."

Rachael's phone rang and David answered, not wanting to distract her from the road.

A male voice spoke rapidly. "The police spotted the missing police van on Jaffa Road just outside the Temple Mount. An officer was blocking the street with his car."

"Thanks," David said and hung up. Quickly he told Rachael what the caller had said.

Rachael nodded. "I'll go there."

"Then drop me off at the Damascus Gate," David said. "That's where Shira and the *ulama* entered the Old City and near where your agent was stabbed. I'll see if I can find them."

They hurtled toward another intersection, scattering cars and pedestrians and causing one car to sideswipe another. David gripped the dashboard tightly, prepared any moment for a collision. Then they were through the intersection. Rachael accelerated, swerving past another car and onto the other side of road. She then swerved back to her side of the road, narrowly avoiding a head-on collision with oncoming traffic.

David spotted the wall of the Old City just ahead. He reached into his shoulder holster and pulled out his gun to ensure the safety catch was off.

As Rachael pulled up at the entrance of the Damascus Gate, David jumped out.

"Here!" Rachael cried out, leaning across the front seat with a picture clenched in her hand. "It's a picture of the guide, Shira. Find her and I'll take care of the police van."

David grabbed the picture and plunged into the crowd surrounding the Damascus Gate as Rachael pulled away in a scream of burning rubber.

✳ ✳ ✳

Hazan got out of the van slowly with his hands raised. The police officer had drawn his gun and was pointing it at Hazan. The police car completely blocked the road, preventing Hazan from passing on either side. The Israeli policeman was kneeling behind his open front door. Hazan kept his hands in plain sight as he called to the officer.

"I heard the bulletin on the radio, but I'm obviously not the guy you're looking for," Hazan called out in Yiddish, thankful again he was fluent in his enemy's language.

"What station are you from?"

"West Jerusalem, station two," Hazan replied, glad he'd taken the time to memorize his identification.

"Where's your partner?" the policeman called out.

"At lunch. Probably having a beer or screwing his mistress."

The policeman laughed and lowered his gun slightly.

"Here comes another police van," Hazan said, pointing behind the Israeli.

The officer turned to look, standing up slightly so that his upper body was no longer completely hidden by the car door. Hazan pulled out his gun and fired multiple rounds. The policeman's head disappeared in a spray of blood and his body collapsed to the ground.

Hazan ran forward and rolled the body away from the police car. Glancing around, he realized that there were several cars stopped in the road—two behind his van and another behind the police car. Fortunately, because it was the Jewish Sabbath, traffic on the road was light. Hazan pointed his gun at the nearest driver and the man ducked beneath the dashboard.

Hazan thought quickly. Clearly, the police were hunting for the van and he would never be able to pass through the checkpoint at the Wailing Wall plaza driving it. He needed to switch vehicles.

Hazan ran back to the van and opened the rear door. Reaching inside, he lifted out one of the bomb cases and carried it over to the police car. Setting it down, he looked inside the police car and found the keys still in the ignition. He popped open the trunk and put the bomb case inside. Then he ran back to the van and grabbed another case. By the time he returned to the police car, the other drivers had managed to turn their cars around and were racing away. Ignoring them, Hazan finished transferring the two duffle bags to the police vehicle.

Hazan slid behind the wheel of the police car, estimating that perhaps three minutes had elapsed since he shot the policeman. He backed up the police car until he was able to turn it around. Then Hazan drove quickly down the hill, feeling triumphant. He was going to make it!

Then he happened to glance up at his rearview mirror to see a car tearing down the road after him.

✳ ✳ ✳

After hanging up with Salwa, Ziad turned on the ambulance's flashing lights and siren. Pulling out of the garage, he accelerated out of the alley and along several side streets until he reached Jaffa Road. He followed the split level street past the Jaffa Gate, before making a screeching u-turn near the bottom of the hill and retracing his path. At the Jaffa Gate, several armed soldiers were manning a barricade. One of them motioned for Ziad to stop while the other two covered him with their Uzis. Ziad rolled down his window.

"Where are you going?" the soldier asked.

"A Saudi Arabian *ulama* just had a heart attack at the Church of the Holy Sepulcher."

One of the soldiers called out. "Sarge, we just got a call from the guard there saying they'd called for an Islamic ambulance."

"Okay." The sergeant stepped aside. "You know where you're going?"

"Of course."

Ziad drove away quickly, humming an old Palestinian folk song about the jilted woman having the last laugh as her former lover lay dying from eating poisoned grapes. He turned left onto a narrow street, driving slowly as he picked his way through the pedestrians that hindered his passage. The siren caused most to move aside, although he saw reluctance on the faces of some once they saw the Palestinian ambulance. He was also forced to squeeze past several cars that nearly blocked the narrow road.

But he was moving steadily forward and the Church was only a few blocks away.

✳ ✳ ✳

Salwa placed her cell phone on the cold stone floor and leaned over the *ulama*. He was lying motionless, his eyes closed and occasionally giving a fake moan. A small crowd had formed, although a tour guide was asking people to stand back and give the sick man some room. One of the guards had rushed back to the Church entrance, saying that he would wait outside for the ambulance. The other guard was standing nearby, looking at her strangely.

"What's the matter," Salwa finally asked, conscious of his stare.

"You called for an ambulance, right?" he asked.

"Yes, yes. A Palestinian one. The *ulama* can only be tended by a Muslim."

The guard looked back toward the entrance, but his companion had already gone outside. "Then why didn't you tell them where he was?"

"What?" Suddenly Salwa realized that when she called Ziad, she had merely told him an ambulance was needed, but not where.

"You never gave the ambulance your location. Why?" The guard was looking at her suspiciously and his hand strayed toward the pistol at his belt.

"Don't be absurd!" Salwa shouted, going on the offensive. "The *ulama* is dying!"

"Let me take a look at him." The guard moved closer and motioned Salwa to one side.

"No," she cried desperately. "You're an unbeliever. A Jew. You can't touch him!"

The guard pulled his gun. "Stand back. Something's not right."

Salwa raised her arms slowly and wondered what to do next.

✳ ✳ ✳

Rachael accelerated her Toyota down Jaffa Road and intently peered at the scene before her. A police van was stopped in the middle of the street, blocked from proceeding by a police car parked diagonally across the road.

Several other cars were also stopped, although Rachael could see the drivers running back up the road toward her. A uniformed policeman was climbing into the police car. A second one was lying spread-eagled and motionless in the middle of the road.

Rachael slammed on her brakes, sending the car skidding violently to one side. She managed to stop perhaps two feet from the abandoned van. She jumped out just as the police car drove away. Rachael stopped only long enough to make sure the van was empty. After getting back in her Toyota, she drove around the van before accelerating after the rapidly disappearing police car.

She reached across the seat to pick up her cell phone, but nearly lost control of the car as she skidded around another turn. She abandoned the effort, realizing she needed to focus on driving. The police car was perhaps a quarter mile away, turning onto *HaOphel Road*, which led to the Dung Gate, the entrance to the Western Wall Plaza. Rachael swore, certain now David was right—the Wailing Wall *was* the target.

Her only hope was that the police at the barricade entrance would be prepared to stop a man posing as one of their own.

✳ ✳ ✳

David ran through Damascus Gate, scanning the crowd for the tourist guide Shira. He wasn't sure which direction she might have gone, but decided he'd head along the *Souq Khan as-Zeit Street* until he reached the place where the Mossad agent had been knifed. He hoped to find someone who had witnessed the attack and perhaps seen the direction in which Shira and Turki Al Faisal had gone.

Perhaps a hundred yards inside the Old City walls, David came across a large group of people milling about. Shoving his way through the crowd, he reached the front. David recognized the prostrate form of the Mossad agent, a knife protruding from his back. An Arab dressed in a cleric's black robe was being physically restrained by several soldiers. Two policemen were questioning the crowd.

"Who's in charge?" David called out in Yiddish, stepping into the open area.

"I am," said one of the policemen. "Who are you?"

"Mossad," David replied, flashing the temporary identification Rachael had given him. "Anyone see who did it?"

"This guy," the policeman replied, pointing to the Arab. From the surveillance photos Rachael had shown him, David recognized Al Faisal's aide.

"It's critical I find out where this man's two associates went."

"Unfortunately, he hasn't said a word," the policeman said. "We'll have to wait until we get him back to headquarters for an interrogation."

"We don't have time." David knew Al Faisal's aide would remain silent even in the face of death threats. He looked around the crowd and shouted, "Anybody see another Arab dressed in cleric's robes with a woman tour guide? A pretty woman with brunette hair, perhaps five foot five or six. I've got her picture."

"Was her name Shira?" called a male voice.

David turned to face an American tourist wearing an 'I Love Jerusalem' t-shirt.

"Yes. This her?" David thrust the picture at the man.

"Yeah, sure. She was our tour guide yesterday. We saw her down the road about 15 minutes ago with a guy wearing a black robe."

"Where were they going?"

"They had just turned up the alley that leads to the Church of the Holy Sepulcher."

"Were they carrying anything?" David asked.

The man frowned, thinking. "I don't think so."

David turned to the police officer. "Follow me. Now."

He darted off through the crowd, shoving past those who didn't immediately move aside. He still was unsure what Shira and the *ulama* were attempting to accomplish. Neither was carrying a bomb, so if they did intend to destroy the church, then the explosives were already there.

It was the only scenario that made sense.

He ran down the street, shouting at people to get out of his way. Fortunately, the crowd parted as if the Red Sea before Moses. His footsteps echoed loudly in the narrow confines of the cobbled street and he could hear the ragged breathing of the trailing policeman. David rounded a corner and collided with a woman, sending both her and her shopping bags flying. He kept going, not even bothering to shout an apology.

He pounded up the slight hill that led to the Church, continuing to yell at people to get out of the way. His lungs burned and legs grew rubbery. His fear created a sinking, acidic feeling in his stomach that he was too late. He cringed at any sudden movement or sound, prepared at any moment for an explosion. David was unable to suppress images of the grainy movie footage of nuclear bomb tests in the Nevada desert and photos of Hiroshima and Nagasaki. He tried not to think about it, nor the fact that he was probably running toward his death.

David burst into the small plaza that led to the entrance to the Church. There, he saw a Palestinian ambulance.

All the doors were open and the ambulance appeared empty.

※ ※ ※

Ziad drove down the narrow alley that led to the plaza in front of the Church of the Holy Sepulcher. After reaching the plaza, he turned off the siren and lights and got out. A uniformed guard came hurrying up.

"Hurry," the guard said. "He's in pain."

"Help me with my equipment."

The guard ran around to the rear of the ambulance. Ziad opened the rear door and grabbed one of the cases.

"Careful," he said, handing the guard the case. "The equipment is fragile."

"Damn, it's heavy!" the guard exclaimed in surprise.

Ziad grabbed the case holding the bomb and followed the guard toward the entrance. At the doorway, Ziad put down the case, saying, "I grabbed the wrong one. I'll be right back."

He ran back to the ambulance and grabbed the duffle bags.. He quickly walked back to the entrance, where the guard was waiting impatiently. He pushed his way inside the Church, past a small group of curious onlookers. Ziad expected to see a prostrate *ulama*, solicitously tended by a distraught Salwa. Instead, he saw a second guard holding a gun on a frightened and speechless Salwa. The *ulama* was lying still on the ground.

"What's going on?" Ziad demanded, putting down the bag. "Why are you pointing a gun at this woman?"

"Papers!" snapped the guard. "Let's see them. Slowly."

"Joshua, what's the problem?" the second guard asked, placing the case he was carrying next to Ziad's.

"Something's not right," Joshua replied. "When this woman called for an ambulance, she never told them where she was calling from."

"You fool!" Salwa snapped. "Of course I did."

Ziad reached inside his white paramedic jacket, looking intently at Salwa. She understood his signal. She stood suddenly and began shouting, drawing the gaze of both guards. Ziad's hand emerged from his jacket holding a gun. He fired twice at the guard holding the Uzi, not even bothering to watch him crash backward to the floor before training his gun on the other guard. The doomed man stood there in shock, his eyes wide with the knowledge of his impending death. Ziad fired three times, warm blood from his victim spraying his face. The guard toppled backwards, his mouth working soundlessly.

The nearby tourists were screaming and surging toward the exit. Ziad quickly glanced at them to see if anyone had a gun, knowing many Israelis carried concealed weapons. Fortunately, most of the tourists were foreigners, predominantly American judging by the screams and shouts in English.

The *ulama* opened his eyes and looked up at Ziad. "Are you ready?"

"Yes."

Ziad assisted the *ulama* to his feet. The three of them were the only ones left standing in the church, although several terrified souls were crouched behind the wall hangings in a far corner in a desperate attempt to hide.

"You must leave," Ziad said to the *ulama*.

The elderly man shook his head. "No, it's too late for me. I'll stay with you. My time is over. I'm dying—I have cancer."

"But I thought Abdullah needed you in Saudi Arabia?"

Turki al Faisal smiled. "He doesn't need me. The Council of Senior *Ulama* knows what to do. I prefer to end it here."

"As you wish."

The *ulama* pulled a *Quran* from his robes and opened it to a previously marked page. He began to read aloud an ancient Arabic prayer that had probably not been read in the Church for hundreds of years. That it was read now, at the end and the beginning, seemed appropriate.

Ziad walked over to the case that held the bomb. He removed the key that hung around his neck and unlocked it. He stared at the mechanism and then reached for the timer switch. He knew that once it was started, there would be no turning back.

Thirty seconds later, the world would be a very different place.

✳ ✳ ✳

Hazan braked sharply, knowing he wouldn't get through the police barricade leading into the Western Wall Plaza if he arrived driving at a breakneck pace. He took several deep breaths, knowing he needed to be calm when talking to the armed guards at the entrance. He glanced again in his rear view mirror, wondering if the speeding car following him would catch up in time.

With relief, he realized the car was at least a half mile behind.

Hazan drove up the approach road that led through the Dung Gate and into the Western Wall Plaza. The road quickly split in two, the fork to the left leading up to the Jewish and Armenian quarters of the Old City. To his right, rose the walled compound of the *Haram ash-Sharif*, or, as most called it, the Temple Mount. The Al-Aqsa Mosque was in the nearest corner, the slender minarets stretching into the dull afternoon sky. Hazan could just barely make out the golden dome of the Dome of the Rock, which stood further back on the Temple Mount. The Wailing Wall extended along the base of the Temple Mount, demarking the ancient plaza that now held the two Islamic holy structures. Hazan knew the radiation poisoning of the Wailing Wall would be a psychological blow from which the Jewish people would never recover.

The entrance road to the Wailing Wall plaza led up a short hill to a barricade. Behind the barricade was a small parking lot, partially filled with police and military vehicles. A thick steel chain separated the parking lot from the stone-paved Wailing Wall Plaza. Hundreds of Jewish worshippers filled the plaza, most clustered in the far right corner at the base of the Wailing Wall. Hazan could hear a rabbi's mumbling, sing-song prayers broadcast through the loudspeakers scattered throughout the plaza.

Hazan braked as he approached the two soldiers standing in front of the barricade. One pointed a gun at him and the other motioned for Hazan to roll down his window. As the soldier approached, Hazan couldn't help thinking that all his training, trials and tribulations had prepared him for this moment.

"*Shalom*," the soldier said.

"*Shalom*," Hazan replied amiably.

"What are you here for?"

"I'm supposed to relieve one of the patrolling guards. Guess he got sick and asked to go home."

"Identification."

"Certainly." Hazan handed over the identification that Salwa had provided.

The soldier examined the paper closely, before looking back up at Hazan. "Did you know this ID has expired?"

"No," Hazan replied, trying to look surprised, his stomach churning. This was it then. He would have to fight his way into the plaza.

Leaning down, he reached for the gun under the front seat.

✳ ✳ ✳

Rachael cursed loudly when the police car she was pursuing arrived at the entrance to the Wailing Wall parking lot. She pressed down on the accelerator, fearful she would not get there soon enough. Rachael saw the next turn in plenty of time, but she miscalculated both the sharpness and her speed. As the Toyota entered the turn, Rachael felt the slide begin. She fought the wheel desperately, trying to correct for the skid. Unfortunately, she overcorrected and the car spun back the other way. Rachael tried to correct and again overcompensated, sending the car into an uncontrollable spin. The car bounced off one steel guard rail, then another, before flipping over and rolling completely several times before coming to a stop.

By that time, Rachael was already unconscious.

✳ ✳ ✳

For a moment, David was confused by the sight of the empty ambulance in the plaza outside the Church of the Holy Sepulcher. Then he heard gunshots. Galvanized by the sound and accompanying screams and shouts, he forced his tired legs forward. As he ran, David reached beneath his shirt and pulled a pistol out of his shoulder holster. He saw the crowd surge through the church entrance, the panicked tourists struggling desperately to get outside. David tried to fight through the crowd, but their panic and sheer numbers overwhelmed him and he was forced to step aside. Once the flood of people slowed, David plunged inside the Church.

With a quick glance, he took in the scene. There were three figures—Turki Al Faisal, the female tour guide and an unfamiliar man dressed in a Muslim paramedic's uniform—standing over an open case.

David brought his gun to bear on the group just as the paramedic turned with a pistol in his hand.

✳ ✳ ✳

The soldier interrogating Hazan looked up at the sound of squealing tires and the crunch of metal against metal.

"Someone missed the turn!" he exclaimed, staring back out at the main road trying to see the accident site. "Damn, the car rolled over completely. Abraham, call an ambulance!"

The second soldier hurried off toward a small guard building. Hazan looked in his rear view mirror, but couldn't see anything as Rachael's car had veered off the road and down the embankment.

"The poor guy," Hazan said, trying to sound sympathetic, although all he felt was relief. He kept his hand near his hidden pistol, waiting for the soldier to mention again that Hazan's ID had expired.

"Second time this week," the soldier said, his gaze still on the road. "Damn tourists take the corner too fast."

"Damn tourists!" Hazan repeated, shaking his head as if he'd made an important observation.

Distracted, the soldier handed back the identification badge to Hazan. "You need to get a new I.D. Two other officers had the same problem earlier. Supposedly, the Palestinians have managed to make copies and they've ordered everyone to get new I.D. immediately."

"Hard to believe," Hazan replied, releasing his grip on the gun beneath his seat and bringing his hand back to the steering wheel.

"Just take care of it by tomorrow. Otherwise, you won't get anywhere without the new papers."

"Where should I park?" Hazan asked.

"Next to the police van," the soldier replied, pointing to a parking space perhaps twenty yards away. "Plenty of space there."

"Thanks."

"Sure thing." The soldier and Hazan exchanged nods.

Hazan couldn't believe his luck. The parking spot was perhaps the closest one to the plaza and the van would shield him from the gaze of the two soldiers at the barricade. *Allah* was indeed looking over him.

He parked the police car and got out. Glancing around to see if anyone was watching, he walked around to the trunk and popped it open. He lifted out the case holding the bomb and placed it on the ground. Removing the key from around his neck, he unlocked the case. The ignition device was ready, surrounded by the plastic explosives. He reached for the timer and turned it on.

The countdown had begun.

✳ ✳ ✳

The Islamic paramedic raised his gun and fired at David. At the first sign of movement, David dove sideways. As he fell, David squeezed off several quick shots. Fortunately, he landed on his left side, absorbing the hard fall with his non-shooting shoulder. He heard the flat crack of his opponent's gun and felt the burning sensation in his left shoulder as a slug hit home. Rolling to a stop, David steadied his right hand and fired three more shots. The paramedic threw up his arms and fell backward, a shower of blood and skull fragments splattering the elderly *ulama*'s robes.

David lay there for several seconds, trying to identify any other threats. The Muslim paramedic was lying still. The *ulama* Turki Al Faisal stood there stupefied, clearly startled by the rapid events and unacquainted with violence. The female guide was screaming as she lay on the ground, her hand groping along the stone floor.

David realized she was searching for a gun. He also noticed the four large cases on the floor nearby, including one that was already open. He guessed the cases contained explosives.

"Stand back!" he shouted in Arabic. "Hands above your head."

Turki Al Faisal glanced around desperately and then went for the open case. David had no choice. He fired twice, his shots striking home and sending the *ulama* reeling backward. He glanced over at the woman, only to discover she had recovered the paramedic's gun and was bringing it around to point in his direction.

He fired again until the clip in his gun was empty.

By the time David stopped firing, all three of his assailants lay still. Blood was everywhere, even splattering the silk tapestry on the wall behind the bodies, a tranquil scene of Christ ministering to his disciples. The white medical cases were streaked with blood. But they were intact. David was intact. There had been no explosion.

He was safe and so was the Church of the Holy Sepulcher.

David staggered to his feet. He walked over to the three bodies, realizing the ambulance driver was still alive. The man was coughing slightly, blowing the red bubbles gathered along his lips. David assumed he was either Hazan Qwasama or Ziad Abbas. The Palestinian looked up. David thought he would see the man in agony, both from the pain and the failure of his plans.

Instead, the man smiled.

David froze, knowing defeat might yet be snatched from the jaws of victory. The dying Palestinian tried to speak, but his voice was too soft.

David knelt to hear the words.

"Second.....bomb...will...........still...de..feat...you....the..Pakistani......bomb....will....de...str..oy....you..

The man smiled again and stopped breathing.

David stood up slowly, wondering what he had meant. He glanced around at the three bodies. The huddled, shapeless forms spoke eloquently, if mutely, about the futility of life if all it had to offer was death. He felt nothing, only a great relief that he was still alive. There was no joy in his victory, no sorrow at the deaths he'd caused. He just was.

David strode to the church entrance, past the bodies of the two guards and ignoring the Israeli policemen who had suddenly materialized holding Uzis. He needed air. He needed to get outside.

As David stepped into the plaza, the sky over the nearby Wailing Wall erupted.

✳ ✳ ✳

Hazan watched in fascination as the timer on the bomb approached zero. Closing his eyes at the last moment, he waited for oblivion with a smile and last prayer for his people.

The detonation of the first bomb instantly ignited the second. The resulting explosion ripped through the police cars and vans in the parking lot, spewing metal, glass, plastic and flesh as far as a kilometer away. Hazan was killed immediately, as were the soldiers at the barricade and anyone else in the parking lot. For nearly a hundred meters in either direction, the blast tore through everything, even pulverizing blocks of stone. The hundreds of worshippers, sightseers and policemen in the southern part of the Western Wall Plaza were killed instantly. Many of those gathered near the Wailing Wall were knocked off their feet, although they suffered only minor nicks or cuts. Although the impact of the blast reached the Dung Gate, it didn't reach the *Ma'Aleh HaShalom Road* as the remnants of the Old City wall served as a shield.

The explosion tore apart the cases holding the finely pulverized radioactive material, which was then distributed by the blast. Then the wind rose, carrying the radioactive dust across the entire Western Wall Plaza and nearby sections of the Old City. The radioactivity was low enough not to cause any immediate damage, although those closest to the explosion who survived the blast would soon die from radiation poisoning. The Western Wall Plaza itself would be uninhabitable without radiation gear for perhaps ten years. The intent had been to not only kill, but to terrify and infuriate.

In the days that followed, that was exactly what would happen.

33

Parissa stretched her legs, tired of waiting for her appointment with Khaled ibn Saud in the stuffy reception area. Standing abruptly, she strolled back and forth, trying to keep her mind on the upcoming meeting. Through David, Parissa had contacted Ramzi Yousef and asked him to use his influence to set up a meeting with Khaled. The Saudi industrialist had agreed, telling Khaled that Parissa had urgent and disturbing information about the upcoming *hajj*.

Parissa intended to confront Khaled with several accusations to see if the Saudi was hiding anything. As the head of the *mutaween*, Khaled might be able to shed some light about the weapons she'd discovered in the warehouse the day before—if he wasn't involved. While at best it was a long shot, she was desperate, unable to think of a better course of action.

The key question remained: was Khaled the man behind everything?

As she paced, her thoughts turned to David, wondering if he'd made any progress on the search for Al Kabbar and his potential nuclear bomb. Their last conversation had been yesterday, when she informed him about the warehouse full of weapons. David had then revealed the real reason for his dogged pursuit of Al Kabbar and the concern about the potential smuggling of a nuclear or dirty bomb into Israel. Although initially upset David hadn't leveled with her, Parissa quickly realized he'd had no other choice. She then agreed to his request to have the Iranian intelligence network also search for Al Kabbar.

Finally, Parissa had asked David if he knew anything about 'medina moonrise', the last words spoken by the dead man in the warehouse. After two fruitless days of utilizing the resources of her agency, she'd turned up nothing.

Unfortunately David had answered in the negative.

"Khaled ibn Saud will see you now,"

Parissa followed the male assistant into a luxurious office furnished with antique furniture, oriental rugs and original oil paintings. Wearing a traditional desert robe, Khaled was sitting behind his desk reading a large, leather bound *Quran*.

"Thank you for seeing me," Parissa said, striding into the room.

Standing, Khaled pointedly ignored her outstretched hand and bowed slightly before motioning her toward an empty chair.

Parissa ignored the snub, realizing Khaled had invoked a traditional greeting as a way of establishing his male dominance.

"I'm not sure what I can do for you. I only agreed to meet you in deference to Ramzi Yousef."

"I appreciate your time," Parissa said as she sat down. "I should let you know I officially represent the Iranian government as well."

"Then why not go through more traditional channels?"

"What I have to say needs to be kept in the strictest confidence. Bureaucratic channels have a way of broadcasting information."

"What did you want to meet with me about?" Khaled's tone was interested but wary. He sat in the chair opposite her and picked up a tea cup.

"We believe an attempt to overthrow the Saudi monarchy will happen during the *hajj* this year." Parissa got right to the point as her intention was to rattle Khaled—both to see his reaction and perhaps pressure him into making a careless comment or mistake. If her and David's suspicions about Khaled were wrong, then perhaps he could become an even stronger ally.

Khaled took her claim in stride. "By whom?"

"Our sources indicate the threat comes from the *mutaween*."

Khaled's impassive expression never changed—either he was already aware of the *mutaween's* involvement or he had nerves of steel. "How is this revolution to come about?"

"We're not sure."

Khaled gave an ironic chuckle as he shook his head. "Rumors, nothing more."

Parissa felt a flash of irritation. "We discovered a warehouse filled with weapons."

Khaled leaned forward, for the first time appearing interested. "Where?"

"In Riyadh, down in the Alamechi industrial district."

"Give me the address and I'll have the army look into it."

"Unfortunately, the weapons are gone," Parissa admitted reluctantly. Zakoria had confirmed it that morning; clearly, the signs of their search—the dead body and smashed doors—had forced the relocation of the weapons. "But they're here in Saudi Arabia—enough to equip a small army."

"Then you've come to me with nothing but rumors and conjecture. As for the *mutaween*, you are, I'm sure, aware that I control them. By implicating the *mutaween*, you implicate me."

"Only if you approve of their plans."

Khaled scowled, his expression darkening. "I've heard of no such thing. There are always rumors about threats against the House of Saud. But to suggest I might be involved in an overthrow attempt against the monarchy is truly insulting."

"My apologies, I didn't mean to insult you." She hesitated, intending to make her next words all the more powerful. "Do you know a man named Al Kabbar?"

This time Khaled's face displayed some expression—recognition, alarm, interest? But Parissa wasn't sure which.

"No, I don't believe I do."

"He's a Saudi involved in the conspiracy."

"More conjecture?"

Parissa ignored his barb. "What about Abdullah? Have you come across his name?"

Khaled sighed theatrically. "Unfortunately, Abdullah is common name. I know many Abdullahs—including the King—but none I'd consider a threat to the House of Saud. What is the source of all this information?"

Parissa smiled and made an indeterminate gesture. "My apologies, but I can't reveal it. As Shia, we have our own eyes and ears in the Islamic Holy Land. Naturally, those men and women must remain unnamed."

Khaled scowled again, his fierce expression clashing with his finely chiseled, handsome features. "I'm sure the goal of your network here in Riyadh is to spread chaos when possible. In my mind, there's not much difference between the Shia and the Israelis. Someday, the Iranians and other Shia will be forbidden to visit our holiest shrines. That day, hopefully, will arrive soon."

Startled, Parissa considered his comment for a moment. Saudi Arabia's official policy promoted co-existence between the two Islamic sects and promised that the Shia could always visit Mecca and Medina. Khaled's comment indicated a rigid, dogmatic position consistent with extremism and religious fanaticism. Something the mysterious man named Abdullah might believe, but certainly not the supposedly balanced, Western-leaning Khaled ibn Saud.

Parissa was beginning to believe that Khaled was the man they were seeking.

Unless he was trying to try to confuse her or was merely posturing knowing that she represented the Shia. But then again, why?

She stood, realizing Khaled's words were essentially a dismissal. In addition, she didn't believe she'd learn anything more at that point.

"Well, you know how to reach me if you need," Parissa said.

"Thanks for your warning," Khaled said, his tone much more friendly than a moment before, as if trying to convince Parissa he was fully sympathetic of her claims and willing to listen. "You can understand my frustration and skepticism when all you bring me is rumors and conjecture. If you get hard, cold facts, then you must immediately call me."

"Of course."

Khaled once again gave a half bow after he ushered her to the door. She glanced back as she left, catching Khaled with a pensive, worried expression—while it was certainly not a friendly one, nor was it threatening.

On her way out, Parissa stopped by the desk of Khaled's assistant. Based on David's description, she knew it was a different man than the one David had seen in the *Fist of Allah* Pakistan training camp.

"Excuse me," Parissa said sweetly. "But are you Khaled's new assistant? I've met another man in the past."

"I'm filling in for Kareem until he gets back."

"Is he on vacation?"

The assistant shook his head. "No, he's taking care of something for Khaled."

"Is he here in Riyadh?"

"No, I'm not sure where he is."

"Well, thanks again for squeezing me onto Khaled's calendar," Parissa offered as she walked toward the exit.

Once outside, she glanced back over her shoulder, half expecting one of Khaled's men to come after her. On the surface, her conversation with Khaled had been unrevealing, the Saudi minister reserved and distant. None of her surprise references—the *mutaween*, Al Kabbar or Abdullah—had elicited much of a response from Khaled.

Which either meant he was the most unflappable person she'd ever met or the man behind everything.

Out of the corner of her eye, Parissa noticed two men in white robes suddenly emerge from a doorway and walk toward her. She knew immediately they were there for her.

Turning, Parissa darted down the street, looking for a defensible position or potential avenue of escape. Unfortunately, she was in Riyadh's historical area, where the buildings were clustered close together and pedestrian traffic exceedingly light. Glancing over her shoulder, she saw the two men break into a run. Turning the corner into an unpaved alley, she reached inside her *abaya* and pulled out a pistol. Unfortunately, the alley terminated against another building and there weren't any doors in the concrete walls lining the alley.

She had reached a dead end.

Parissa quickly took refuge behind a large garbage dumpster. As she settled into her hiding place, the two men ran around the corner of the building.

Both held pistols.

Parissa fired without hesitation, taking advantage of the element of surprise. Her first few shots took out the taller of the two men, knocking him to the ground. The second man dove to his left, seeking shelter behind a pile of wooden crates. Parissa held her fire, knowing she had only a precious few shots left. Her opponent laid down a steady barrage, clearly trying to keep Parissa pinned down.

Then he ceased firing. The moments ticked by, the only sound a faint murmuring from her assailant's hiding place. Parissa suddenly realized he was calling for reinforcements.

Clearly time wasn't on her side.

Glancing around the corner of the dumpster, she saw movement behind a cardboard box. She fired two shots. There was a scream and a pistol spun out into view. Parissa emerged from her hiding place and moved cautiously up the alley. A man lay groaning behind the pile of boxes.

Parissa knelt down and placed her gun against his head.

"Who sent you?"

He just shook his head, his expression fearful.

"Who sent you?" She smacked her gun against his head.

"Abdullah," he gasped.

"Who is he?"

"No one knows."

She could see by his expression he was telling the truth. "What do you know about 'medina moonrise'? What does it mean?"

"I'm not sure."

She cocked the pistol. "Then guess."

"I overheard something about the Red Sea. Just a mention, nothing more."

Parissa thought furiously. What could medina moonrise have to do with the Red Sea? Was it the name of a hotel, bar or restaurant? Then it hit her; Medina Moonrise must be the name of a boat. But why would a boat be important? Given Saudi Arabia's relative isolation and vast distances, most people chose to fly into the country. So why use a boat?

The answer was simple: to smuggle something into Saudi Arabia while avoiding the tight security at all airports.

Raising her gun, she struck the man on his head. He slumped to the side, still breathing but unconscious. Rising to her feet, Parissa smoothed her robe and put away her gun. She glanced over at the second man, but he was lying there unmoving, clearly dead.

Suddenly, she swayed unsteadily, a dull roar in her ears. With her adrenaline abating, Parissa felt nauseous and began to shake. She had never fired a gun before in anger, let alone killed anyone. Now, she'd killed one man and shot another. Everything felt dreamlike, as if she were floating outside her body looking down at a scene that involved a pure stranger.

Parissa knew later she would need to come to terms with her actions. For now, she didn't have the luxury.

Stumbling out of the alley, Parissa weaved down the street toward the taxi that had brought her there. She needed to call David immediately to convince him to come to Saudi Arabia. Parissa was now certain that Al Kabbar had used 'Medina Moonrise' to smuggle a nuclear or chemical weapon into Saudi Arabia.

With a sick feeling of certainty, she also knew where Al Kabbar was headed.

34

In the pale light of the waning afternoon, the Grand Mosque was extremely impressive and imposing. The setting sun glistened off the white stone walls, reflecting the crowns of gold on the 11 minarets surrounding the Grand Mosque plaza. The enormous open air interior held several golden domes and was surrounded by a 150 foot-high wall made of white granite and inlaid with intricate designs of colored stones. A large, multi-tiered depression near the center of the Grand Mosque held the *Kaaba*—the cube-shaped, 15-meter-high black structure that Muslims always faced during their prayers. The *Kaaba* was supposedly built by Abraham and his son Ishmael and contained the Black Stone, an ancient Islamic relic that dated back to Adam and Eve.

That evening, the Grand Mosque and encircling plaza held over a million worshippers dressed in an *ihram*, each head uncovered before *Allah* as a sign of modesty. Numerous loudspeakers enabled the prayers to carry clearly in the sweltering evening, occasionally followed by the murmuring replies of the sea of adherents.

Abdullah was standing on the balcony of a luxurious apartment building overlooking the Grand Mosque and surrounding plaza. He was impressed neither by the grandeur nor the religious significance of the Grand Mosque, but by the throngs of worshippers. As a masterful manipulator of people, Abdullah was envious of Islam's influence and the Prophet Mohammad's ability to control Muslims nearly fifteen hundred years after his death. There seemed to be no limit to what Muslims would give for *Allah* and their faith. For one of the few times in his life, Abdullah reluctantly acknowledged a force more powerful than himself, detesting the unaccustomed feeling of weakness, even inferiority.

Al Kabbar came out onto the balcony. He was wearing an *ihram*, the two pieces of white cloth worn by pilgrims.

"Any word?" Abdullah asked, although he knew the answer from Al Kabbar's excited expression.

"We've done it! Al Jazeer just announced that a radioactive bomb went off in Jerusalem near the Wailing Wall."

"Just the one?" Abdullah asked, in disbelief that his plan might have failed.

"The announcer also said several people were killed at the Church of Holy Sepulcher trying to set off a second bomb."

Furious the second bomb had been unsuccessful, Abdullah struck the railing with his fist in a rare display of anger. He wondered what had gone wrong or if perhaps Ziad's nerve had failed at the last moment. Feeling Al Kabbar's gaze on him, Abdullah brought his emotions under control. "Then we've succeeded. Even if the second bomb didn't detonate, it was discovered."

Al Kabbar smiled broadly. "It's a great moment for Islam. *Allahu Akbar!*"

No, Abdullah wanted to say. It's my triumph—*Allah* was merely an observer. Abdullah didn't believe in providence or good fortune, only the superiority of some men over others—himself above all others.

The two men stood together in silence for some time, although with vastly different emotions.

"Is the rest of the plan on schedule?" Al Kabbar finally asked.

Without answering, Abdullah turned away from the railing and beckoned Al Kabbar inside, closing the sliding glass door behind. The luxurious apartment interior resembled an ancient Egyptian Pharaoh's living quarters—silk curtains and drapes, gold embossed furniture and plush Persian carpets. Abdullah owned the two story penthouse condo; in fact he had financed and constructed the building several years ago.

Abdullah sat gratefully on the floor, leaning back against the large pillows that comprised the sitting area. He reached over and poured some wine into a bejeweled glass. Ignoring Al Kabbar's frown of disapproval, he took a sip, savoring the rich flavor of the '79 Rothschild. Abdullah then began discussing the second part of his plan, smugly enjoying Al Kabbar's open admiration and interest. Tonight, for just a short time, he would boast of his cleverness. After so many years of planning, he deserved it, even if his audience was less than desired.

"As you know, the bombs in Jerusalem were the first part of the plan. Before the second part occurs, we must manipulate both Western and Middle Eastern media. I've arranged for video tapes to be delivered to the international news agencies claiming that the bombs were the work of a new Islamic terrorist organization simply called *Jihad*. This new organization will advocate a holy war against the West and their lackeys, the Israelis."

Abdullah took another sip of wine before continuing. "During the next two days, numerous stories will appear in the media, inflaming the passions on both sides. In the West and Israel, Muslims will be blamed for the explosion. In the Islamic world, people will be told it wasn't Muslims, because the Al Aqsa Mosque was also damaged and radiation pollutes both it and the Dome of the Rock. Muslims will believe it must've been the Jews who set off the bombs against their own people in order to blame Muslims and justify the seizure of more land from the Palestinians."

Al Kabbar's eyes lit up. "Once again, the Jews will be accused of playing the false role of victim to justify their actions."

Abdullah nodded. "Exactly. Two days from now, you'll detonate the nuclear bomb you brought from Pakistan. Just think of the scenario. Neither side trusting each other, the Wailing Wall contaminated by a dirty bomb. An attack also made against the Church of the Holy Sepulcher, one of the holiest Christian monuments. Then, two days later, a nuclear bomb destroys the Grand Mosque in Mecca. At least a million will die."

Abdullah paused for dramatic effect, caught up in the magnificent horror and boldness of the plan. He waited until Al Kabbar met his gaze before continuing.

"Every Muslim will believe it was either the Jews or Christians, most likely the Americans, who destroyed Mecca in retaliation for the recent attack on their shrines. Who else possesses portable nuclear weapons? Who else but the descendants of the Crusaders and killers of the Palestinians, Chechens, Afghanis and Iraqis? Furious at the destruction of their shrines, the Christians and Jews responded with swift and terrible retribution—the detonation of a nuclear device in the Grand Mosque, Islam's holiest place. Perhaps it was a government sponsored attack or just a rouge element of the armed forces. It doesn't matter which one is blamed—Jew or Christian, the government or a rogue element of the military. Every Muslim will be enraged and demand revenge."

Abdullah took another sip of wine, enjoying Al Kabbar's rapt attention. "The West and Israel will deny any involvement. But they obviously are guilty. After Mecca is destroyed, the entire Muslim world will be ready to die for Islam and committed to driving the Americans and Jews from the Middle East."

Al Kabbar looked away. "So many will die."

"What are a million dead for the glorious new chapter of Islam? The Prophet Mohammad would gladly have traded the lives of a few for the salvation of many."

"But what if Muslims doubt the culpability of the West or Israel?"

Abdullah smiled, his eyes remaining cold and calculating. "That's where my Jewish-Palestinian-American comes in handy."

"This man, is he the one I nearly killed in Pakistan?"

"Yes. It's fortunate you didn't kill him. He still has a role to play. As a CIA spy, he's just the man to give final proof of the West's complicity in Mecca's destruction."

Al Kabbar chuckled. "I'm glad he'll bring about the very thing he is trying to prevent."

"We need him here in Mecca. And I know how to do it."

"What do you want me to do now?" Al Kabbar asked.

"Stay here, out of sight and out of trouble. I must go, but I'll return tomorrow."

"Then I'll take the opportunity to pray for our forgiveness in the Grand Mosque. To destroy the Grand Mosque is a terrible crime."

"But necessary."

Al Kabbar walked back over to the sliding glass door to stare out at the Grand Mosque. "It's so beautiful. I remember the first time I came here." His voice softened as if recalling the images of those long ago years. "I was only five years old. My family was too poor to fly, so we took the bus. All the passengers were in such a festive, happy mood. Making the *hajj* to Mecca brought us all closer together—as Muslims, as a family, but, most importantly, closer to *Allah*. It was the single greatest experience of my life. I don't want to destroy the Grand Mosque."

"Places can be rebuilt," Abdullah said gently, irritated of the need to constantly reassure Al Kabbar. "We need to spark our people, raise them up from the stupor imposed by the secular Arab governments and the Jewish and Christian unbelievers with their music, pornography, loose morals and dangerous ideas."

Al Kabbar remained silent for few moments before sighing. "I know, you're right. I'll wait patiently for your return."

Abdullah smiled. "I'll be back soon."

Abdullah reluctantly embraced Al Kabbar and then left. Once inside the private lobby elevator, he relaxed and leaned against the wall. He slid his hand inside his shirt and flipped on the safety switch of his concealed pistol. For a moment, he had feared Al Kabbar would change his mind and refuse to continue. Abdullah had been prepared to kill him if necessary. But he still needed Al Kabbar, who had one last task to perform—detonating the nuclear bomb in Mecca when Abdullah was safely a hundred miles away.

Abdullah sighed contentedly, his only regret that he had left behind a nearly full bottle of the Rothschild. It didn't really matter. Soon, he could relax and enjoy the successful completion of his plan after years of planning. At this point, Abdullah was certain nothing could stop him.

After all, no one ever had.

✳ ✳ ✳

After Abdullah left, Al Kabbar returned to the balcony, letting his gaze roam over the Grand Mosque and throngs of pilgrims, feeling blessed. He was still stunned by Abdullah's real identity, which had finally been revealed to him that evening. For the first time, Abdullah spurned the false beard and *keffiyeh* he had always worn during their previous meetings.

Now Al Kabbar understood why Abdullah was the right one to lead their endeavor.

Despite Abdullah's comforting words, Al Kabbar was racked by one last spasm of doubt about their plan. He prayed harder than ever before for guidance, knowing it wasn't too late to abort Abdullah's plan. The nuclear bomb was sitting in one of the bedrooms. He had only to pick up the bomb and walk out the door. Then, Al Kabbar could take the bomb and leave Mecca. From there, he could travel to a hundred potential targets. The American embassy in Saudi Arabia. Their military bases in Kuwait, Qatar, United Arab Emirates and Iraq. The royal residences of the House of Saud. He could take the nuclear bomb to America, to Europe, perhaps even to Israel. There were so many others who deserved to die, but he was about to kill devout Muslims praying at Mecca. Perhaps even take the life of his friends and relatives making the *hajj* this year.

Al Kabbar felt his resolve weakening, realizing his acquiescence was due largely to Abdullah's persuasiveness. He closed his eyes to pray for guidance before opening them to receive his answer. In the distance, he saw fireworks streak across the sky, the explosions casting a fiery light upon the alabaster walls of the Grand Mosque. He heard the accompanying booms of fireworks, as if the thunder of the artillery of approaching armies and marching feet of a million men. It was an awesome spectacle, marking the start of the Festival of Sacrifice, 'Id al-Adha.

Al Kabbar felt as if *Allah* had spoken. It would take violence and destruction to bring peace on earth and the triumph of the one true faith. Although Islam had been born in peace, it had been spread and defended by the point of the sword. For the first time, he was completely at peace with his decision.

It was time once again for violence.

35

David picked his way through the hospital corridor, stopping to examine every woman patient in an effort to find Rachael. The hallway was crowded with the injured and dying, many lying unattended on the floor. Most had been hurt in the blast that had ripped apart the Wailing Wall Plaza, some in the mad scramble that ensued. Blood was everywhere, dripped along the floor, smeared against the wall or caked in the hair and clothes of the injured. The scene was mass bedlam, the cries of the wounded mixing with the calls of those who had rushed to the hospital to search for their loved ones. Doctors and nurses ran back and forth, trying desperately to attend to every patient.

David's upper left arm still throbbed from his gunshot wound. After killing the false Palestinian ambulance driver, female tour guide and Turki Al Faisal, David had been examined by an American doctor who was one of the terrified tourists hiding inside the church. Fortunately, the bullet had just grazed David's arm. The doctor quickly cleansed and dressed the wound, ironically using some of the emergency supplies found in the Palestinian ambulance. The doctor had then hurried off to see if he could do anything for the victims of the explosion near the Wailing Wall.

Meanwhile, Israeli soldiers and policemen had sealed off the Church of Holy Sepulcher to question witnesses. After flashing his temporary Mossad ID, David had related his story. He had then tried calling Rachael, but her cell phone went unanswered. He was worried about her, as she had obviously failed to stop the other terrorist bomber.

Finally, David had tried going to the Wailing Wall Plaza to look for Rachael. He was stopped by the IDF soldiers who had sealed off the blast area. There, he learned that the explosive device had contained radioactive isotopes and Israeli soldiers in radiation gear were evacuating the Old City and surrounding areas. David's offer to help was refused. Unsure what else to do, he had gone to the nearest hospital to search for Rachael, hoping she was alive and among the wounded.

He continued to walk down the hall, trying to spot a familiar face.

"David!"

He turned and saw Rachael sitting with her back against the wall, holding a compress against her shoulder. Aside from her shoulder, she appeared to be fine. Then David saw her dazed expression—a horrified, sorrowful look with a vacant gaze, her eyes taking in everything and nothing. David knelt down and placed his hand gently against her cheek. Rachael started to sob uncontrollably, her breaths coming in large gasps, tears rolling down her cheeks.

"Oh God David, I failed."

"Are you alright?" he asked, not wanting her to dwell on it.

"I failed David. I saw him driving up ahead, but couldn't catch him."

"It's all right Rachael. You did your best." He sensed her failure had triggered the years of cumulative stress and traumatic experiences. She was teetering on the edge of intense guilt and remorse, restrained only by the fact that she hadn't yet fully absorbed the terrible tragedy. Like a tremendous blow to the head, the full impact was delayed.

"They're dead. All of them because of me."

"Don't talk that way," David said angrily, trying to stem her recriminations. "There wasn't anything you, or anyone, could've done. This time, they won."

Rachael turned away, her tears continuing unabated. David reached out to touch her gently on the shoulder. "Rachael, I have something important to ask you."

"All dead because of me."

"Listen to me!" David shouted.

"Dead," she mumbled. "All dead."

He grabbed her shoulder and shook her hard. "Rachael, you've got to focus! Tell me what happened."

"I'll try," she mumbled. Visibly struggling to control her emotions, Rachael haltingly told her story—how she'd seen the terrorist drive off from the aborted roadblock and given chase before losing control of her car and crashing. While trapped in the wreckage of her car, she'd heard the explosion and seen the plume of smoke rise from the Wailing Wall Plaza. Two passing motorists had pulled her from the wreckage and driven her to the hospital. Physically, she was fine, aside from a few cuts and bruises and a deep cut on her shoulder.

David knew the real damage was mental and emotional. Rachael would probably never forgive herself—it wasn't her failure to stop the bombing as much as the fact that her accident had prevented her from even making an effort. No one had forced her to crash by holding a gun against her head or swerving their car into hers. Rachael had simply taken the turn too fast and missed it. David sensed the knowledge would eventually consume her from within, a cancerous tumor that would grow unchecked even as she desperately tried to make amends. He doubted there was any amount of prayer or even redeeming actions that could provide a cure. With a sharp prescience, David realized a large part of Rachael had died that afternoon and the years ahead would grow increasingly bitter and empty.

"So you never actually talked with this terrorist?" David asked.

"No."

Quickly, David told her what the dying Palestinian had told him about the Pakistani bomb. Rachael stirred uncomfortably and looked at David with concern.

"Damn! There *is* a Pakistani bomb after all. Where the *hell* is it?"

"I don't know."

"We'd better find out."

David knew the time had come to challenge and revive her. "Don't worry, you rest up. I'll handle it."

"Like hell you will," she said, throwing off the blanket. "Let's get the fuck out of here."

✳ ✳ ✳

David drove through a Jerusalem gone berserk. Cars loaded with belongings jammed the roads, the inhabitants fleeing a city rumored to be poisoned by deadly amounts of radiation. The years of open warfare had never shaken the resolve of either the Israelis or Palestinians to remain; now, both fled Jerusalem from an insidious, unseen enemy that recognized neither friend nor foe. Drivers shouted and cursed at each other, many bundled in heavy layers of clothing in a hopeful and desperate effort to ward off radiation. Small groups of young Israeli men roamed the streets, savagely beating Palestinians and burning Palestinian businesses and homes. The radio reported that a large vigilante army of Jewish settlers, off-duty policemen and reservist soldiers was rampaging through eastern Jerusalem, unchecked by the authorities. Open warfare seemed possible, in fact, was almost a reality.

David was stuck in traffic on his way back from Rachael's house, having driven her there to get a change of clothes. They drove without speaking, each lost in their own thoughts. David was desperately trying to figure out what target the Pakistani nuclear bomb would be used against. According to the dying Palestinian, there was a second part to this terrorist plot. David feared it would be as horrific as the destruction of the Wailing Wall Plaza. By now, he knew the bomb that had exploded was a 'dirty bomb', as was the one he'd prevented from detonating in the Church of the Holy Sepulcher. David was certain Al Kabbar must have the Pakistani nuclear device. So far, both he and the bomb remained missing.

Where, when and how the second part of the plan would unfold, David had no idea.

David's cell phone suddenly rang. Filled with trepidation, he answered. "Yeah."

"David?" A woman's soft voice with the hint of an accent. David grew warm, as he recalled Parissa's upturned face meeting his.

"Parissa! It's good to hear from you."

"Can you talk? Is this line secure?"

"Yes. Where are you?"

"Saudi Arabia. I saw the news about the bomb. Are you in Jerusalem?"

"Yes. We tried to prevent the explosion, but failed."

Her voice grew concerned. "The other men that were shot? At the Church. Was that you?"

"Yes. I'm fine. Why are you calling?"

"David, it's gotten very tense here." Her voice was filled with concern, even fear. "The military leader of the *mutaween* returned from Egypt yesterday. He's been calling his key subordinates, telling them to be ready."

"Ready for *what*?"

"I don't know. But I think Khaled is the man we're looking for." She quickly filled him in on her meeting with Khaled. "I think he sent Al Kabbar to get a nuclear bomb."

David gripped the phone tightly. "Parissa, the Palestinian ambulance driver I killed today said something about another bomb."

"I think I know why. Today, I finally figured out what "Medina Moonrise" means. It's a boat moored in a Saudi harbor on the Red Sea. My people located it this morning and searched it. The boat was empty, but they found the body of the Captain."

David felt his stomach churn in anticipation. "And?"

"David, we found traces of radiation in the boat. We think they transported a nuclear bomb to here."

A wave of nausea hit David. "Shit! So there *is* a Pakistani nuke floating around somewhere."

"Yes. Al Kabbar must've brought it here from Pakistan."

"It fits," David acknowledged, the pieces falling into place.

"If the bomb is in Saudi Arabia, then the second part of the plan *must* involve Saudi Arabia. Get here as fast as you can."

"I'll be in Saudi Arabia shortly. I'll call you back and let you know our plans."

"*Our* plans?" Parissa asked suspiciously. "Who are you talking about?"

"An ally. Someone who knows Saudi Arabia and can tap into a broad network."

Parissa's sigh spoke volumes. "The Israelis?"

"Yeah."

"I don't like it, but I don't think I have a choice. I'll be in touch. David..." she hesitated then spoke quickly. "Be careful, okay?"

David couldn't resist grinning. "Don't worry, I will. We'll see you shortly."

David hung up and looked over at Rachael, who had overheard enough to become both interested and worried. David quickly filled her in on the conversation.

"Do you think they plan to set off a nuclear bomb in Saudi Arabia?" she asked. "Why there instead of here? Israel is the enemy, not the Saudis."

"I don't know," David said. "Perhaps they intend to use the nuke against a U.S. military base or the living compounds of foreign oil workers. Most likely the target is the Royal Palace as part of an attempt by the *mutaween* to overthrow the Saudi government. Turki Al Faisal was involved in the bombing today and it was his son who was arrested with a draft copy of a *fatwa* illegitimizing the House of Saud. The *ulama* must've drafted the *fatwa*."

Rachael understood his meaning. "So they use a nuclear bomb against a U.S. or House of Saud target. Afterwards, the Council of Senior *Ulama* issues a *fatwa* against the House of Saud claiming they can't protect Islam's holy sites and the revolution starts."

"Exactly," David replied, although he couldn't shake the feeling their theory wasn't quite right. "I need to go to Saudi Arabia. Clearly Al Kabbar is there."

Rachael nodded. "I'll go with you. You'll need help and I know my way around. We've got a great network there."

"I expected nothing less," David replied, glad she was focused on the mission and not the bombing. "We'll just be one more husband and wife team on the *hajj*. I hope you speak Arabic fluently and know your Islamic prayers."

Rachael nodded. "If I weren't a woman, I could pass as an *imam*."

David allowed himself a brief chuckle. "Now that'd be a real shame for the men of this world."

For the first time since the explosion, Rachael managed a ghost of a smile. "I thought you'd never notice."

✳ ✳ ✳

David stopped outside his hotel room, realizing the thread he had placed along the bottom of the door had been disturbed. Since David had asked the front desk to suspend housekeeping services, he knew it wasn't a maid. Pulling out his gun, he gently tried the door. It was locked. Keeping his gun raised, he inserted his keys into the door. It opened slowly. As David stepped cautiously inside, he sensed rather than saw the figure hiding behind the door. He spun around abruptly and drove his shoulder into the soft body, causing the intruder to crash backward into the wall and fall in a heap to the floor. David pointed his gun at the back of the prostrate man.

"David, wait!"

He hesitated, then recognized the voice and figure of Ramzi Yousef.

David breathed deeply, trying to release the violent tension gripping him. Shocked, he realized he had reacted without thinking, prepared to kill without preparation or remorse. He had come a long way since his first tentative days as a CIA agent. Until that moment, he had viewed himself as a reluctant businessman-warrior, temporarily taking up arms to defend his adopted country. When it was over, David had always imagined himself returning effortlessly to his old life, figuratively beating his sword into a plow. He realized now that he would be unable to reclaim the past, that his recent experiences had already changed him and left an indelible stain.

David leaned over, offering the older man his hand. "My apologies, Ramzi. What the hell were you doing behind the door?"

"I wanted to make sure it was you."

The older man leaned heavily on David as he got to his feet. The Saudi then made his way over to the bed and sat down.

Yousef rubbed his shoulder ruefully. "You're well trained."

"Sorry. You caught me by surprise. What are you doing here?"

"I came to find you. Things are heating up in Saudi Arabia."

"What's happened?" David asked resignedly, bracing himself for more bad news.

"The *mutaween* are on the move. Their leaders are meeting with Khaled ibn Saud in Mecca as we speak. All leave has been canceled and the bulk of their forces have begun gathering in Mecca."

"Do you know why?"

"Due to the Jerusalem bombing. As you know, the bomb damaged the Al Aqsa Mosque and spread radiation around the Temple Mount, including contaminating the Dome of the Rock. The entire site will be off limits to anyone without protective clothing for years until the radiation subsides. Riots have already broken out in Cairo and Damascus and in Saudi Arabia by the pilgrims on the *hajj*. Once again, Muslims are blaming the Jewish people for the desecration."

"That's absurd. The Wailing Wall was partially destroyed by the blast and is also contaminated with radiation. There's no holier site in Judaism."

Yousef shrugged. "I didn't say it made sense. Unfortunately, that's the reaction in the Arab world and the hysterical reports on Al Jazeera haven't helped."

"What else have you learned about Khaled ibn Saud?"

Yousef pulled a pipe out of his suit pocket and a bag of tobacco. "I've had my men tail Khaled since we last spoke."

"So have we, but it's led nowhere."

"He's been careful, I'll give him that," Yousef replied. "But I got lucky. I managed to plant a spy amongst his house servants."

David wasn't surprised—Yousef's financial resources were substantial and his prominence in Saudi Arabia probably gave him better contacts than the CIA.

Yousef lit his pipe. "First, it appears Khaled's connected to a terrorist training camp in Northern Pakistan."

"The one run by the Fist of *Allah* madras in Peshawar?" David asked.

Yousef looked surprised. "You knew?"

"I guessed." David decided not to reveal his information for the time being. "How'd you find out?"

"My man in Khaled's household installed several listening devices in the house. Two days ago, he overheard Khaled talking about a secret shipment from Pakistan that had just arrived in Saudi Arabia."

"Shit!" David exclaimed. "The Pakistani nuke?"

Yousef looked alarmed. "What do you mean?"

David debated about telling Yousef about the Pakistani bomb. He knew both Reynolds and the Israelis would be livid at the disclosure. Still, at this point, David felt he had no other option. The nuclear bomb was somewhere in Saudi Arabia and he needed Yousef's help.

For the next few minutes, David revealed the Palestinian ambulance driver's dying words and Parissa's information.

Yousef's normally impassive expression was deeply troubled, even stricken. "If a nuclear bomb explodes in Saudi Arabia, it'd have devastating consequences. Even if used against non-Muslims or the American military, a nuclear bomb would underscore the Saudi government's weakness and its inability to protect Mecca."

"When do you think they'd strike?" David asked.

"Now. The *hajj* ends in two days. It'd be the best time to disrupt the country and issue a *fatwa*."

"How do you see the scenario unfolding?"

Yousef rubbed his chin thoughtfully. "Suppose a bomb is set off and creates mass panic. The House of Saud loses all credibility, both in their ability to protect the populace and, most importantly, Mecca. Then the Council of Senior *Ulama* issues a *fatwa* that proclaims that the House of Saud is weak and illegitimate. Without question, that would spark a revolt, particularly with millions of pilgrims in the country."

"But Turki al Faisal is dead. He was the senior *ulama* on the Council."

Yousef shook his head. "It doesn't matter, not if other members on the council collectively issue a *fatwa*."

"Would they use the bomb against the crowds of pilgrims?" David asked, wondering about other potential targets.

"For what purpose? They'd be killing thousands of devout Muslims. No, the most likely targets are an American one such as the embassy, a foreigners' housing complex or the House of Saud royal residences."

"Can you find out?"

Yousef smiled grimly. "I can try. My man is still in place in Khaled's household. You need to come to Saudi Arabia in case we uncover something."

"Isn't this a job for the House of Saud's personal guards or Saudi intelligence? Surely we need to tell the Saudi Arabian authorities or even the King personally."

Yousef shook his head gravely. "I don't know who to trust. Don't forget that Khaled is a member of the House of Saud *and* the head of the GDI. There could be factions within both organizations that support what he's trying to do."

"*If* he's the one leading the revolt." David said, although Parissa's warning about Khaled was still fresh in his mind.

"I'm sure of it. Besides, going to the Saudi authorities would only expose our suspicions and perhaps cause the terrorists to either accelerate their time-table or change their plans."

"Are you certain Mecca isn't the target?" David asked again.

Yousef stood angrily. "Muslims, even the worst possible kind, would never set off a bomb in Mecca. It's against everything they believe in."

"Fifteen years ago, Muslim radicals seized the Grand Mosque by force. Blood was spilled, even near the *Kaaba*."

Yousef considered David's words, before finally relenting. "I suppose it's possible."

"I wouldn't rule out anything at this point."

Yousef put away his pipe. "Will you come to Saudi Arabia?"

David thought quickly—after Parissa's phone call, he had already planned on going. He still wasn't sure what he could do. If the *mutaween* were already implementing a plan to overthrow the Saudi government, the military and House of Saud's personal guard were the only ones capable of thwarting the attempt. David realized he should focus on finding the Pakistani nuclear bomb by tracking down Al Kabbar. After all, David was the only one who could identify the man. Without question, David knew he needed to be in Saudi Arabia.

Despite his decision, David was strangely reluctant to divulge his plans to Yousef. For some reason, he felt uneasy about the Saudi industrialist. Yousef was too smooth and persuasive and had a quick, plausible answer to every difficult question. At that point, David was inclined to trust no one.

"Why did you fly here instead of calling me?" David asked.

"Because I wasn't sure you'd come."

"I still don't know if I can. I need to check with some people."

Yousef walked to the door and stopped to look back at David. "If you come, call me on my cell. In the meantime, I'll see if my people can find out the location of the bomb."

"Let's hope I'm wrong."

"If there is a nuke and it goes off, *Allah* help us all. There'll be no stopping a *jihad*."

David knew Yousef was right. He had to get to Saudi Arabia as soon as possible.

36

"There!" Rachael called out, pointing to shore. "The Iranian."

Ahead on the sandy beach, David saw the flicker of headlights, the three rapid and two slow flashes giving the all-clear signal.

"She's on time," David replied, immensely relieved. "I told you Parissa would come through."

"I still can't believe we're trusting the Iranians and not your own people in Saudi Arabia."

"The CIA's been compromised," David replied. "I know Parissa isn't."

Unconvinced, Rachael shrugged and busied herself assembling their gear—two large duffle bags containing a Muslim pilgrim's clothes and enough weapons for a small army. In the five hours since leaving Jerusalem, she had spoken infrequently and then only in response to questions. Her anguish and ongoing self recrimination weighed heavily, expressed with her gaunt, strained expression and hunched shoulders. David knew that catching Al Kabbar would alleviate some of her guilt.

Hunching over the outboard engine of the rubber dinghy, David steered toward the flickering light. The agile craft plowed through the rough water, smacking the waves with enough force to send water spraying over the gunwale. The night sky was clear and bright with a steady wind. The approaching Saudi Arabian coast was dark and silent, the nearest village several miles away.

David kept his hand on the throttle until the dinghy ran aground just before reaching the rocky beach. Rachael jumped out into the knee deep water and grabbed one of the duffle bags. David killed the engine and hoisted the remaining bag. He could see two figures standing near the dark silhouette of a large SUV.

"What about the dinghy?" Rachael called out as she reached the shore.

"Forget it. By the time someone finds it, we'll be a hundred miles from here."

David glanced over his shoulder, but was unable to make out the small U.S. Navy patrol boat that had dropped them off. Jumping into the water, he slogged through the surf to shore. There, he found Parissa and Rachael silently staring at each other, arms crossed defensively over their chests. Clearly both women were apprehensive about teaming up with a long time adversary, even if it was a temporary alliance.

"Hello, David," Parissa said, walking over to give him a hug. She wore a warm smile, visibly pleased to see him again. Her windswept hair softened her haggard expression and puffy, tired eyes. David enjoyed feeling her body against his and the smell of her hair. As he let go, David was aware of Rachael's sudden interest, both as a Mossad agent and a woman. Clearly she instinctively sensed that he and Parissa had more than just a working relationship.

"Thanks for meeting us," David said.

"It'll cost you at some point," she replied lightly. "Any problems getting here?"

"No. It went as planned. We took a helicopter from Jerusalem to the patrol boat. The trip here was rough, but fast."

"Are the borders still closed?" Rachael asked.

"Yes, for the last 20 hours," Parissa replied. "The Saudi government has banned anyone from entering the country. Hundreds of thousands of pilgrims on the *hajj* have supposedly been turned away. The Saudi government continues to blame the closed borders on the Jerusalem bombings, which they say increased the likelihood of riots or more terrorist attacks."

David scowled, fearful that sealing the borders was the first step in the overthrow of the House of Saud and establishment of a fundamentalist Islamic regime. "Even the U.S. military flights are still suspended. By boat was our only alternative."

"Is the rest of the Middle East still in turmoil?" Parissa asked.

David nodded. "There've been violent demonstrations in most Muslim countries protesting the damage to the Al-Aqsa Mosque and the radiation contamination of the Dome of the Rock. Hundreds have died. The rioters and most Muslim clerics are blaming the U.S. or Israel."

"Any word on Al Kabbar?" Rachael asked.

Parissa shook her head. "None. Then again, we don't have much to go on."

"Damn!" David exclaimed, although he had expected the response. He knew it would take a miracle to find Al Kabbar in the vast expanse of Saudi Arabia.

"Enough talk," Rachael interjected. "If we're going to find him, we need to get going."

"This way," Parissa said, motioning toward the SUV parked nearby.

David shouldered his duffle bag and moved across the sand to the vehicle. Parissa introduced them to her driver, an Iranian agent named Zakoria. A heavyset man with a permanent scowl, bad teeth and thin lipped mouth, Zakoria merely grunted a greeting. Both Iranians were wearing a pilgrim's *ihram*, the white cloth slightly rumpled from their long drive. David rummaged through the duffle bags, removing appropriate clothing for Rachael and himself. They changed quickly. David strapped on a shoulder holster, taped a small gun to the small of his back and a third just above his ankle. Then he threw the remaining gear in back of the Chevy and climbed into the rear seat with Rachael.

"Any other news?" David asked.

"The Saudi military is on alert, although no one will say why," Parissa said.

"The *mutaween*?"

She glanced up in the rear view mirror to catch David's gaze. "Nothing yet. Their leaders met about twelve hours ago in Mecca. Since then, nothing more. The *mutaween* so far are merely performing their typical tasks, such as enforcing the dress code during the *hajj*. We guess that there might be as many as 20,000 in Mecca alone. There are scattered reports of *mutaween* gathering in other key cities."

"How is security for the *hajj*?"

"Tight, the tightest I've ever seen. The police are everywhere, as is the military."

David grunted, wondering if he were missing anything. He leaned over the front seat. "Parissa, what about Khaled ibn Saud?"

She shook her head. "No word. He hasn't been seen for two days."

"Maybe Ramzi Yousef knows where Khaled is."

David pulled out his cell phone and called Yousef, but there was no answer.

"How far are we from Mecca?" David asked, putting away his phone.

"Four hours of hard driving," Parissa answered. "Mecca will be unusually empty this year for the *hajj*. The Saudi radio estimated that only half of the expected pilgrims, about a million, arrived in Saudi Arabia before the borders were sealed."

"What's been the reaction to the borders being sealed?"

"There've been several demonstrations by pilgrims angry that their family members on the *hajj* were turned away at the border. But they seem to be spontaneous."

"Parissa, where's the likely flash point—Mecca or Riyadh?"

Parissa turned to look at David, her dark eyes filled with concern. "Mecca. Everything in this country revolves around Mecca. Control it, and you control the country."

"Besides, most members of the House of Saud will be in Mecca for the *hajj*," Rachael added.

"Yesterday was the ritual stoning, right?" David asked.

"Yes. Today, most pilgrims will undertake the final *tawaf.*"

David knew the *hajj* took place over the span of four or five days. First, the pilgrims put on the *ihram*, so that all were equally humble before *Allah*. On the first day, pilgrims completed their first *tawaf*, or seven counter-clockwise circles around the *Kaaba*. Then pilgrims left Mecca for Mina, a small nearby village where they meditated and prayed. On the next day, most traveled to the nearby Mount Arafat, where the Prophet Mohammad had delivered his Farewell Sermon. After sunset, they traveled to *Muzdalifah*, a nearby open plain, to gather a fixed number of pebbles for use on succeeding days. The following day, the pilgrims traveled back to Mina to cast seven pebbles at each of the scattered white pillars. The stoning was symbolic of mankind's defiance of the devil and an attempt to cast away evil and vice while the seven throws represented infinity.

Following the casting of the pebbles, most pilgrims sacrificed a sheep or goat as part of the *'Id as-Adha*, or Festival of Sacrifice. Finally, the pilgrims returned to Mecca to perform the final rite of the *hajj*—the *tawaf*, or seven-fold circling of the *Kaaba*, with a prayer recited during each circuit. This rite implied that all human activity must have *Allah* at its center and symbolized the unity of *Allah* and man.

All of which meant that since most Muslims considered the final *tawaf* the high point of the *hajj*, any attack or uprising was likely to occur that afternoon.

"Then we'll go to Mecca," David said, confirming the course of action he and Rachael had already discussed. "Any disagreements?"

The car remained silent, the only sound the roar of pavement beneath their wheels.

"Good. Wake me when we get there," David said, nestling down against the seat and falling asleep almost immediately.

✳ ✳ ✳

David woke to the sound of his cell phone ringing. Feeling groggy, he fumbled with the pocket in his robe, finally extracting his phone after several more rings.

"Yes."

"David, it's Yousef."

David glanced around the car, noticing that Zakoria was still driving and both Rachael and Parissa were rousing themselves from sleep. His back ached and his mouth felt as if it were filled with cotton.

"Where are you?" David asked.

"Mecca. You need to get here as soon as possible," Yousef said, his tense voice conveying the urgency.

David covered the mouthpiece of his phone. "Where are we?"

"Five miles outside Mecca," Zakoria replied.

Glancing out the window, David noticed the traffic was fairly heavy, even given the early morning hour. The road was filled with buses, vans and cars, most filled to capacity. Ahead, he could see the glow of lights from the Grand Mosque, which remained open all night during the *hajj* for worshippers.

"Yousef, we're just arriving in Mecca."

"Who's we?" the Saudi magnate asked.

David decided that for now, he would hide the fact he was with three other agents and their identities. "One of our local CIA agents."

"Who?"

"It doesn't matter. What do you know?"

"Khaled ibn Saud arrived here an hour ago. He's in an apartment building overlooking the Grand Mosque. I hate to say it, but you may be right about the bomb being here in Mecca."

David thought quickly—if Khaled were involved with the plot to overthrow the Saudi government, perhaps he might lead David to Al Kabbar and the Pakistani nuclear bomb. David decided the best solution was for them to split up and have him and Rachael follow Khaled while Parissa and Zakoria pursued any leads their intelligence network generated.

"Give me the address," David said.

Yousef did, also giving David a phone number to reach him if necessary. "Be careful, Khaled's a dangerous man. There are *mutaween* guards outside the apartment building."

"I'll be in touch," David promised before he hung up.

He outlined his plan to the others. Although Parissa initially protested, she eventually reluctantly agreed to return to the Iranian safe house in Mecca and monitor the information gathered by their field agents.

Parissa's phone suddenly rang and she answered it. She listened without interruption, a puzzled expression appearing on her face. After hanging up, she turned to face David.

"That was one of my people. The *mutaween* are moving en masse."

"To Mecca?" David asked.

"No. *Leaving* Mecca," Parissa replied. "At least twenty bus loads so far."

"Where are they going?"

Parissa looked worried. "That's the strange part. About 50 miles away."

"What's there?" David asked, although he had already guessed the answer.

"Absolutely nothing. Which would suggest…"

"…they've been warned to evacuate Mecca," David finished for her. "Which means that a nuclear bomb will shortly destroy the city."

They looked at each other with horror and dismay. David felt a surge of fear and helplessness and his stomach lurched nastily as the bile rose in his throat.

Time was running short and their only lead, Al Kabbar, was nowhere to be found.

37

Alone in Abdullah's luxurious condominium overlooking the Grand Mosque, Abrahim Al Kabbar paced furiously back and forth trying to decide on an appropriate course of action. Both concerned and anxious, he hadn't heard from Abdullah since their meeting. About an hour ago, Al Kabbar had attempted to make a phone call, only to find the line was dead. He had taken the private elevator down to the lobby to find another phone, where two of Abdullah's guards had politely but firmly asked him to return upstairs immediately. Al Kabbar knew their request was a veiled threat if he refused.

In short, he was Abdullah's prisoner.

Since his return from the lobby, Al Kabbar had nervously roamed around the penthouse, wondering what was keeping Abdullah. Glancing around the richly appointed furnishings, he wondered how a man as devout as Abdullah could surround himself with such luxury, including the well stocked liquor cabinet. For the first time, Al Kabbar was concerned that perhaps Abdullah was not what he appeared.

The phone suddenly rang. Surprised, Al Kabbar hesitated before answering. "Yes?"

"Are you ready?" Abdullah asked.

"Where have you been?" Al Kabbar demanded angrily, fighting his urge to lash out.

Abdullah's tone was brusque. "Taking care of arrangements. I asked if you were ready."

Al Kabbar breathed a sigh of relief, his anger dissipating. It was time. "Of course."

"Take the bomb downstairs. A driver will be waiting for you in the lobby. He'll take you where you need to go."

With that, Abdullah hung up.

Relieved, Al Kabbar thrust aside his concerns about Abdullah. His time had come. Soon, very soon, he would join *Allah* in heaven and be rewarded for his sacrifice.

* * *

Abdullah replaced the phone and smiled. The last few pieces of his magnificent puzzle were about to come together. He walked out onto the balcony of the Intercontinental Hotel where he had rented an entire floor and looked toward the adjacent building where Al Kabbar was staying. He nodded approvingly when the penthouse lights were extinguished, knowing Al Kabbar had taken the elevator to the lobby. There, a guard would ask Al Kabbar to wait for perhaps twenty minutes. The wait was very purposeful and deliberate. Abdullah wanted Al Kabbar to be seen—by the CIA agent named David. Seen, but not caught. Afterwards, the guard would take Al Kabbar to a warehouse about a mile away. There Abdullah would meet one last time with the doomed terrorist and his nuclear bomb.

But first, Abdullah must make sure the final piece of his plan was in place.

He picked up the phone and made another call.

* * *

David stared at the front entrance of the apartment building where Ramzi Yousef had said Khaled ibn Saud was staying. He and Rachael were sitting in a Mercedes that Parissa had lent them. They had been there for nearly an hour, Rachael tense and silent and lighting cigarette after cigarette, exhaling the smoke out violently as if she could somehow erase her memories of Jerusalem. David left her alone, knowing there was nothing he could say to ease her mind.

David was both puzzled and worried. So far, they hadn't seen Khaled or anyone else interesting. Moreover, he hadn't even seen the *mutaween* that Yousef warned were guarding the building. Nor had he spotted Yousef's men who were supposedly following Khaled as well. Then again, the Grand Mosque was only a block away and the street and sidewalk were thick with vehicles and pedestrians. Although this enabled them to observe the building unnoticed, the crowds also made it difficult to pick out any *mutaween* guards.

"There must be something else we can do," Rachael complained bitterly, extinguishing another cigarette. "Sitting here and hoping to see Al Kabbar seems too passive."

"I'm open to suggestions," David replied diplomatically, knowing Rachel was venting her anger and helplessness.

Rachael scowled. "You know I don't have any."

"Then keep an eye out."

Rachael shifted irritably in her seat and remained quiet. David wondered how much time was left—if the *mutaween* were already leaving Mecca to assemble in the desert outside the city, then it was highly likely the bomb would be detonated that evening. *If* there were a bomb, he reminded himself for the hundredth time. Yet, despite his desperate hope, he knew the threat was real.

A crowded bus bearing the insignia of the *mutaween* drove past. David wondered if the bus were fleeing Mecca to take the *mutaween* to a gathering point outside the city. He suddenly shivered with fear—it took all his courage to remain there knowing that a nuclear explosion could occur at any moment. He forcefully subdued his panic—the bomb wouldn't be detonated as long as Khaled ibn Saud remained in Mecca.

He swept his gaze back toward the apartment entrance. Still nothing. Where the hell was Khaled ibn Saud or the *mutaween* guards?

"David," Rachael said, her voice strained. "I think we've got trouble."

❊ ❊ ❊

About a mile away in an Iranian intelligence center located in a drab low-rise office building, Parissa was reading reports gathered by Iranian agents from around Saudi Arabia. One of three centers the Iranian intelligence agency maintained in Saudi Arabia—the other two were in Medina and Riyadh—the building served both as a gathering point for field agents and a research facility that reviewed field reports and intercepted communications. The Shia Iranians closely watched the predominantly Sunni Saudis, as the considerable enmity between the two sects extended back over 1400 years.

Rubbing her chin thoughtfully, Parissa stared down at the papers scattered across her desk trying to make sense of the recent reports. For the past four hours, she had devoted her agency's entire resources to finding Al Kabbar and his nuclear bomb. So far, she'd failed. Al Kabbar had vanished without a trace, as had Khaled ibn Saud.

In general, the intelligence reports were extremely troubling. In the past 24 hours, the Saudi military had moved several detachments to positions outside key cities. In addition, two loyal companies of the House of Saud's personal guard had been suddenly sent to Mecca. She had also learned the *mutaween* continued to withdraw from Mecca and several senior members of the Council of Senior *Ulama* had also recently left Mecca.

Parissa surmised that those leaving Mecca either knew, or their superiors knew, a nuclear bomb would soon be detonated. She also suspected the House of Saud's personal guard had been sent to Mecca so they would perish in the explosion. Clearly, certain commanders in the personal guard and the military had been co-opted. The important question was how many? Were there even enough loyal officers remaining to put down the coming rebellion?

Wearily rubbing her eyes, Parissa glanced up as the local station chief entered the room. He wore a bitter scowl, still upset their superiors in Tehran had temporarily placed Parissa in charge of his operation. Stalking across the room, he thrust several pieces of paper at Parissa.

"What is it?" she asked, scanning the lines of Farsi.

"You wanted to know the whereabouts of Khaled ibn Saud's family."

"You found them?"

The man nodded. "The first page gives you their locations. The second page gives the location of the other family you asked about."

Parissa bit her lip as she examined the two pages. She glanced up again, comprehension finally dawning. Of course! It was so obvious! Lunging forward, she grabbed her phone and dialed David's cell phone number.

"C'mon David, pick up!" she pleaded silently. "Pick up!"

There was no answer. Equally ominous, her call failed to roll into David's voice mail.

"Get me a car and driver," she snapped, standing so quickly her chair crashed to the floor. "I must get to the Grand Mosque."

For once, the Intelligence Station Chief didn't hesitate. "Of course."

He turned and ran out of the room.

Cursing loudly, Parissa glanced down once more at the papers in her hand. Confronted with the truth, it now all seemed so simple.

Unfortunately, David didn't know it yet.

✳ ✳ ✳

"Rachael, what's the problem?" David asked, concerned about her stricken expression.

"On my side, there are two men approaching us from behind, perhaps 15 meters away. There's a third man on the other side of the street about the same distance back."

David glanced in the rear view mirror, trying to pick out the men in the crowd streaming past. He noticed two tall, well dressed Arabs walking slowly, their hands hidden beneath the folds in their robes. "Why them?"

"Instinct. They were standing together talking for a few minutes before they split up. I noticed that one has a pistol."

David wasn't about to take any chances. "Let's move."

He started the Mercedes and put it into gear. Suddenly, a white Jeep SUV pulled up alongside, effectively boxing them into the parking space.

"Get out!" David shouted.

He jumped out of the Mercedes and pulled out a pistol from his shoulder holster. Glancing over his shoulder, he noticed the two men behind them had stopped and were watching him warily. David looked over at the Jeep that had pulled alongside. It was empty except for the driver, who ducked down below the dashboard when he saw David's gun.

Rachael emerged from the Mercedes, a gun in her hand. David knew the crowded sidewalk prevented them from moving rapidly, but their adversaries were stuck as well. Thinking quickly, David pointed his gun in the air and fired several shots.

The effect was instantaneous. People began screaming and shouting while they pushed and scrambled to get out of the way. The crowd surged away from them, preventing the two men from moving forward. David glanced across the street and saw a third man pushing his way through the crowded sidewalk, a gun in his hand.

"C'mon!" David cried.

They ran for it. Fortunately, the crowd had split up—some running with David and Rachael and the remainder headed in the opposite direction, which precluded the three men from following quickly. David glanced hurriedly around for somewhere either to hide or aid their escape. The street was solidly lined with modern four or five story apartment buildings with retail stores at the street level.

"Rachel, over there!" David pointed to a narrow alley about 20 meters away between two apartment buildings.

"Got it!"

Lungs burning and legs rubbery with apprehension, David followed Rachael into the alley. They had gone about ten meters before David realized a tall brick wall loomed ahead at the end of the alley.

They had reached a dead end.

"David, the door!"

About ten meters away, there was a service entrance into the rear of the apartment building where Khaled was supposedly located. David tugged hard on the door, but it was locked. Glancing over his shoulder, he saw one of their pursuers enter the alley with his gun raised. Rachael fired twice, causing the man to duck back behind the corner of the building.

David fired several shots to splinter the door around the lock. Kicking it open, he motioned Rachael forward. She ducked inside and he followed. They found themselves in a long concrete service corridor that led into the bowels of the building. They ran, passing two garbage dumpsters and several other doors, including one marked 'Boiler Room'.

"Who do you think they are?" Rachael managed to ask between gasps.

"Gotta be the *mutaween*," David replied, desperately trying to figure a way out of their predicament.

"Let's find out."

David slowed as he approached the door at the end of the corridor. "What's your plan?"

"I think only one man follows us while the other two circle around to the front of building to cut us off."

David nodded agreement—it made sense, it was what he would've done. "Then we should hide and wait for the first guy?"

"Yes."

They turned and sprinted back to the boiler room. Rachael ducked inside first. As David closed the door, he noticed the alley door swing open. He left the boiler room door ajar just enough so he could hear their pursuer approaching. Leaning up against the doorframe, David tried to slow his breathing. Rachael was standing bent over silently gasping for air, her hands on her knees. A curtain of steam hung over the musty smelling room, which was filled with heating ducts, water pipes and two large furnaces.

David placed his ear to the door and listened. He heard nothing, then a single set of running footsteps. Rachael had been right; the other two men must have circled back to the building's front entrance. He waited for their pursuer to reach their hiding place, assuming the man would check inside before going on. The pounding footsteps slowed and then stopped. There was the sound of ragged breathing outside in the corridor. David flattened himself against the wall and pointed his gun at the door.

Suddenly, the door flew open. A handsome, tall, dark skinned man in a robe stood there, his gun pointed at them.

"Drop it!" David and Rachael yelled simultaneously.

The Arab hesitated before dropping his weapon, which clattered to the floor.

"Inside," David demanded.

The man walked tentatively inside, his gaze darting back and forth.

Rachael put her gun against his head. "Who are you?" she hissed.

He blinked rapidly, his expression fearful. "GDI."

Surprised, David and Rachael exchanged glances. David had expected their pursuer to say he was part of the *mutaween*. The GDI was the intelligence organization headed by Khaled ibn Saud, but had a reputation of unswerving loyalty to the House of Saud. Either this man was a rogue agent and answered only to Khaled ibn Saud or something was wrong. For some reason he was unable to identify, David suspected the latter.

"Why are you chasing us?"

The man remained silent. Once again, Rachael placed her gun against his temple. "I've got nothing to lose," she said grimly. "Tell us why."

The Saudi's eyes darted around wildly, looking for a way out. Realizing he was trapped, he licked his lips nervously before responding in a rush. "We got a tip that an American agent would detonate a bomb near the Grand Mosque to retaliate for the Jerusalem bombing."

"What the hell?" David exclaimed, looking at Rachael.

Before she could reply, David heard a loud commotion outside in the corridor. He realized the two remaining pursuers were approaching. Raising his gun, he brought it down hard on their captive's head, causing him to crumple to the ground.

"Think there's another way out?" Rachael asked.

"There better be."

They sprinted across the room, circling around behind the large furnaces. There, they found another door. Opening it, David peered out cautiously before motioning Rachael forward. They stepped out into the first level of an underground garage. Straight ahead, the exit ramp was bathed in sunlight that spilled down from the street and a number of cars were parked on their right. David stood still for a moment, debating whether to sprint up the ramp to the street or steal a car for their escape.

Suddenly, an engine roared to life and a gold BMW sedan pulled out of a nearby parking spot and accelerated toward them. David shielded his eyes from the headlights, lowering his arm as the car drove past. With blatant curiosity, the solitary rear seat passenger stared at David.

Stunned, David recognized Al Kabbar. On the seat next to him was a large metal case.

The BMW accelerated up the exit ramp and disappeared.

✻ ✻ ✻

"The CIA agent has disappeared," the voice on the phone said.

"Where?" Abdullah asked, lowering his glass of wine and restraining the urge to pound the table in frustration.

"I don't know. They're hunting for him. There was also a woman with him."

"An American?"

"They don't know."

"And Al Kabbar?"

"He got away. But it was close, they almost caught him."

Abdullah put the force of his anger in his response. "Find the American and the woman. Get the police to issue an all-points bulletin. If you fail…"

"I won't."

Abdullah slammed down his phone, nearly breaking the handset. Cursing loudly, he leaned back to think. The final act of his perfectly written play had been disrupted. With the assistance of this mysterious woman, David had escaped the trap Abdullah had painstakingly set. The CIA agent was supposed to catch a glimpse of Al Kabbar in the lobby of the apartment building, and, like a bee to honey, come rushing forward. Then, the GDI, with the assistance of Abdullah's men, was supposed to seize David. But the timing had been off. Spotting David in his car outside the building, the GDI had clumsily approached, causing him to flee prematurely. The damn fools!

His only consolation was that David had seen Al Kabbar.

Abdullah cursed his impetuousness in letting David even get near to Al Kabbar. He never should have directed the CIA agent to the same building. His thoughts turned to an unforeseen problem. Who was this woman? An American or Israeli agent? If she were Israeli, it would be an incredible stroke of good fortune for his plan. In fact, the more he considered it, their escape could turn out to be fortuitous. David and his female partner had injured a GDI agent and now were officially classified as threats to Saudi Arabia and hunted as fugitives.

The only difficulty was finding him again.

Abdullah leaned back against the chair and considered his alternatives. There was another way in which he could trap the CIA agent. But this time, he'd do it himself.

Looking at his watch, he frowned in consternation. He would be forced to push back the timing of the explosion.

Then again, he had planned for this day for years. Another hour or so wouldn't make any difference.

❋ ❋ ❋

Stunned, David stared at the taillights of Al Kabbar's BMW as it disappeared from view. Rachael immediately sensed something was wrong.

"What is it?" she asked, pulling on his arm.

"The passenger," he managed to say, furious he hadn't reacted more quickly. "It was Al Kabbar!"

"Here? Now?"

David looked desperately around the garage and spotted an elderly man getting into Mercedes S-Class sedan about ten yards away.

"C'mon." David raced across the intervening distance. The elderly man looked up in surprise, his expression becoming terrified when he noticed the gun in David's hand.

"The keys. Now," David snapped.

Trembling, the man handed David the keys and backed away, breaking into a stumbling run as David opened the driver's door. Rachael raced around to the other side and got in. David revved the engine and the Mercedes shot forward toward the exit ramp.

Suddenly, the boiler room door burst open and one of their pursuers emerged. Raising his gun, he fired at the speeding Mercedes. David ducked instinctively as the bullets shattered the rear window. Turning around, Rachael returned fire through the open window. David accelerated up the ramp toward the street, grateful the garage horn had warned pedestrians to clear the sidewalk.

As the car shot into the street, David was forced to slam on the brakes. The one-way road was filled with slowly moving cars, vans and buses. Throngs of pedestrians filled the sidewalks and spilled out into the street. Honking incessantly, David forced his way past several vehicles. Rachael rolled down her window and shouted at the cars obstructing their progress.

"See Al Kabbar's BMW?" David shouted, concentrating on weaving his way through traffic.

"Perhaps a half block ahead," Rachael called out. "They're stuck in traffic as well."

David cursed and swung the wheel, shooting the Mercedes into a slender gap between the traffic and the cars parked alongside the road. Suddenly, there was the crunch of metal on metal as a limousine slammed the Mercedes against a parked car. At the collision, the limousine stopped. But David kept driving, his gaze searching desperately for the gold BMW. He finally spotted it up ahead, moving faster now that traffic had begun to thin.

Al Kabbar's BMW darted through an intersection just as the traffic light changed. Stuck behind several cars that refused to run the yellow light, David was forced to slam on his brakes.

"Damn it!" he swore, pounding the steering wheel in frustration.

There they remained as the intersection filled with cars. The gold BMW rapidly disappeared from view.

They had lost Al Kabbar and the case in his possession.

✳ ✳ ✳

Abrahim Al Kabbar leaned back against the luxurious leather seat, wondering if he were mistaken—the man in the condominium garage had looked extremely familiar. Although Al Kabbar knew he'd seen the man somewhere before, he was unable to recall where. He could tell by the stranger's expression—a mixture of anger, hatred and surprise—that he recognized Al Kabbar. Al Kabbar had also seen the stranger's hand reach inside his robe, as if for a gun.

With a feeling of relief, Al Kabbar knew he'd barely escaped confronting an enemy.

He was impatient to get to his rendezvous with Abdullah. Nearing the end of his journey, Al Kabbar was extremely weary. There was something inside that cried out for the relief of death, for sinking into the comforting arms of eternal bliss. The feeling had grown steadily during the last few days, as if he suffered from an infection spreading throughout his body. He was weary of the years of fighting to free Islam from the unbelievers. He wanted to enjoy the fruits of his labor in heaven. He was looking forward to his reward of 30 virgins and worshipping the Prophet Muhammad and *Allah*.

Al Kabbar had pursued this struggle for eight years, giving up any chance for a family, close friends or even a peaceful night's sleep. He had killed and seen men kill. He had bled, lied, cheated and nearly died for the cause.

Now, he was ready for the fight to end, for the peace and contentment he deserved.

It was time.

✳ ✳ ✳

At Parissa's urging, her driver drove recklessly toward the address that David had given her earlier that evening. The heavy traffic moved slowly, most foreign pilgrims unfamiliar with the roads. She could only hope David and Rachael were still staking out the apartment building that Ramzi Yousef had told them about. Picking up her cell phone, she tried to call David one more time. To her surprise, this time David answered.

"Where are you?" Parissa asked.

"On the move in a stolen Mercedes."

"What happened?"

Quickly, David updated her on the events of the past half hour.

"Do you think there was a nuclear bomb in the case Al Kabbar had?"

"Everything we know points to it. So, yes, absolutely."

Parissa felt a surge of grim satisfaction, as it fit with her newfound knowledge. "David, why do you think Al Kabbar was there at the apartment building?"

"To meet with Khaled ibn Saud, of course. Khaled must've still been upstairs when Al Kabbar left."

"How did these men from the GDI learn where you were?" Parissa asked. "You told no one."

There was a prolonged silence and she could hear Rachel and David discuss something, although she couldn't make out the words.

"I was hoping you could tell me," David finally said, in both an accusatory and questioning tone. "There were only two people who knew we were there—you and Yousef. He was the one who gave us the address and he was right—we found Al Kabbar with Khaled. Which leaves you as the possible leak."

"But David, you never *saw* Khaled. Your only evidence he was even there was based on what Yousef told you."

Parissa could tell David was mulling it over. Then she asked another question designed to get him closer to the answer she had already uncovered. "Why were the men who chased you from the GDI instead of the *mutaween*?"

"I don't know," he replied slowly.

"I think I do. Let me tell you what I've uncovered in the past hour."

Parissa proceeded to lay out a compelling story that led to only one conclusion, something that in hindsight should have been obvious to all of them since the beginning.

✳ ✳ ✳

At Rachael's suggestion, David decided to ditch the Mercedes and steal another car. Rachael correctly pointed out their pursuers had seen them drive off in the Mercedes and the rear window was shot out, making it easily identifiable by anyone looking for them. David drove around until he reached a quiet residential neighborhood perhaps three miles from the Grand Mosque. They parked the Mercedes and walked along the street until they found an unlocked late-model Audi parked outside a dark house. David slid into the front seat and within a minute was able to hotwire the car, courtesy of his training at Langley. The Audi roared to life and David smiled grimly at Rachael.

"Not bad for a Turkish rug merchant."

"Just as long as we aren't caught. According to Islamic law, you'd lose your hands."

"With Al Kabbar and a nuclear bomb floating around Mecca, that's the least of my worries,"

As David accelerated, he pulled out his cell phone and dialed a number he now knew by heart.

"Yes." The man's voice was as David remembered—calm, smooth and powerful.

"Yousef, it's David."

"It's about time! I've been worried about you. My men told me about a shoot out at the address I gave you for Khaled."

"Your men were there? Where?"

"Across the street in another apartment building. They paid the manager to use an apartment to observe Khaled's building."

"Is Khaled still there?"

"No. He's just left. But my men tailed him to another location. He's in a warehouse a couple of miles from the Grand Mosque."

David breathed a sigh of relief, certain Parissa's suspicions were correct. "Good work. Is Al Kabbar with him?"

"Perhaps. Ten minutes ago, a gold BMW pulled up to the warehouse and a single passenger got out. Based on the description you gave us earlier, it could be the same man."

David tempered his excitement knowing they were a long ways from capturing Al Kabbar. "Tell me where Khaled is."

Yousef gave an address and David relayed it to Rachael. She nodded, indicating she knew how to get there.

"Yousef, we're on our way," David said. "Thanks for keeping tabs on Khaled."

"I'm as worried about this as you. Good luck."

"To be on the safe side, you might want to leave Mecca."

The Saudi gave an embarrassed laugh. "I'm already headed out of town. Just in case. I'm a businessman, not a martyr."

"Let's hope we find Al Kabbar or Khaled ibn Saud in time."

"I'm not a religious man," the industrialist replied. "But I've been praying very hard today. Good luck."

David hung up and turned to Rachael. "Looks like we're on track. Parissa was right. How long until we get there?"

Rachael smiled grimly. "With the way you drive? We'll be there in ten minutes."

.

38

Al Kabbar glanced around the warehouse, wondering why Abdullah had insisted that he come there. It seemed an unlikely place to set off the nuclear bomb. Located two miles from the Grand Mosque, the warehouse was a cavernous structure with a high roof supported by a series of steel beams. The first floor was without any walls and overflowed with cartons stacked on pallets, most containing imported food. In the center of the building, there was a large circular open area that extended to the roof. On each of the three overlooking floors, a railed walkway perhaps five feet wide encircled the open area.

Sitting impatiently on a crate near the freight elevator in the center of building, Al Kabbar wondered what was keeping Abdullah. Had he been arrested or even killed? Al Kabbar looked down at the Pakistani nuclear bomb case that had cost so many lives to reach this point. Concerned time was growing short, Al Kabbar decided to review how to arm the bomb even though he'd memorized the instructions. Al Kabbar removed a tattered piece of paper from beneath his robe and smoothed it out on the floor. He suddenly realized he didn't even need to look at the instructions—he could close his eyes and the words appeared.

He was ready to begin.

"Don't move!"

Al Kabbar froze, unsure what to do. He surreptitiously moved his hand toward his gun, but stopped as a bullet whistled overhead.

"Hands over your head. Move away from the case."

Al Kabbar did as he was told.

"Turn around. Slowly. Keep your hands high."

Al Kabbar turned to look into the face of the man he had left tied to a chair in the burning *madras* in Pakistan.

"You!" Al Kabbar exclaimed, stunned. Although he had known the American agent was still alive, he'd never expected to see him again. Now, too late, he realized the familiar face he'd seen earlier in Abdullah's garage was the American's.

Was he about to be stopped just before reaching his goal?

✳ ✳ ✳

David took a step forward, still keeping a safe distance between them. After days of intensely tracking Nawaz's murderer, he was excited, nervous and wary—it wasn't over yet. Al Kabbar's face was as David remembered—the flat, squat nose, thin lips and cold, steely eyes. He felt a grim satisfaction at the Saudi's surprise and transparent fear.

David kept his gun trained on Al Kabbar. "That's right asshole. I haven't forgotten you either."

"How'd you find me?" Al Kabbar asked, despair in his voice.

"I told him," called out a new voice.

Both David and Al Kabbar turned and looked up at the source of the interruption. There, standing on the second floor walkway overlooking the open area was a tall man in a cleric's robe, a hood obscuring his face. Four armed men stood next to him, their automatic rifles pointed at David.

"Please David, drop your weapon and step back," said the calm, powerful voice David knew so well.

David knew there was no alternative. He dropped his pistol and raised his hands. Al Kabbar rushed forward and picked it up.

"Thank you David." The man reached up and pulled back his hood. Yousef Ramzi smiled down at him. "You've been so accommodating."

"Yousef!" David exclaimed, his expression twisted with surprise. "What the hell..."

"It's a long story, my friend. One I'll be happy to share with you." Yousef made his way over to an open air freight elevator with two guards while the remaining two men continued to train their guns on David. The elevator whirred and descended. Yousef walked out and motioned to a nearby empty crate.

"Please, sit down."

"Screw you," David replied angrily, remaining standing.

"I'll enlighten you in a moment." Yousef turned to Al Kabbar. "It's time for you to go back to the Grand Mosque."

"Then I don't set the bomb off here?" Al Kabbar asked.

"No, at the Grand Mosque as we agreed. I asked you here merely to draw in the American. One of my men will drive you to your destination. Set the explosion for one hour from now. By then, I'll be far away, ensuring the *jihad* has started."

"You'll kill the American?"

"Immediately."

Al Kabbar nodded, clearly relieved. "Good. Farewell Abdullah. May I see you at *Allah's* side."

Al Kabbar closed and locked the Pakistani case. Picking it up, he walked out without glancing back, followed by one of the gunmen.

"Shall we talk?" said Yousef, turning back to David. His gray eyes sparkled with excitement and his stance was that of a victorious boxer. Yousef looked much younger than David remembered, perhaps energized by the success within his grasp.

"Yes Yousef, I'd like to get filled in. Or should I call you Abdullah?"

Yousef gave a slight bow. "I was wondering if you'd figure it out. My alter ego, Abdullah, has been very useful. You should feel privileged; few know that we are the same person. But after tonight, I'll have no further use for him."

"Are you sure you want them to hear our conversation?" David said, motioning at the three remaining gunmen.

Yousef chuckled. "It was Al Kabbar I was worried about. These men work for me. There's no need to hide the truth from them."

"And Al Kabbar?"

Yousef shrugged. "He's just a sharp tool that must be directed at a target for maximum effect. It wouldn't be wise to have him know what I'm about to tell you."

"That your only interest is money, not the *jihad* or Islam?"

Yousef took a sharp breath and stared thoughtfully at David. "Very astute. When did you figure it out?"

"Your motives are as old as man himself. Greed, pure and simple."

Yousef laughed sourly, not pleased with David's deductions. "Yes, it's true. My motives, and those in this room that work for me, are really simple. But my plan, now that was a complicated thing of beauty."

"Care to fill me in?" David asked through gritted teeth, anxious to keep Yousef talking.

Yousef laughed loudly, a slightly maniacal sound that contrasted with his normally straitlaced demeanor. "Yes, yes I would. I shall enjoy this part, where the villain discloses everything to his dogged, yet outclassed hunter."

David just stared back.

Yousef gestured broadly, clearly enjoying the moment. "Where to begin? Well, I suppose it all begins and ends with money. I'm extraordinarily wealthy, but crave the absolute power only the obscenely rich achieve. In short, I want to become the wealthiest man in history, more so than any Pharaoh, King or Pope. My plan is a foolproof way to achieve my goal."

"How?"

Yousef waved his arm vaguely. "By creating havoc and profiting from that turmoil. You see, the key is my fellow Muslims. A thousand years after the Crusades ended, they are still fighting the war. They see an arrogant West as a threat, both militarily and culturally. They watched the U.S. unilaterally attack a Muslim country, Iraq, and support a brutal Israeli state that murders their Arab brothers. This feeds upon itself—pride, rage and religion are a volatile stew—and leads to a growing interest in Islam."

Yousef pulled out a pipe and poured some tobacco in the bowl. "The first blast in Jerusalem set the stage. Most Muslims believe it was a well deserved payback to the Christians and Jews. Others thought it was a clever Israeli or U.S. ploy—either to give the Israelis an excuse to punish the Palestinians further or damage the Al Aqsa Mosque and Dome of the Rock. There was one question on every Muslim's mind: what would the *infidels* do next? Surely they'd respond!"

"Strike at the heart of Islam by destroying the Grand Mosque with a nuclear bomb?"

Yousef smiled broadly. "Precisely. Everyone knows only the Christian nations and Israel have portable nuclear bombs. So, in retaliation, one—perhaps even both—strikes back at Mecca, the very heart of Islam. The explosion tonight will have tremendous repercussions."

David nodded understanding. "Chaos. Mass riots. Probably war throughout the Middle East. Both Israel and the U.S. forces in the Middle East will be attacked. Muslim governments will either be forced to invade Israel or be overthrown. Most will probably be overthrown anyway. Certainly the Saudi government won't survive; it'll be replaced by an Islamic one."

"Again, precisely. After the explosion, I've arranged for several members of the Council of Senior *Ulama* to issue a *fatwa* proclaiming the Saudi government is incapable of acting as the trustee for Islam's holiest places and must be removed. The new government will stop selling oil to the *infidels,* as will other Islamic Middle East governments."

"So how do you benefit?"

"Oil prices will skyrocket, stock markets collapse. I have positioned myself to benefit from both."

"How?"

"Very simple really. I've placed trades in every single financial market around the world. I've done it carefully and over time so that no one would suspect anything and I wouldn't disrupt the markets. In the oil market, I've bought contracts to take future delivery of oil at a fixed, low price. I've also bet that stock markets around the globe will crash by shorting stocks and buying puts. By using the options and futures markets, I've managed to leverage the investment of my entire $20 billion fortune. I've conservatively calculated that I own or control over a trillion dollars in stocks and oil."

Even though David had already figured out Yousef's intent, he was staggered by the size and sheer audacity of his plan. "Your profits would be astronomical."

Yousef smiled. "Yes. The first bomb generated an $80 billion dollar profit, which I've already reinvested into more options and futures. The profits from the second bomb will be far greater. In the end, I could earn as much as $500 billion."

"But hundreds of thousands will die!" David exclaimed. "You can't be that merciless."

Yousef's eyes glittered strangely in the light, a fleck of spittle on his lower lip. "Why not? To some, it's a mad plan. But why? History is full of dictators who wage war to satisfy their thirst for conquest and wealth. Countless millions have died in these wars. Al Quada would gladly detonate a nuclear bomb in New York City if they could, killing millions. I'm seeking to become the wealthiest man in history. With that wealth comes virtually unlimited power. And that comes with a price."

David realized that Yousef's logic, although twisted, made sense. In the bloody annals of history, men had killed millions for much less. "Why did you bring me to Saudi Arabia? Why did you tell me where Al Kabbar was tonight?"

"Simple. I wanted one last piece of evidence pointing to the complicity of the U.S and the West in the destruction of Mecca. Obviously, the bomb had to be a small device, brought in by someone. You're that person—you're perfect.

Part Jewish, an American and a CIA operative. I couldn't have asked for a better fall guy. That's why I tipped off the GDI about you earlier tonight. We'll spray you with radioactive particles as if you handled a nuclear bomb before turning you over to the GDI. You'll be vilified as the man who brought the bomb to Mecca and killed a million Muslims. There'll be no doubt in any Muslim's mind that America and Israel are to blame."

"What makes you think the GDI won't believe me when I tell them you planned everything?"

Yousef waved his arm dismissively. "Two reasons. First, I'm a respected member of Saudi society. Second, because you'll die shortly after your arrest. Unfortunately, you'll be killed while trying to escape. But the authorities and, most importantly, Muslims, will have someone they can blame. Your rather unique past will quickly be revealed."

"Why did you try to kill me the first time I came to Saudi Arabia?"

"At the time, I was worried that Khaled might thwart my plans. I didn't want him teaming up with the CIA."

David knew Abdullah's plan was perfect. "Why'd you let me see Al Kabbar?"

"Originally, I intended to use you against Khaled ibn Saud as well. Everything you'd learned pointed to him. That's why I told you he was in the apartment building. My plan was for you to see Al Kabbar in the lobby and then get arrested by the GDI, after I told them where to find you. Then, you would've implicated Khaled. Of course, before you could be questioned further, a grief stricken Muslim would kill you. But the damage would've been done to Khaled."

"Why implicate him?" David asked, stunned by the thoroughness and complexity of Yousef's plan.

"Because he's the one man who could bring order out of chaos. Unfortunately, the GDI was too efficient and arrived before you spotted Al Kabbar. That was the weak link in my plan. I never meant for us to have this conversation. But now that my plan has changed, I can satisfy your curiosity."

"I'm impressed," David said bitterly.

Yousef laughed with delight. "It took years of planning, but it's finally paid off."

David gave a long, slow smile. "You forgot something.'

"You're right. I have." Yousef looked at the guard standing next to him. "Bring out the woman."

David had a horrible, sinking feeling. The guard walked out of sight behind a stack of crates. He quickly reappeared, prodding Rachael forward with a gun in the small of her back. Her face bore the bruises of several blows and her hands were tied with rope. Her bloody robe was ripped near the shoulder. Rachael stumbled as the guard pushed her from behind. She looked at David, soundlessly mouthing, 'I'm sorry'.

"I hadn't forgotten you were in Saudi Arabia with a woman agent who helped you escape my trap and the GDI earlier this evening," Yousef said, immensely enjoying the spectacle. "We found her upstairs in one of the hallways observing you and our friend Al Kabbar. I take it she was your backup?"

David just stood there refusing to answer.

Yousef took the pipe out of his mouth and blew out a cloud of smoke. "You knew I was the mastermind when you came to the warehouse tonight. How?"

Despite his shock at seeing Rachael captured, David kept his cool. He knew he couldn't reveal his source—Parissa was the one who had warned him.

So far, Yousef was apparently unaware of her.

"I realized it couldn't be Khaled," David replied, lying to protect Parissa's identity. "I found out his family is still in Mecca tonight for the *hajj*. Your family left Mecca yesterday for Riyadh. If Khaled had been behind the nuclear bomb, he would've removed his family to safety far from Mecca. If he wasn't the mastermind, then it had to be you, since you implicated Khaled in the first place."

Yousef smiled. "Nicely done. But that doesn't help you now."

David felt desperate. Yousef and the man holding a gun on Rachael stood about ten feet away. The two men on the second floor walkway continued to train their guns on the group. David's only edge was that Yousef had forgotten to search him—the Saudi was a businessman, not a man of violence.

He still had his gun strapped to his ankle. That and Parissa.

Suddenly, several shots rang out. One of the guards on the second floor pitched forward, his body catching the waist high railing and causing him to flip up and over. He fell soundlessly 20 feet to the main floor. The remaining guard on the upper floor looked desperately around for the gunman. Stunned by the sudden turn of events, Yousef and the man guarding Rachael froze.

David didn't hesitate. He reached down and pulled out the gun strapped to his ankle. He fired twice, hitting Rachael's guard in the chest. The man collapsed. The guard on the second floor balcony was shooting down one of the hallways. David raised his gun and snapped off several shots. The guard dropped his gun over the railing and stood there swaying, before literally sitting down as if in surprise.

"Don't move," barked Yousef.

David turned to find Yousef holding a gun pointed at Rachael's head. His hand appeared steady and sure. David knew better than to underestimate his adversary—after all, this was a man who was prepared to kill hundreds of thousands.

"Tell your friend to come out and drop his weapon with his hands raised," Yousef ordered. "Now!"

David didn't take his eyes off Yousef. "Parissa, come on out."

Parissa materialized on the second floor balcony, cradling a semiautomatic rifle. She walked over to the railing and looked down at the three of them. Surprised, Yousef glanced at David. "Another woman agent. I commend you. Now David, you and the woman drop your guns."

David smiled grimly. "I can't do that."

Yousef pressed his pistol against Rachael's temple. "Drop it or she dies."

David sighed theatrically. "Yousef, what's one life against a million? Rachael understands. She'd do the same if our roles were reversed. I can't let you leave. Not until you tell me where Al Kabbar went and how to stop the bomb."

Yousef nodded, his expression growing desperate. "I'll cut you a deal. I'll tell you where Al Kabbar went if you let me leave. Later, you can try to convince the Saudi authorities of my involvement. But I walk now."

"How can I trust you?"

"You don't have a choice. Kill or arrest me and you'll never find the bomb."

David nodded. "All I care about at this point is finding Al Kabbar. It's a deal."

Yousef smiled. "Al Kabbar has gone to a condo in a building near the Grand Mosque."

"Why there?"

"The condo was rented by a dummy organization that'll be traced back to the CIA. One more finger pointing at the Americans."

"The address."

Yousef began to back up toward the exit, pulling Rachael with him. "My freedom first. I'll call you on your phone."

"Okay."

Yousef stumbled over the body of the dead guard, slightly separating him from Rachael and giving David a target. He raised his gun and snapped off two quick shots. The bullets struck Yousef's shoulder and spun him to the ground, his gun clattering across the floor. David walked up to the industrialist and looked down. A spreading crimson stain sullied Yousef's robe and his brow gleamed with sweat.

"I thought we had a deal," Yousef managed to whisper through the pain twisting his features.

"I don't do deals."

Yousef coughed and moaned.

"The address!" David demanded.

Yousef shook his head. David kneeled and looked into the industrialist's eyes. "Give me the fucking address."

He pointed the gun at Yousef's kneecap and fired. The Saudi shrieked with pain.

David pointed the gun at Yousef's other knee. "The address!"

Yousef mumbled an address. David pointed the gun at the Saudi's foot and fired again. Yousef screamed again and repeated the same address.

Satisfied, David stood and looked at Rachael and Parissa, who had come down from the second floor. "Let's go."

"What about him?"

David looked down at the bleeding man. "We'll call Khaled on the way and tell him where to find Yousef. Maybe he'll live, maybe not. Quite frankly, I couldn't care less."

With that, David headed for the door to stop Al Kabbar.

39

They raced through the crowded streets leading to the Grand Mosque, weaving in and out of the traffic. David drove, flinching at every red light he ran and the dozen or so near accidents. He had tried to call Khaled ibn Saud and explain the situation, but the head of the GDI was unreachable. David knew they would have to be careful since the GDI was probably still looking for both him and Rachael. The Israeli agent sat in the rear seat nursing her head and shoulder wound, her jaw tightly clenched against the pain.

"The address. Are you sure it's near the Grand Mosque?" David asked.

Parissa nodded. "Yes. I recognized it because it's near one of our intelligence centers."

"You Iranians have put together quite an operation," Rachael said accusingly.

"We still have many enemies in the world," Parissa replied pointedly, glancing in the rear view mirror.

"Let's keep our focus on finding Al Kabbar," David interjected, knowing the exchange only hinted at the gulf separating the two lifelong enemies. The two women were only temporary allies—if there were a tomorrow, they would once again be adversaries.

David leaned on the horn and they shot through another intersection, scattering cars and pedestrians.

"There," Parissa shouted. "The building on the left."

David noticed a gold BMW parked in front. The same car he'd seen outside Abdullah's warehouse before his confrontation with Al Kabbar.

The moment had arrived.

✳ ✳ ✳

Abrahim Al Kabbar got out of the BMW and looked up at the building in which Abdullah insisted he detonate the nuclear bomb. The glass and steel office building was soulless and uninspiring, like something that belonged in an American business district. Behind the building, the glow of the Grand Mosque lit up the sky and he could hear the chanted prayers of the worshippers as they completed the *tawaf*. Suddenly, Al Kabbar longed to be praying beside them and cleansed once more of his sins, particularly given what he was about to do.

Al Kabbar spontaneously decided he'd ignore Abdullah's instructions and take the bomb into the Grand Mosque. There, he would complete the *tawaf* before detonating the bomb. Then at his death, he would have recently atoned for his sins. Feeling much better about his decision, Al Kabbar turned to the driver.

"I've decided to go to the Grand Mosque."

"But Abdullah ordered me to take you to an office in this building!"

"I know. Wait for me here. I'll return soon."

The driver shrugged and got back inside the car, clearly unaware of the deadly nature of Al Kabbar's mission.

Al Kabbar walked slowly through the crowd, taking in the pilgrims' joy and piety. He noticed many with tears in their eyes, emotionally fulfilled after a lifetime of dreaming about the *hajj*. He saw families worshipping together, strangers sharing bread and wives walking respectfully behind their husbands. He remembered his first trip to Mecca, when filled with awe and the presence of *Allah*, he had devoted his life to Islam. Even then, he had been resentful of the *infidel* American presence in Saudi Arabia and throughout the Middle East. He was delighted the bomb would be blamed on the haughty CIA agent who had nearly captured him earlier in the warehouse. Al Kabbar's only regret was that he would die before the American.

He walked slowly across the vast white stone plaza surrounding the Grand Mosque, relishing the sights and sounds of so many pious Muslims. At the King Fahd gate, Al Kabbar was surprised to find so few pilgrims waiting to enter inside. Clearly the closure of the Saudi Arabian border had prevented many pilgrims from arriving. Relieved, Al Kabbar knew the sparse crowds would enable him to easily reach the recessed plaza surrounding the *Kaaba*. There, he could complete the *tawaf* and pray for his soul. For in the midst of the mass of pilgrims, Al Kabbar was beginning to feel his own humanity.

He moved forward to the entrance, but a guard stopped him.

"I'm sorry. But you can't take the case in here."

"I'm a cameraman for Al Jazeer," Al Kabbar said. "This is my video equipment."

"Your ID please."

Al Kabbar pulled out the fake identification and pass Abdullah had given him several days ago. "As you can see, my pass is signed by Turki Al Faisal. I'm allowed to take my video equipment wherever I want during the *hajj*, including inside the Grand Mosque."

The guard grunted and handed back the identification. "Go ahead."

Al Kabbar picked up the case and walked through the entrance, bypassing the metal detectors.

He was minutes from his destination.

✳ ✳ ✳

Mounir el-Moutassadeq was ecstatic. Since he was a boy, he had dreamed of attending the *hajj*, thereby fulfilling one of the five basic tenets of Islam. After scrimping and saving for ten years, he had finally been able to afford the journey—not an insignificant achievement for a young street peddler from Cairo. Together with his wife, two brothers, their wives and twenty friends, he had taken a tour bus from Cairo across the desert to the Red Sea, then a rat infested, leaky boat to Saudi Arabia before taking another tour bus to Mecca.

The experience was everything Mounir had hoped. His excited fellow pilgrims were filled with an otherworldly peace and serenity at undertaking the *hajj*. He had already gone to Mina, a small city east of Mecca to spend the day praying and meditating. Afterwards, he'd spent the night in a temporary city of 40,000 tents constructed by the Saudi government. On the second day, he'd gone to the Mount Arafat where the prophet had delivered his farewell sermon. Then back to Mina, where he'd cast his seven stones at the white pillars symbolizing Satan and his attempt to persuade Abraham from sacrificing his son as *Allah* had commanded. Mounir had then sacrificed a sheep and given the meat to fellow pilgrims even poorer than himself before shaving his head.

There was one final important rite left—the *tawaf*, the seven-fold circling of the *Kaaba* displayed inside the Grand Mosque with a prayer recited during each circuit.

Mounir had never seen anything as beautiful and magnificent as the Grand Mosque. The eleven slender minarets were grouped around the enormous white alabaster walls, which were strikingly inlaid with semi-precious stones. The glow of the lights and the murmuring voices were spellbinding, almost ethereal in the desert night.

He took his wife's hand and gazed happily into her eyes.

"This is truly the greatest night of my life."

They parted at the King Fahd Gate—his wife to circle around the outside of the Grand Mosque to reach the woman's entrance. Mounir waited patiently while he was searched and then passed through the metal detectors.

Finally, giving thanks to *Allah*, he stepped inside the Grand Mosque.

✳ ✳ ✳

Parissa pulled up next to Al Kabbar's gold BMW and David leaped out of the Audi, a gun in his hand. He ran around the back of the BMW and approached the driver's side door, crouching low to stay out of the driver's line of sight. Parissa and Rachael were crouched behind the open front doors of the Audi, their guns pointed at the BMW. So far, the driver was unaware of their presence. David was disappointed to see that there was no one in the rear seat.

David rapped hard on the side of the BMW. Seeing David's gun, the driver carefully rolled down the window.

"Get out slowly, hands up. One false move and I kill you."

The door opened slowly and the driver emerged, his hands held high. He appeared shocked to find David had escaped. Moving forward, David frisked him and took his weapon.

"Where's Al Kabbar?" David hissed, as Parissa and Rachael joined him.

"I don't know."

David pointed the gun at the man's knee. "I've already shot Yousef tonight. I won't hesitate to shoot you too."

The man swallowed hard. The look in David's eyes brooked no argument.

"The *Kaaba*. Al Kabbar went to the *Kaaba*."

"Was he carrying a metal case?" David asked.

"Yes, yes. A change of clothes, he said."

"You stupid son of a bitch!" David raged. "That's not a suitcase, but a nuclear bomb!"

He pushed the Saudi aside, replaced his gun in his shoulder holster and began running toward the Grand Mosque.

Allah be merciful, David prayed for the first time in years. Let me get there in time. Let me find one man in the midst of 500,000—the men all dressed alike, all clean shaven and the vast majority, Middle Eastern.

Realistically, David knew it would take a miracle.

✳ ✳ ✳

Al Kabbar pushed through the throngs of people, but the black metal case hindered his passage. He had already walked through much of the open interior of the Grand Mosque until he drew parallel with the King Abdul-Aziz Gate. From there, he could see the multi-level recessed courtyard that held the *Kaaba*. The women's section was on the far side. Moving through the crowd, Al Kabbar reached one of the escalators that took him down to the floor that held the *Kaaba*. As he stepped on the escalator, a young man jostled him, hitting the bomb case. It slipped from Al Kabbar's hand and struck the moving escalator.

Al Kabbar held his breath but nothing happened.

"Fool," he snapped and reached down to pick up the case.

The young man gave a contrite shrug. "My apologies, friend. Why are you bringing your case to the *tawaf*?"

"None of your business," Al Kabbar replied tersely, although he knew his hostile behavior was inconsistent with the peaceful principles of the *hajj* and would draw attention.

"Again, my apologies." The young man smiled and turned away.

Al Kabbar stared down at the *Kaaba*, a tall black structure that held the cornerstone of Abraham's ancient temple. Thousands of men were walking in a circle around the *Kaaba*, chanting *"B-ismi-llahi r-rahmani r-ra! Allah-o-Akbar."* In the name of *Allah*! *Allah* is great!

Now that the moment was close at hand, Al Kabbar was once more assailed by doubt. He tried to squelch his qualms and ignore the smiling, content and joyful crowd and instead focus on the task at hand. After all, he'd made his decision and now he had a job to do.

He decided to skip the *tawaf*, afraid a guard might decide to search his case. Reaching the bottom of the escalator, he moved off to the side and walked toward a relativity uncrowded corner of the *Kaaba* plaza.

✳ ✳ ✳

Mounir knew something was amiss with the stranger he bumped into on the escalator. He had first noticed the man at the entrance of the Grand Mosque. The stranger was walking briskly and carrying a black metal case, intent only on getting inside without appreciating the religious experience. Mounir was deeply concerned about the stranger's intense demeanor and large suitcase. He knew Islamic militants had seized the Grand Mosque 30 years ago, violating the holy sanctity by smuggling guns inside and shedding blood.

Mounir was certain the rude stranger was planning a violent demonstration and the black case held some sort of weapon.

He looked around in vain for a Mosque guard. Failing to find one, Mounir decided to follow the man with the case. He was terrified of losing sight of him, realizing he'd never find him again in the crowd. Mounir stayed close as the stranger made his way through the Grand Mosque and down the escalator to the same floor as the *Kaaba*. He watched as the man turned away from the *Kaaba* and toward the outer wall without even attempting the *tawaf*.

By now, Mounir was certain the stranger was up to no good. He hurried after him, intent on preventing whatever was planned.

✳ ✳ ✳

David plowed through the crowd, Parissa and Rachael following close behind. As they reached the King Fahd entrance to the Grand Mosque, a guard pointed Parissa and Rachael towards the women's entrance. David flashed his fake police ID and was ushered inside. Walking quickly, he desperately scanned the crowd for Al Kabbar. He despaired of finding him in the crush of humanity. David realized his only hope was that Al Kabbar had headed for the floor that held the *Kaaba* in the center of the Grand Mosque.

Pushing through the worshippers, David bulled his way toward the *Kaaba*. His throat was dry and his breath came in ragged gasps, as if a vice were squeezing his chest. He had never known such terror—he flinched at every sudden noise or movement. David willed himself forward, all the while fearing his mission was hopeless and trying to ignore the knowledge that the world was about to end.

As David rode the escalator down to the floor that held the *Kaaba*, his eyes scanned the crowd. Most of the men surrounding the *Kaaba* were engaged in the *tawaf* and were walking in a circle around the *Kaaba*, chanting *"Bismillah! Allahu-Akbar. Allahu Akbar wa lil Lahi Alhamd."*

Al Kabbar was nowhere in sight.

David realized Al Kabbar could never stop and arm the bomb in the midst of those engaged in the *tawaf*. Therefore, if Al Kabbar were on the same level, he was near the outer walls where people were resting, either having just completed the *tawaf* or about to begin.

As the escalator reached the main floor, David plunged into the crowd and headed for the closest wall.

✳ ✳ ✳

Al Kabbar reached the outer wall and gazed up at the three floors that overlooked the *Kaaba*. The railings held back numerous people, most of whom were praying as they gazed at the *Kaaba*. Al Kabbar found a small open area against the encircling wall and put the nuclear bomb case on the ground. Kneeling, he pulled out the key that hung around his neck and opened the case. Staring at the timing mechanism, Al Kabbar recalled the priming instructions. He glanced around at the men standing nearby to see if anyone was paying attention, but most were either lost in prayer or gazing at the *Kaaba*.

Al Kabbar began to set the detonator to explode in two minutes.

✳ ✳ ✳

Mounir saw the stranger put his case on the ground and kneel to open it. Moving closer, Mounir peered over the man's shoulder to see that the interior was filled with wires and a digital clock face.

Even though he had never seen one before, Mourin knew it was a bomb.

He rushed forward to tackle the unbeliever, shouting wildly, "In the name of *Allah*, help me. He's got a bomb!"

✳ ✳ ✳

David was feeling desperate by the time he reached the wall that encircled the sunken plaza. Suddenly, there was a commotion about fifty feet away and he could hear a voice shouting frantically. As other voices joined in, David pushed his way past the milling crowd toward the tumult. Suddenly, a shot was fired, followed by three more. The crowd panicked, some diving to the ground seeking cover and others trying to flee. Several men crashed into David, nearly knocking him to the ground. After regaining his balance, he reached into his shoulder holster and pulled out his gun.

The crowd parted. David could see a man standing near a black metal case, a gun in his hand, another pilgrim lying unmoving on the ground nearby. The gunman was turning in circles, pointing the gun at the crowd and forcing everyone to stand back. David recognized Al Kabbar and raised his gun. As he pulled the trigger, someone jostled his arm and the shot went wide of his target.

Turning at the sound of gunfire, Al Kabbar caught sight of David. The Saudi returned fire. A bullet caught David's shoulder and spun him around. Crying out in pain, he fell to the ground as another bullet tore into his leg.

David's vision grew fuzzy and he felt his fingers loosen on the butt of his gun.

He saw Al Kabbar lower his gun and kneel down once more next to the case. Through the pain and haze, David managed to regain his grip on his gun. Steadying his arm against the ground, he fired. Once, twice and then again and again, until the hammer clicked on an empty chamber.

Then the blackness took him.

.

Epilogue

Palmyra, Syria

Plane Crashes in Saudi Arabia, Killing 31
Senior Muslim Clerics Among the Dead

Riyadh, Saudi Arabia (Reuters)—A chartered Saudi Airlines passenger jet crashed today near Riyadh, killing all twenty five passengers onboard and the crew of six. The Boeing 737 apparently experienced engine trouble while attempting to land during a sand storm. All of the passengers were Wahhabi Muslim clerics returning from the *hajj* at Mecca, including eight members of the Council of Senior *Ulama*, a group of religious leaders that advises the House of Saud.

King Abdullah issued a statement at a hastily called press conference. "We are devastated by this loss. The clerics killed today were important religious figures and honorable and pious representatives of Islam. While it's a sad day for Saudi Arabia and all Muslims, *Allah* is truly blessed to have such men join him in heaven."

The Riyadh airport tower received a distress call during the plane's final approach, although it was unclear as to the nature of the emergency. Several witnesses claimed that the plane exploded before plummeting to the ground, but a Saudi Airlines spokesman denied the reports, as did King Abdullah.

"I am aware that there are some unfounded rumors regarding the crash," the King said in his statement. "Therefore, I am appointing the head of the GDI, Khaled ibn Saud, to look into the accident. Khaled will oversee an immediate and thorough investigation. I have also asked him to look into the unsubstantiated rumor that last week an Israeli nearly succeeded in setting off a bomb in the Grand Mosque during the *hajj*. While I hesitate to mention these rumors for fear of giving them additional credence, I feel it is my duty to inform all Muslims there is no truth to them."

At the press conference, Khaled ibn Saud also took a moment to comment on the death earlier this morning of Ramzi Yousef, Saudi Arabia's wealthiest industrialist. "Ramzi Yousef was a good friend and his untimely demise from a heart attack is a terrible tragedy. Today was truly a black day for Saudi Arabia."

David lowered the *International Herald Tribune* front page and tossed the paper into the back seat of his rental car. He didn't need to read anything more. He knew the Muslim clerics had been murdered. Not surprisingly, Khaled ibn Saud had moved quickly in the seven days since David had killed Abrahim Al Kabbar in Mecca. All of the dead clerics must have been part of Ramzi Yousef's conspiracy to overthrow the House of Saud. David was impressed Khaled had discovered their names so quickly; then again, the House of Saud could use interrogation tactics unavailable to the police in most democracies. Killing the clerics was a simple but effective way to remove the cancer threatening the Saudi monarchy; it also served as a warning to potential future conspirators. David knew Khaled ibn Saud would allow the rumors of what really happened to sweep through Saudi Arabia, even as the government maintained the official position that the plane crash was accidental.

As for Ramzi Yousef, David wondered if he were truly dead or if the industrialist was locked away somewhere in a Saudi prison, still being interrogated. Not that David cared either way. Yousef deserved the worst mankind could offer—there was no torture or depravation cruel enough to match his attempted crime. David still found it hard to believe Yousef had been willing to kill so many innocent people and plunge the world into conflict just to satisfy his greed.

Then again, as Yousef pointed out, money was power, and history was replete with ruthless dictators who had killed millions while attempting to enlarge their empires.

"Are you coming to join me?"

David looked up at the sound of Parissa's voice and smiled. For the past few days, they had traveled together through the newly democratic Syria, visiting the ancient sites and behaving like a typical couple on vacation. Currently, they were in Palmyra, a fascinating ruined city of a post-Roman civilization.

"In a minute," he called out.

Parissa smiled and pushed back the stray strand of hair that fell across her face. She was achingly beautiful in the afternoon light—her dark, mysterious eyes and high cheekbones suggested a long-lost aristocracy while her slender, shapely body moved effortlessly and economically, almost as if floating. Her mouth was soft and inviting, the curious half-smile foreshadowing sudden laughter or a mischievous retort. There was a playful, loving side to Parissa that had surprised David—and helped him forget the terrors of the past few weeks. Although the bullet wounds in his shoulder and leg had begun to heal, his psyche had not. There were too many deaths and violent moments to forget. Surprisingly, it wasn't the actions of Al Kabbar or even Ramzi Yousef that David was unable to forget.

It was his own.

In the lonely hours before morning, David was unable to sleep. Every night during the darkest hours, he would rise, walk outside and gaze up at the sky. There, he saw the faces of his victims—the men in Pakistan, the three terrorists inside the Church of the Holy Sepulcher and lastly, Al Kabbar. Although each had deserved his or her fate, David believed he should feel guilty over killing another human being. For that was what kept him up at night—not that he'd killed his enemies, but that he felt nothing, not even a twinge of remorse.

His coldness and ability to kill quickly and efficiently raised questions that for now David avoided, but was unable to completely ignore.

In looking back at his life, David realized he'd never been particularly close to anyone—not his family, friends or lovers. In that, he was a product of his upbringing. Even with Parissa, he avoided intimate conversations by changing the subject or initiating another round of lovemaking. The long, revealing conversations over a bottle of wine were missing, leaving a chasm between them that was unfilled by either their physical closeness or shared experiences. Only last night, Parissa had exploded, accusing him of holding her at arm's length. Sadly, it was a charge David was unable to refute. For the moment, he was incapable of anything more. Much as he wished otherwise, he knew his relationship with Parissa wouldn't venture much further.

After their vacation in Syria, David intended to return to Istanbul to pick up the pieces of his life. Such as it was. Upon his return, he knew he'd sink even further into the espionage world. In mafia parlance, he'd made his 'bones' and the CIA considered him a rising star. Even though he feared he was becoming his father's son—dedicating his life to a cause at the cost of his personal life—David knew he'd welcome the increased demands for his time. At this point in his life, he craved simplicity, not complicated questions. The CIA offered a form of refuge—a one-dimensional world of black and white, of us versus them.

As for his father, David sensed one day they'd meet again. Next time it would be as adversaries, for they had chosen different sides. Despite his best efforts, David was unable to completely resolve his feelings about his father, which remained jumbled and confused. He knew what his father had become—a terrorist—but there were still the ties of father and son. Instead, David subdued his emotions and tried to think of his father as he had for 20 years—with fond memories, but knowing he was out of David's life forever.

David got out of the rental car and locked the door. He could see Parissa standing on the crest of a nearby hill surveying the ruins of Palmyra—the hundreds of impressive columns, broad boulevards and reconstructed buildings. In the distance, a rust-colored ridge of sand and rock rose from the surrounding desert, an ancient Muslim stone fortress straddling the peak. David began to walk toward Parissa, knowing she'd soon regale him with stories about the past glories of Palmyra. An undergraduate history major, Parissa knew all the fascinating details of civilizations that had prospered and disappeared, leaving behind only mounds of dust-covered debris.

Later that evening, they'd have dinner at a candlelit table beneath a cool desert night sky emblazoned with stars. They would share a bottle of wine and pretend they were just two tourists visiting Syria, not competing intelligence agents destined to soon part and return to their respective masters.

But at least for tonight, all that would be forgotten.

After dinner and a second bottle of wine, he and Parissa would return to their room. There, they'd make love and everything would be all right—at least for the moment.

For now, that was all David could expect.

ABOUT THE AUTHOR

Jeff Westmont was an investment banker for over twenty years and currently runs a small hedge fund. He has a Wharton MBA and a BA in Economics from the University of California at Davis. He has traveled to more than 40 countries around the world, including Syria, Lebanon, Egypt, Israel, Jordan and Iran. He lives in San Francisco with his wife Sarah and two sons, Joshua and Zachary. *Countdown to Jihad* is his first novel and he is working on his second.